KU-060-870

Hart of Empire

SAUL DAVID

HODDER &
STOUGHTON

First published in Great Britain in 2010 by Hodder & Stoughton
An Hachette UK company

1

Copyright © Saul David 2010

The right of Saul David to be identified as the Author of the Work has been asserted by him in accordance with the Copyright, Designs and Patents Act 1988.

All rights reserved. No part of this publication may be reproduced, stored in a retrieval system, or transmitted, in any form or by any means without the prior written permission of the publisher, nor be otherwise circulated in any form of binding or cover other than that in which it is published and without a similar condition being imposed on the subsequent purchaser.

All characters in this publication are fictitious and any resemblance to real persons, living or dead, is purely coincidental.

DUMFRIES & GALLOWAY LIBRARIES

AS215919	
Askews & Holts	Feb-2013
AF	£12.99

A CIP catalogue record for this title is available from the British Library.

Hardback ISBN 978 0 340 95365 5
Trade Paperback ISBN 978 0 340 95366 2

Typeset in MT Sabon by Hewer Text UK Ltd, Edinburgh

Printed and bound in the UK by Clays Ltd, St Ives plc.

Hodder & Stoughton policy is to use papers that are natural, renewable and recyclable products and made from wood grown in sustainable forests. The logging and manufacturing processes are expected to conform to the environmental regulations of the country of origin.

Hodder & Stoughton Ltd
338 Euston Road
London NW1 3BH

www.hodder.co.uk

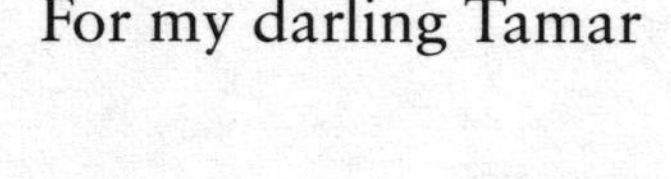

For my darling Tamar

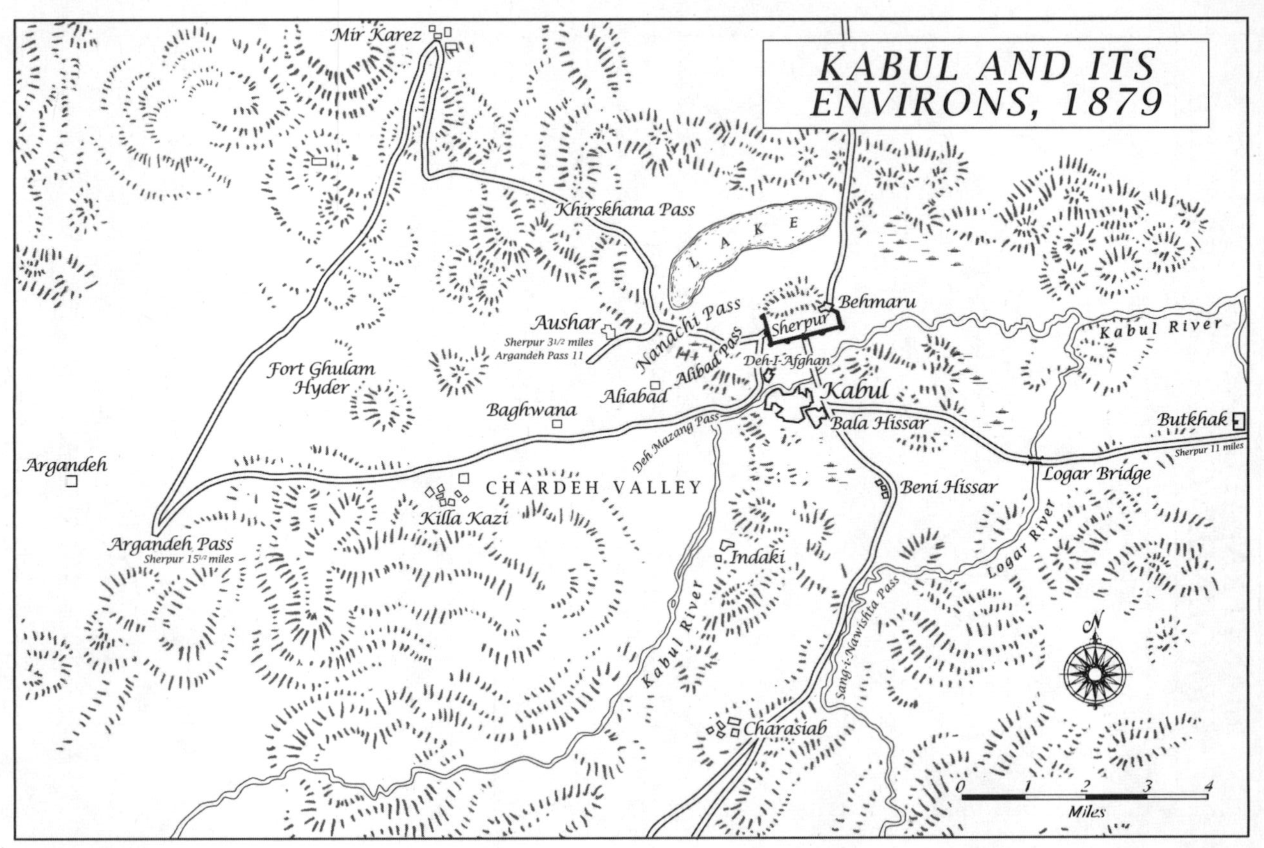
KABUL AND ITS ENVIRONS, 1879
Mir Karez
Khirskhana Pass
LAKE
Behmaru
Sherpur
Kabul River
Aushar
Sherpur 3½ miles
Argandeh Pass 11
Nanachi Pass
Alibad Pass
Deh-I-Afghan
Fort Ghulam Hyder
Aliabad
Kabul
Baghwana
Bala Hissar
Butkhak
Deh Mazang Pass
Sherpur 11 miles
Argandeh
Logar Bridge
CHARDEH VALLEY
Beni Hissar
Killa Kazi
Argandeh Pass
Sherpur 15½ miles
Indaki
Logar River
Sang-i-Nawishta Pass
Kabul River
N
Charasiab
0 1 2 3 4
Miles

EASTERN AFGHANISTAN AND SURROUNDING COUNTRIES, 1879

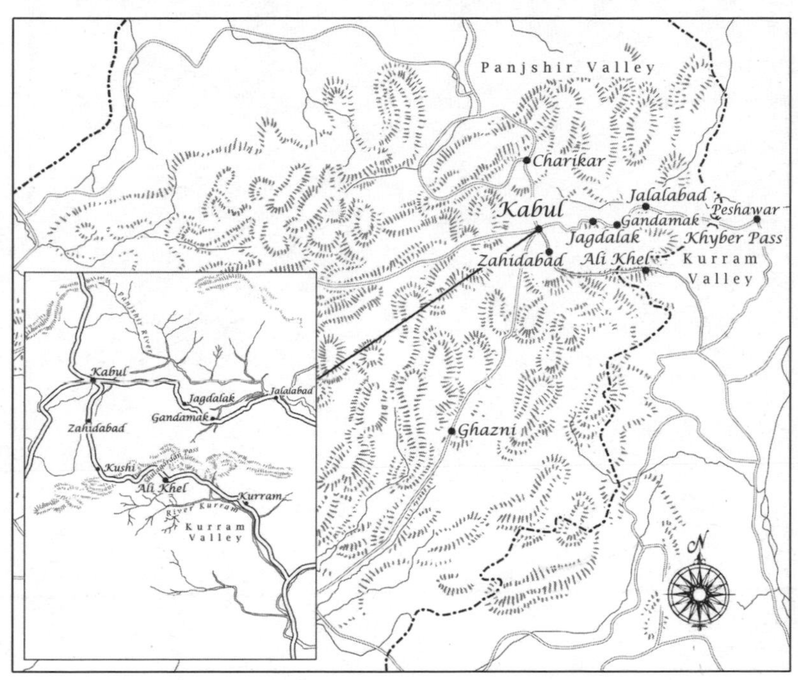

Preface

Copy of an undated letter given to the eighteen-year-old George Hart in the autumn of 1877 by Josiah Ward of Ward & Mills, a London firm of Solicitors-at-Law, shortly before George joined the 1st King's Dragoon Guards as a young officer fresh from Sandhurst:

To my son George Arthur Hart, Esq.,

To encourage you in your early military career, I have put aside the sum of £30,000. But it will only be made over to you, in the amounts mentioned, if you manage to comply with the following conditions before your twenty-eighth birthday, a lapse of ten years:

1. *Marry respectably, that is to a lady of gentle birth – £5,000.*
2. *Reach the substantive rank of lieutenant colonel in the British Army – £5,000.*
3. *Be awarded the Victoria Cross – £10,000.*

If you comply with all three conditions within the time allotted, you will receive an additional sum of £10,000. This money is in the safekeeping of my solicitor, Josiah Ward of Ward & Mills, and will be disbursed by him once reasonable proofs of compliance have been provided.

I

Haymarket, London, late spring 1879

'Thirty-three black!' announced the croupier.

George shook his head slowly, scarcely able to believe his luck. He preferred gambling at cards but neither baccarat nor *chemin-de-fer* had been kind to him today and he had switched in desperation to roulette, placing his last fifteen pounds of chips on black. It had won and, for want of a better strategy, he had bet on the same colour for five more spins, each time doubling his money, so that with this latest success, he now had the princely sum of £960. One more win would give him the two thousand or so that he desperately needed. He took another gulp of whisky and decided to let the money ride. All or nothing.

But something in his drink-fuddled brain told him it couldn't be black again, not seven times in a row, though he knew the odds on each new bet were the same for either colour. At the last moment, as the croupier was about to spin the wheel, he leant forward and moved all his chips to red. Then he closed his eyes and prayed.

As the ball was released, George glanced nervously round the dingy gambling den, its candelabra casting ghostly shadows over the few remaining players. He was alone at his table but for the croupier, a small, wiry man with greasy hair and a lopsided bow-tie, who was staring at the wheel as if his life depended upon it. Maybe it did, because his brow glistened with beads of sweat and his hands were gripping the table so tightly that the knuckles were white.

George looked back at the wheel and, almost imperceptibly, the croupier moved his right thumb below the level of the table, felt for a small button and pressed it. Seconds later the ball ran out of momentum and fell into the bed of the wheel, rattling along the numbers before finally coming to rest.

'Zero green,' announced the croupier, with as straight a face as he could muster, before raking George's neat pile of chips from the red diamond at the side of the baize.

Oh, my God, thought George. It's fallen into the only number I didn't consider, the one that gives the house its advantage. But even as his racing heart and clammy hands registered the consequences, he noticed the visibly relieved croupier grinning at someone behind him. He swung round to see the rotund proprietor, Mr Milton Samuels, advancing towards him.

'So sorry for your loss, Captain Hart,' said Samuels, thumbs crooked in his bright checked waistcoat. 'You win some . . .'

George's eyes narrowed. He had lost money before, of course, but Samuels had never felt the need to console him. Something was wrong. He looked from boss to employee, and back again, and felt sure he had been cheated. 'Don't give me that flannel, Samuels,' he said, a hard edge to his voice. 'You're not sorry at all. And why would you be when you've just fleeced me of everything I own?'

'Now, now, Captain Hart, there's no need for that.'

'Isn't there?' said George, his voice rising. 'So, you keep your temper when you've been rooked, do you?'

The room had fallen silent, all eyes on the altercation.

Samuels glanced beyond George to the stairs. 'I assure you, sir, that nothing untoward—'

'I saw your croupier gripping the side of the table and suspect you may have fitted some mechanical device to ensure the ball landed on green.'

George strode towards the croupier's end of the table, intent on discovering the truth, but Samuels intercepted him, his arms outstretched. 'I don't want no trouble, Captain Hart, so if you leave quietly we'll say no more about it.'

'I shall go nowhere without my money.'

'That right, Cap'n?' said a new voice, behind him. Before George could turn he felt an iron-like grip on his throat as an arm pinned him from behind. The more he struggled, the more the pressure increased. He could feel blood pounding in his ears and knew he was close to blacking out. But then the pressure on his throat eased a little and, coughing and spluttering, he regained his senses.

'Like I was saying,' snarled Samuels, 'I don't want no trouble but you would insist. All right, Paddy, throw him out.'

George felt as helpless as a rag doll as he was dragged backwards up the stairs, through the entrance and propelled on to the pavement, the boisterous Haymarket crowd parting for yet another drunk. Furious, he scrambled to his feet and advanced towards O'Reilly, the huge doorman who had thrown him out and was now standing coolly on the steps, his arms crossed. 'Don't be a fool, Cap'n. I'll make mincemeat of you, so I will, and it'd be a shame to damage that handsome figurehead of yours.'

George knew he was no match for the former prize-fighter, and was likely to receive a thrashing, but he was so angry and drunk he didn't care. He swung a right hook that missed as the battle-scarred Irishman swayed out of range, moving his large frame with the speed and grace of a cat. Overbalancing, George stumbled forward into a hammer of a counter-punch, O'Reilly's right fist slamming into his solar plexus, driving the air from his lungs and dropping him to his knees. He had never been hit so hard.

'You won't get away with this,' he said, gasping for breath. But he knew that they would, for he could hardly complain to the police about an illegal gambling den.

'Go home and sober up, Cap'n, though I'll wager home for you is far from these shores.'

Normally such an insulting reference to his dark skin, which made him look more southern Mediterranean than British, would have provoked a violent response. But the blow George had received had knocked much of the fight out of him and, as he crouched on the pavement, he realized he had only himself to blame for his humiliation. He rose to his feet, dusted himself down and, with a last scornful glance at O'Reilly, set off in the direction of his hotel in Knightsbridge. It was a fair distance and he would normally have hailed a cab but he had decided to walk to save money and to clear his head.

Halfway down Piccadilly – oblivious of the fashionable swells in their frock coats, checked waistcoats and tight blue trousers, and the ladies in dolman-style cloaks and narrow-brimmed bonnets – he pulled out his mother's letter and read it a second time.

17 Connaught Square
Dublin

Dearest George,

It was wonderful to have you to myself again for those few short weeks of your convalescence, and to hear all your news.

I am so proud that your gallantry in South Africa has been rewarded with a regular commission, and that you now have a second chance to make something of your military career.

I am grateful for the £500 you sent on your return to England. I have never been good with money, and since your father stopped paying your allowance it has been a constant struggle to keep my creditors at bay. In truth the £500 was quickly eaten up by debts and I have been forced to resort to moneylenders. But their interest is exorbitant and they have warned me that if I do not pay the £2,000 I shall owe by January next year they will force me to sell the house. I hate to burden you with this, my darling, particularly after your recent generosity, but I don't know where else to turn.

Your loving mother,
Emma

George folded the letter and groaned. He knew he had been a fool to try to raise the money his mother needed by gambling, but what was the alternative? After having kitted himself out with his new regimental uniform he had been left with barely two hundred pounds. Now, thanks to his idiocy, that money was almost gone and tomorrow he would return to South Africa to join his new regiment. It was almost a relief.

He set off at an unsteady walk and, twenty minutes later, was in sight of his hotel on Queen's Gate when he registered footsteps behind him. They grew gradually louder, and as the pedestrian caught up, George moved aside to let him pass. Instead he felt a tap on the shoulder.

'What do you—' As he turned, George froze in mid-sentence. There, standing before him in a top hat and cape, was a ghost. The ghost of a man he had killed in a fight the year before: the same huge frame, clothes and blotchy red face. It couldn't be, yet he seemed real enough in the flickering light from a nearby gas lamp. 'It can't be . . .' he whispered. 'You're dead.'

'Not me,' snarled the man, 'my brother Henry. I'm Bob Thompson.'

'You're his *brother*?' George was aghast.

'Yes. And I'm here to see you pay.'

George looked down at the man's hands, expecting to see a weapon. They were bunched into fists. 'Now just a minute. I can understand your anger, but your brother drew a sword on me. I had to defend myself.'

'That's not what you told the police. They said they were about to arrest you when a lady gave you an alibi. And yet you've just admitted to me that you did kill my brother.'

A voice in George's head was screaming at him to stop incriminating himself and say no more, but perhaps because of the drink, or the shock, or perhaps because in truth he was haunted every day by his distress at having killed a man and run from the fact, he spoke again: 'It was self-defence, I swear.'

'Then why not swear to the police, and let a jury decide?'

'Because I cannot believe I'll receive a fair trial. I fought your brother because he was trying to apprehend a young girl I was travelling with. She had just left the employment of my former commanding officer, Colonel Harris, who wanted her back. But she feared he would ravish her – he had tried once before, which was why she left.'

A shadow passed over the big man's face. 'So my brother was acting on Harris's orders?'

'Exactly.'

'And you say he drew a sword on you?'

'A sword-stick, to be exact.'

Thompson swore. 'John always were a bully, quick to use his fists. But he never killed no one, not to my knowledge.'

'Well, he almost killed me. As I say, he left me no alternative.'

'I don't believe you,' said Thompson, shaking his head. 'I reckon you were taking a beating and you pulled a pistol.'

'That was not how it was. He drew his weapon first. I tried to reason with him, but he wouldn't let us go. So I told the girl to run, which was when your brother tried to stab me. I shot him in self-defence.'

'So you keep saying, but old Bob can't speak for himself, can he?'

'No.'

'Which is why I'm asking you nicely, *Captain* Hart, to hand yourself in. Our poor old mother won't rest until she knows justice has been done.'

'I'm sorry for her, I truly am. But no jury influenced by Harris will believe I was justified in using a pistol against a sword-stick, though I know I was. If I admit to killing your brother I'll swing, and I don't deserve that.'

'And that's your final answer?'

'It is.'

'You bloody coward.' Thompson lurched forward, swinging a left-handed haymaker at the side of George's head.

But George, though drunk, was the nimbler of the two, easily slipping the punch and countering with one of his own, a straight right that caught Thompson flush on the jaw with a crack that echoed down the empty street. It was a blow made all the more potent by the humiliation he had already suffered at the gambling den, and Thompson reaped the consequences. He staggered and fell backwards into a sitting position, his eyes glazed.

'Like your brother, you left me no choice,' said George. Suddenly sober, he walked briskly away.

2

George's heart was still pounding as he entered the lobby of his small, discreet hotel at the bottom of Queen's Gate. It had been an evening to forget and he wished he was already on the ship to South Africa.

'Room thirty-two. Any messages?' he asked, more out of habit than expectation.

'Yes, sir,' said the tail-coated concierge, handing over his key and a thick white envelope. 'This came for you an hour ago.'

Recognizing at once the crest of the Commander-in-Chief, George tore open the letter and read:

The Horse Guards
Pall Mall

My dear Captain Hart

There is a matter of some urgency I would like to discuss with you this evening at my private residence, 6 Queen Street, Mayfair. Would you be so good as to arrive no later than half past nine? I look forward to renewing our acquaintance then.

I am, etc.

George Cambridge, Field Marshal

George pulled out his pocket-watch and cursed. It was ten minutes past the hour, which gave him just twenty minutes to change his clothes, hail a cab and get to the Commander-in-Chief's house in Mayfair. He grabbed his room key and ran for the stairs, taking them two at a time.

A quarter of an hour later George's cab was snarled in traffic on Piccadilly, a swearing, tangled mass of horse-riders, private carriages and hansoms jostling for position. The evening was going from bad to worse. 'How much longer?' he asked the driver, perched high above him.

'Don't worry, sir,' shouted the cabbie, as he steered his horse left off Piccadilly into Half Moon Street. 'Almost there.'

A couple of minutes later the cab drew up outside a substantial but far from palatial Georgian townhouse, the home of HRH the Duke of Cambridge and his morganatic wife, the former actress Mrs FitzGeorge. George had not heard from the duke since their interview two months earlier, and could only assume there were some last-minute instructions or messages the War Office wanted him to convey to South Africa. But why not summon him to Pall Mall, as before? Why ask a lowly captain to his private residence? George was intrigued and not a little flattered.

He was also hoping to meet Mrs FitzGeorge, who was, like his mother, a famous beauty of the stage; she was said to have secretly – and illegally – married the duke *after* she had had three illegitimate sons by him. They had since had another and all four were serving officers, known by the royal suffix 'Fitz', signifying bastard. Because of her humble origins as the daughter of a Bow Street printer, Mrs FitzGeorge had neither been accepted by society nor acknowledged by the Queen, the duke's first cousin.

George Hart himself occupied an ambivalent position in the British class system: dark-skinned and illegitimate, he had been sent to Harrow and Sandhurst and was now masquerading as an officer and a gentleman. He assumed they would have much in common.

The door was opened by a florid-faced butler who, having taken George's hat and coat, led him upstairs to the first-floor drawing room. 'Captain George Hart,' he announced.

'At last,' said a voice George recognised as the duke's. 'Show him in.'

The room contained three men in evening dress. The duke was standing by the empty fireplace, a portly figure with bald pate and white mutton-chop whiskers. Seated on a sofa to his left was a younger man George did not know, also bald but with a full beard and pince-nez hanging from his neck. Opposite him, on a second sofa, he saw the unmistakable figure of Lord Beaconsfield, the Prime Minister, with his thin, pinched face, prominent nose and goatee beard.

'You look as if you've seen a ghost, Captain,' said the duke, with a chuckle. 'I can assure you, Lord Beaconsfield is flesh and blood. As is Lord Salisbury,' he added, gesturing towards the second man. 'Come over and all will be explained.'

George was taken aback – the Prime Minister *and* the Foreign Secretary – but he did as he was bidden, bowing slightly as he shook the duke's hand. Salisbury rose to greet him, but Beaconsfield remained sitting. 'Forgive my *impolitesse*, Captain,' he said, 'but I've been unwell and my doctor advises rest – as if that were possible in these troubled times.'

'I quite understand, Prime Minister.'

'Now, before we start,' said the duke, 'would you care for a drink?'

George knew it was unwise to accept, but felt it might calm his nerves. 'Whisky, please.'

'What you're about to hear is a matter of national security and must not be repeated without our authority. Secrecy is paramount. Do you understand?'

George nodded as he took his drink from the butler, who then left the room, closing the double doors behind him.

'First may I congratulate you, Captain Hart,' began Beaconsfield, 'on surviving the catastrophe at Isandlwana. I don't mind telling you that receiving the news of that defeat was one of the darkest moments of my life. The government might have fallen there and then without the glimmer of sunshine provided by the heroic defence of Rorke's Drift. I gather you fought there too?'

Unwelcome memories of the vicious fighting, particularly the death of his friend Jake, swirled into George's head. 'I did, my lord,' said George, as if in a trance, 'until I was wounded.'

'Of course,' said Beaconsfield, nodding, 'and I trust you're fully recovered.'

'I am. Thank you.'

'From what His Royal Highness tells me, you have performed a double service for your country – first, by your acts of valour during the fighting, and second, by exposing the inadequacies of the military command in South Africa. My instinct on hearing the news of Isandlwana was at once to relieve Lord Chelmsford of his command. But the duke argued against this, as did Her Majesty the Queen, on the grounds that it would be unfair to condemn the man before the full details of the battle were known. Well, now they are, thanks to you, and a few days ago Her Majesty finally sanctioned the Cabinet's recommendation to replace Lord

Chelmsford with Sir Garnet Wolseley, who will leave on the SS *Edinburgh Castle* tomorrow. I hear you are booked on the same passage.'

'Indeed I am,' said George, barely able to conceal his delight that Chelmsford had finally received his comeuppance. He was eager to return to South Africa – to take revenge on his Zulu cousin Mehlokazulu for killing Jake at Isandlwana, to settle scores with Sir Jocelyn Harris, his former CO, for drumming him out of the 1st Dragoon Guards and to avoid retribution for killing Thompson – but he had dreaded serving again under Chelmsford and his deputy Crealock. Now that threat had been lifted.

'I can see from your expression that you approve of the Cabinet's decision,' said Beaconsfield, leaning forward. 'Quite right. But you may not have the opportunity to make Sir Garnet's acquaintance. We have in mind for you a quite different form of military service in another country that should suit your unique talents. Lord Salisbury will explain.'

Nonplussed, and not a little irked that his return to South Africa was in doubt, George swung round to face the Foreign Secretary. 'Have you ever heard of the Prophet's Cloak?' asked Salisbury, in a deep, gravelly voice.

'No,' replied George, 'but I imagine it has something to do with the Muhammadan religion.'

'Exactly so. The Mussulmans believe it was once owned by the Prophet Muhammad himself and as such is one of their most sacred relics. How it found its way to Afghanistan has never been properly explained. Some say it was given as a present to an Afghan chief called Kais who fought on behalf of the Prophet in the seventh century, others that it was brought to the country from Bokhara in the late eighteenth century by Ahmad Shah Durrani, the founder of the ruling dynasty. Today it resides in a locked silver box, itself protected by two outer wooden chests, in the shrine of Kharka Sharif in Kandahar in the south of the country. If we could be sure it would stay there, and never see the light of day, we would not be having this conversation. But experience tells us it can and will be brought out in times of national emergency. It was last donned by Dost Mahomed, the late Amir of Kabul. Does that name sound familiar?'

'Of course, my lord. Every schoolboy knows of Dost, and of how Britain was forced to restore him as ruler after the disasters of the first Afghan war in the forties.'

'Quite right. Dost understood the symbolic power of the cloak as a means of rallying the faithful against the foreign invader, which brings me to the point. While you were battling the Zulu, a quite separate war was being fought in Afghanistan. And, like your war, it was launched by a pro-consul who exceeded his brief. When Lord Lytton took up his post as Viceroy of India in seventy-six he was instructed by the Cabinet to prevent the ruler of Afghanistan, Sher Ali, falling under Russian influence. One by one the khanates of Central Asia have fallen to the Russians, who now stand on Afghanistan's northern border. Our greatest fear is that they will continue their march south and use Afghanistan to invade India. Lord Lytton's task was to encourage Sher Ali to accept a British resident in Kabul who could keep an eye on the Russians.

'What he was not authorized to do was send a mission up the Khyber Pass without Sher's permission, which was what happened last autumn. Inevitably the mission was turned back by the Afghans and war was the result. It might have been avoided, but only if Sher had apologized and agreed to accept a resident. It was vital to our prestige that he agreed to some form of reparation. He refused. These Orientals are very proud.'

The sequence of events was not dissimilar to that which had preceded the Zulu war. Yet there was one vital difference, and George voiced it in the hope that it would end all talk of cloaks and holy war. 'All this is fascinating, my lord, but was not the recent Afghan war brought to a satisfactory conclusion, unlike the fighting in Zululand, which continues? Or that is the impression one has from the newspapers.'

'And newspapers never lie, do they?' asked Salisbury, with more than a hint of sarcasm. 'But you're mostly right, Captain Hart. For once our military operations went like clockwork – though the Afghans fought well against Roberts at Peiwar Kotal – and by January this year it was mostly over. Sher Ali had fled north and both Kandahar and Kabul were in our hands. Then in February we heard of Sher Ali's death and the accession of his son, and former prisoner, Yakub Khan, who had enough sense to open negotiations with us. He signed a treaty last week at Gandamak, ceding a strip of Afghan territory that includes the Khyber Pass and the Kurram valley, agreeing to our original request for a British resident in Kabul, and guaranteeing British control over Afghan foreign policy and freedom of commerce. In return he will receive an annual subsidy of sixty thousand pounds and the promise of British support in the event of war with a foreign aggressor.'

Salisbury paused to let the details sink in, but George was confused. 'Forgive me, my lord,' he said, 'but I don't see what this has to do with me or the cloak. Surely with the war over and the treaty signed you have everything you want – a British resident, a pliant amir and Russian influence nowhere to be seen.'

Beaconsfield could remain silent no longer. 'Appearances can be deceptive, Captain Hart. But in truth the situation in Afghanistan is far less satisfactory than the newspapers would have you believe. How do we know this? Because the Foreign Office has a spy in Kabul, and his last report warned that Yakub is despised by the majority of his countrymen for concluding such a shameful treaty, and that an extremist cleric from Ghazni . . .' Beaconsfield turned to Salisbury for help. 'What's his name?'

'Mullah Mushk-i-Alam, Prime Minister,' said Salisbury, 'which apparently means "Perfume of the Universe".'

'Extraordinary! Well, this fellow, according to our spy, is trying to rouse the faithful against our presence in Afghanistan and all who condone it, including Yakub. And the easiest way for him to achieve this is to don the Prophet's Cloak and declare himself the spiritual leader not just of Afghanistan but of the whole Mussulman world. It goes without saying that it is in our vital interest to prevent this happening – which is where you come in. We want you to travel to Afghanistan, find the cloak and bring it back to Britain.'

Until now George had listened to both men in respectful silence. They were, after all, the most powerful men in the country, which, by dint of the Empire's pre-eminence, meant the world. But this request was insane. No, he decided, it was worse than insane – it was guaranteed to get him killed. 'I'm flattered that you've considered me for such an important mission, Prime Minister,' he began, careful not to sound ungrateful, 'but, with all due respect, I fail to see how I fit the bill. I'm still young and learning my profession, I've never been to Afghanistan, and I've no experience of espionage. Surely it would make more sense to send an agent of the

Indian government who knows the country and can speak the lingo.'

'You might think so, Captain Hart,' said Salisbury, 'but we and the Indian government don't always see eye to eye. For the last few years they've been pursuing a quite different—'

Beaconsfield raised his hand. 'I don't think we need to go into that, Salisbury. Suffice to say, Captain Hart, we have our reasons. As for your fitness to undertake this mission, I can think of no one better. Yes, you are young, but you were the best in your class at Sandhurst and your feats in Zululand confirm you as an officer of outstanding promise. You've shown bravery, endurance, resourcefulness and integrity, all qualities that are needed for the Afghan mission. I'm told you pick up languages easily, that you are an excellent horseman – and you have one important advantage over almost any other British officer for an undercover operation of this nature, and that is – how shall I put this? – you're . . .'

'Expendable?' suggested George, one eyebrow raised.

'Why on earth would you think that?' asked the Prime Minister.

'I apologize, Prime Minister, I was being flippant, though it strikes me that you'd be much less likely to send a titled member of the Brigade of Guards than a misfit like me.'

Beaconsfield smiled. 'There's more to it than that.' He turned to the duke, who was still standing by the fireplace, a glass of whisky in hand. 'Your Royal Highness, would you mind if I had a word in private with young Hart?'

'Not at all. I'll be next door.'

'You too, Salisbury.'

The Foreign Secretary frowned. 'Is that really necessary, Prime Minister?'

'Yes.'

Once the pair had left the room, Beaconsfield turned back to George, a faint smile playing on his lips. 'You may be surprised to hear this, Captain Hart, but you and I have much in common.'

'We do?' asked an unconvinced George.

'Yes. We're both . . . cuckoos in the nest. We may look the part, say the right things, but we don't really belong. My father was a practising Jew who baptized his children into the Church of England so that they could get on in society. Did you know that?'

'I did not.'

'It's true, and just as well for me because I couldn't have climbed the greasy pole if I hadn't become an Anglican. Until a few years ago Jews couldn't vote, let alone stand for Parliament. But don't misunderstand me. I didn't always want to be a politician. Before I became an MP I tried my hand at business and writing novels. I wasn't very successful at either, which mattered to me because I always want to be the best at anything I do, and I suspect you feel the same. Am I right?'

George hadn't given it much thought before now, but he couldn't deny he had always been fiercely competitive and had worked twice as hard as his peers at Harrow and Sandhurst.

'I thought so. The truth is, Hart, people like ourselves don't fit neatly into English society and never will. They know it and, more importantly, we know it, which is why we will move Heaven and Earth to prove ourselves superior. Harrow and Sandhurst can't have been easy for someone of your background yet you excelled, and clearly have determination as well as brains, a combination not usually found in a pink-cheeked ensign of the Grenadier Guards. You believe we've selected you for this mission because you're nobody and therefore expendable. Far from it. You possess a range of qualities that are rarely found in someone of your age and education – not least a handsome figurehead, which, alas, I was not blessed with – and that is why we – I – would hate to lose you.'

Not as much as I'd hate to lose myself, thought George, as he tried to read between the Prime Minister's honeyed lines. Did they really have that much in common? Or was Beaconsfield, consummate politician that he was, simply telling him what he wanted to hear? He couldn't decide. And something about the undercover mission made him uneasy. 'I'm flattered, of course, my lord,' said George, after a lengthy pause, 'but there's much to consider. I appreciate your intention is to avoid more bloodshed and turmoil, but would it not be best to withdraw from Afghanistan and leave the Afghans to their own devices?'

'Thus allowing the Russians to advance to the very borders of British India? We cannot allow that to happen.'

'But would it, my lord? Surely the Russians would find the Afghans every bit as tough a nut to crack as we have. Is it not better to have Russians dying in the Hindu Kush than our own soldiers in the Khyber Pass?'

'Of course. But we cannot guarantee the Afghans will win such a war. And if they do not we shall face a mortal threat in India. No, Hart, the only sensible option is to retain a British envoy in Kabul to keep an eye on things. But the position of our current resident, Sir Louis Cavagnari, is in danger of being undermined by religious radicals, as I've explained, and the best way to prevent this is for us to get our hands on the Prophet's Cloak.'

George rubbed his chin. 'I see the sense of that, my lord,

but I can't help feeling uneasy. The cloak is clearly a religious artefact of great importance to the Afghans. Won't our removing it make it harder for them to accept us as an ally?'

'Of course, but only if they know we're responsible – which they will not, if you're careful.'

'It doesn't seem right to interfere in someone else's religion. Or sensible. After all, isn't that what caused the Mutiny of fifty-seven?'

'Partly, though I suspect many Indian sepoys were simply using the defence of their religion as a pretext to overthrow our rule. In any event, we've learnt our lesson. This is not about meddling with the Muhammadan religion but about safeguarding our vital interests in the region. As long as the Afghans keep the Russians out, they can worship whom they damn well please. Well, I've said my piece and now, I think, it's best if the others rejoin us. Andrews!'

The butler put his head round the door. 'My lord?'

'Be so good as to ask your master and Lord Salisbury to come back in.'

Once the pair had resumed their former places, Beaconsfield continued, 'I think, gentlemen, that Captain Hart is ready to give us his answer. Is that right?'

'Not quite, my lord,' said George. 'You still haven't explained the "important advantage" I have over my peers for a mission of this kind.'

Beaconsfield chuckled. 'I would have thought that was obvious. Why, it's the colour of your skin, of course. Put you in Afghan clothing and you'll pass for a native in no time. What do you say, Salisbury?'

The Foreign Secretary nodded vigorously. 'I agree. They'll never know you're British.'

That's because I'm not, thought George. Well, not entirely. But he was not about to explain to these powerful men that a mixture of Zulu, Irish and British blood ran in his veins. What would be the point? Far better to stick to the story his mother had told him as a boy: that she was of Maltese descent. That way he could continue the charade that he was an officer and a gentleman with only a touch of the tarbrush. After all, if Beaconsfield – the son of a practising Jew – could become Prime Minister, what was to stop George Hart rising to the very top of his profession, if he kept quiet about his African past?

'I am, of course, happy to second you to the Foreign Office for the duration of the mission,' interjected the duke, 'and if you're successful there's a good chance, a very good chance, that Her Majesty will approve your promotion to the rank of major.'

'So will you do it?' asked Beaconsfield.

George paused. Every bone in his body was urging him to say thank you, but no thank you. It wasn't just the qualms he felt about purloining an article of such religious significance, or that he had unfinished business in South Africa: he had been looking forward to joining the 3rd/60th Rifles and becoming a proper regimental officer with men under his command. Yet, on the other hand, promotion to major would take him tantalizingly close to the rank of lieutenant colonel and five thousand pounds of his father's money. Neither could he deny that Lord Beaconsfield had a point: he indeed possessed many of the attributes required for such a mission. This gave him, he realised, a crucial bargaining chip that might help him solve his mother's financial worries. And something else swayed him, something to which Beaconsfield had just alluded: the determination to excel at soldiering, the only profession that interested him, and to prove himself as good as, if not better than, all those officers who were unmistakably 'white'. His heart was thumping as he drained his glass, then set out his terms.

'I will, Prime Minister, but on one condition.'

'Now, Captain,' said the duke, gruffly, 'I hardly think you're in a position to set conditions.'

'On the contrary,' said Beaconsfield. 'It seems to me he's in a very strong position to do so. We need him but does he need us? Let us hear what he has to say.'

'I won't go into the details, Your Royal Highness, my lords,' said George, 'but for personal reasons I need a substantial sum of money by January next at the latest. Therefore I will undertake the mission if you promise to pay me two thousand pounds.'

'*What?*' said the duke, red-faced. 'You have the gall to demand money to serve your country? Have you lost your reason? You're a British officer, not some soldier of fortune.'

'Your Royal Highness, please,' said Beaconsfield, his hand raised. 'Let me handle this. Two thousand pounds, you say? That's quite a sum, but not impossible to come by.' He turned to the Foreign Secretary. 'Salisbury, could we procure this amount from the Secret Service Fund? After all, Captain Hart will be undertaking special duties for your department.'

Salisbury frowned at the irregularity of the request, but he knew Beaconsfield well enough to grasp when he was being asked and when he was being told. 'I'm sure that could be arranged, Prime Minister, but I'd like to add a caveat of my own – that we pay the two thousand pounds if Captain Hart's mission is successful and he returns to this country with the cloak intact.'

'Will that satisfy you, Hart?' Beaconsfield asked.

'It sounds fair.'

'Excellent.' Beaconsfield rose stiffly from his chair. 'Now I must be getting back to Number Ten. It's late.'

'I must go too,' said Salisbury.

George stood to shake hands. 'Good luck in Afghanistan, Hart,' said Beaconsfield.

'I'll second that,' added Salisbury, 'but remember this. Officially the government knows nothing of your mission. If anything goes wrong you're on your own. Is that understood?'

'Yes, my lord.'

'Very well. You'll be briefed tomorrow at the Foreign Office, nine sharp.'

As the door closed on the departing politicians, the duke turned to George. 'You've made the right decision, Hart. You wouldn't have enjoyed serving under that pretentious snob Wolseley who, had it been up to me, would never have been appointed. I wanted Napier, but the Cabinet said he was too old and that only Wolseley would do. Bloody fools! What do they know of military affairs?'

George was surprised that the duke was prepared to criticize openly the two men who had just left his house.

'Oh, make no mistake,' continued the duke, 'I admire Dizzy and his set as politicians, and would see them in government before any of the ghastly alternatives, particularly that old prig Gladstone. They, at least, act in the best interests of the service and the Empire. And Dizzy clearly has a high opinion of you or he wouldn't have asked you to undertake such an important mission. But enough of that. You should be getting along, too. Before you go, though, I have a favour to ask.'

'Your Royal Highness?'

'It's . . . a personal matter,' said the duke, colouring slightly.

'You'll be travelling to Afghanistan incognito, and not in any official capacity, but if you cross paths with my son Major Harry FitzGeorge, who's serving on General Roberts's staff, could you somehow encourage him to write more frequently to his mother? An odd request, I know, but she worries.'

'Of course,' said George, with a smile. 'All mothers do.'

'Yes, but some have more reason than others. With Harry and his brothers, it's one scrape after another,' said the duke, shaking his head. 'I imagined the military life would straighten them out, but it hasn't made a blind bit of difference. They're constantly in debt and I've lost count of the times I've had to pay off their creditors. If they had been anyone else's sons they'd have been cashiered years ago. But I'm convinced Harry in particular has good in him, and not a little aptitude for soldiering – lately he has shown signs of having put behind him the wildness of his youth. Why, only last week I received a letter from General Roberts complimenting Harry on his excellent intelligence work during the recent war. Naturally his mother is delighted.'

George could not imagine why the duke was talking so freely about his errant sons. 'If we do meet I'll do my best to carry out your request, sir, though I won't be at liberty to repeat this conversation.'

'No, of course not,' said the duke, his head cocked to one side. 'But I'm grateful to you for trying, and wish you the best of luck in Afghanistan. I once met an officer who was on the retreat in forty-two. He wouldn't talk about the horrors of the march, but he did say the Afghans were easily the toughest, most treacherous and pitiless foe he'd had the misfortune to encounter. So my advice is, expect the worst and trust no one. Oh, and one more thing, Captain.

You may not agree with everything we're trying to achieve in Afghanistan, but remember where your loyalties lie.'

George was already nervous about the mission, and this was not the pep talk he had hoped for. But the duke's sentiments were genuine, and he marvelled again at the contrast between the public's perception of him as a cold, unimaginative bureaucrat and the warm-hearted family man before him. 'I'll endeavour to remember that, sir,' he said.

3

Off Karachi, Sind province, midsummer 1879

The sun was setting as George got his first glimpse of British India from the poop-deck of the steamer *Windsor Castle*: a barren shoreline of low hills and stunted shrubs, soon giving way to the hustle and bustle of a working port as the ship approached Karachi, the capital of Sind and the nearest British-controlled port to Afghanistan.

It had taken just twenty-five days to cover the six thousand nautical miles that separated Karachi from Gravesend, though the sweltering weather and snail's pace through the Suez Canal had replicated the tedium of his earlier voyage to South Africa. This time he had kept to himself, exchanging the barest pleasantries with his fellow first-class passengers, the usual mix of army officers, civilian officials, businessmen and their families to be found on any passage to India. To anyone who enquired, he gave his name as James Harper, an employee of the Anglo-Indian Trading Company who was keen to investigate new opportunities in Afghanistan made possible by the recent treaty.

To back his cover, the Foreign Office had provided him with a false passport and a letter of introduction from the company chairman to the Amir of Kabul. He also carried with him a money-belt, containing sixty gold sovereigns, and a brand new six-shot Adams revolver. He regretted the loss of his grandfather's Colt at Rorke's Drift, but this weapon had the advantage of an extra shot and, because it did not need firing caps, was easier to reload.

George had spent much of the trip reading up on the history of Afghanistan, its people, customs and language. He now knew the country to be a largely roadless tract of grey-green mountains and dusty deserts, yet its strategic position astride the route from Persia and central Asia to India meant it had been fought over and traded through for thousands of years. Many of history's great conquerors – the Persian kings Cyrus and Darius, Alexander the Great and Genghis Khan – had passed through Afghanistan on their way to India. More recently the British had tramped in the opposite direction in the hope of bringing the Afghans to heel.

The chief obstacle to control, George discovered, was that Afghanistan was so ethnically diverse, with a multitude of races and nationalities, each with rival interests and antagonistic ambitions. In the south and east were the Pashto-speaking Pathans, descendants of the original Afghans from Syria, transplanted to the country in the time of Nebuchadnezzar; further north, beyond the Hindu Kush, lived Mongol-looking Hazaras, Turkic-featured Uzbeks and their neighbours the Tajiks, and to the west, in the mountain fastness of Nuristan, a tall people with fair hair, blue eyes and freckles.

Since 1740 the country had been nominally ruled by the shahs and amirs of Kabul, members of the Sadozai and Barakzai tribes of Pathans, but rarely had they established complete control. The exception was Dost Mahomed, scourge of the British and grandfather of the current ruler, who had died in 1863, thus ushering in a new era of internecine strife. The only thing Afghans seemed to have in common was the Muhammadan religion.

The more George had read about the Pathans – whose honour code, the *pashtunwali*, guaranteed life to friends and death to strangers – the less confident he had become that he would leave Afghanistan in one piece. To have any chance of survival, much less of carrying out his mission, he knew he needed a guide he could trust, and determined to find one at the earliest opportunity. But first he would have to acclimatise to the heat of the sub-continent which, though past its hot-season worst, was still severe enough to discourage most Europeans from venturing out between the hours of ten and two.

Fortunately it was early evening, with a light breeze cooling the deck, as the *Windsor Castle* passed slowly between Shark Island and the breakwater, coming to a halt in Karachi harbour off the wharfs of Kiamari Island. No sooner had the anchors dropped than the ship was surrounded by a swarm of native boats, their turbaned skippers loudly hawking their services as they fended the competition away. George watched with amusement as an aggrieved captain boarded his rival's boat and pushed the occupant overboard. The sodden victim took it in good part and, back on his vessel, continued searching for passengers to take to shore. George admired the fellow's stoicism and, having fetched his valise from his cabin and said goodbye to the ship's captain, he climbed down the rope-ladder, called the man to him and leapt aboard.

They agreed the extortionate fare of four annas – the equivalent of sixpence, more than most boatmen would earn in a day – and George was soon ashore and striding up the wharf towards the village of Kiamari where a second riot ensued as pairs of palanquin-wallahs vied for his custom. He selected the sturdiest duo he could find and, climbing inside the covered rickety litter, told them to head for the Hotel Metropole on Frere Road; a fellow traveller had assured him it was the best in town. The pair hoisted the litter to waist level and set off at a trot. Their route took them down Napier mole – named after Sir Charles Napier, who had conquered Sind in 1843 – past the Customs House and on up Bunder Road, the dividing line in Karachi between the narrow, people- and refuse-choked streets of the native town and the broader, tree-lined avenues and spacious bungalows of the European quarter. Bunder Road itself was something of a hybrid with its tall two- and three-storey public buildings, stores and hotels in the Indo-Gothic and Anglo-Mughal styles so beloved of the post-Mutiny period.

George had read of this, but nothing could have prepared him for the towering grandeur of the Metropole: set in its own lush gardens, three storeys high and as wide as a country mansion, it was distinctively Indian, with its Mughal arches, minarets and cupolas. Having paid off the palanquin, he gazed up in awe at the scale and splendour of the place. 'Welcome to the Metropole, *huzoor*,' said a voice to his left.

He swung round to see the smiling, bearded face of a turbaned doorman, six feet six if he was an inch, his smart white tunic, or *kurta*, and pyjama trousers held in place with a broad red sash. 'Thank you,' said George, as he entered the hotel's large vaulted lobby, his boots ringing on the polished marble floor.

* * *

George spent the next few days getting used to the heat and humidity, buying supplies and planning his route north. The quickest option was rail, a branch line between Karachi and Multan, eight hundred miles distant, having opened the year before. But George knew that if his mission was to have any chance of success he needed to learn Pashto, the language spoken in most of southern and central Afghanistan, which would take time. He decided to journey by train as far as Kotri, ten hours away, then continue up the Indus river by steamer, a more comfortable and leisurely means of travel.

He still required a tutor, and it dawned on him that if he could find a guide-cum-bodyguard who could also teach him the language he could kill three birds with the same stone. His initial enquiries drew a blank, until he overheard a comment by one porter to a colleague on his first day in the job: 'Work hard and you should do well. The food is good and the tips are the best in Karachi. But don't forget to give ten per cent of your pay, tips included, to Ilderim Khan,' he said, pointing to the giant doorkeeper.

'And if I don't?' asked the newcomer.

'You may not live to regret it. Ilderim's a Pathan from beyond the Khyber.'

He'd be ideal, thought George, who knew that the Khyber Pass led directly to Kabul, and that its tribesmen were among the fiercest in Afghanistan. It did not occur to him to ask why a member of such a proud race was employed as a humble doorkeeper, but Ilderim provided the answer anyway. 'Yes, *huzoor*,' he replied, to George's simple enquiry, 'I was born in the Khyber but I left twenty years ago to join the Corps of Guides.'

George had been at Sandhurst with a young subaltern destined for the Guides, and knew of the regiment's reputation as the finest in the sub-continent. Any young Indian soldier from the North West Frontier of the Punjab would have given his eye teeth to serve with it, hence the presence in the regiment of Pathans, Punjabi Muslims and Sikhs. But an Afghan recruit, George knew, would have been regarded by his people as a traitor. 'Why the Guides? Why not an Afghan regiment?'

Ilderim's brow darkened. 'If you'd seen the Afghan Army, *huzoor*, you wouldn't ask such a question. Its soldiers are a rabble, low-born, half trained and undisciplined. The Guides are different. I first heard of them from a cousin who was born near Peshawar and joined the corps in forty-six when it was raised to protect the frontier. On the few times I met him at family gatherings, he'd fill my young head with tales of the Guides' exploits during the Mutiny, particularly the legendary march from the Punjab to Delhi when the infantry covered almost six hundred miles in just twenty-two days. I could hardly wait until I was eighteen and old enough to enlist.'

'And did you ever regret your decision?'

'No, *huzoor*. Those thirteen years in the corps were the best of my life. I didn't want to leave. I was forced to after injuring my shoulder in a bad fall. It was my troop commander who found me this job.'

'Do you like working here?'

Ilderim frowned. 'It pays for my bed and board, and the occasional prostitute.'

'But it doesn't compare with soldiering.'

'No.'

'Well,' said George, flashing his broadest smile, 'I might have the solution. How would you like to work for me? My name's James Harper. I'm employed by the Anglo-Indian

Trading Company and in two days I leave for Kabul to find new business. But as it's my first time in the country I need a bodyguard-cum-guide-cum-language tutor. Your background and military training suggests you would be just the man.'

Ilderim raised his eyebrows. 'You say you're a businessman, *huzoor*? You look more like an officer to me.'

'Are you calling me a liar?'

'I know a soldier when I see one.'

George's jaw dropped. He could not believe how easily Ilderim had seen through his cover story, but knew it would be counterproductive to lose his temper. 'I *was* a soldier, but I'm not any longer. Are you satisfied?'

'It means nothing to me, *huzoor*, but I will say this. Soldier or no, your grasp of Pashto is shakier than a Hindu's rifle aim. I heard you practising earlier. Not good.'

'Bloody cheek!' said George, laughing. 'Though I won't deny I've much to learn, which is where you come in. Clearly you think highly of yourself so I'll pay you double what you're earning here, and a bonus of a hundred rupees when we return to Karachi. What do you say? It must be better than opening doors for fat businessmen and their ugly, uptight wives.'

Ilderim grinned wolfishly. 'They're not all ugly, *huzoor*, or so uptight they won't ask for Ilderim to deliver a glass of warm milk to their room. But what you say is true – it's no job for a warrior. So I'll eat your salt if you treble my pitiful wage and offer a bonus of two hundred rupees.'

'Is there no limit to your effrontery?' asked George. 'Two and a half times and one hundred and fifty rupees. Take it or leave it.'

'I will take it.'

'Then let us shake on it,' said George, and regretted this excess of bonhomie as Ilderim's huge fist closed painfully over his.

Two days later, after a hearty breakfast of lamb chops and curried fowl, George was striding across the lobby to the main staircase when he was hailed by the clerk at the desk. 'Excuse me, Harper Sahib, a letter has arrived for you from South Africa.'

George's heart gave a little skip. Perhaps it was from Fanny Colenso, the daughter of the Bishop of Natal, with whom he had fallen in love the previous year, only for her to tell him that she did not reciprocate his feelings. Instead she would devote her life to clearing the name of her lover Colonel Durnford, killed at Isandlwana and a convenient scapegoat for the defeat. But the childlike handwriting on the cream envelope told him it was from Lucy Hawkins, the former housemaid he had been trying to protect when he had killed Henry Thompson in Plymouth. He had written to both women before his departure with the barest outline of his mission and his alias, saying that the Metropole would forward any mail. How typical, he thought, that Lucy was the first to respond. She had done well for herself since their first parting at Cape Town in March 1878, and was now running a successful saloon in the diamond town of Kimberley. She loved him still – and had said as much as he lay in hospital in Pietermaritzburg, recovering from the wound he had received at Rorke's Drift. He had told her he was in love with Fanny Colenso.

Did he still feel the same? He suspected as much from his initial disappointment that the letter was not from Fanny; yet he could not deny the depth of his feelings for Lucy, whose generous gift of a diamond had helped to pay off his mother's previous debts. They had been through much together and there was no question that he found Lucy attractive. She was a natural beauty, with her delicate oval face, green eyes and curly chestnut hair. What self-respecting man would not desire her? She also had spirit and determination – traits that George prized above all others – and, despite her lowly birth, a natural intelligence that would take her far in the world. It already had. He admired her hugely, he concluded, but that wasn't the same as love. Or was it?

Back in his room he read her letter:

The Lucky Strike
Long Street
Kimberley
Cape Colony

Dearest George

I can hardly write I'm shaking so much. This morning I received a letter from that monster Colonel Harris, threatening to expose us both as murderers unless I return to England and re-enter his service, in line with the terms of the loan he agreed with my father. I don't know what to do. I daren't mention this to my protector, Mr Barnato, for fear he'll turn me out. I'm terrified Harris will pay me a visit. Please advise me.

Your loving friend
Lucy

Anger flared in George's breast. Poor Lucy, he thought, hounded by that brute. He knew, though, that Harris was bluffing and said as much in his reply, counselling Lucy to sit tight and destroy any subsequent letters. Harris had no evidence against them, he added, and would find it impossible to refute the alibi that George's former lover, Mrs Bradbury, had given them to atone for a previous wrong. As for Harris paying her a visit, it was impossible for him to do so while the Zulu war was still being fought and likely to continue for some time. Meanwhile George promised to return to South Africa as soon as he could to reassure her in person. He signed off 'with much love' and, for the first time, meant it.

Later that morning, as George was handing in the letter for posting and paying his bill at the front desk, he caught sight of a tall, fair-haired man on the far side of the lobby he was sure he recognised from the voyage. The man was smartly dressed in a cream linen suit and apparently reading a newspaper – but George was convinced he was being watched because every time he glanced in that direction the man looked back to his paper. He was about to go over and ask him his business when the hotel manager, an unctuous European called Beresford, interrupted his train of thought: 'I trust you have had a pleasant stay, Mr Harper, and that everything was to your satisfaction?'

'What's that?' said George. 'Um . . . yes, very satisfactory, though I can't say I've enjoyed being woken every morning by the Muhammadans' call to prayers.'

'No, sir, but there's little we can do about that. If the Mutiny taught us anything it's that you tamper with the natives' religion at your peril.'

'I'm sure. I wasn't suggesting . . .' George trailed off as he remembered the man observing him. He looked over again but he had gone.

4

Kotri railway station, Sind, midsummer 1879

The whistle sounded twice as the train approached the small town of Kotri, an oasis of whitewashed buildings fringed with orange, lime and mango trees on the right bank of the Indus. George could feel only relief that the tedious ten-hour journey was over and that he no longer had to stare at the drab, featureless desert that covered much of southern Sind.

The small station was packed with passengers, and as the train juddered to a halt with a squeal of its brakes and a great whoosh of steam, they surged forward, some clambering onto the roof, others passing children and sacks of their possessions through open windows, one or two even using the doors.

George stepped down from the cool haven of his first-class carriage into this seething mass of humanity, keeping a tight hold on his kit-bag as turbaned traders offered their wares from behind carts heaped with colourful spices, and railway officials, in their blue tunics and caps, tried in vain to keep order. He had been warned about the chaos of an Indian railway station but nothing, he now realized, could have prepared him for such a sensory overload. A voice hailed him. '*Huzoor!* Wait there!'

It was Ilderim, towering head and shoulders above the

other passengers, but still a good fifty yards further down the platform, having just got out of third class. As he moved towards George the crowd seemed to part, intimidated as much by his size as by the steel-rimmed wooden club, or *lathi*, he clutched in his right hand.

On reaching George he rattled off instructions to a waiting gaggle of porters: two were to carry their bags while a third collected their horses from the livestock carriage and met them at the ghat, or landing place. 'This way, *huzoor*,' he said to George. 'We'll take a gharry to the river. It's not far.'

From the back of the pony-drawn carriage George got his first view of the famed Indus, the two-thousand-mile river that flowed from the Tibetan plateau to the Arabian Gulf, whose Greek name had been given to the entire subcontinent. Its span at Kotri was more than half a mile, yet it was close to bursting its banks, thanks to the recent onset of the monsoon and the melting of the summer snows. The ghat below teemed with native craft, some with thatched roofs, and all crammed with merchandise bound for or just arrived from the booming port of Karachi. The exception was a small steamer with a rear paddle-wheel, and a barge attached to either side, that was tied to a rough wooden jetty.

'Is that *it*?' asked George, having imagined something much grander.

'Yes, *huzoor*. A fine vessel, no?'

George was about to answer in the negative when his attention was drawn to a tall man boarding the steamer by a rickety gangplank. He was wearing a light-coloured suit and George could have sworn he was the man from the hotel. 'Ilderim, have you seen that man before?' he asked, pointing at the steamer.

'Which man, *huzoor*?'

'The European who just boarded.'

'There are many Europeans on deck. Which one?'

'The one in the cream suit. I'm sure he was watching me at the hotel.'

'I have no memory of him, *huzoor*.'

'Well, perhaps you weren't on duty – or he didn't leave you a tip. But, believe me, he was there.'

'And you'd like me to keep an eye on him, *huzoor*?'

'Yes, please, if it's not too much trouble.'

Ilderim frowned at his employer's attempt at a joke. 'Consider it done.'

But Ilderim had little opportunity to make good his promise because, for the first week of the voyage up the Indus, the mysterious European spent most of his time in his cabin, even taking his meals there rather than in the communal saloon. Only occasionally did he venture on deck, and only at night when the stifling heat made even the first-class cabins all but unbearable. Ilderim had spotted him once or twice from the shore where he and George, after one torturous night on board, had taken to sleeping rough, wrapped in thin mosquito nets to discourage the swarms of insects. It was as well for them that the steamer only travelled by day to minimize the chances of grounding on the many sandbanks that lay just below the river's fast-flowing surface, and at night was usually anchored alongside a wood station so that fuel for the hungry boilers could be replenished. One by one the other passengers had followed their lead until only the stranger remained on board at night, which made George more suspicious still. When he quizzed the skipper, a light-skinned Anglo-Indian called Skinner, he received a curt reply: 'Where he sleeps at night is his business.'

As the days passed George began to think less of the

stranger and more about his mission. His grasp of Pashto was increasing by the day and even Ilderim – who took little pleasure from his duties as language tutor, or *munshi*, which he seemed to regard as beneath him – was forced to concede that he was a fast learner. George knew that he would have to be fluent if he was to have any chance of getting his hands on the cloak, and redoubled his efforts, spending many hours studying in his cabin.

When he was not working he would sit in a deckchair as the steamer crawled up-river, at speeds rarely exceeding four miles an hour, through immense forests, sandy plains and the occasional tract of cultivated land. They passed so many villages of rudely constructed flat-roofed huts, whose inhabitants looked almost as destitute as their dwellings, that George was hard-pressed to think of a more impoverished setting – until, that was, Ilderim pointed out to him the numerous small craft loading and unloading goods in little creeks beside each village. 'Don't be fooled, *huzoor*. They can trade, thanks to the river, and have more than most. To see real poverty, you must visit the interior.'

The only place of any size and interest on their journey was the sacred town of Sukkur, in upper Sind, which they reached towards the end of the second week. Its main attraction – the needle-shaped minaret of Mir Masum Shah, completed in 1614, and said to house the bones of numerous Mussulman saints – was visible for miles around. George decided to pay it a visit without Ilderim. He had just completed the last of its eighty-four winding steps, and was enjoying the spectacular view over Sukkur's colourful bazaar when footsteps heralded another sightseer. It was, to George's great surprise and not a little alarm, the suspicious stranger who, for once, had left his cabin. He was an odd-looking man, with small, light blue eyes and a slightly crooked jaw, his blond hair parted in the centre. Like George, he wore a broad-brimmed slouch hat, open-necked shirt and trousers, though he also carried a small bag, which could have housed a weapon.

'Are you following me?' asked George.

'Not at all,' said the stranger, with a chuckle. 'Why do you ask?'

'Because every turn I take you're right behind me – the ship from England, the Hotel Metropole in Karachi and now the steamer to Multan. You probably caught the same train as me to Kotri.'

'I did. I won't deny it. But it's hardly a coincidence. Anyone travelling to Peshawar from England would have gone that way. Mail packet to Karachi, a few days' stay in its best hotel while they waited for the first steamer up the Indus from Kotri. I'm not following you, just taking the same route.'

Put like that, George had to concede that it wasn't such a coincidence – but that didn't explain the stranger's odd behaviour. 'Then why have you been acting so suspiciously? I saw you watching me in the hotel lobby, and since we boarded the steamer you've hardly left your cabin.'

'And you've put two and two together, and concluded I'm following you.'

'Exactly.'

'Now, why would I do that? Have you something to hide?'

George reddened. 'No! I just don't like being spied on.'

'Well, you've nothing to worry about then, have you? At the hotel I looked over when I heard you asking about the train to Kotri because I was going the same way. As for my strange behaviour on the boat, there's a quite innocent explanation. I've been working on the facts and figures for a major new piece of business my company is trying to secure in Peshawar.'

'And what business would that be?'

'Why, carpets, of course. You must know that Peshawar is *the* emporium for Asian carpets – the Shatuz is particularly in demand in London at the moment, though the Persian is never out of fashion.'

'You're a carpet dealer?'

'I am. Thomas Overton of the Anglo-Persian Carpet Company, to be precise. And you are?'

'James Harper of Anglo-Indian Trading.'

'Never heard of them. What do you trade in?'

'Dried fruit and nuts from the Punjab and Afghanistan. The well-to-do in the Home Counties can't get enough of them.'

'Is that so? Well, well, well. It seems we're in a similar line of work.'

'Yes, indeed.'

'Well, I must be getting back to my books, sir. Enjoy the view but don't stay out too long. You may be waylaid by dacoits.'

'Dacoits? I don't think I've come across that word in my language book.'

'Which language?'

'Pashto.'

'"Dacoit" is an Urdu word for petty thief or robber. This part of Sind is crawling with them – another reason not to sleep on shore.'

'I'll bear that in mind,' called George, as Overton began to descend the stone staircase.

Later, back at the boat, George told Ilderim of his meeting with Overton, and that he hadn't believed a word the man had spoken. 'Carpet dealer, my foot! He's no more a carpet dealer than I'm a . . .'

'Businessman?' suggested Ilderim.

'What do you mean? I *am* a businessman. No, I was going to say Eurasian. But never mind that. The point is, I don't trust Overton – if that's his name. I fear he means to disrupt my plans.'

'Your *business* plans, *huzoor*?' said Ilderim, pointedly.

George took the hint, and was tempted to tell him the truth, or at least that he was an agent of the British Foreign Office. But on reflection he realized he hardly knew his Afghan companion, and the fewer people who were privy to his mission the better. 'Yes, of course. It may be he works for a rival company. Anyway, as I said before, I'd appreciate it if you'd keep a close eye on him.'

Ilderim said he would, but George could not help feeling that his bodyguard was taking his duties less than seriously. He preferred flirting with the young Sindi women who were travelling with their families in steerage, packed like sardines into the two airless barges that flanked the steamer. One in particular had caught Ilderim's eye, a black-haired beauty with kohl-dark eyes and a suggestive pout, and more than once George had caught him ogling her from the upper deck as she washed her clothes by the riverbank.

'Is she not fine, *huzoor*?' Ilderim had asked, with a wolfish grin.

'Very fine. But she happens to have a father in tow so keep your hands to yourself.'

As it happened, Ilderim could not, but his excuse was a good one. A day after George's brief conversation with Overton, the steamer was negotiating a particularly narrow channel between two large sandbanks when it came to a loud shuddering halt. Its passengers and staff were knocked off their feet and its wheel thrashed the water to no avail. It had run aground.

The captain could not say how long it would take to free it: a day, if they were lucky, possibly three. It depended upon the height of the river. The poorer passengers took him at his word and, despite the danger from the crocodiles that infested the river above Sukkur, set up camp on the nearest sandbank. Before long, the makeshift shelters had spread across several hundred yards of sand and mothers busied themselves at their cooking fires while their youngsters splashed in the shallows.

George and Ilderim had found a secluded spot a little further on and were in the process of unrolling their bedding when they heard a high-pitched scream from the direction of the main camp. Ilderim pulled his long, razor-sharp Khyber knife from its scabbard and tore off down the sand, with George, pistol in hand, a good twenty yards at his rear. A crowd had gathered on the shore, pointing and shouting at an adolescent girl, transfixed with fear, on a narrow sand-bank. Also on the sandbank, barely twenty yards from her, was a huge crocodile.

Without breaking stride, Ilderim stuck his knife between his teeth and hurled himself full length into the water, his long arms eating up the short distance to the stranded girl. George followed, holding his pistol above the water, but was barely halfway across as Ilderim clambered on to dry land. The crocodile had closed to within a couple of yards of the girl, who was screaming hysterically but making no attempt to escape. So intent was the beast on its prey that it failed to notice the big Afghan approaching from behind. As it opened its gaping jaws to strike, Ilderim threw himself on to its back and plunged his knife through the hard scales of its right flank. The great beast snapped its jaws and thrashed in agony, but Ilderim clung on, stabbing it repeatedly until it lay still.

George ran forward and fired a single bullet into the crocodile's head.

'Aargh!' groaned an exhausted Ilderim, his right ear ringing with the gun's report. 'Not so close, please.'

'I was making sure it was dead.'

'It was. Is the girl all right, *huzoor*?'

George turned to see her enfolded in the embrace of the dark-haired beauty Ilderim had been ogling. She, too, had swum across, and her soaking wet *salwar kameez* left little to the imagination. 'Are you sisters?' asked George.

The elder girl smiled but did not reply.

'She doesn't speak English, *huzoor*,' explained Ilderim, who had risen to his feet. He was still holding the bloody knife and the right arm of his white tunic was red with crocodile blood. 'Or Pashto. I'll try in Urdu.'

After a brief conversation, Ilderim turned back to him. 'They're sisters, travelling with their family to their ancestral home near Multan. The young woman is called Soraya. The little one is Umra. She has a habit of wandering off, but no harm done.'

'Thanks to you,' said George. 'That was very brave, what you just did.'

'Any man would have done the same.'

'I think not. Did you see anyone else take on the crocodile?'

'You did.'

'But I had a pistol,' said George, clapping Ilderim on the back. 'Let's get back, shall we, before any more crocodiles appear?'

Having safely escorted the pair back across the water, Ilderim and George were applauded by the crowd and warmly embraced by the girls' father, a great bear of a man with a notable belly and a pair of upturned moustaches. 'You saved my child's life,' he declared in Urdu with great solemnity. 'I am for ever in your debt. Name your price. Anything I have is yours.'

'Anything?' asked Ilderim.

'Anything.'

Ilderim's eyes twinkled with mischief. 'He says I can name my price for saving his daughter. Do you think he'd be agreeable if I asked for the other—'

George raised an index finger. 'Don't even think it!'

Out of the corner of his eye George noticed Overton on the upper deck of the steamer. He was aiming a rifle at the far bank, as if on the look-out for the plentiful game that lined the river, but there were no wild geese, ducks or peafowl in sight. George had an uncomfortable feeling that *he* might have been Overton's true target.

That night, as he slept beside Ilderim on the sandbank, George dreamt the steamer had hit a rock and was sinking. Everyone was leaping into the water to save themselves, and as he followed suit he noticed, too late, that the river was crawling with crocodiles. He woke as a pair of huge jaws were about to slam shut on his arm. It took him a moment to realize that something was indeed tugging on his shoulder. Thinking it must be Ilderim, he uttered an oath and pushed the hand away, but it was insistent. 'What the devil—' He froze in mid-sentence.

It was a clear moonlit night and he could distinctly see a revolver levelled at his chest. The man holding it was not Overton, as he'd half expected, but a swarthy, turbaned rogue with rotten teeth and a great jagged scar from jaw to ear. A couple of steps behind him crouched a younger accomplice, his face pitted with smallpox scars, also holding a pistol. 'Where's your money, Feringhee?' demanded the older man in English.

'I have none,' said George, loudly, hoping to wake Ilderim. But when he sneaked a look at the bedroll on his left it was empty.

'You lie. Feringhees always carry money. Find it or you die.'

George searched in his jacket pockets and produced a handful of notes and coins, which the robber counted. 'Thirty-three rupees, you dog! Where is the rest?'

'That's all I have,' said George, determined not to hand over his gold sovereigns, which were in the bottom of the pack he was using as a pillow, and hoping against hope that Ilderim would return from his midnight ramble.

'You have three seconds to find some more money,' said the robber. 'Then I shoot.'

George looked the man in the eye. He stared back unflinchingly, almost daring George to defy him. 'I have a little in here,' said George, handing over his pack.

The robber passed it back. 'You find it.'

As George rummaged among his clothes he felt the cold metal of his Adams revolver and, for a fleeting moment, was tempted to use it. But he suspected that his chance of shooting both robbers before they got him was extremely low. If he handed over some of the sovereigns they would probably be satisfied and leave. He took the latter option and eased five gold coins from the money-belt at the bottom of the pack. 'Take these and go,' he said, passing them to the older man.

'What are they?'

'Gold.'

The robber's eyes lit up as he inspected one of the shiny coins in the moonlight. 'This picture on the *mohur*, what is it?' he asked, referring to Pistrucci's depiction of St George slaying the dragon.

'It's of one of our mightiest warriors.'

The man grunted in approval, then turned the coin over. 'And who is this?'

'Our queen, Victoria, who is *your* empress.'

The robber chuckled. 'No, my friend. We Sindis have never been ruled by a woman.' He turned to his accomplice. 'Allah has blessed our endeavours this evening, Jabar, and we have far more than we came for. Kill the Feringhee and let us go.'

It was said so matter-of-factly that George thought he must have misheard until the pockmarked Jabar raised his pistol and pointed it directly at his head. 'Now, hold on . . .' he shouted, as a single shot ripped through the still night.

Jabar's pistol remained unfired as a bullet exited from his chest in a spray of blood and tissue. The younger man looked down at the gaping wound in astonishment and horror, then toppled forward. As his body hit the ground, the older robber spun round in one fluid motion and loosed off three shots in the direction of the gunman, then took off into the night, leaving his stricken accomplice on the sand.

Shocked by the sudden violence, George stood rooted to the spot, amazed by his survival. If it had not been for the acrid smell of gunpowder in the air, and the slickness of Jabar's blood on his face, he might have believed he had imagined the whole thing. But groans from the direction of the original shot brought him to his senses. Oh, no, he thought. Please – not Ilderim.

He grabbed his pistol, ran over and found a man in the foetal position on the sand, clutching his stomach, a rifle by his side. It was Overton. '*You* saved me!' said George, wide-eyed. 'Why would you do that? I thought you had it in for me.'

'No,' said Overton, breathing in little gasps. 'Far . . . from it.'

'Lie still and I'll look at your wound.'

'No point, it's in the stomach . . . I'm a goner. But first there's something I must tell you. My name is Overton but I'm not a carpet trader . . . I work for Military Intelligence and I . . . I was sent to keep an eye on you and make sure you reached Afghanistan safely.'

'Who sent you?'

'The Duke of Cambridge.'

'Why?'

Overton paused, as if deciding how much to tell George. 'Let's just say,' he gasped, 'there are vested interests in India who . . . who would prefer you *not* to complete your mission.'

'What vested interests? Are they businessmen? Do they work for the Indian government?'

'They *are* the government.'

George was appalled. How could that be? Overton's response, punctuated by increasingly long gasps for breath, was that Lytton and the hawks in his Indian administration were pursuing a quite different agenda in Afghanistan from that of the British government. They preferred an aggressive Forward policy with the aim of dismembering the country so that the borders of British India could be extended to the natural barrier of the Hindu Kush.

'Are you saying,' asked George, aghast, 'that Lytton and his crew *want* the Mullah Mushk-i-Alam to get his hands on the Prophet's Cloak?'

Overton nodded. It would, he said, guarantee a religious uprising and that in turn would give the Indian government the excuse to invade, topple Yakub and impose British rule. George had to stop that at all costs.

George could see the twisted logic in what Overton was saying, and why Disraeli and Salisbury had avoided using an agent of the Indian government, but he still wanted to know why they had kept him in the dark.

'I suppose they feared,' said Overton, grunting with the exertion, 'that you wouldn't have accepted the mission if you'd known the truth.'

I probably wouldn't, thought George, then remembered something he wanted to ask. 'You said earlier you were sent by the duke to keep an eye on me. Was it his idea, or was he acting for the politicians?'

Overton had shut his eyes. His breathing was much shallower now, his face deathly pale. 'Overton? Can you hear me?'

At first there was no response, and George feared he was dead. But he could see a slight quiver on Overton's lips and at last there came a whispered reply: 'It was his idea . . . his alone.'

George was mystified. Why would the duke send someone to shadow him without telling his political superiors? It didn't make sense – unless the Commander-in-Chief had a personal interest in his safety and the success of his mission. But what could it be?

He looked back at Overton and saw that he was perfectly still. He felt his neck for a pulse. There was nothing. 'Poor fellow.'

Behind him someone was approaching. He whipped round, gun at the ready, to see a bare-chested Ilderim clutching his Khyber knife. '*Huzoor*, are you injured?' said the Afghan, genuine concern on his face.

'I'm fine, but no thanks to you. Where the devil have you been?'

Ilderim looked sheepish. 'I . . . ah . . . had someone to meet.'

'In the middle of the night? Who?'

'Forgive me, *huzoor*, but I couldn't resist.'

'Couldn't resist? Couldn't . . . Oh, no!' said George, having suddenly twigged. 'Please don't tell me you were off whoring with Soraya when you should have been protecting me.'

'Shame on me, *huzoor*, but how was I to know this dog and his accomplices would try to kill you tonight?' said Ilderim, pointing at Overton's body.

'This *dog* saved my life.'

Ilderim took a step closer to examine Overton's face. 'But is this not the man who was following you?'

'He was sent from England to protect me. I got the wrong end of the stick.'

'The wrong end . . . ?'

'Never mind. The point is, if he hadn't intervened those dacoits would have killed me.'

'I saw one body at our camp, *huzoor*. How many were there?'

'Two.'

'And the other escaped?'

'Yes – after he'd shot Overton here, and with my money.'

'I beg your forgiveness, *huzoor*,' said the big Afghan. 'I have failed you miserably and if you seek to replace me I will understand.'

'Don't tempt me, Ilderim. But we've come this far and, having seen you in action, I know how useful you'll be in any future scrum. If you're present, that is, and can keep your mind off the ladies and your trousers on.'

'I can and I will, *huzoor*, on my father's life.'

'Good. Now, you can start by fetching a spade from the steamer. We need to bury these bodies.'

'At once, *huzoor*.'

'And, Ilderim?'

'Yes?'

'Don't dwell on tonight. You couldn't have known what was going to happen and we've all made mistakes with the fairer sex,' said George, thinking of his own ill-starred liaison with Mrs Bradbury, which had cost him his first commission before the Zulu war. 'I just hope your Soraya was worth the trouble.'

Ilderim grinned. 'She was, *huzoor*. In the moonlight her body gleamed like—'

'Enough!' interrupted George. 'I don't need the details. Just be sure her father doesn't find out.'

5

Khyber Pass, North West Frontier Province, late summer 1879

The sun was high in a beautiful cobalt blue sky, the temperature already above a hundred degrees, as George and Ilderim rode through the famous stone gateway at Jamrud – almost medieval in appearance with its round towers and crenellated parapet – and into the Khyber Pass proper. They had left Peshawar at sunrise, having arrived there by train a day earlier. The remainder of the journey up the Indus to Multan had passed without incident.

'Look around you, *huzoor*,' said Ilderim, from the back of his sturdy pony, gesturing to the craggy, dun-coloured hills on either side of the track. 'This was Afghan territory the last time I rode this way. Now it's part of British India, but the tribesmen haven't changed. They're still Afridis – on both sides of the border.'

'Is that your tribe?' asked George.

'I'm a Ghilzai from beyond Michnee Pass. Thankfully my father's lands are still in Afghanistan.'

'Are they close to our route?'

'Not far.'

'Then we must pay your family a visit.'

Ilderim shook his head vigorously. 'No, *huzoor*, that will not be possible.'

'Why ever not?'

'Because my father and I did not part on good terms.'

'But that was many years ago,' said George, reining in his horse and forcing his companion to stop. 'Surely he'd be pleased to see you.'

'I think not.'

'Suit yourself, but I don't see why we should spend any more time roughing it than we have to.'

They rode on in silence up the twisting track, past small fortified villages of mud and stone, perched like eyries on the barren, rocky hillsides of an ever-narrowing valley. Vegetation was sparse and the soil thin and barren. Every now and again they would look up and see a lone Afghan horseman, rifle slung on his back, watching them from the sun-baked ridge above.

'He's from the Akakhel clan of the Afridi,' said Ilderim of one. 'They've been guardians of this stretch of the pass for centuries, and are constantly feuding with the other clans. The only time they band together is when a foreign power tries to use the pass without paying a subsidy.'

'Like the British in forty-two?'

'Yes, though my own people were the first to close the passes beyond Jalalabad.'

Near the summit at Shagai, 3,500 feet above sea level, the pass was barely more than twenty feet wide with steep rocks at either side, a death-trap for any advancing army. But beyond the route levelled and widened into the Landi Kotal plateau – the site of an ancient caravanserai for travellers and soldiers – before narrowing again as the track fell through a series of hairpins and defiles towards the new border crossing at Torkham. There, a red-faced sergeant of the 92nd Highlanders, perspiring freely in his khaki tunic and heavy kilt, detained them long enough to inspect George's papers and warn him against travelling at night.

Though it was early evening they pressed on regardless, and were toiling up yet another precipitous defile, the loose shale and stones causing their mounts to slip and slide, when Ilderim uttered an oath and pointed ahead. Strung out across the summit, blocking their path, were eight horsemen, their slung rifles clearly silhouetted against the darkening sky. 'They're Ghilzai,' said Ilderim. 'Let me do the talking.'

As they got closer George could see that each rider was clad in the tribesman's standard garb of *kurta*, pyjama trousers and a black turban, and was armed to the teeth. Obtruding from the *chadar*, or cummerbund, round his waist were the handles of a knife and pistol, while two cartridge bandoliers across his shoulders provided ammunition for his rifle. Most had Sniders, the breech-loading single-shot rifle first issued to British troops in the sixties and since superseded by the more robust and accurate Martini-Henry. George was relieved to see they were still slung and trusted Ilderim's tribal connection to get them safely through.

'Greetings, brothers,' said Ilderim, cheerily, in Pashto as they approached to within a few yards of the waiting horsemen, whose deadpan expressions betrayed neither friendliness nor hostility. 'Is it far to Jalalabad?'

'Yes, very far,' responded the leader of the group, a bearded ruffian with a hawk nose and high cheekbones. 'Who are you and what are you doing in Afghanistan?'

'My name is James Harper,' responded George, 'and I'm—'

'Hold your tongue, Feringhee,' barked the Afghan. 'I wasn't speaking to you.'

'We have business in Kabul,' said Ilderim, 'and plan to stop in Jalalabad on the way.'

'What business?'

'My companion works for the Anglo-Indian Trading Company and is hoping to develop trade between Afghanistan and Britain for the mutual benefit of both countries.'

'You lie. Trade is an excuse for the British to take control. Did not their interest in Hindustan begin with trade?'

'I can assure you,' said George, 'that my company has no—'

'Quiet! If you speak again, Feringhee, you will lose your tongue. Is it not bad enough that our exalted amir has relinquished the Khyber and allowed the Franks a presence in our capital? Soon, if we let them, they will take over and convert us to Christianity – which is why it is our duty to kill all Feringhees and their Afghan accomplices.'

The leader drew his pistol and aimed it at Ilderim. 'Prepare to meet Satan, you Angrez lapdog!'

'Wait!' shouted Ilderim, who was sure he recognized the cheek mole on the man about to kill him. 'You're Gul Shah. Your father served mine. I'm Ilderim Khan, son of Abdulla Khan, Malik of Khajuri.'

George was about to draw his own pistol, though he knew it would only delay the inevitable, but stayed his hand for the Afghan's response.

'You're *Ilderim*?' the man asked, jaw dropping. 'The malik's only son?'

'I am.'

'Is it possible? The last time I saw Ilderim he had fluff on his chin, yet indeed you resemble him. There is one way you can prove it. Tell me how I got this scar on my temple.' He tapped the side of his head with the revolver.

Ilderim smiled. 'We were hunting for eagles' eggs. You fell and hit your head.'

'That's right,' said Gul, nodding. 'And you stole my prize.'

'You'd have done the same,' countered Ilderim. 'It's good to see you, old friend. Tell me, is my father well?'

'He is. But he still hasn't forgiven you for betraying your people and serving the British. I will spare you and the dark-skinned Feringhee for now, but your father will decide your punishment. Come – Khajuri, as you know, is many miles to the west. It will be dark long before we arrive.'

With Gul and three of his men preceding them, and four more behind, there was little chance of escape, but George was more relieved than concerned. As they rode he told Ilderim that he was looking forward to seeing his ancestral home, and felt sure his father would forgive his youthful indiscretions. 'You're his flesh and blood, after all.'

'You do not know my father,' growled Ilderim. 'When I told him, aged eighteen, I was going to join the Guides, he flew into a rage and said it would be over his dead body. I stole away one night and never returned.'

'That explains your lack of enthusiasm when I suggested a visit. You could have told me, Ilderim.'

'We all have secrets, *huzoor*, even you.'

George wondered again if he should tell him the truth about his mission. But now was not the time.

An hour later, his legs stiff from so long in the saddle, George had just urged his horse up and over yet another steep, scree-covered incline when he saw ahead the ominous outline of a squat mountain fortress with a main entrance gate and a tower at each corner. 'Khajuri?' he asked Ilderim.

'Yes. It seems like only yesterday that I was stick-fighting with Gul in the courtyard, but it must have been thirty years ago.'

'Come!' shouted Gul, kicking his pony into a canter. 'Your fate awaits you.'

They clattered over the wooden drawbridge and into a courtyard lit with burning torches. Grooms hurried forward to hold their horses as they dismounted. 'Follow me,' said Gul to Ilderim, pistol in hand. 'Your father will be dining in the great hall.'

With Gul leading the way, they passed through a large wooden door, studded with iron, and down a stone passageway to where another door and a guard with a rifle barred their progress.

'Tell the malik I've brought his son and a Feringhee,' said Gul.

The sentry nodded and entered the hall, closing the great door behind him. At last it opened to reveal a towering figure of a man with a jet-black beard and a craggy, lined face, his chin glistening with animal fat. 'I have no son,' he said coldly, looking from Ilderim to George. 'Kill them.'

The words were so peremptory, so shocking, that George just stood there open-mouthed. Then he spoke. 'What do you mean you have no son?' he said in Pashto. 'He's standing before you.'

Abdulla turned his fierce dark eyes on George. 'You dare to address *me*, Feringhee?' he said, with quiet menace.

'Yes,' said George. 'I do. Your son is a warrior famed for his valour. You should be proud of him.'

'Proud?' spat Abdulla. 'Of a man who betrayed his people? Never!'

'How did he betray his people?' demanded George. 'Did he take up arms against them? No, he became a soldier of the British, like countless others. When was it a crime for an Afghan to become a mercenary?'

'Always – if his employer is British. They have twice invaded our country and deposed our rightful ruler. Now, instead of Sher Ali, we have his faithless son, Yakub Khan, who has allowed the British a residency in Kabul. Soon they will conquer the whole country.'

George measured his response. He knew that his and Ilderim's lives hung in the balance, and that to preserve them he would have to convince Abdulla that Britain was not intent on annexing his country. The only way to do this, he decided, would be to tell the truth about his mission. Only then might Ilderim's military service be forgiven.

'That is not true,' said George. 'The British government's only interest in Afghanistan is to prevent Russian encroachment, which might threaten the security of India. If Yakub Khan can guarantee this, he will be left to govern as he sees fit. How do I know this? Because I heard it from the mouth of our wazir, Lord Beaconsfield.'

'You lie, Feringhee. Why would your wazir tell a mere boy like you – and a dark-skinned one at that – about matters of such importance?'

'I have been sent here on a secret mission. I told your son I was a businessman called James Harper, but my real name is George Hart. I'm a captain in the British Army and I've been sent to Afghanistan to try to prevent a tribal uprising that will topple Yakub and provoke a fresh invasion, with more bloodshed.'

On hearing this Ilderim turned to George. 'I knew you were a soldier, *huzoor*. Didn't I say it when—'

'Quiet!' shouted Abdulla. 'I'm speaking. So tell me, Feringhee, how do you plan to stop the uprising? Because there will be one, and soon.'

'My task,' said George, looking Abdulla in the eye, 'is to prevent the Mullah Mushk-i-Alam from donning the Prophet's Cloak and rousing the faithful.'

'The Feringhee dog is a British spy!' interjected Gul Shah, raising his pistol. 'He says it himself. Let me kill him now and there's an end to it.'

'Stay your hand, Gul,' growled Abdulla. 'I will hear him out first. It is true that the mullah plots a holy war and would have the whole country under *sharia* law. I know this much from my cousin who lives in Ghazni. It is also true that the cloak would bring many Ghazis to the mullah's side. So your aim is not a foolish one, even if your hopes of success are slender. I, too, have no wish to see the mullah rule supreme: he would weaken the authority of tribal chiefs like me. But I have even less desire to see the British rule in Kabul, and will do everything in my power to prevent it.'

'Then you must spare me, forgive your son, and let us continue on our mission because there are those in Simla who would welcome a rising as an excuse to invade Afghanistan – and this time they will stay.'

'You talk in riddles,' said Abdulla, shaking his head. 'First you say the British don't want to invade. Now you insist they do. Which is it to be?'

'Both. The British government in London doesn't, but the Indian government at Simla does. The viceroy and his friends are convinced the security of India would best be served by annexing Afghanistan. London feels that would only result in more blood spilt and treasure spent, which is why it hasn't told Simla about my mission. If Simla finds out it will certainly try to interfere.'

'So I must let you go if I want Afghanistan to remain free?'

'Yes, and your son too. I can't find the cloak without him.'

Abdulla tugged at his beard while he digested George's words. 'I will think more about what you have said and soon make a decision. But I have one final question. If I let you go and, by the grace of Allah, you recover the cloak, prevent an uprising and avert a British invasion, what then? What will you do with the cloak?'

George hesitated. The cloak was of great spiritual and cultural import to the Afghans and they would not take kindly to its removal, yet his mother desperately needed the money he would earn if he delivered it to London. He was in a quandary and, for the moment, decided to lie. 'It will be kept safe until the country has settled down and Yakub's rule is secure. Only then will it be returned to its special casket in the shrine of Kharka Sharif in Kandahar.'

'I'm not a devout man, but this cloak belongs to we Afghans and must not leave the country. If you can swear to me now, on the life of your mother, that you will neither harm nor remove it, I will grant you your freedom.'

'I swear,' said George. If he kept his word it would cost him two thousand pounds.

'Good. Now let us—'

'Malik, think what you do!' implored Gul Shah, waving his pistol. 'How can you trust a Feringhee?'

'Quiet, I say!' snapped Abdulla. 'If this man can keep the mullah from power and the British outside our borders, then the risk will have been worth taking. And my nose tells me this Feringhee speaks the truth.'

'If that is so,' Gul scowled, 'he will be the first.'

'Maybe so,' said Abdulla, 'but he has already done me a service by returning my son to me.' He turned to Ilderim. 'Promise that you'll never disobey me again. If you can do that, the past is forgotten.'

Ilderim, eyes filled with tears, took a step forward. 'I promise, Father.'

'Then embrace me,' said Abdulla, arms outstretched.

The two huge men stood locked together as Gul glowered and George breathed a sigh of relief, marvelling at the speed with which an Afghan could change his mind.

'Come inside and eat,' said Abdulla, having released his son. 'You must all be hungry.'

They ate in the eastern style, lying on cushions and bolsters, and using their fingers to scoop lamb and rice from wooden bowls. Abdulla was affable now, telling George of when his son had won the tribal wrestling competition, the proudest moment of his life. 'Six months later he left home without a word. But he is here now,' he said, smiling at Ilderim across the room, 'and all is well. A man is nothing without a son to lean on, and a son without the advice of a grey-bearded father is like a pilgrim lost in the desert. Wouldn't you agree, Feringhee?'

'Heartily,' replied George. He gulped his sherbet drink 'I have never met my father. He abandoned me as a child, though he paid for my upkeep and has set aside a substantial sum of money for me if I achieve certain goals.'

'What kind of man abandons his child?' demanded Abdulla.

'I asked my mother that very question. Her answer? "The sort that's married" – he already had a wife.'

'May an Englishman not take many wives?'

'No – it's against the law. And because of this I've never had a father's advice, though there were times when I would have been glad of it,' he said ruefully.

'All sons need direction. But you said your father set you tasks. What are they?'

'To marry well, reach a high military rank and win the Victoria Cross, our highest gallantry award, before the age of twenty-eight.'

'And what age are you now?'

'Almost twenty.'

'Then you have more than enough time. It seems, Feringhee, that even in his absence your father shapes your life.'

'He tries to. And the money would be useful – but for my mother not me. I have no aspirations to be rich.'

'Yet you are bold enough, at nineteen, to come to a foreign country to steal a sacred treasure.'

'I had no choice.'

'Perhaps not, but if your father knew of it he would surely applaud you. It takes much courage even to try such a thing.'

'That and stupidity. I seem to have plenty of the latter.'

With the meal over and the evening entertainment about to begin, Abdulla leant close to George. 'A word of advice, Feringhee,' he whispered. 'If anything happens to my son in your service, you will pay with your life.'

'Then I will do my best to deliver him back to you without a scratch.'

The main door to the hall swung open to reveal a tall, lean tribesman, his clothes streaked with dust.

'Ahmed Jan! At last!' exclaimed Abdulla. 'What news from Kabul?'

'Before strangers, Malik?' asked Ahmed Jan, motioning towards George and Ilderim.

'One is my son Ilderim, the other his companion. They leave for Kabul tomorrow and need to know what's afoot.'

'What's afoot, Malik, is mutiny.'

'In which regiments?'

'The six recently arrived from Herat. They haven't received pay for two months and are angry that Yakub Khan has signed the treaty with the Angrez. I heard one soldier abuse a fellow whose regiment had been defeated by the Angrez last year. He said that if the Herat regiments had fought, the outcome would have been very different.'

'What deluded fools they are to imagine they wouldn't scatter like sheep at the first sight of an Angrez bayonet. And now they plan mutiny, do they? How came you by this news?'

'My cousin serves with one of the Herat regiments. He told me not all are disaffected, but the leaders threaten those who waver with death. Their plan is to kill their officers and attack the compound inhabited by the Angrez envoy and his escort. None of the Feringhees will be spared.'

George felt a chill down his spine. The Foreign Office spy he was due to meet, his sole contact in Afghanistan, worked at the British Residency in Kabul as an interpreter for the envoy, Sir Louis Cavagnari. He had to get to him before the mutiny erupted or he would never discover the whereabouts of the cloak. 'Do you know when this will happen?' he asked Ahmed Jan.

'No, my cousin couldn't say. But it will be soon.'

'Then Ilderim and I must leave at first light.'

'As you wish, Feringhee,' said Abdulla. 'But first some entertainment.'

He clapped his hands and a light-skinned young dancing girl appeared, wearing satin trousers and a tight, transparent bodice that seemed too flimsy to restrain her ample bosom. Her face was partially obscured by a gauze veil, but above it shone a pair of green almond-shaped eyes, a legacy of Alexander's Greeks. As the flautists and drummers began to play, the girl's body writhed and quivered, her hands twirling before her.

George couldn't take his eyes off the undulating spectacle before him. Faster and faster the musicians played, with the dancer keeping pace, seemingly with ease, though her face glistened with perspiration. Suddenly the music stopped and the girl froze, then slumped to the floor, her chest heaving.

Abdulla turned to George. 'Isn't she magnificent?'

'She certainly is. What's her name?'

'Ishtar – it means "Star of Heaven". Her parents were killed in a tribal feud when she was just four. She has lived under my protection ever since. No Ghilzai dances better. Would you like to meet her?'

'Certainly.'

'Ishtar, come to me,' called Abdulla.

The girl walked over, her breasts swaying provocatively, and stood before the cushions, arms crossed and chin held high. She was very tall, with a tiny waist and full hips, and George could just detect a tiny diamond sparkling in her belly button.

'This Feringhee is my guest,' said Abdulla. 'Sit with him awhile and, if he likes you, he may choose to take you to his bedchamber.'

'No!' said George. 'That's not what I meant when I said I'd like to meet her.'

'You don't like her?' asked Abdulla, affronted.

'Of course I do. Who wouldn't? But does she like me?'

'Like you? What difference does it make? Ilderim!' he shouted, motioning for his son to come closer. 'You must hear this.'

Ilderim rose and walked over. 'What is it, Father?'

'The Feringhee won't accept my offer of Ishtar.'

Ilderim looked grave. 'You understand, *huzoor*, that to spurn an Afghan's hospitality is the greatest insult you can offer?'

'I know, and I would never do that,' said George, calmly. 'I wish to be sure that Ishtar has a say in the matter.'

'You have much to learn about our customs,' said Ilderim. 'Ishtar owes her life to my father. If he asked her to jump into a freezing river she would do it. Spending the night with a pretty youth like you is nothing. She might even enjoy it. Eh, Ishtar?'

The girl did not reply and, because she was still veiled, George was unable to read her expression, though her eyes seemed faintly amused.

'So what do you say, Feringhee?' asked Abdulla. 'Will you lie with her or not?'

George had been in some ticklish positions in his young life, but none quite as bizarre as this. He was certainly attracted to the girl, and would have liked to take her to his bed if she was willing. But how could he know she was before he accepted Abdulla's offer? The only solution, he decided, was to tread a delicate middle ground.

'I will,' said George, standing up and taking Ishtar's hand. 'And as it's late, and we have an early start, I hope you will not take offence if I retire at this very minute.'

Abdulla roared with laughter. 'You change your mind like a woman, Feringhee, but no matter. Leave us and enjoy yourself. The servants will show you the way.'

'Good night, then,' said George.

He and Ishtar followed a servant along a passageway, then up a spiral staircase to a chamber in one of the towers. It was a simple whitewashed room with few furnishings beyond a carpet, a chest and an iron bedstead, and was lit by a single flaming torch set in the wall. Beside the bed lay George's kit-bag. He turned to Ishtar. 'You may stay or go. If you go, I won't tell the malik.'

She unhooked one side of her veil to reveal a beautiful shapely mouth. Slowly her full lips parted in a smile. 'I will stay, Feringhee, not because you want me to but because I choose to.' With that she took two paces forward and raised her lips to his.

Surprised by her boldness, George felt a momentary stab of guilt as he was reminded of the two women he had left behind in Africa – one with whom he was in love, or had been, and one who was in love with him and increasingly in his thoughts. Yet he was tied to neither, he told himself, and Ishtar was too inviting an opportunity to dismiss. His qualms assuaged, he leant forward and kissed her hungrily, pulling her towards him and down onto the bed.

6

They left at dawn, and were escorted by Gul Shah and his men as far as the Kabul road where they continued on alone. Ilderim broke the silence. 'Thank you for what you did last night, *huzoor*,' he said, as they slowed their mounts to a walk. 'I am for ever in your debt.'

'Not a bit of it,' replied George, trying to keep a straight face. 'It is I who am in your debt, or at least your father's. I have never known such hospitality. Your dancer . . .'

Ilderim snorted. 'I did not mean Ishtar but your talk with my father. One moment he is angry enough to kill us both, the next he is ordering food and embracing me like the long-lost son I am. It was your doing, *huzoor*, and I shall not forget it.'

'Oh, *that*,' said George, feigning surprise. 'Well, I did it to save both our skins. But, joking aside, it was fortunate that your father sympathized with my mission because he and the British government in London have the same basic aim in Afghanistan – to keep the mullah from power and British troops out.'

'Yes, *huzoor*, very fortunate. But why didn't you tell *me* about your mission? I knew you were no trader. A soldier always knows his kind.'

George grinned. 'You spotted me, all right. But I didn't

dare tell you because I was afraid you wouldn't come with me if you knew the truth. I suspect most Afghans would happily slit the throat of an infidel if he dared to look upon the cloak, let alone touch it.'

'Maybe so, *huzoor*. But you have my father's blessing and that is enough for me. I will remain with you until you have the cloak, or are killed, whichever comes first.'

'Thank you, Ilderim. I appreciate your loyalty.'

Now it was Ilderim's turn to smile. 'It's not loyalty, *huzoor*. I'm doing it for the money.'

'Spoken like a true Afghan!'

'So where next, *huzoor*?'

'To Kabul. My only contact in the country is Pir Ali, a *munshi* in the employ of the British resident. He will have information about the cloak. I must also speak to Sir Louis Cavagnari himself, without revealing my true identity, and warn him of the impending mutiny. But it's a race against time. If the mutineers attack before we reach the Residency, and Pir Ali is killed, we have no hope of locating the cloak. So, let's not dawdle,' said George, and dug his heels into his horse's sides.

An hour later, as they watered the animals in a shallow stream, George looked across at his companion. 'I confess, Ilderim, I never dreamt I'd spend my twentieth birthday here.'

'So young, but why didn't you talk of this last night? My father would have given you two women to mark the occasion.'

George laughed. 'One was quite enough!'

It was late afternoon the following day when George and Ilderim came in sight of the walled city of Kabul. They had camped overnight at Gandamak, where the recent treaty had been signed. It had been the site, too, in 1842, of the British 44th Regiment of Foot's last stand. Riding in from the east, with the Siah Sang range of hills on his right, it seemed to George that the city occupied a near impregnable position: to the south and west it was protected by mountains, to the north by the Kabul river, while the east, directly ahead, was guarded by a wall, twenty feet high and twelve feet thick. Its south-eastern corner was commanded by a towering fortress, rising more than 150 feet above the plain.

'That must be the Bala Hissar,' said George, pointing towards the fort. 'Now I know why the British were so criticised for relinquishing it in thirty-nine.'

Ilderim nodded. 'We have a saying: "He who holds the Bala Hissar holds Kabul." By that we mean the upper fortress, or citadel, which contains the magazine and the dungeon known as the "Black Pit". The lower fortress, which you enter first, is not as formidable and houses the stables, barracks and royal residences.'

'One of which, I'm told, Yakub has given to Cavagnari to use as his residency. Well, at this distance it looks quiet enough. I think we're in time.'

They rode on through a richly cultivated valley of clover and lucerne, the crops' verdant green a relief from the general brownness of the land, and up a road lined on both sides with closely planted willow trees. Just short of the city walls they turned sharply to the left and began the climb to the fortress. Their first view was of a huge wall of crumbling masonry, twenty feet high but built on a rock of similar height so that a precipitous face of forty feet was presented to any attacker. Every hundred yards or so a bastion, bristling with cannon, jutted out from the main wall, and in the intervals between rose the high, flat-roofed buildings of the palaces. The road curved gently to the right and soon came to the main gatehouse, almost medieval in appearance, with its two round towers, vaulted archway and castellated top. It, too, had seen better days, the inner supports having crumbled away and the defensive position overhead lacking its protective parapets.

As they approached, a big, bearded havildar, or sergeant, of the Afghan Army, with a Snider rifle on his shoulder, stepped forward.

'I'm a British businessman,' said George in Pashto. 'I've come to speak to the resident.'

The Afghan soldier spat pointedly on the ground and said something in a language George didn't understand.

Ilderim shouted back at him in the same strange tongue and the soldier responded in kind. Worried that the argument was getting out of hand, George was about to tell Ilderim to calm down when the havildar, his face still defiant, waved them through the gateway.

'What was that about? And what language was he speaking?' asked George, as they entered the lower fortress, a veritable rabbit warren of dilapidated mud and brick buildings and squalid alleyways, hidden behind tumbledown walls, interspersed with patches of wasteground. Directly ahead, higher up the hill, stood the citadel.

'The insolent dog answered you in Persian, *huzoor*, though he speaks perfectly good Pashto.'

'Why?'

'Because he dislikes Feringhees.'

'Is he from one of the Herat regiments?'

'He is.'

'So Ahmed Jan was right. There is trouble brewing. What did he say?'

'He said that we should hurry if we wished to visit the resident because he wouldn't be here for much longer. When I asked him what he meant by that, he refused to say, but I think we know.'

'There's not a moment to lose. Which way?'

'The Residency stands against the southern wall of the Bala Hissar, and directly below the south-east wall of the citadel. To reach it we must pass by the amir's garden. It's not far.'

Using the citadel as a guide, they soon came to a small unkempt square that was being used as an artillery park: six field guns and as many mountain guns were parked in front of a dozen dirty tents, the gunners lounging and chaffing in the sun. Ilderim questioned one man, who was not wearing uniform and looked more like an unwashed coolie than a soldier, and was told they had come too far. They retraced their steps and eventually found the narrow lane that ran along the southern edge of the amir's garden. On their right was the high wall that marked the garden's boundary and on their left rude open-air stables, little more than simple enclosures in the mud wall, in which were tethered the horses of the royal household.

The lane brought them to the rear of an enclosed three-storey building that Ilderim explained was part of the Residency compound, but that to reach the main gate they had to work their way round to the right. They did so, and at last came to an open gateway guarded by two soldiers wearing large turbans, long khaki *kurta*s with red facings on the collar and cuffs, and riding boots. 'Rest easy, *huzoor*,' said Ilderim, 'they're Indian soldiers from my old corps.'

'Guides?'

'Yes.'

'Do you know them?'

'Perhaps,' said Ilderim, as if he was speaking to a child. 'But I can't tell at this distance.'

As they got closer, George received his answer from one of the Guides, a burly *naik*, or corporal,with a hooked nose and a trim beard. 'Can it be true?' He took a step forward and peered intently at Ilderim. 'Why, it is. The hero of a thousand fights, Subadar Khan! What are you doing in Kabul, sir?'

'And salaams to you, too, Akbar Shah, as insolent as ever, I see. Whatever possessed your officer to raise you to *naik*?'

Akbar Shah chuckled, showing a fine set of betel-stained teeth. 'He believes, like many, that it's better to guard sheep with a wolf.'

'And is *he* a wolf?' asked Ilderim.

'No, sir, but he *is* a lion. He saved my life when I was unhorsed in the charge at Futtehabad, in April, by cutting down my three assailants. We had already lost the commandant and Hamilton Sahib took charge. There is none braver and he deserves the Queen's Cross.'

'He has been recommended for the Victoria Cross?' asked George.

'I have indeed,' said a voice to their right, with a distinctly Irish accent. The speaker was a stocky officer of middle height with a pale, freckled face and a centre parting. He was dressed in a khaki patrol jacket and breeches, with a sword and pistol holster attached to his shiny leather Sam Browne cross-belt, and was holding a white sun helmet topped with a metal spike under his left arm. 'I'm Lieutenant Walter Hamilton, commanding the Resident's Escort. What can I do for you?'

George gave his cover story and said he had come to discuss

business opportunities with the resident. His intention was to use the interview to warn Cavagnari of the impending attack and then to make contact with Pir Ali.

'The resident is very busy but if you follow me, Mr Harper, I'll see what I can do. Leave your horse here. Your guide can secure him to the picket line and is welcome to refreshments in the soldiers' mess.'

'Thank you,' said George, dismounting. 'His name is Ilderim Khan. Does that ring any bells, Lieutenant?'

'Should it?'

'He was a subadar in your regiment.'

'Was he?' exclaimed Hamilton. He gave Ilderim the once-over but showed no sign of recognition. 'Well, I don't remember him. He must have been before my time. Come this way, Mr Harper. Akbar Shah will look after Ilderim Khan and see to your horses.'

The outer compound was bounded on its south side by the huge outer wall of the Bala Hissar, and on the north by a low mud wall that was commanded along its length by flat-roofed houses. In the centre of the compound stood the cavalry lines and stables, and at the far end the infantry barracks. Just beyond the barracks was the gated entrance to the inner courtyard, which, again, was manned by four Guides. They presented arms as George and Lieutenant Hamilton passed through the gate and turned immediately right towards the Residency, a handsome two-storey brick and plaster house, with two small wings and a covered balcony on each floor. 'Not a bad place to live,' commented George.

'I wouldn't know,' said Hamilton, with a grin. 'I'm slumming it with the other officers in the Mess House opposite.' George looked back to see an even grander three-storey suite of rooms enclosing the far end of the inner courtyard, the back wall of which he had seen from the lane that flanked the amir's garden. However, as it backed on to two lanes it was harder to defend, while Cavagnari's house was built into the fortress's outer wall. Even to George's relatively inexperienced eye, it was obvious that the compound – overlooked on three sides by flat-roofed houses and higher ground – was a death-trap.

'Coming?' said Hamilton, rousing George from his gloomy thoughts.

He followed the officer through the door of the main house, across a marbled entrance hall and into a small antechamber beyond. 'Take a seat,' said the lieutenant. 'I'll let Sir Louis know you're here.'

An hour passed and, with the light failing, servants came to light oil lamps. George was pacing the room, wondering how best to phrase his warning, when another servant entered. He was short and wiry, with a keen, intelligent face, and wearing a small white cap of the type favoured by Bengali Muslims. 'A thousand apologies, sahib,' said the man in English. 'The resident cannot see you today and asks that you come back another time.'

'No!' said George, loudly. 'That's not good enough. I must see him today. Tell him it's a matter of the utmost urgency.'

The servant looked puzzled. 'But Hamilton Sahib said you had come to discuss business?'

'That too. But I have something more serious to talk to the resident about and I will not leave until I have spoken to him.'

'I will try.'

Minutes later the servant was back. 'The resident will see you now.'

George was led up a flight of polished wooden stairs to

a large, airy office on the first floor. A middle-aged man with thinning hair and a spade beard sat at a desk strewn with papers, writing a letter. He was impeccably dressed in a starched shirt with a wing collar, a loose bow-tie and double-breasted frock coat sporting three medals, one of which George recognized as the campaign award for the Indian Mutiny. Like many ambitious officers in India, Cavagnari had served a brief time with his regiment before switching to the political service.

'Thank you, Pir Ali,' said Cavagnari to the servant, with just the faintest touch of the Irish brogue in his voice, 'that will be all.'

George was startled to hear the name of the Foreign Office spy he had come to see. He had assumed the departing *munshi* was just another servant, and now he knew better he chided himself for missing the opportunity to talk to him.

'Well?' snapped Cavagnari. 'What's so important that it must interrupt a letter to Lord Lytton? You do know who Lord Lytton is?'

'Of course,' replied George, trying hard to keep the irritation out of his voice. 'And what I have to say would be of interest to the viceroy.'

'Go on.'

'The Afghan regiments, lately arrived from Herat, are planning to mutiny, and when they do they'll attack the Residency. They intend to kill everyone.'

'How did did you come by this information?' asked Cavagnari.

'I heard it two days ago from a Ghilzai whose nephew serves in one of the mutinous regiments.'

'So it's hearsay?'

'Well, yes, but—'

'No buts. You've heard a rumour and now you're repeating it as fact. So, tell me, if you're so sure of your source, when is this mutiny to take place?'

'I don't know, but it will be soon. Why, only today as we passed through the gatehouse—'

Cavagnari raised his hand. 'You come here without an appointment, demanding an audience, and when I grant you one against my better judgement, you repeat some gossip from the bazaar about a mutiny and a threat on my life. Do you think I'm some griff, wet behind the ears, who knows nothing of these people?'

'Of course not. I was simply trying to—'

'Save your breath. Who exactly are you, anyway? You say you're a businessman, but you look too young for that. Tell me, how long have you been in India?'

'About two months.'

'*Two months*? I've been here for more than twenty years, most of that time on the frontier, and I know the Afghans. They're cowards – oh, they're brave enough when they have numbers on their side, but put 'em in a fair fight and they'll slip away every time.'

'But this won't be a fair fight!' said George, in exasperation. 'The Afghan troops from Herat are more than six thousand strong. How many men do you have?'

'I have seventy-five, under one of the finest officers in the Indian Army, which is more than enough to deter a mutinous rabble. But it won't come to that because the Afghans know that if anything happens to me the Indian Army will be back in force.'

It occurred to George that Cavagnari, a staunch advocate of Lytton's Forward policy, might welcome an attack as a means of provoking a British response. But even he, George decided, wouldn't be stupid enough to ignore the risk of an attack, and put his own life in danger, in the interests of government policy. Or would he?

'I'm not saying the Afghans welcome our presence,' continued Cavagnari. 'Of course they don't. And it's true the regiments from Herat have been going about the city with drawn swords, using inflammatory language against us and the amir. But their chief gripe is with their arrears of pay. Once Yakub pays up, they'll be as meek as lambs. When you've been in this part of the world as long as I have, Harper, you'll know that barking dogs never bite.'

'I'll have to take your word for that, sir,' said George. 'But a wise man would still take the precaution of preparing the Residency for a siege and asking Simla for more troops.'

'A *wise* man? How dare you condescend to me?' Cavagnari blustered. 'The troops I have are unpopular enough. Bringing in more would be like waving a red rag before a bull. I think it's time you left. Pir Ali!'

The *munshi* reappeared. 'Sahib?'

'Show Mr Harper out.'

'At once.' He turned to George. 'This way, Harper Sahib.'

George followed Pir Ali out of the room and, as they reached the top of the stairs, put his arm on the *munshi*'s shoulders. 'I must speak with you in private. My real name is Captain George Hart. I've been sent by the Foreign Office on a secret assignment.'

Pir Ali seemed mystified. 'I'm sorry, sahib, I don't understand.'

So convincing was Pir Ali's disavowal that for a second George feared he had the wrong man. Then he remembered the password. 'Himalaya,' he said, without explanation.

Instantly Pir Ali's demeanour changed. 'Welcome, sahib. Follow me.'

At the bottom of the stairs, Pir Ali led George along a short corridor and into a small, windowless room. A table was piled high with papers. 'My office,' explained Pir Ali. 'Now what can I do for you, sahib?'

'You can start by convincing your arrogant, short-sighted chief that you're all living on borrowed time.'

Pir Ali laughed. 'I've been trying to do that for months. My instructions from the Foreign Office are to watch for any signs of disaffection, and to warn Cavagnari Sahib accordingly, which I have. But he ignores me. It's as if he welcomes an explosion.'

'My thoughts exactly,' responded George. He explained his assignment to secure the Prophet's Cloak.

'I fear your task here has been compromised,' said Pir Ali, ruefully. 'Only the other day I overheard Cavagnari Sahib tell his secretary, Jenkyns Sahib, that it was vital he got his hands on the cloak before the Foreign Office did. It was the first time I'd heard him speak of it.'

'But how could he have found out?'

'Perhaps the Indian government has a spy in the Foreign Office. It wouldn't surprise me. But Cavagnari Sahib didn't mention you by name so he may not know your identity.'

George breathed a sigh of relief. 'That's something. If he did suspect anything just now, he didn't let on. Then again, he could hardly have been ruder. What do you think he plans to do with the cloak?'

'I couldn't say, sahib. It's possible he intends to give it to the mullah. That way a rebellion is certain. It will be followed by a British invasion. The resident has often talked of annexation as the only way to guarantee India's security. I suspect he covets the post of governor. You must never forget, Hart Sahib, that the cloak means power.'

George nodded. 'That's why I must get to it first. I was told you'd know how to find it. Do you?'

'I did. But I heard only yesterday that it had been moved from the shrine of Kharka Sharif in Kandahar.'

'Do you know by whom, and where it is going?'

'No, I do not. But the people who have it are either acting for Cavagnari Sahib or the mullah. I will ask my contacts. Now you had better go, sahib, or you'll arouse suspicion. Come back tomorrow and I should have some news for you.'

'I'll do that, but please don't take any unnecessary risks. The success of my mission depends on your information. One more thing: where can I spend the night?'

'Try the Shalimar Hotel on Faizabad Street. It is cheap and clean, and out of the way. But don't go out after dark. It is not safe in these troubled times.'

7

George took Pir Ali's advice and shared a room with Ilderim at the ramshackle Shalimar Hotel. They regretted it the following morning, having been eaten alive by fleas, and it was as much as George could do to prevent Ilderim assaulting the owner.

Ilderim was still cursing as they rode back up the hill to the Bala Hissar, but the faint sound of fifes and drums caused George to interrupt: 'Hush! Listen!'

Ilderim cocked an ear. 'It sounds like soldiers, *huzoor*.'

They both swung round in their saddles and looked out across the dusty plain that separated the city from the Sherpur cantonment to the north. Advancing steadily up the road that skirted the city and led directly to the Bala Hissar they saw a great straggling mob of soldiers. The head of the column had just crossed the Kabul river, barely a mile distant, and would be with them in fifteen minutes. 'They must be the Herat troops,' said George. 'We'd better warn the resident.'

They clattered to a halt at the gatehouse. There was no sign of the surly havildar, but his replacement looked no more pleased to receive them. Once again Ilderim did the talking and they were soon waved through. At the Residency George was pleased to note that the guard had been strengthened, with six on duty at the entrance to the outer compound and another six on the inner gate. 'It seems our warnings weren't entirely disregarded,' he said to Ilderim, as they dismounted.

'Maybe not, *huzoor*, but what can twelve do against many thousands?'

They explained to the guards they had an appointment with the *munshi* and hurried into the main house where George almost collided with the resident who, having just returned from his morning ride, was still wearing his jodhpurs and hacking jacket. 'Ah, it's Harper, the Cassandra,' sneered Cavagnari, 'come to warn us the sky is about to collapse. I thought I made my feelings plain yesterday.'

'You did, perfectly,' said George, ignoring the sarcasm. 'But events have moved on since then. As we rode up the hill from the city just now we could see the Herat troops marching across the plain.'

'What of it? Like as not they're coming to receive their pay.'

'And what if there isn't money to pay them?'

'Then they'll come back when there is.'

George frowned. 'I believe you're being a little optimistic. If you only knew the temper of the troops you'd be taking every precaution. They'll be here in minutes.'

'I've heard enough of this,' said Cavagnari. 'Jemadar!' An immaculately dressed Sikh officer appeared from a side room. 'Escort this pair out of the compound without delay, please.'

The jemadar was about to comply when the sound of shouting caused him to pause. Cavagnari strode over to the door and opened it. The shouts and yells were much louder now, as if they were getting closer. He turned to the native officer. 'Jemadar, take two men and find out what's happening.'

'Sir.'

Minutes later the jemadar returned, his chest heaving with exertion. 'Sahib, come quick! Hundreds of unruly soldiers have entered the outer compound.'

'Why didn't the guard stop them?' asked Cavagnari.

'They didn't want to shoot for fear it would make matters worse.'

'Where's Hamilton?'

'He's at the cavalry lines, sahib, trying to stop the crowd looting.'

'I must speak to them,' said Cavagnari. 'Pir Ali!'

The *munshi* appeared from his office and acknowledged George with a slight dip of his head. 'Yes, sahib?' he said to Cavagnari.

'Come with me. I need you to translate.'

'Shall we come too?' asked George.

'If you must.'

They hurried through the gate into the outer compound and past the infantry barracks. Up ahead, stretching from the cavalry lines to the low mud wall, stood a thin picket of Guides, rifles at the ready. Beyond them raged a huge crowd of infuriated half-savage soldiery in their undress uniform, clutching clubs, wooden staves and stones, and shouting curses and threats.

They ran forward to the centre of the thin khaki line where they were met by Lieutenant Hamilton, who had reinforced the initial guard with another twenty men. He gestured towards the mob. 'They're demanding their arrears of pay, sir.'

'Are they indeed?' said Cavagnari. 'Cheeky blighters. I'll soon set them straight.'

'Sir Louis,' said George, 'if you have the money it might be the safest option to pay them.'

Cavagnari gave George a withering look. 'Nonsense. They're the amir's soldiers, not mine. If he doesn't stand on his own two feet now, he never will. Stand aside!'

The guard complied, enabling Cavagnari and Pir Ali to walk through the picket and stop within ten yards of the mutinous soldiers who, having recognised the resident, had fallen silent.

Prompted by Cavagnari, the *munshi* spoke to the crowd: 'His Excellency Sir Louis Cavagnari, Envoy and Minister Plenipotentiary to His Royal Highness the Amir of Kabul, wishes me to tell you that, even if he wanted to, he could not furnish your arrears of pay because he does not have enough money.'

The angry yells began again.

'But,' continued Pir Ali, forced to shout to make himself heard, 'he will speak to the amir today to try to ensure that you are paid what you are owed as soon as possible. In the meantime he asks you to cease this disorder and return quietly to your barracks.'

The crowd responded by jeering and throwing rocks, one of which narrowly missed Cavagnari's head. But Pir Ali was not so fortunate, a missile catching him flush on the forehead. The crack as stone met skull was quickly followed by the boom of shots from the Guides' Sniders. Three Afghans fell to the ground, as did Pir Ali, while the crowd scattered in all directions.

George and Ilderim rushed forward and dragged Pir Ali to safety as the crowd rapidly funnelled out of the compound.

'Will he live?' asked Cavagnari, as they placed Pir Ali's unconscious body gently on the ground.

'I don't know,' replied George, feeling his wrist. 'His pulse is weak. He took quite a blow to the head.'

'Hamilton, order four of your men to carry Pir Ali back to the Mess House so Dr Kelly can examine him. Then withdraw the rest of the guard to the barracks and the inner courtyard. Make sure all the doors are barricaded and the roofs manned. They've dispersed for the moment but they might return.'

'I'd say that's very likely, sir,' said George. 'My guess is they've gone to loot the armoury and rouse their fellows.'

Cavagnari cleared his throat. 'It seems, Harper, you were right all along. I apologize for doubting you. How long do think we've got?'

'An hour, maybe less. Your best course is to appeal to the amir for protection. If he sends some of his own regiments to intervene, the Herat troops would never dare to attack.'

'I'm sure you're right. Hamilton, who would you recommend as a messenger?'

'Sowar Taimur, sir. He's descended from the Sadozai amirs of Kabul and speaks the lingo. If he takes off his uniform, he shouldn't arouse too much suspicion.'

'Taimur it is, then. Tell him to collect the letter from my house in five minutes. And can you also provide Harper and his guide with Sniders and ammunition from the armoury? We'll need their help if the mob returns.'

'Sir.'

As Cavagnari returned to his house, Hamilton turned to George. 'Are you armed, Mr Harper?'

George patted the shoulder holster he was wearing under his jacket. 'I have a revolver.'

'What about Ilderim Khan?'

'He has his Khyber knife.'

'Much good that will do him. Has either of you used a Snider before?'

'No,' said George, 'though I have fired a Martini-Henry.'

'I have handled neither, *huzoor*,' put in Ilderim. 'When I was a Guide we used muzzle-loading Enfields.'

Hamilton laughed. 'One ahead of his time, one behind. But no matter, you're both familiar with firearms and a quick demonstration will set you straight.'

'If I may ask,' said George, 'why *are* you still armed with the Snider? The British Army stopped using it years ago.'

'Which is why we have it now. Since the Mutiny, there's been an understandable mistrust of native soldiers and a deliberate policy to keep them at a slight disadvantage by issuing them with the previous generation of firearm to that used by the British Army. So when British troops got the Martini-Henry a few years ago, our men were given their Sniders.'

'Doesn't that benefit our enemies?'

'Not in Afghanistan. Oh, I know what they say about the Snider – that it's a breech-loading conversion of the old Enfield rifle, whereas the Martini-Henry was custom-built. And that's all true. But the Snider still has a couple of major advantages: it's accurate to a thousand yards, which is further than the Martini-Henry, and its slug packs a greater punch.'

'What about rate of fire? Is it as quick as the Martini?'

'Almost.'

'Really?' George raised his eyebrows.

'In skilled hands, anyway. Look, I'll show you.'

He took a rifle from the nearest soldier and showed George how to cock the hammer before using a lever on the left of the breech to slide the side-hinged block to the right. The old cartridge, he explained, could then be extracted either by hand, or by turning the rifle on its back to allow it to drop out. Finally a new cartridge could be inserted and the block returned to its original position for firing. 'Effective, isn't it?' said Hamilton.

'Not really,' said George. 'With the Martini-Henry you just pull the lever behind the trigger guard and the weapon is ready to reload. But beggars can't be choosers. I'm sure it will suffice.'

George squinted down the sight of his Snider, took a deep breath and gently squeezed the trigger. A metallic click sounded as the hammer struck the firing pin, but no explosion. He lowered the weapon and went through the loading procedure that Hamilton had taught him. But no matter how many times he did it he couldn't get the hang of it. Part of the problem was that you needed two hands, and that made the whole process far clumsier than loading the Martini-Henry. There was also the issue of recoil: he'd suffered many a painful shoulder from firing the .45 calibre Martini-Henry; but the Snider was .577 and reputedly had a kick like a mule's. Not that he'd know until he actually fired it.

He glanced at his pocket-watch. Ten minutes to nine, and already the glare from the sun was making it hard to focus. He could feel a trickle of sweat rolling down his back and sensed it was going to be a long, hot day. He and Ilderim had been kneeling with Lieutenant Hamilton and a party of Guides behind a makeshift parapet on the flat roof of the Mess House for more than forty-five minutes and still there was no sign of either the messenger or the mutinous troops. Of more immediate concern to George, however, was the state of Pir Ali's health. The unconscious *munshi* had been put to bed on the second floor of the Mess House but there had been no news of him since.

He stood up to stretch his cramped limbs and to get a better view of the Bala Hissar's layout. Directly below him, away to the west, stretched the Residency's mostly deserted outer compound, though the Guides' cavalry horses were still picketed at the far end; the only troops were the twenty or so men guarding the infantry barracks, the roof of which was a nerve-racking but manageable leap of about ten feet from where George was standing on the south-west corner of the Mess House. Due south of George was Cavagnari's house, and behind him, to the north-east, a garden that led to the amir's palace, no more than 250 yards away.

A voice spoke behind him: 'He should have been back by now, Hamilton. What's keeping him?'

It was Cavagnari. He and his secretary, Jenkyns, a tall Scotsman with a neat moustache, had climbed up to the roof for a better view.

'I don't know, sir,' replied Hamilton. 'I suppose it's possible he's been detained.'

'By the amir? Never. He wouldn't dare. But unless we hear back soon we'll have to send another message. And another, until that rascal Yakub responds.'

'Just give me the word, sir. My sowars are ready for anything.'

'Can I ask, sir,' interrupted George, 'how is Pir Ali? Has he come round yet?'

'I'm afraid not. Dr Kelly thinks his skull is fractured and that he may not live.'

George's heart sank. Without Pir Ali's contacts he knew that locating the cloak would be like finding a needle in a haystack. But he had only a moment to dwell on the matter before Hamilton pointed to a gathering cloud of dust beyond the fortress's main gate. 'Sir, we have company.'

'My God,' breathed Cavagnari. 'How many must there be to raise a cloud like that?'

At first all they could hear was the din and rush of hurrying feet, but soon the sound swelled to an audible chant from countless throats. '*Ya Charyar! Ya Charyar!*'

'What are they saying, Ilderim?' asked George.

'It's the Ghazi war-cry,' explained Ilderim. 'It means "Hail, the four Prophets of Muhammad", and promises death to the non-believer.'

As if to confirm Ilderim's words, a mob of soldiers and civilians came pouring down the road that led from the main gate and spilt through the lanes that fed into the far end of the Residency's outer compound. Some clutched the green flag of *jihad*, others a variety of ancient and modern weapons: muskets, swords, rifles, pistols, clubs and knives. There were hundreds of them, and they kept coming.

'Sights at four hundred yards,' roared Hamilton, above the din. 'Hold your fire until they reach the cavalry lines. Steady . . . steady.'

Memories of the desperate fight at Rorke's Drift flooded back to George as he waited, heart thumping, for the order to fire. How he and most of the tiny British garrison had survived wave after wave of Zulu attacks he would never know, but this time the odds were even worse, the position less defensible and the enemy better armed.

'Fire!' shouted Hamilton.

George pulled his trigger and the stock slammed viciously into his shoulder. He had no idea whether he had hit his target but, given the number of bodies he had fired into, it didn't seem to matter. As the boom of the first volley echoed behind him, and the smoke from the black powder cartridges began to clear, he could see gaps in the charging mass. But still they came.

Hamilton ordered a second volley, and a third, and each time the Residency's rooftops erupted into smoke and flame. By the fourth volley the charge had been broken, and upwards of a hundred bodies, some still, others writhing in agony, littered the ground between the cavalry lines and the infantry barracks. Many hundreds more had taken cover and were firing back from the roof of the stable block, some godowns to the left and the low mud wall to the right.

'Independent firing,' called Hamilton. 'But only shoot if you have someone in your sights. Our ammunition is limited and Heaven knows how long they'll keep this up.'

Cavagnari looked across from his own position in the firing line. 'How limited, Lieutenant?'

'Fairly, sir. Each man has seventy rounds on him, and we have five thousand in reserve, which works out at another seventy per man. It sounds sufficient, but we'll soon run through it if we're not careful.'

George nodded in agreement. For him it was *déjà vu*. At Rorke's Drift he and the other hundred and forty or so defenders had shot off forty thousand rounds in just under twelve hours. At Isandlwana, a few hours earlier, the problem hadn't been quantity but supply: the increasingly desperate, and ultimately doomed, attempt to get the bullets out of their boxes and up to the firing line. 'May I suggest,' said George, above the zip and whine of incoming bullets, 'that you ensure the ammunition boxes are unscrewed and the packets ready for distribution? If they rush us we'll need the bullets to hand.'

'The advice of a civilian is always welcome, Harper,' replied Hamilton, his voice heavy with sarcasm, 'but not required in this instance. The boxes are no longer secured by screws – Isandlwana taught us that lesson – and I've already divided them between the various houses and ordered the sliding tops to be removed.'

'A wise precaution, Hamilton,' said Cavagnari, 'but Yakub is bound to intervene long before we run out of ammunition.'

'Hamilton Sahib!' shouted a sowar manning the opposite side of the roof, with a view of the royal palace.

'What is it, Dowlat Ram?' asked Hamilton.

'Horsemen are coming from the amir's palace.'

'At last!' exclaimed Cavagnari. 'I knew Yakub wouldn't leave us in the lurch. How many are coming, sepoy?'

'Three, sahib.'

'Only three? You must be mistaken! Let me see for myself.'

Cavagnari kept low as he crossed the roof, followed by Jenkyns, Hamilton and George in the same crouching stance. All four joined Dowlat Ram behind the low barricade. 'There, sahib,' said the sepoy to Cavagnari, pointing to a trio of riders advancing up the lane that led from the royal palace.

'Well, that explains it,' said Cavagnari. 'See the big rider in front? That's General Daoud Shah, Commander-in-Chief of the Afghan Army. If anyone can restore order, he can.'

The lead rider was a huge man whose broad shoulders and huge frame almost dwarfed the Arab horse he was riding. He was simply dressed in a drab black *kurta* and trousers, with matching cap, and only his jewel-studded sword-hilt hinted at the high office he held. George held his breath as Daoud and his two aides approached the rear of the mob, which, by now, had entirely surrounded the Residency compound, and was tightly packed into the lane that ran along the back of the Mess House. Without breaking stride, the horsemen rode into the crowd and tried to force their way through. At first the mob gave way, but as soon as the soldiers among them recognized Daoud they surged angrily around his horse and those of his aides. Daoud tried to force the crowd back with the flat of his sword, but weight of numbers told and he and his aides were dragged from their mounts. As George and the others looked on in horror, the enraged mob struck at the defenceless officers with clubs, stones and even their fists.

'Should we fire into the crowd, Sir Louis?' asked Hamilton.

'Too dangerous. You might hit Daoud. But by all means shoot those on the fringes. It just might disperse them.'

Hamilton gave the order and a volley rang out from that side of the roof, bringing down ten or so rioters and causing the others to flee for cover. They left behind the three apparently lifeless bodies of the Afghan officers.

'My God!' exclaimed Cavagnari. 'If they're prepared to kill their own general, what hope have we?'

Barely had he finished speaking than a fusillade of shots began to ricochet off the roof behind them, the sound not unlike a swarm of angry bees. George knew at once that the mutineers were firing from above, which could only mean the upper fort. He looked up and saw the tell-tale puffs of smoke along the ramparts. 'They've taken the citadel, Sir Louis!' he shouted. 'We're sitting ducks if we stay here.'

'Harper's right, sir,' said Hamilton.

'Let's get below then,' said Cavagnari, dashing for the open trapdoor in the middle of the roof. Halfway across he staggered and fell to his knees.

Hamilton ran to his assistance. 'Are you badly hit, Sir Louis?'

Cavagnari put his hand to his forehead, which was covered with blood. 'A ricochet. I'll live. Get the others below.'

Hamilton gave the order and, one by one, his men followed Cavagnari through the trapdoor and down the ladder. As George waited his turn, a bullet zipped past the back of his head, causing him to duck. When he looked up the sowar next to him was lying slumped against the barricade, his sun helmet beside him and a neat blue hole in the side of his head where the Snider bullet had entered. Most of the far side of his skull had been blown away, and fragments of skin, bone and brain tissue were spattered over the face and helmet of the soldier beyond him. 'Aaaiee!' cried the man in anguish, as he wiped his face with his sleeve.

George couldn't help gagging as he stripped the dead sowar of his ammunition pouches and rifle before making his escape down the ladder. Ilderim, Jenkyns and Hamilton brought up the rear. In a corner room on the first floor below they discovered Dr Kelly, a short Irishman with a red beard, tending Cavagnari and the wounded Guides on the floor. Pir Ali lay unconscious beside them, while a sowar fired through the half-barricaded window.

'How's Sir Louis?' shouted Hamilton.

'It's just a flesh wound,' said Dr Kelly. 'The bullet glanced off his skull, but it gave him quite a bump and he needs rest.'

'I certainly do not,' said Cavagnari. 'We need every rifle we can muster. Just patch me up, Doctor, quick as you can. In the meantime, Hamilton, you'd better put a man on each window and a couple covering the trapdoor. They're bound to get onto the roof sooner or later.'

'Sir.'

'What about the gate from the inner courtyard to the lane beyond?' asked George, who had noticed that exit during his first visit. 'If the mutineers get through there we're finished.'

'One man's keeping an eye on it,' said Hamilton. 'But you're right. I'd better send a couple more.'

'I'm happy to go,' offered George. 'I'll take Ilderim Khan with me.'

'Very well. Meanwhile I'll check on the rest of my men in the infantry barracks. So you're a businessman, are you, Harper? Strikes me you've had some form of military training, even if it's just with the militia. Am I right?'

George smiled.

'I thought so. Follow me.'

They left the Mess House by the main entrance and at once split up. Hamilton turned right and headed for the main gate that led to the infantry barracks; George and Ilderim made for the opposite gate, a much smaller one set in the back wall behind the godown that served as the Residency's armoury. They were just in time. As they rounded the godown they saw the strut securing the wooden door shake with the impact of a heavy blow from an axe or a makeshift battering ram. The lone sentry was lying prone on the ground with blood seeping from a head wound. 'Quick, Ilderim!' said George. 'I'll hold them off while you find something to bolster the door.'

While Ilderim searched, George raised his Snider to the small gap between the door and the wall and fired. A scream was followed by a volley of return shots, causing George to hurl himself sideways out of the line of fire. 'Ilderim!' he shouted. 'Hurry!'

'I'm coming, *huzoor*!' The big Ghilzai appeared from the back of the godown, dragging a large bullock-cart, known as a hackery, and with George's help placed it against the damaged door.

'Well done, Ilderim. That should hold it for now.'

A great boom sounded. Door and hackery exploded inwards in a maelstrom of flame, dust and flying timbers, knocking both George and Ilderim off their feet. George's last memory before he lost consciousness was of lying on his back, looking up at a sky filled with smoke and burning sparks. When he came to the smell of burning flesh and hair filled his nostrils, and all he could hear, above a ringing in his ears, was his name being called. He opened his eyes to see Ilderim's face, black with soot and dripping blood from many tiny cuts.

'*Huzoor*, can you stand?'

'I think so.' With Ilderim's help, he staggered to his feet. His left thigh muscle screamed with pain – it had probably taken a blow from flying timber but the bone did not appear to be broken. His face was sore and bleeding, but otherwise he was unharmed. The smell of burning flesh, he now discovered, was coming from the sepoy's corpse, which lay pinned beneath a flaming hackery wheel. The rest of the cart had simply disappeared, as had the door beyond, leaving a jagged hole in the wall.

'They must have brought an artillery piece down from the citadel,' mumbled George, his senses still dulled by the explosion.

'Yes, *huzoor*, and it won't be long before they gird their loins to attack. I must get help. Can you hold a rifle?' asked Ilderim, handing George his own loaded Snider.

'Of course.'

'Take cover behind the godown and wait for my return.'

George did as Ilderim suggested, and was covering the hole in the wall when a bearded mutineer poked his head through and, satisfied the gap was undefended, signalled to his comrades to join him. All the while George was glancing back and praying that Ilderim would hurry. He knew that if he fired he would never have the chance to reload, and would be forced to rely on his revolver, which was useless for anything beyond point-blank range. But still there was no sign of Ilderim and, with more mutineers in the doorway, it was now or never. George fixed his sights on the foremost mutineer and fired, the bullet hitting the man in the chest and driving him backwards into his comrades. As George tried desperately to reload, his fingers scrabbling to open the packet of rolled-brass cartridges in his ammunition pouch, the mutineers spotted him and charged.

Dropping the rifle, George drew his pistol and was about to fire when a fusillade of shots slammed into the charging Afghans, dropping the trio in front and causing the others to turn tail. George looked back to see Ilderim rise up from one knee and run forward. Behind him came a bandaged Cavagnari, Hamilton, Jenkyns and four sepoys. Cavagnari stopped next to George while the others covered the gap in the wall. 'You all right, Harper? Your face is a little singed.'

'I'm surprised you can tell,' said George, with a grin. 'It was courtesy of the mutineers' field gun.'

A loud bang – and another section of the wall disintegrated into yet more smoke, dust and flying masonry. George and Cavagnari ducked. 'Right on cue, sir,' said George. 'We've got to disable it. If we don't, it'll blow our defences to pieces.'

'You're right. Hamilton!'

The lieutenant trotted over. 'Yes, sir?'

'Find ten volunteers. We're going to spike that gun.'

'We?' said Hamilton, eyebrows raised.

'Yes, *we*. You don't think I'd ask you and your men to do something I would not? You forget I fought during the Great Mutiny. This is a mere riot in comparison.'

'I didn't mean to imply you couldn't fight, only that you've already been wounded and shouldn't risk yourself further.'

'That's for me to decide. I got us into this fix by ignoring every warning,' he said, glancing at George, 'and it's my responsibility to see us safe. So rustle up some volunteers and let's get on with it.'

George put his hand up. 'You want to go too?' asked Hamilton.

'Yes. I served for a time in the King's Dragoon Guards. I know how to spike a gun.'

'I thought as much. While you do the business we'll keep the Afghans busy.'

Minutes later the raiding party was lined up on either side of the gap in the wall: Cavagnari, Jenkyns and three Guides to the right; Hamilton, George, Ilderim and two more Guides to the left. Hamilton sneaked a look. 'The gun's about a hundred yards away, at the bottom of the lane. It's manned by six mutineers with more in support. Once we've killed the gunners, Mr Harper will spike the gun. No one is to stop for the wounded. Understood?'

The group nodded.

'Good. Wait for the next shot. We'll charge as they reload.'

Excitement coursed through George as he waited for the signal. Why me? he asked himself. But he knew the answer: he never felt more alive than at moments like this. His blood felt as if it was boiling, his brain on fire. Danger for him was an addiction, and death the only cure.

'All right. Let's go!'

Pistol in one hand, sword in the other, Hamilton tore up the street, with George and the others close behind. At first the mutineers were so shocked by this desperate sortie that they just stood and gaped. Then someone shouted a warning and they opened up with everything they had. The air seemed alive with bullets, one striking the ground a foot in front of George, and another wounding a Pathan sepoy in the leg. 'Leave him!' shouted Cavagnari.

With just twenty yards to the gun, a second Guide was shot, then a third. Hamilton avenged them by shooting two gunners with his pistol and impaled another with his sabre. The rest fled down the lane towards the royal palace. 'All yours, Harper,' said Hamilton, as Cavagnari and the others took up defensive positions around the gun.

Placing his pistol on the ground, George took out a long thin spike and a mallet from a satchel round his neck and proceeded to hammer the spike into the field gun's vent-hole so that it could no longer be fired. Bullets whistled overhead but he ignored them. 'Done,' he shouted, after three lusty blows.

'Everyone back to the compound!' roared Hamilton. 'I'll cover you.'

'So will I,' said Cavagnari.

'What about our casualties?' asked George.

'They're dead,' said Hamilton, pointing to the two Guides near the gun. 'But Harawant Singh, the sepoy on the road, needs a helping hand. Now go!'

Ilderim beat George to it and lifted the wounded sepoy on to his shoulder. But as he set off for the compound a second bullet hit the sepoy on the head, spattering the back of Ilderim's white *kurta* with crimson blood. 'He's dead. Leave him!' exhorted George.

Ilderim did so, and he and George were the last, but for the rearguard, to reach the safety of the breach. When they looked back, Hamilton and Cavagnari were running up the lane, bullets striking all around them. So much for the Afghans' prowess with a rifle, thought George. They couldn't have hit a haystack at fifty paces.

Just yards from safety Cavagnari's body twitched, as if it was attached to an invisible thread, and toppled to the ground. George and Ilderim ran forward to help and, covered by Hamilton, managed to half carry, half drag the unconscious resident back inside the courtyard. 'How is he?' asked Jenkyns.

'Not good,' said George, indicating the spreading stain of blood on Cavagnari's shirt front. 'Let's get him upstairs to Dr Kelly.'

8

The Residency, Kabul

Kelly looked up from inspecting the livid exit wound, a hole the size of a sovereign, on the right side of Cavagnari's chest. 'It's mortal, I'm afraid. He's lost too much blood.'

'Is there nothing you can do?' implored Jenkyns.

'I'm sorry, William. The best I can do is ease the pain with a little morphine if he comes round. But I doubt he will.'

As if oblivious to the noise of battle outside, the room was quiet as the senior men came to terms with the loss of their chief. George broke the silence. 'Any sign of your messenger, Hamilton?'

'What's that?' said the lieutenant, wiping away a tear. 'No, no sign.'

'Don't you think you should send another?'

'I suppose we should. If you write it, Jenkyns, I'll see that one of my men carries it.' Then Hamilton turned to the doctor. 'I see the rooms next door are overflowing with wounded, Ambrose. Do you know how many?'

'Twenty-two. And that's just in this building. There'll be more in the resident's house and the barracks, with goodness knows how many dead.'

'I don't mean to teach you your business, Hamilton,' interjected George, 'but it strikes me we don't have enough men left to defend all three buildings. Wouldn't it be better to withdraw everyone into the barracks? It has a parapet on the roof and the best all-round field of fire.'

'You're right,' said Hamilton, putting his sun helmet back on. 'I'll see the messenger off first, then give the order.' He left the room.

What of Pir Ali, Doctor?' asked George. 'Any change?'

'I'll check.' Kelly knelt down next to the *munshi*'s prone form and checked his wrist pulse. 'I'm afraid not. He's still out cold and his heartbeat is very weak. I don't think he'll pull through either.'

George shook his head slowly. 'I doubt any of us will.'

The sound of firing broke out from the floor above. Seconds later a Sikh jemadar appeared in the doorway. 'The Afghans are on the roof! Where is Hamilton Sahib?'

'He's down in the courtyard, sending off another messenger,' said George. 'How many men have you got left on the floor above?'

'Only seven, sahib, and two of those are wounded. The Afghans are firing down from the trapdoor and have driven us into the corridor. We can't hold them for long.'

'Christ. We've got to get the wounded across to the infantry barracks before it's too late. Can any of them walk, Kelly?'

'A few. But don't you think we should wait until Hamilton returns? With Sir Louis incapacitated, he's the senior military officer and the order should come from him.'

'This isn't the time for military niceties, Doctor!' snapped George. 'If we delay even a few minutes it may be too late.'

'I'm sorry, Mr Harper,' said Kelly, his jaw jutting forward in defiance, 'I don't take orders from a civilian.'

George was so angry he was about to draw his pistol and put it to Kelly's head, but then he realized there was another way to persuade him. 'What if I told you I'm not a civilian, but a captain in the British Army on special duty for the Foreign Office? That makes *me* the senior officer.'

'*You*? On special duty?'

Another burst of firing sounded from the floor above. 'Yes, and I don't have time to explain so you'll have to take my word for it. Now, get the wounded moving while we hold them off above. The serious cases will have to be left.'

'Left? To be butchered by the Afghans? I won't do it.'

Boots sounded on the stairway below and, seconds later, Hamilton appeared in the doorway. He had a bloody gash over his right eye and was helmetless. 'The mutineers have broken into the compound below. They bored loopholes in the wall and shot the men guarding the gates.'

'What about the messenger?' asked George.

'He scaled the wall, but I wouldn't wager a rupee on his survival. Our only hope of getting to the barracks now is over the roof.'

'I'm afraid it's too late for that, Walter,' said Kelly. 'They're on the roof too.'

Hamilton's face drained of all colour. 'My God, we're trapped.'

'Not necessarily,' said George. 'My guess is that only a handful of insurgents have made it up ladders and onto the roof. The last thing they'll be expecting is for us to risk an assault from below. So if we do it now, using every able-bodied man, we might take them by surprise. What do you say?'

Hamilton frowned. 'I don't know . . . it sounds very risky. Might we not be better to sit tight and hope the amir comes to our assistance? Even if we do retake the roof, how are we to move Sir Louis and the other badly wounded?'

'We can't,' said Kelly, 'and Harper knows it. Though I doubt that's his real name. He has just told me he's a British captain on undercover duty, and therefore your superior.'

Hamilton looked from George to Kelly and back again. 'Is that true?'

'Yes. You guessed I'd had military training and I confirmed that. What I didn't tell you was that I'm still a soldier. I don't want to pull rank but I will if I have to.'

'Now, just hold on a minute. You say you're a serving captain, but why should I believe you?'

'Because—'

'Hamilton Sahib!' a voice hailed from below.

The lieutenant ran out to the landing and looked down the stairs. 'What is it, Mehtab Singh?'

'The Afghans in the courtyard have set fire to the building. The flames are spreading.'

George joined Hamilton on the landing from where they could both see, through the window overlooking the front of the building, the first plumes of black smoke. 'That settles it. It's the roof or nothing.'

'All right.' Hamilton turned to the Sikh jemadar who, with Ilderim and Kelly, had joined them on the landing. 'Mehtab Singh, gather all the able-bodied and any wounded who can walk on the top-floor landing. Leave the rest with a pistol so they can decide how it ends.'

'Sahib.'

George returned to the bedroom in which Cavagnari and Pir Ali lay unconscious. He knelt next to the *munshi* and shook him gently by the arm. There was no response and he had to accept that Pir Ali was all but dead, and that he would never learn what the spy had found out about the cloak, if anything. He left the room and climbed the stairs to the top-floor landing where he found the remnants of the garrison gathered. They were a motley crew, eighteen in total, including six walking wounded. Some of the Guides were heavily bandaged, others had lost their turbans, but all were armed with a rifle and fixed bayonet. Hamilton, Jenkyns and the doctor had both a sword and a pistol, George a pistol, and Ilderim his rifle and Khyber knife.

'This is it, men,' said Hamilton, the crackle of burning timbers clearly audible from the ground floor, 'it's all or nothing. We're dead men if we don't clear the roof, so let's give it everything. Mehtab Singh and I will lead the way through the trapdoor and, if we survive, provide covering fire for the rest of you. Are there any other volunteers for the covering party?'

A forest of arms went up. 'You and you,' said Hamilton, pointing to George and Ilderim. 'The rest of you are to jump as soon as you reach the gap between the two roofs. Don't hesitate. It looks a long way, but it's manageable. And remember, no quarter to mutineers.'

'No quarter!' roared his men, as they shook their weapons.

'Follow me!' Hamilton tugged open the door of the room that led to the roof, and fired his pistol once before tearing up the stairs, his boots clattering on the wooden steps. Mehtab Singh was close behind him, followed by George and Ilderim. More shots rang out as Hamilton and Mehtab Singh passed through the trapdoor, then a scream of pain. When George poked his head through he fully expected to see two bodies and a host of armed mutineers waiting to despatch him. But the only casualty was a prone Afghan clutching a stomach wound. Both Hamilton and Mehtab Singh were still alive, the latter shot in the left arm, and were firing at the backs of six retreating Afghans as they ran across the roof to the rear of the house. George leapt clear of the trapdoor and opened fire, as did Ilderim, and one of the Afghans slumped to the floor. The others scrambled onto and down the ladders they had used to scale the Mess House from the flat roofs of the houses behind.

Hamilton poked his head through the trapdoor. 'For God's sake, hurry! The roof's clear but it won't be for long.'

The first Guide emerged and was directed by Hamilton to the front right corner of the building where the gap to the lower roof of the Sikh infantry barrack was a nerve-racking perpendicular angle of ten feet. 'Jump!' roared Hamilton.

The soldier hesitated for a moment, then took a short run up and leapt into the abyss. Others followed, though by now the mutineers were firing from both the tops of the ladders and the upper Bala Hissar – bullets were ricocheting all over the Mess House roof. One Guide was hit in the back as he was about to jump, and tumbled three floors to the alley below, his body hitting the stone paving with a sickening thud.

George was certain the shot had come from a mutineer poking his head above a ladder so he waited, pistol outstretched, for the man to reappear and when he did he shot him. With a groan, the mutineer fell. By now black smoke from the fire had obscured much of the Mess House, enabling Jenkyns, Kelly and the surviving Guides to make it across safely to the barracks. 'Your turn,' shouted Hamilton, to George and Ilderim.

George was in the act of holstering his pistol when a body stirred beside him. It was the wounded mutineer. Before George could react, the mutineer had grasped his fallen rifle and was pointing it at George's chest. At point-blank range he knew the Afghan could not miss. He waited for the explosion, his body tensed against the bullet. But as the Afghan squeezed the trigger a blade flew through the air, entered his back and exited his chest, its bloody red point emerging a full two inches. The Afghan dropped his rifle and toppled sideways.

'That makes up for last time, *huzoor*,' said Ilderim, as he ran forward, placed a foot on the mutineer's back and, with a loud grunt, pulled free his Khyber knife. He then wiped it clean on the mutineer's *kurta* before replacing it in his belt. All the while George was staring at his assailant's body, finding it hard to believe that he had cheated death by the narrowest margin for the second time in a matter of weeks.

His shoulder was tugged. '*Huzoor!*'

'What?'

'It's our turn. Let's go.'

At the edge of the building Ilderim threw his rifle to some Guides waiting below. Then he and George took a short run up and jumped together. Ilderim made the distance with feet to spare, though he stumbled forward on landing. George miscalculated and landed with both feet on the parapet. For a second it seemed his momentum would carry him forward to safety. But then his right foot slipped on a loose piece of masonry and he began to fall backwards. He threw up his arms in a futile attempt to regain his balance and a strong hand gripped his wrist to pull him, sprawling, on to the roof. The swarthy, bearded face of one of Hamilton's Pathans smiled down at him. 'A lucky escape, sahib.'

'Yes, and not my first.'

A bullet pinged through the air, close to George's head, and he and the Pathan ducked behind the parapet where they were joined by Ilderim. George looked up to the Mess House roof, waiting for the final pair to make the leap. The building was burning fiercely now, and screams were coming from the second-floor rooms where the wounded were being engulfed by flames. George turned away, unable to watch. As he did so another jumper landed beside him with a thump, and rolled forward. It was Hamilton.

'Where's Mehtab Singh?' asked George.

'Dead. He was shot in the head as we made our way across the roof. Sepoy,' said Hamilton, addressing the Pathan next to George, 'is Jemadar Jewand Singh still alive?'

'Yes, sahib, he's down in the courtyard with the wounded.'

'And the others who jumped across?'

'There too, sahib.'

'Good. And where is most of the firing coming from?'

'All over, sahib, but particularly from the houses beyond the mud wall,' said the Pathan, pointing, 'and the cavalry lines and stables.'

Hamilton lifted his head a few inches to get a better view of the outer compound beyond the barracks. 'There seem to be even more bodies out there than before. Did they try to rush you again?'

'Twice, sahib, but a few well-aimed volleys had them running like sheep.'

'Well done.' Hamilton turned to George. 'Come with me, Harper, and bring Ilderim Khan. This place is pretty solid, with gates at either end of a central courtyard dividing the Sikh block below us from that of the Muhammadans. But the outer gate opposite the cavalry lines is weak and needs to be strengthened. If we can do that we might even hold out till nightfall, or at least till Yakub comes to our rescue.'

'Do you still think he will?' asked George. 'It's been at least three hours since Daoud Shah was dragged from his horse.

Yakub must know. So why hasn't he sent his own troops to restore order?'

'I don't know. But one thing is certain: if he leaves us to our fate, a British Army will march on Kabul, depose Yakub and take control of the country. He must know that too.'

'Yes,' said George, nodding, 'which makes me suspect he's thrown in his lot with the mutineers. Either that or he knows his own troops won't obey orders to save the Feringhees.'

'That's possible, but it's not a scenario I want to contemplate because the closest British troops are eighty miles distant in the Kurram valley. Even if they knew our predicament, they could never get here in time.'

A loud boom echoed from the far side of the compound, close to the cavalry lines, followed by an explosion at the front of the barracks block, shaking the whole building and throwing up a cloud of masonry and dust. They all ran to the parapet at the front of the Sikh quarters, from where they could clearly see, at a distance of no more than 150 yards, a team of Afghan gunners reloading an artillery piece behind a low mud wall to the left of the main gate into the compound. The handful of Guides on either side of the officers was trying to target the gunners, but the return fire from hundreds of Afghan riflemen made a carefully aimed shot practically impossible.

'Christ, they've brought up another gun,' said Hamilton. 'We'll have to knock that one out now.'

'How, in Heaven's name, will we do that?' said George. 'We'll be cut down if we try to cross the compound.'

'We did it once, and we can do it again. What time is it?'

George pulled out his pocket-watch. 'A quarter to twelve.'

'Then we'll rush the gun at midday,' said Hamilton. 'That should give us enough time to prepare.'

George was far from convinced that this charge would succeed. But then an idea formed in his head: a means of extricating both himself and Ilderim from their horrific predicament with, if all went well, a chance of saving the garrison. 'I've had an idea, Hamilton, but I think we should discuss it with the others.'

'Yes indeed,' said the lieutenant, lowering his head as another bullet whizzed by. 'Let's go below. The steps are just over there.'

They descended a single flight of dusty steps from the roof and emerged on the right side of the barracks' vaulted entrance, facing a second stairway that led to the roof of the Muhammadan block. Hamilton pointed to the flimsy outer door, made from unseasoned planks. 'I had that made when we arrived in July to mask the stairs to the roof but there doesn't seem to be much point in barricading them now. If the gun gets its range it will disintegrate like matchwood.'

Another explosion shook the barracks wall, bringing dust and plaster down on their heads. 'As I said,' he added, 'we have little time.' He hammered on the huge iron-hinged inner door.

'Who is it?' demanded a Guide on the other side.

'Lieutenant Hamilton.'

The door opened to reveal the burly figure of Naik Akbar Shah. 'Sahib, it's good to see you in one piece.'

'You too, Akbar Shah. Now, where can I find Jemadar Singh and the other sahibs?'

'In the Sikh block with the wounded.'

'Good. Shut this gate and don't let anyone through without challenging him first.'

'Sahib,' said Akbar Shah, saluting.

They hurried down the left of the two arcades – formed

by stone pillars and a sloping veranda roof – that ran along both sides of the long, open courtyard and entered the Sikh block by the main door. The scene inside was grim. Most of the beds – straw mattresses on simple iron bedsteads – were occupied by wounded Guides, some silent, others moaning softly. The air was hot and fetid, the ceiling punkahs not having moved since the desertion of the Afghan servants at the start of the siege. Clouds of flies added to the torment. Dr Kelly was working on a patient on a trestle table in the centre of the room while Jenkyns and the jemadar stood at loopholes with rifles at the ready.

Kelly looked up as they strode into the room. 'I'm glad to see you all made it safely. That was very brave what you did up there.'

'Thank you,' said Hamilton, 'but we didn't all make it. Mehtab Singh was shot before he could jump.'

'What's that you say, sahib?' enquired the jemadar, a white-bearded Sikh in a long drab-coloured *kurta* with red facings and beige silk lace and braid. 'Is Mehtab Singh dead?'

'I'm afraid so. Which makes you the senior native rank, Jewand Singh. Tell me, how many fit men do we have left?'

'No more than twenty-five, sahib, and another dozen who could hold a rifle if they had to.'

'Give them one, and order them to man the loopholes. Then find a dozen volunteers – good men, mind – for special duty.'

'What duty, sahib?'

The building shook as yet another shell slammed into the front wall of the barracks.

'*That* duty,' said Hamilton, pointing towards the sound of the explosion. 'If we don't disable that gun we're finished.'

'Now, wait a minute, Hamilton,' said Jenkyns, propping

his rifle against the wall. 'With Sir Louis gone I'm the head of the mission and I don't think the gain is worth the risk. We're bound to lose men, like we did the first time, and even if we succeed in spiking the gun they'll simply replace it with another.'

'Not if we *don't* spike it,' suggested George.

All eyes turned to him. 'Whatever do you mean?' asked Jenkyns.

'What if we recover it intact and use it against the mutineers? Then even if they do bring up another gun we'll have something to counter it with.'

Hamilton rubbed his chin. 'Do you know? That's not such a hare-brained idea. I trained for a short time as a gunner and know the firing drill. But we'll have to make sure we get our hands on powder for the vent-hole as well as cartridges and shot.'

'You're all stark raving mad,' said Jenkyns. 'The chances of us even reaching the gun, let alone dragging it back with the requisite sundries, are virtually nil and I won't allow you to try.'

'Forgive me, sir,' said George, 'but it's not your decision to make. This is a military matter and I, as a captain, have seniority. My feeling is we have to try because if we don't we're doomed. Do you agree, Hamilton?'

'I do.'

'Then I hope you'll also agree with my second suggestion: that Ilderim and I come with you as far as the gun, then escape in the confusion and try to make our way to the royal palace. If I can speak with the amir, I'm sure I can persuade him to send some troops.'

Ilderim turned to George, eyebrows raised. 'This is the first I hear of this plan, *huzoor*.'

'The thought only came to me a few minutes ago. Will you do it?'

Ilderim sighed. 'Yes, I'll do it. Not because I think it will succeed, but because it's better than sitting here like rats in a trap.'

'More like rats leaving a sinking ship,' said Jenkyns, mopping his brow with a handkerchief.

George spun round to face Jenkyns, fury in his eyes. 'How dare you question my motives after all I've done today? You'd prefer to go yourself, would you?'

'Well, er, no . . . I didn't say that. I just think it would be better if we stuck together.'

'If we stick together, as you put it, we'll die together. Sooner or later. It's as simple as that. Yakub's our only hope.'

'Harper's right,' said Hamilton. 'It's worth a try. The loss of two men will hardly tip the balance in the short-term, and it might just save us. Kelly, what's your view?'

Throughout the altercation the doctor had continued working on his patient, a sepoy with a serious bullet wound in his thigh. Now he passed a bloodstained hand across his forehead. 'I don't see what all the fuss is about. Harper and his man are not on the staff here so they can come and go as they please.'

'True,' said George, 'but do you agree the attempt should be made?'

'Yes, and I'd like to volunteer for the raiding party.'

'Isn't your place with the wounded, Kelly?' asked Hamilton.

'In normal circumstances, yes, but if we don't recover the gun the wounded are dead men.'

'Jenkyns?' said Hamilton.

'What?'

'Will you come with us?'

'I don't see that I have any choice.'

'That's settled, then.' Hamilton looked at his watch. 'It's just before twelve. At five past we'll leave by the front door, pass to the left of the cavalry stables and work our way through the servants' quarters at the end of the compound. That way we only have to break cover for the last fifteen yards or so to the gun, which is in a walled enclosure beside the main gate. We'll drag the gun back the same way. Everyone who can hold a rifle, meanwhile, will give us covering fire. What's your plan, Harper?'

'While you secure the gun,' said George, 'we'll sneak into the lanes beyond and work our way back to the royal palace. A map would be useful. Does anyone have such a thing?'

'I can draw you one,' said Hamilton. 'I've ridden through every lane in the Bala Hissar and can remember most of them.'

'Excellent. Meanwhile I'll change into native garb. I'm just sorry I didn't grow a beard.'

'No matter, *huzoor*,' said Ilderim. 'You simply wrap part of the turban round your face.'

'And I'll get Akbar Shah to kit you out in mufti,' added Hamilton.

'Thank you,' said George. 'Best of luck, everyone. It's a mad scheme, I know, but it might just work.'

Five minutes later, George and the rest of the raiding party were crouched behind the rickety front door, waiting for Hamilton's signal. But for the lack of a beard, George looked every inch the Afghan in his turban, long *kurta*, baggy trousers and turned-up native shoes. And Ilderim had shown him how to leave a strip of material hanging from his white turban so that, in an emergency, he could cover his face.

George felt the familiar surge of nervous anticipation that any soldier experiences before combat, but he was more excited than afraid. It was as if he had been born to this sort of undercover work and he couldn't wait to get outside the compound where, even surrounded by enemies, he could rely on his dark skin, his linguistic ability, and Ilderim, of course, to see him through.

'Ready!' said Hamilton. 'Follow me!' He yanked open the door and headed obliquely left for the alley that passed between the cavalry stables and some rickety godowns that backed on to the fortress's outer wall. Jenkyns, Kelly, Naik Akbar Shah, Ilderim, George and eleven Guides followed, in that order, and for twenty yards or so they ran without hindrance. Then a single shot rang out, followed by more, until a storm of bullets was tearing up the ground around them and ricocheting off the wall to their left. Covering fire exploded from the barracks.

The raiders all crouched as they ran, to present smaller targets, but it did not save Akbar Shah, two ahead of George, who was hit in the right side, the bullet passing through his chest and exiting close to his left nipple. He crumpled to the ground, still clutching his Snider, and Ilderim at once went to the aid of his former comrade. But George knew it was futile. 'Leave him!' he bellowed. 'He's already dead!'

Ilderim took one look at Akbar Shah's sightless eyes and realised that George was right. Pausing only to close his eyelids, he tore after the others, his long limbs eating up the ground until he was almost level with the rearmost Guide. Hamilton and those at the front, meanwhile, had reached the relative safety of the alley beside the cavalry lines. Any Afghans who had been stationed there had long since fled, and Hamilton took the opportunity to pause while Ilderim and the stragglers caught up. 'Anyone else hit?' asked the lieutenant.

'Yes, sahib,' said a Sikh Guide, holding his right arm.

'You'd better stay here and wait for us to return. The rest of you, come with me. And don't bunch together or you'll make it easy for them.'

Hamilton burst into the open, sword in one hand, pistol in the other, determination etched on his young face. The others followed, but with slightly bigger gaps between them, and again they made a few yards before the Afghans opened fire. George felt a tug on his left arm and, looking down, realised a bullet had passed harmlessly through the baggy material. A second Guide went down, then a third and, just as they reached the edge of the row of huts that housed the Residency servants, Dr Kelly was shot in the right side of his chest and spun onto his back. George and Ilderim dragged him behind the cover of the huts. 'Go on!' gasped Kelly. 'I'm a dead man, and so will you be if you linger.'

They left him, and followed the others down a maze of dusty, refuse-choked lanes towards the main gate. At the last hut Hamilton again waited for the others to catch up. The party was now down to Hamilton, Jenkyns, George, Ilderim and seven Guides. 'Is the doctor hit?' Hamilton asked George, breathlessly.

George nodded.

'For his sake, let's not fail. One last effort and we're there.'

Boom! The gun sounded just around the corner and a shell exploded against the front wall of the barracks. Hamilton sneaked a quick look round the corner of the hut. 'They're reloading. Let's go.'

With Hamilton leading the charge, they covered the remaining twenty yards to the gun in a matter of seconds,

'Very commendable, brother, but the Feringhees are still holding out and we need every man we can muster. Climb up behind Ewuz Khan, over there, and you'll soon be avenging your cousin.'

'A generous offer, rissaldar, but let others enjoy the spilling of Angrez blood.'

The native officer raised his eyebrows. 'You recognize my mark of rank, brother. That's unusual for a civilian.'

George silently cursed his error. 'I . . . I once served in the army.'

'Which regiment?' asked a burly trooper to George's right.

'And where is your weapon?' asked another.

'I . . .'

The rissaldar touched George's chest with the point of his sword. 'Uncover your face, brother, so we can see you.'

George lifted his left hand to the knot at the side of his face, and with his right drew his pistol from its hidden holster. He shot the rissaldar in the neck, the bang causing the other horses to rear and shy. Before the riders could regain control, George had hauled the wounded officer from his horse, grabbed his sword and vaulted into his saddle. He rode towards the house. 'Ilderim!' he shouted. 'Where are you?'

'I'm here, *huzoor*,' replied Ilderim, firing his rifle from behind the mulberry tree. George turned to see another saddle empty, but the other four riders were bearing down on him, swords outstretched. He shot one and ducked as the second rider made a wild cut at his head that missed by inches. As the Afghan passed, George looked up to see the last two riders just feet away, their eyes wild and their teeth bared, as they looked to avenge their comrades. He fired at the nearest and missed, cursing himself for not aiming at the horse, and was just in time to parry a sword thrust aimed at his chest. The two horses closed and George fought desperately to defend himself from a flurry of thrusts and slashes, one of which sliced through the top of his hand and forced him to drop his sword. From the corner of his eye he saw the last rider's *tulwar* arcing down towards his head. He tried to sway out of range but, hemmed in by the other horse, there was no room for manoeuvre. With the blade just inches away, the rider reared in his saddle and dropped his sword. Ilderim had shot him.

Aware now of the threat from the hidden rifleman, the last two riders disengaged and galloped off down the road, leaving George nursing an injured right hand, which he bandaged with his handkerchief. 'Is it bad, *huzoor*?' asked Ilderim, as he emerged from behind the tree.

'It's not good,' said George, wincing as he tried and failed to flex his fingers, 'but I don't think I'd have a head on my shoulders if you hadn't shot that swordsman. That's twice you've saved me today.'

'If you want to thank me, *huzoor*,' said Ilderim, with a grin, 'you can always increase my pay.'

George shook his head, laughing. 'Typical Afghan. Now get up behind me. Yakub's palace isn't far and there may still be time to save the others.'

The royal palace was off the next lane. As they approached the towering gatehouse, a burly guard in chain mail stepped into their path with palm outstretched. 'No one enters on the amir's orders.'

'Tell the amir,' said George, 'that I must speak to him on a matter of the utmost importance.' His explanation was deliberately oblique because he did not know how sympathetic the royal guards were to the mutineers' cause.

'And you are?'

'Abdulla Khan, Malik of Khajuri.' George had said the first thing that came into his head, and the guard did not look convinced.

'Wait here,' he said, and disappeared through a wicket-door to the left of the two wooden gates.

'A bad idea to say you're my father,' whispered Ilderim. 'He's an old man.'

'The guard won't know that.'

Five tense minutes later, the guard returned with his officer, similarly dressed but wearing a sword. 'I'm Walidad Khan, Commander of the Palace Guard. What is your business with the amir?'

'I have news of the fight at the Residency.'

'What news? Do the Feringhees hold out still?'

'Yes, as you can hear,' said George, gesturing towards the sound of gunfire. 'But the end is close and it might profit the amir to stop the slaughter.'

Walidad Khan scowled. 'Why should he? The infidels should not have come, and deserve their fate. But I will tell him you are here. Leave your horse and come with me.'

They dismounted and followed the guard commander through the wicket-gate and past more sentries into an enchanted garden of fountains, shaded pavilions, fruit trees and octagonal parterres of sweet-smelling flowers. At the far end of the garden lay the palace itself, a three-storey building similar in design to Cavagnari's Residency, but much bigger. It, too, had covered arcades with lattice-work balconies on every floor, and two wings that jutted out from the main building to form a central courtyard.

More sentries, armed with long spears, barred the entrance. But on seeing the commander of the guard they stood aside. George and Ilderim were led through the hall and up a staircase to the two interconnecting durbar rooms. On the floors were spread thick Persian carpets, bolsters and the thin mattresses known in the East as *rezais*, while gaudy glass chandeliers hung from the ceilings. The walls were covered with cheap prints in elaborate frames, including one of Tsar Alexander III of Russia, and a copy of the *Graphic* newspaper lay on a British-made chair. 'Wait here,' said Walidad Khan.

Ten minutes passed and no one came. 'Where the devil is he?' asked George. 'The Residency is being destroyed a few hundred yards away and he behaves as if it's a normal day. I'm damned if I'll wait here doing nothing.' George turned for the door but was stopped in his tracks by a man entering the room ahead of Walidad Khan. He was of middle height, in his early thirties, with a conical-shaped head, slightly receding black hair, and a weak chin that was only partially obscured by his beard. He was wearing what appeared to be a white ceremonial uniform with gold stripes on the trousers, gold epaulettes and a profusion of gold lace.

'I'm Yakub Khan, Amir of Kabul. Who are you and what news do you have of the resident?'

'Thank you for receiving me, Your Highness,' said George, removing the piece of turban from his face. 'I'm James Harper, a British trader, and I've just come from the Residency.'

Yakub looked stunned. 'A British trader? How did you escape?'

'In disguise, as you see. Your Highness, you must send troops to stop the slaughter. Cavagnari is dead and the others soon will be unless you act now.'

'Cavagnari dead!' said Yakub, putting his head into his

hands. 'Those foolish soldiers have no idea what they've done.'

'It's not over yet, Your Highness. If you act now you can save the others. Did you not receive the messages we sent earlier?'

'I received them, Mr Harper, which is why I sent Daoud Shah, my commander-in-chief, to talk to the mutineers and try to return them to their duty.'

'But he failed, Your Highness. His own soldiers set upon him like wolves. Are you aware of that?'

'How could I not be? He was brought back to the palace, badly injured, by some soldiers who took pity on him. It was then that I sent my uncle Sirdar Yahia Khan and my son to appeal for order, and later some well-known mullahs. But all to no avail.'

'Why did you not order your own guards to intervene?'

'My dear Mr Harper, I don't think you understand the difficulty of my position. I have only one regiment I can rely on, the Kuzzelbashes, the descendants of Persian warriors who conquered Kabul in the last century. They are a thousand strong, but the mutineers number many thousands. If I send the Kuzzelbashes to intervene, they will be destroyed and I with them.'

'You don't know that for certain, Your Highness. It's a risk, I know, but it's one you have to take. Simla will never forgive you if you don't even *try* to save the garrison.'

'This is not my fault,' he said, in an anguished tone. 'I was forced to sign that accursed treaty, or you British would never have withdrawn your troops. Yet my people can't forgive me for allowing a British resident and his escort to reside in Kabul. And now I'm caught between the two. What should I do?'

George despised irresolution and knew that every minute Yakub prevaricated was costing another life. Yet he also felt that the amir's predicament was genuine, and that he needed to be cajoled rather than bullied. 'I appreciate it's hard for you to ask your men to fight other Afghans, Your Highness, but you personally guaranteed the safety of the British mission. You must do something to help.'

'How can I? Daoud Shah told me that it's not only mutineers who are attacking the Residency but ordinary civilians too. Should I order the Kuzzelbashes to fire on my own people?'

'You must. Who would you rather make an enemy of – the rabble from the bazaar or the British?'

'The rabble, of course, but it's not as simple as that.'

'It is. As soon as the Indian government hears about this attack it will despatch troops to punish those responsible. When that happens, your only hope of keeping your throne is by convincing the British that you did all you could to save the garrison.'

Yakub sighed. 'Very well. I'll send my men. Much good it will do. Walidad Khan!'

The guard commander appeared. 'Highness?'

'Form up the Kuzzelbashes and lead them at once to the Residency. I want you to put a stop to the fighting. How you do that is up to you.'

'Is that wise, Highness? The mutineers are many and we are few. And the firing seems to be lessening. It might be at an end by the time we get there.'

'All the more reason to make haste.'

'Yes, Highness,' said Walidad Khan, saluting. He glared at George as he left the room.

Minutes later he was back.

'I gave you an order,' said Yakub.

'I was about to carry it out, Highness, but then all firing ceased and I received a message from a lookout on the roof that the Residency had fallen.'

George's heart sank. 'Are you certain of this?' he asked Walidad Khan.

'Yes, sahib. I went up to the roof to see for myself.'

George turned to Yakub. 'If you'd only acted earlier you might have saved them.'

'I am not to blame,' said Yakub, angrily. 'Did I put those faithless soldiers up to this? No. But I vow to you now that those responsible *will* suffer.'

'That will be of little consolation to Hamilton and the others,' said George. He turned to Walidad Khan. 'Is there any hope of survivors?'

'No, sahib, the buildings are all on fire.'

'Can you show me?'

The commander looked at the amir and received a nod of assent. 'This way, sahib.'

Up on the palace roof, with the sun low in the sky and the light beginning to fade, they could see great plumes of smoke rising from the Residency compound, which was barely a quarter of a mile away. The Mess House was little more than a charred ruin, but the other two buildings were burning fiercely, a sign that the defenders hadn't been long overcome. Both inside and outside the compound a huge crowd was celebrating its victory by chanting and firing rifles into the air. 'Those poor souls,' said George. 'It doesn't look as if they managed to get the cannon back to the barracks.'

'No, *huzoor*,' said Ilderim. 'I can see it by the entrance, where we left it.'

George looked in that direction, but it was too far to make out any detail. 'What else can you see?'

'Some mutinous dogs near the gun. They're cutting at something with their knives.'

'Is it a body?'

'Maybe so, *huzoor*. They've put it on a spear and are holding it up for the crowd to see.'

The mutineers' chanting grew louder. George felt sick. 'Can you see what it is?' he asked, though he knew the answer.

'It's a man's head, *huzoor*, but there's no beard. It must be Hamilton Sahib's.'

George turned and vomited.

9

Royal Palace, Bala Hissar, Kabul

George woke with a start, his heart thumping and his body bathed in sweat. He blinked his eyes open, desperate to erase the nightmarish image of Hamilton's headless body lying by the abandoned gun, but it was still dark. He groped for matches and lit the oil lamp by the bed. Slowly his breathing returned to normal.

As he lay on his back, staring at the ceiling, he agonized over his next move. He was tempted to use the murder of Cavagnari and the others as an excuse not to continue with his mission now that an uprising had taken place and a new British invasion was inevitable. Yet he also knew that the rising, thus far, was only in Kabul and that the Mullah Mushk-i-Alam could still use the Prophet's Cloak to spread the flame of *jihad* across the country. His mission, therefore, was still very much alive. Yet Pir Ali's death in the Residency had cost him not only his main contact in Afghanistan, but all hope of discovering the whereabouts of the cloak. All he knew for certain was that it had been moved from its shrine in Kandahar by either Cavagnari's agents, or those of the Mullah Mushk-i-Alam, and was probably bound for the mullah's home town of Ghazni. He and Ilderim would go there next, he decided, but first he had to recover from his wound and let the tumult in Kabul die down a little. As things stood, no European in Afghanistan was safe.

Resolved as to his future course of action, George blew out the lamp and fell asleep. He was woken at dawn by a servant. 'Sahib, His Highness would like to speak with you in the durbar rooms.'

'This very minute?'

'Yes, sahib, it's a matter of some urgency.'

George dressed and made his way downstairs to the first of the durbar rooms where he found the amir, dressed informally in a dark blue *kurta* and white pyjama trousers, reclining on a cushion and eating an apricot. A large bowl of fruit lay at his elbow. 'Ah, Mr Harper, do take a seat,' said Yakub, wiping juice from his chin with a sleeve. 'Did you know we Afghans produce the finest apricots in the world, to say nothing of our pomegranates, peaches, grapes and plums, or that our dried fruit and nuts, particularly walnuts, are our chief exports and are prized all over India?'

'I did know that, Your Highness,' said George.

'Would you like to try one?'

'Not just now. I prefer savoury food in the morning.'

Yakub chuckled. 'You never did explain how you and your Afghan guide came to be at the Residency yesterday. How long have you been in Afghanistan?'

'Not long,' said George, as he sat down. He paused, wondering whether it was worth continuing with his cover story, then decided that he would have more influence over the amir if he came clean and admitted his links to the British government. 'I didn't tell you the truth yesterday, Your Highness. I'm not a trader. My real name is Captain George Hart and I was sent to Afghanistan by the Foreign Office to keep an eye on the resident.'

'To spy on your own side? Why was that necessary?'

'Because, Your Highness, there are those in the Indian government who think that the only sure way to stop a Russian invasion of India is by annexing all or part of Afghanistan. Lord Lytton is of this mind, as was Sir Louis Cavagnari. The British government, on the other hand, is anxious to avoid the expense and loss of life that would result from a renewed war, which was why they sent me to try to prevent another conflict.'

'You don't think, Captain, that the resident had anything to do with yesterday's riot?'

'Not directly, Your Highness, but once the fire had begun he made little attempt to put out the flames. He could have agreed to the mutineers' demands and paid their arrears but he chose not to, almost as if he welcomed a crisis that he hoped would provoke an armed British response.'

Yakub shook his head. 'Sir Louis always professed himself a friend of the Afghans. I had no idea that he was really a serpent in the bosom. But it seems, Captain, that you and I want the same thing – to prevent the rebellion spreading and the need for another British invasion. To that end I wish to ask your advice. Last evening I sent a letter explaining yesterday's unfortunate events to your superior General Roberts, who commands the British garrison at Ali Khel in the Kurram valley, just eighty miles from Kabul. In it I detailed the unprovoked attack on the Residency by the troops, the people from Sherpur and the country around the Bala Hissar, and the city people of all classes. I also mentioned the attempts I had made to stop the fighting by sending Daoud Shah to speak to the rebels. This morning I have written a second letter that I would like you to read.'

George scanned the proffered sheet of paper. After half a page of flowery compliments, it came to the point:

Yesterday, from 8 a.m. till evening, thousands assembled to destroy the Residency. There has been much loss of life on both sides. At evening they set fire to the Residency. All yesterday and up till now, I and five attendants have been besieged. I have no certain news of the resident, whether he and his people have been killed in their quarters, or been seized and brought out. Afghanistan is ruined; the troops, city and surrounding country have thrown off their yoke of allegiance. Daoud Shah is not expected to recover; all his attendants were killed. The workshops and the magazine are in cinders – in fact, my kingdom is ruined. After God, I look to the government for aid and purpose. My true friendship and honesty of purpose will be proved as clear as daylight. By this misfortune I have lost my friend, the resident, and also my kingdom. I am grieved and perplexed.

'So tell me, Captain Hart,' said the amir, as George looked up from the page. 'Will it do?'

'Well, that depends on what you're trying to achieve, Your Highness. If you seek to reassure the Indian government that you're as much a victim as the defenders of the Residency, that you're still a friend of the Indian government and that you look to the British for assistance, your letter will serve admirably.'

'Thank you. That is exactly how my advisers and I were hoping it would be read.'

'But,' added George, 'I don't think you've been entirely honest in it. I know for certain that the resident is dead, and the others almost certainly are. As for your point about being besieged, you and I both know that's not true. I accept you were in a very difficult position but at no stage was the palace sealed off by the rebels. Your decision not to send your guard to intervene until it was too late was because you feared such an action would be counterproductive, not because it was a physical impossibility.'

The amir sighed. 'My friend, let's not quibble over minor details. As you are aware, I am in a delicate situation. I need the help of you British to restore my authority – particularly here in Kabul where I hear reports that my treacherous uncle Nek Mahomed Khan has usurped the government – yet I can't be seen as your lapdog. So please allow me to . . . how do you say it? Gild the lily just a little. That way I satisfy the Indian government and, hopefully, also my own people.'

George nodded. 'I take your point. I believe the Indian government was wrong to invade your country last year, and that we still haven't learnt the lesson of our previous attempt to install a pro-British ruler in Kabul.'

Yakub smiled, showing a fine set of even white teeth. 'You refer to Shah Shuja's brief reign in the eighteen forties, and you are right to make the comparison. More's the pity that a far-sighted man like you is not viceroy, instead of Lord Lytton. But it would be dishonest of me not to admit that last year's British invasion was to my benefit. Without it, my late and unlamented father would still be amir and I would be languishing in a Ghazni prison. So, I'm grateful to the British, but I'm also aware of the tightrope I must tread if I'm to keep my throne.'

'I'll do everything I can to help. But never forget that Simla and London have different agendas. One will use the news of the massacre here as an excuse to invade while the other strives for peace. Yet the British government is hamstrung because, apart from me, it has no representatives in the region – the Indian government has many and most are pro-war hawks like General Roberts. Your letter is well judged, but whether it will satisfy Roberts that you had nothing to do with the massacre is another matter.'

'Then perhaps, Captain Hart, you could write a letter of your own to the general, saying much the same thing.'

'I could, but it won't cut any ice. General Roberts doesn't know me from Adam – and has not been informed of my mission, for obvious reasons.'

'Then I will send this letter and, if Allah wills it, all will come right.'

'*Inshallah*, Your Highness. May I offer you one more piece of advice?'

'Please do.'

'Try to re-establish your authority in Kabul, and apprehend those responsible for the massacre without delay. Then you will have removed from General Roberts his chief motive for invasion – revenge.'

'That won't be easy, Captain Hart. As things stand, my power remit barely runs beyond the walls of this palace, let alone the Bala Hissar. But I will do my best, and I hope you will remain here to advise me.'

'I will stay until my hand is healed and I can ride again. By then you should have heard from General Roberts and the picture will be clearer.'

George left the durbar room in two minds about the amir. In some ways Yakub appeared to be a weak and indecisive man who told you what he thought you wanted to hear, and who needed others to make up his mind for him. That was the conclusion George had come to after their first meeting, but now he was not so sure. The amir was not a man for a crisis, that much was plain, but could that be attributed to flaws of character or to the fact that he was trapped in an impossible situation, caught between Scylla and Charybdis, his own people and the British? George could not decide.

He was mulling this over as he climbed the broad wooden staircase to his bedchamber on the second floor, and barely noticed the finely dressed Afghan lady, flanked by two guards, who was moving in the opposite direction. Only as she passed, and the faint perfume of jasmine reached his nose, did he turn and catch a fleeting glimpse of two beautiful brown eyes above a gauze veil. He sneaked a look back and judged her to be of medium height, with a full, rounded figure her garments did little to disguise.

Over the next week or so, as the rebellion showed no sign of fizzling out and the palace remained shut off from the rest of Kabul, George had more brief sightings of the mysterious lady. He learnt from Ilderim that she was none other than the amir's younger sister, Princess Yasmin, and that she was kept in close confinement because she had refused to marry the Afghan chief her brother had chosen for her. George was well aware of the sensitivity of such an issue, particularly as it involved such a high-born lady, but he was bored by his enforced inactivity and, intrigued by the princess's predicament, determined to find out more. One afternoon, he went up to her apartments on the top floor of the palace. There, he discovered her two guards asleep. Without regard for the consequences, he crept past them and tried the door. It was unlocked, so he slowly pushed it open and slipped inside.

The room was large and airy, with shutters at the far end that opened onto a covered balcony. The floor was covered with rich carpets and scattered with cushions, and on one wall hung a huge looking-glass. A cushioned swing dangled from the ceiling, still gently swaying as if it had recently been used. There was no sign of the princess, yet George could hear a female voice from the room beyond.

'Sufi, I've told you a thousand times I do not like the colour scarlet. It reminds me of the accursed Angrez. Change it, please.'

The door opened and in walked the princess, book in hand. She was simply dressed in a silk *shalwar kameez*, consisting of loose trousers and a long-sleeved tunic, her raven hair pulled back in a high top-knot. Her face was uncovered, and the scowl she wore could not hide the beauty of her high cheekbones, aquiline nose and delicately arched eyebrows. She looked to be in her early twenties, but might have been younger. At last she noticed George and gasped. 'How dare you enter my room without leave? Who are you and what do you want?'

George bowed. 'I apologize for the intrusion, Princess, but I heard you were under house arrest and knew I would never be allowed to speak to you. I waited until your guards were distracted – they're asleep – and came in as quietly as I could. My name is Captain George Hart and I'm one of the "accursed Angrez". I escaped from the Residency during the attack and came here to ask your brother for help.'

'Did he provide any?'

'He was about to, but then we heard the place had fallen with all lives lost.'

She nodded. 'Yakub can never make up his mind until it's too late. But in this instance I sympathize with him. What was he supposed to do? If he saves the Angrez he alienates his people. A nobler act would have been to throw in his lot with the rebels and declare a war of national liberation. Yet he does neither, and skulks here in his palace while my upstart uncle Nek Mahomed Khan and the bazaar rabble control Kabul.'

'It sounds as though there's little love lost between you and your brother.'

'Are you surprised, Angrez? He rules like a woman, and bows to the opinion of his advisers, particularly that snake Shah Mohammed Khan, the wazir, who insists I marry my aged cousin Safed Khan for *dynastic* reasons. When I refused they put me under constant guard, and said the confinement would continue until I was safely married in October. Do they know me so little,' she said, raising her chin defiantly, 'that they imagine I will meekly succumb after a spell under lock and key? The fools! I would rather die than marry a man I didn't love.'

'I'm certain it won't come to that. Once your brother realizes the strength of your feeling, he will relent.'

She laughed scornfully. 'Have you any understanding of what life is for a woman in Afghanistan? We are little more than chattels.'

'Surely it's different for a royal princess?'

'No. I live in a palace, wear pretty clothes and have plenty to eat, but I have no say in my future – and when I marry the man chosen for me I become his property, and will have to live by his rules, never to be seen in public without a veil. You're a fortunate man, Angrez. Only members of my family and eunuchs have seen me like this. So have a care: if you're discovered here you will certainly forfeit your manhood.'

'Unlikely, Princess. I'm more useful to your brother in one piece.'

'Truly? Tell me how.'

'As an intermediary between him and General Roberts, who commands the nearest British troops in the Kurram valley. At this very moment Roberts will be massing his men on the border, thirsting for revenge, but your brother knows that if they enter Afghanistan he must choose between them and the rebels, and either way he'll forfeit his crown. So his only hope is to persuade Roberts not to invade, which is where I may be able to help him.'

'I don't follow, Angrez. Why would you discourage an invasion? It's no secret that your masters in Simla would like to add my country to their Raj.'

'That may be true, Princess, but I wasn't sent by the Indian government. I was sent by London.'

'Are they not one and the same?'

'No, Princess,' said George, and explained the Foreign Office's determination to avoid being drawn into another costly war.

'An admirable objective,' scoffed Yasmin. 'But I don't see how you can keep your countrymen from invading. They'll demand revenge for the massacre, and my brother is hardly in a position to arrest those responsible.'

'We'll see,' said George, though he saw her point. He paused. 'Since we're discussing the avoidance of war, may I ask what you know about the Prophet's Cloak?'

'Only that it's kept under lock and key in a mosque in Kandahar. It's long been said that whoever controls the cloak controls Afghanistan.'

'Do you believe that?'

'Yes.'

'Then why hasn't your brother tried to get his hands on it?'

'Because the imams would never allow it to be removed from their care unless the country was threatened by foreign invaders.'

'Is that not the case now? Is it not possible that the Indian government will send troops to exact revenge for the Residency massacre?'

'That's true, but the imams must decide.'

'But if the cloak was taken from them, who would benefit?'

'Whoever planned to lead a holy war against the British, I suppose,' said Yasmin. Or, thought George, whoever had a vested interest in such a war – namely, the Indian government.

'Who are you talking to, Princess?' asked a voice from the next-door room.

When Yasmin made no reply, a dark-haired beauty appeared, holding a green sari. 'Princess,' she cried, 'you're not veiled! Who is this man?'

'Quiet, Sufi, you'll rouse my gaolers!' warned Yasmin. 'This man is Captain Hart, a survivor from the Residency. He insists he has the best interests of Afghanistan at heart, but I'm not convinced.'

'I didn't say that, Princess,' interjected George. 'I told you that I'm working for the British government to prevent another war. If that benefits most Afghans, then all well and good.'

'But that's not your chief aim – no, why would it be? You're an Angrez, after all.'

'Not exactly. My mother is half Irish and half African.'

'African? How can that be?'

'It's a long story – but I'm not a blinkered Englishman who views the world only from his perspective. I do see the broader picture which is why, irrespective of my mission, I can sympathize with your brother's predicament.'

'Much good that will do him. Truth is, he should never have become the amir. He's too weak to be of use to his country.'

'What about you, Princess? Would you make a better ruler?'

'Indeed I would.'

Inwardly George agreed with her. The woman standing before him seemed to possess the two qualities that a successful monarch most requires: good judgement and resolve. Afghanistan would indeed have been better served if she, not her brother, had been born to rule.

10

Royal Palace, Bala Hissar, Kabul, two weeks later

George entered the durbar rooms to find Yakub Khan talking to a short, thick-set man with a long, handsome beard, a hawk nose and a haughty, scornful expression, whose rich clothes marked him out as a nobleman. 'Ah, Captain,' said Yakub, wringing his hands. 'This is my wazir, Shah Mohammed Khan. We've just been discussing General Roberts's reply to my letters, which arrived this morning. It's not good news. Will you read it and give me your opinion?'

George strode up to Khan and took the proffered letter. It stated:

Ali Khel, 18 September 1879

Your Highness,

In accordance with your own request that a British officer should be deputed as resident to your court, and on condition that you would yourself be responsible for the protection and honourable treatment of such a resident, Major Cavagnari and three British officers were allowed to go to Kabul, all of whom within six weeks have been ruthlessly murdered by your troops and subjects.

Your inability to carry out your treaty engagements, and your powerlessness to establish your authority, even in your own capital, having thus become apparent, a British army will now advance on Kabul with the double object of consolidating your government, should you loyally do your best to fulfil the terms of the treaty, and of exacting retribution from the murderers of the British mission.

But although Your Highness has laid great stress in your letter of 4 September on the sincerity of your friendship, my government has been informed that emissaries have been dispatched from Kabul to rouse the country people and tribes against us, and as this action appears inconsistent with friendly intentions, I consider it necessary for Your Highness to send a confidential representative to confer with me and explain your object.

Yours, etc.,
Sir Frederick Roberts, V.C.

George looked up from the letter. 'Your Highness, I warned you that Simla would want revenge, and that the only way to forestall this would be for you to put down the rebellion and punish the leaders. Yet you have not done this.'

'How can I, when I have so few reliable troops?' cried Yakub, throwing his hands into the air. 'Even my uncle, Nek Mahomed Khan, whom I appointed governor of Kabul, sides with the rebels. The faithless scoundrel! It is he who is rousing the tribes against the British, not I. But at least I've regained control of the Bala Hissar and, in time, will disarm the regular troops and raise new levies. Then I can act against those responsible for the late abominable outrage. But how can I convince General Roberts of this?'

'You must do as he asks,' advised George, 'and send an

emissary to give your side of the story. But the man you choose must be a senior member of your government, such as the wazir, or Roberts will not take him seriously.'

'I?' spluttered the wazir. 'Must I cross the rebel lines and put myself at the mercy of General Roberts? I will not.'

'You must,' pleaded Yakub. 'Captain Hart is right. The emissary must be an important man whom I trust implicitly. You are that man.'

'If I go, the British will not let me return.'

'Stuff and nonsense!' said George. 'Roberts wouldn't dare to hold you against your will. Not while his stated aim is to re-establish the amir's authority.'

Yakub turned to George. 'If Shah Mohammed refuses, will you go instead? Roberts will believe you if you tell him I had nothing to do with the rebellion, and did all in my power to save the resident.'

'I can't do that.'

'Why not?'

'Because I don't believe it to be true. Anyway, as I said before, Roberts doesn't know me.'

'It's of no matter, Captain Hart. You simply say you're a British traveller who was caught up in the fighting at the Residency, and are carrying a letter for General Roberts from the Amir of Kabul. Remember we both want the same thing: to prevent an invasion that will almost certainly provoke a full-scale war. As things stand, I have only to overcome the mutinous regiments and a few disaffected civilians. But if Roberts and other British columns invade, the tribes will surely rise across the country in a *jihad* against the infidel and those who are friendly towards them, which includes the present government.'

He's right, thought George. We do want the same thing

– if for different reasons – and I might just get away with the businessman cover story. But now I'm recovered from my wound, can I justify a trip to the Kurram valley that will inevitably delay my departure for Ghazni and the continuation of my mission?

He decided he could: it would waste a little time and there was no guarantee he would be able to stop Roberts's march, but if he didn't try, full-scale war was almost inevitable – whether or not he captured the cloak. And the added advantage of travelling to the Kurram was that Roberts, one of the leading exponents of the Indian government's Forward policy, was as likely to know its exact whereabouts as anyone.

'Very well. Ilderim and I will leave after dark.'

'Thank you, Captain. I'll see you're given my letter to General Roberts before you leave. My family will be for ever in your debt.'

That night, mounted on sturdy ponies and armed with carbines, pistols and Khyber knives, George and Ilderim rode unchallenged out of the Bala Hissar's main gate, dropped down to the plain and took the road south, skirting the spine of bare and rocky hills called the Sher Darwaza Heights. They were approaching the village of Beni Hissar, nestled close to the hills, when a voice ahead called, 'Stop! Who are you and what is your business?'

They drew rein. George could just make out a small group of armed men blocking the road and, though he had grown an impressive beard and was disguised in his Ghilzai border ruffian garb, he prayed they weren't mutineers. 'What ails you, brother?' responded Ilderim. 'Can a man no longer return to his home at night unmolested?'

'No, he may not. Where have you been these last few weeks since we butchered the Feringhees and their lapdog guards at the Residency? The country is crawling with spies, all seeking to pass information between that traitorous dog of an amir and the Angrez, and we've been ordered to question everyone who passes. So, I ask you again, what are you doing on the road at this time of night?'

With his worst fears confirmed, and fearing discovery, George moved his right hand closer to where his pistol was concealed. But Ilderim seemed unconcerned, and continued his comradely banter: 'Brothers, put aside your weapons! We're returning to our home village of Zahidabad in the Logar valley. We've been celebrating the marriage of my cousin in Kabul, and afterwards we spent a while in a bawdy house on Charahai Street. Aiee! If you could have seen the Tajik woman I enjoyed. What thighs! What . . .' Ilderim cupped his hands in front of his chest, an idiotic grin on his face.

'I have been there,' interjected one of the mutineers. 'The trollops are indeed magnificent, and from all corners of the country. Why, I once paid for two Hazaras who kept me—'

'Quiet, Anwar!' snapped the officer of the guard. 'Will you lower yourself to this debauched fool's level? Though it's plain he hasn't the sense to be a spy so we need detain him no longer. On your way, then, fellow! And next time you choose to visit the fleshpots of Kabul, take a room for the night.'

'I will, brother,' cackled Ilderim. 'And as I'm enjoying the pleasures therein, I'll be sure to think of you.'

George held his breath, convinced that Ilderim had gone too far. But the mutinous officer, no doubt yearning for the warmth of his bed, ignored the jibe and waved them on without comment.

Once safely out of earshot, George asked Ilderim if he'd ever visited the whorehouse in question. 'Sadly not, *huzoor*, but I hear it is the best in Kabul. When the country has quietened down, what say we visit it together?'

'You're incorrigible.' George shook his head. 'We've just cheated death again and all you can think about is chasing women!'

They pressed on and, having safely negotiated the Sang-i-Nawishta defile, through which the Logar river passes into the Kabul valley, they eventually came to Zahidabad where they stopped to water the ponies. They had covered twenty miles in two and a half hours. But with another sixty to go to reach Ali Khel, Roberts's headquarters in the Kurram valley, including a strength-sapping ascent up the ten-thousand-feet high Shutargardan Pass in the Sufaid Koh mountains, they did not delay long.

It was getting light as they neared the village of Kushi, the last settlement of any size before the climb to the Shutargardan, and George was able to observe the terrain that Roberts's army had crossed the previous year. The road passed over a stony plain, devoid of vegetation, that was flanked on either side by low slate-coloured hills. Directly ahead, no more than eight miles beyond the village, stood the towering, snow-capped peaks of the mountains.

The road continued along the same flat, barren terrain for a further five miles beyond Kushi until it reached the foot of the mountains where the Shinkai Kotal provided the first steep climb. Thereafter the track descended to a stony riverbed before rising sharply through a series of narrow gorges and rocky climbs to the Shutargardan. As their exhausted ponies plodded through yet another narrow defile, flanked on both sides by sheer rock faces that at one point closed to within a few feet of each other, George was forced to conclude that a tiny force of determined tribesmen could have prevented a far bigger army getting through any of these features.

'*Huzoor*,' said Ilderim, snapping George out of his reverie, 'there are soldiers ahead.'

George looked up the hillside to see, beyond the next hairpin, a group of khaki-clad men working on the road with picks and shovels. 'Are they Afghans?'

'Sikh pioneers, Indian troops. I can tell by the shape of the turbans.'

'At least we don't have to run the gauntlet of any more mutineers. But the presence of Indian troops here, on Afghan territory, means the preparations for the invasion are already well under way. We must hurry,' said George, urging his pony into a trot.

As they rounded the next bend, a voice shouted, 'Stop and identify yourselves!'

George could see Sikh riflemen concealed in rocks at either side of the road. The speaker was a young British officer, standing in the road, his palm outstretched.

'I'm James Harper, a British businessman,' called George. 'I've come from Kabul with a letter for General Roberts from the amir.'

'Have you now? You don't look very British to me.'

'Of course not. I'm in disguise.'

'And your companion? Is he in disguise too?'

'He's an Afghan in my employ.'

'And you've just come from Kabul, you say? How did you manage that? The last report we received was that the city was given over to mutineers and bandits.'

'We were stopped once, but my guide convinced them we were natives of the Logar valley. We were lucky.'

'I must ask you to hand over your weapons until we can verify your story.' The officer turned to a strapping Sikh who was wearing cross-belts over his dust-coloured tunic, puttees below his baggy trousers and native shoes. 'Havildar Singh, disarm these men, please, and escort them up to the general at the pass.'

'Is General Roberts already so far forward?' asked George.

'Of course not. He's at Ali Khel. I'm referring to Brigadier General Baker. He's in command of the advanced troops on the Shutargardan. We've been holding the pass since word reached us of the massacre at the Residency. Do you know of any survivors?'

'Yes. Ourselves.'

Flanked by Havildar Singh and four of his men on foot, George and Ilderim rode the last couple of miles to the summit of the pass, a desolate, snowy, rock-strewn clearing where Baker's men had established their entrenched camp on the recently established frontier between British India and Afghanistan. As they approached, George could see the strength of the huge rectangular position, defended by an outer trench and a four-foot mound of earth, topped with rocks and stones, that was bristling with riflemen and cannon. Once past the outer picket of 72nd Highlanders – big men with bronzed, bearded faces, white sun helmets, scarlet tunics and green and blue tartan trews – Singh led them through the main gate and along row after row of white bell tents to the centre of the camp where Baker had sited his headquarters' marquee. The sun was shining brightly, but the air was cold. Singh and his men were breathing hard after the exertion of the climb.

'Dismount and wait here,' said Singh, before announcing his business to the sentries and disappearing through the tent flap. Seconds later he reappeared. 'The general sahib will see you now, Mr Harper. Your guide can wait outside.'

George entered the tent and it took a second or two for his eyes to adjust to the gloom. Three officers were poring over maps on a trestle table in the centre. The oldest of the three, a tall, bulky man with steel grey hair and a neat moustache, looked up. 'I'm Brigadier General Baker. Who might you be and what are you doing here?'

George explained that he had been visiting the Residency in Kabul to talk to Cavagnari about business opportunities when the attack had begun on 3 September. Thereafter his account of the battle – Cavagnari's wounding, the sorties against their guns, his and Ilderim's eventual escape to the royal palace – was exactly as it had happened. 'Once I'd recovered from my wound,' added George, 'I told the amir I was anxious to reach the safety of British lines in the Kurram valley, and that I'd be happy to carry a message from him to General Roberts.'

'May I see the message?'

'Of course,' said George. 'Have you a knife handy? It's sewn into my tunic.' One of Baker's staff officers handed him a pen-knife, which he used to unpick the lining of his *kurta* and recover the letter. He gave it to Baker, who inspected the writing and seal, before passing it to the officer on his right.

'What do you think, Innes? I'm damned if I know. The bloody thing could have been written by anyone.'

Innes inspected the letter. 'I agree with you, sir. The whole story sounds a little unlikely.' He turned to George. 'You say you're a British merchant? Have you proof of this? A passport, for example?'

'I left all my papers in my hotel room.'

'Very convenient, Mr Harper. You sound British, all right, but you look as if . . . you come from foreign parts.'

'My mother's part Maltese.'

'Is she? Well, I'm not entirely convinced.'

'Neither am I,' said Baker. 'But I'll pass you up the line and Major FitzGeorge, General Roberts's chief of intelligence, can make up his own mind.'

'Do you mean Major *Harry* FitzGeorge?' asked George.

'I believe that's his name. Why? Are you claiming an acquaintance?'

'We have mutual friends in England.'

Baker looked doubtful. 'I see. Well, we'll keep you here overnight and tomorrow you'll be escorted as far as Karatiga with some mules we're sending back for telegraph wire. That's about ten miles from here. Ali Khel is a further twenty, but you'll have to wait until another supply column is ready to leave because it's too dangerous to travel without an escort. Only today I received a warning from the local Mangal tribesmen that our columns would be attacked if we didn't pay protection money. I fancy it's bravado, but you can never tell. And if you do get through safely, I hope, for your sake, you can persuade Major FitzGeorge that your story is true. If not, you may end up swinging from a rope.'

George dozed in his saddle as the column of eighty unladen mules, accompanied by their Indian muleteers and a modest escort of one *naik* and nine sepoys of the 5th Punjab Infantry, plodded up the slope of a feature known as the Soorkai Kotul, roughly halfway to Karatiga. In places the track was little more than stones and boulders, and it had taken them two hours to cover just five miles, with the muleteers regularly resorting to curses and blows to keep their animals moving.

Ilderim leant across and shook George by the arm. '*Huzoor*, wake up.'

George blinked open his eyes. 'What is it?'

'I've just seen movement in the trees ahead, near the summit. It might be an ambush.'

George peered up at the fir-covered slopes on either side of the track. 'I can't see anything, but those trees would offer splendid cover. I'll have a word with the *naik*.'

He nudged his pony forward to the head of the column where the *naik* and four of his men were marching with rifles slung; the remaining five infantrymen were acting as rearguard. 'My man thinks he saw someone in the trees,' said George to the *naik*, a jolly-looking man with an impossibly large turban. 'Shouldn't we stop the column while you send forward a couple of your men to investigate?'

'No need, sahib. One of our own posts is barely half a mile from here. The Afghans wouldn't risk an attack with troops so near. Now, please go back to your place in the column. There's nothing to fear.'

George rejoined Ilderim. 'The damned fool won't listen, and here we are stuck in the centre of the column without even a weapon to defend ourselves.'

'I have weapons, *huzoor*,' said Ilderim, with a grin. 'A pistol and a knife. I keep them under my saddle for times like this.'

'Good – we might need them.'

Barely had George spoken than a single shot echoed from the woods to the flank, followed by a fusillade. Muleteers screamed as they were hit and their animals stampeded in panic. 'Dismount and take cover, *huzoor*,' shouted Ilderim, as he swung himself off his mount and felt under the saddle for his weapons.

George rolled to the ground and sprinted behind a large boulder, on the edge of the riverbed, where he was joined by Ilderim, who handed him his six-shot Adams revolver and a small pouch of ammunition. 'How did you get this back?'

'I took it from the havildar's pack when he wasn't looking.'

'Well done,' said George, peeking round the boulder and firing at the puffs of smoke in the trees. As he did so the top of the boulder seemed to explode, stinging his cheek with fragments of rock. He looked down to see where the bullet had struck, and quickly concluded that it could only have come from the far slope, against which line of fire the boulder offered no protection. 'They're on both sides, Ilderim,' he yelled, above the din of musketry, screams and braying mules. 'We've got to get to the line of trees or we're done for.'

'Stay close to me, *huzoor*!' shouted Ilderim. Clutching his Khyber knife, he scrambled up the steep bank of the riverbed and set off for the treeline, no more than thirty yards away. George trailed in his wake as bullets zipped and whined overhead. With just ten yards to go Ilderim pitched forward as if poleaxed, his huge frame hitting the stony ground with an audible thump.

George dropped beside him. 'Where are you hit?' he shouted.

Ilderim pointed to his right ear. 'Not so loud, *huzoor*. I tripped – must have been a tree root.'

'Idiot! Hurry, or the next bullet will find its mark.'

George hauled Ilderim to his feet and the two stumbled forward to the trees where they almost collided with two Mangal tribesmen, in long white *kurta*s and sleeveless black tunics, coming in the opposite direction. George shot one before he could raise his Snider, but the other had his Khyber knife out, intending to finish off the unarmed muleteers, and at once closed with Ilderim. George was afraid to shoot again, for fear of hitting his companion, and for a few moments the result of the fight seemed to hang in the balance. But Ilderim's bulk soon began to tell and, having missed once too often with a wild slash, the tribesman left himself open to a counter-thrust and Ilderim drove the fearsome eighteen-inch blade deep into his chest. '*Kafirs!*' he groaned in defiance, as his life ebbed away.

Placing his foot on the man's chest, Ilderim hauled the blade free and wiped it clean on his victim's baggy trousers. Then he spat on the corpse. 'Mangal pigs! They never could fight with knives.'

'For God's sake, grab his rifle and get down beside me,' implored George, who was already holding the other Snider. 'The wood is crawling with tribesmen and they won't give up until they have the mules.'

Ilderim did as he was told and the pair watched helplessly from the edge of the trees as the Mangals closed in on their prey, shooting at the column until all resistance had ceased, and then advancing with their knives. George was sorely tempted to shoot at two tribesmen who emerged just yards to his left, but that would give away their position so he was forced to hold his fire as the merciless Afghans butchered the wounded. Unwilling to witness such horrors, he looked away, but the agonized screams and cries told their own story.

George and Ilderim stayed hidden while the Mangals stripped the corpses, rounded up the mules and their ponies, and made off into the hills. Only when they were convinced it was safe did they emerge from the woods to check for survivors. The scene reminded George of the pitiless killing he had witnessed in Zululand as he came upon body after gashed and naked body, the ground soaked with blood and buzzing with flies. About to give up, he noticed a slight movement and heard a groan. It was a muleteer with a bullet wound in his back. George turned him over and could see that he was still breathing in short gasps. 'Ilderim!' he shouted. 'This man is still alive.'

'I have one here too,' replied Ilderim, from further up the track.

Just as George was wondering how they could move the wounded men, a patrol of khaki-clad Indian soldiers appeared over the brow of the Soorkai Kotul. They were led by a young British officer whose eyes widened in horror as he took in the scale of the massacre. 'I'm Lieutenant Macinkstray of the Fifth Punjabs,' he said to George. 'We heard the firing but they attacked our post at the same time, killing one of my men, and we were unable to come to your assistance. How many wounded have you?'

'Only two. They despatched the others with their knives and took all the mules.'

'The wretches! How did you survive?'

'We made it to the treeline and hid.'

'And you are?'

'James Harper, a British merchant, and this is my guide Ilderim Khan, late of the Guides. We've just come from Kabul with vital intelligence for General Roberts.'

'Then it's doubly fortunate you survived. We can take you as far as Karatiga and they'll arrange your onward journey from there. You should reach Ali Khel tomorrow.'

'Can't we be there any sooner?' asked George, conscious that every hour was precious.

'Not if you want to arrive in one piece. For that you'll require an escort.'

11

Headquarters camp, Ali Khel, Kurram valley, late September 1879

It was not until noon the following day that George and Ilderim, mounted on fresh ponies and escorted by a troop of Bengal Lancers, finally reached Ali Khel, the main British base in the Kurram valley. The village itself lay in a saucer-shaped valley, on the left bank of a tributary of the Kurram, and was a typical Afghan cluster of sturdily built mud houses flanked by orchards of fruit trees. The British camp was sited on the opposite side of the stream, a huge tented city that in recent days had steadily expanded to include the many diverse regiments and corps that Roberts was assembling for the re-invasion of Afghanistan: tall Sikhs in outsize turbans, wiry Gurkhas with their fearsome *kukri*s, sturdy Highlanders in kilts, Bengal sappers with their picks and spades, bearded Pathans, and small but tough British infantrymen from the agricultural poor and the industrial slums. The total force under Roberts's command was 7,500 men, though some had already been sent forward to garrison posts as far as the Shutargardan.

At the centre of the camp were two mud-brick buildings that, before the arrival of the British, had been the home of a local farmer. Now they served as Roberts's headquarters, and it was into the smaller of the two structures, formerly a barn, that George and Ilderim were led. 'Wait here,' said the Lancers officer. 'I'll inform Major FitzGeorge of your arrival.'

Ignoring the reek of sheep dung, Ilderim lay down on the straw-covered floor and soon fell asleep, his snores echoing round the single-room building. But George was too aware of the importance of the impending interview to rest, and spent the time pacing the room, rehearsing what he was about to say. The success of his mission and the British government's foreign policy in the region were, he knew, dependent to a great degree upon his ability to convince both Major FitzGeorge and General Roberts that Yakub Khan was an ally they could trust. He was so absorbed in thought that he didn't hear the rough door being pulled open.

'I take it you're James Harper, the man who *says* he escaped from the Residency?' said a haughty voice behind him.

George spun round to see a tall, strikingly handsome officer, with a waxed moustache and piercing blue eyes, standing in the doorway. He looked to be in his thirties, and was wearing the staff officer's garb of dark blue patrol jacket, dark blue trousers with a red stripe, and shiny black riding boots. On his head he wore a yellow and blue pill-box hat with a small peak, and on his face a look of such utter conceit that George took an instant dislike to him.

'That's right. And you are?' he asked, though he knew perfectly well.

'Major Harry FitzGeorge. I'm in charge of intelligence here, hence the questions. Where's your companion?'

George motioned to Ilderim's sleeping form.

'We'll let him be, shall we?' said FitzGeorge. 'You're the one I want to speak to. I hear you had a spot of bother en route from the Shutargardan.'

'You could call it that, though I imagine the thirty-two dead soldiers and muleteers would quibble at the description.'

'My, my,' said FitzGeorge, 'you *do* have a sharp tongue. So tell me, *Mr* Harper, exactly what you and your Afghan guide were doing in Kabul on the day of the massacre, and how the pair of you – and you alone – escaped from the Residency.'

Even before he spoke, George could sense that his interrogator was suspicious but he ploughed on regardless, repeating his cover story and the exact sequence of events from his and Ilderim's arrival at the Residency to their flight to the royal palace. As George finished he could see FitzGeorge shaking his head in disbelief. 'I'm sorry, Harper,' he replied, 'but I'm finding your tale a little hard to swallow. You say you were in Kabul on business and just happened to be visiting the Residency when the violence occurred. And yet you, a civilian with no military training, survived when Lieutenant Hamilton, a Victoria Cross winner, lost his life. Forgive me if I speak my mind, but you bear no resemblance to the usual representative of a British trading company.'

'What do you mean?'

'You're a little too eastern-looking. It generally pays to send a white man if you want to do business in these parts. That way you won't confuse the natives.'

'I'll have you know I was educated at Harrow,' said George, indignantly.

'I'm sure you were – but that means nothing these days.'

George sighed. 'All right, have it your way, Major. You don't believe I'm who I say I am but at least take seriously the letter I carry from the Amir of Kabul. You can easily verify it by comparing the handwriting and seal to the previous letters you've received, one of which I read before it was sent.'

'Show me the letter.'

George took it from his trouser pocket and handed it to FitzGeorge, who turned it over in his hand.

'It looks similar, I grant you. I'll return once I've checked with the chief.' With that, FitzGeorge left the barn.

Ten minutes later he was back with a stern-eyed older officer, identically dressed, but a good six inches shorter, with a small wiry frame and an unruly salt-and-pepper beard. He was holding the opened letter. 'I am General Roberts. I'm told you brought this message from the Amir of Kabul, having previously escaped from the Residency. Is that so?'

'It is, General.'

'The letter looks genuine enough. What can you tell me of Sir Louis's fate?'

'He was mortally wounded during a sortie to silence an artillery piece. We took him back to the Residency but he died later.'

'You're certain of that?'

'I am.'

Roberts bowed his head. 'Poor Sir Louis. I had a bad feeling when we parted in July, but he seemed gay enough and talked of all he might accomplish in Kabul. As we descended from the Shutargardan we came across a solitary magpie, which Sir Louis begged me not to mention to his wife because she would be sure to consider it an unlucky omen. And so it was.' Roberts's eyes flashed. 'But I will ensure that he didn't die in vain, that his mortal remains receive a Christian burial, and that the cowardly dogs who murdered him get their just deserts. The amir hopes to placate me with honeyed words,' said Roberts, shaking the letter he was holding, 'but it won't work. I hear from other sources that he did nothing to prevent the massacre, and that he now plays for time in the hope of raising the whole country to oppose our re-invasion.'

'That's not the case, General, and I'll do my best to explain. But first may I read the letter?'

'By all means,' said Roberts, passing it to him. 'It's a typical example of eastern deceit, promising much yet delivering little.'

George skipped the flowery compliments and read only the heart of the letter. It stated:

I am dreadfully distressed and grieved at the recent event, but there is no fighting against God's will. I hope to inflict such punishment on the evil-doers as will be known world-wide; and to prove my sincerity, I have written twice on this subject. I now write to say that I have preserved myself and my family by the good offices of those who were friendly to me, partly by bribing, partly by coaxing the rebels. Some of the cavalry I have dismissed, and night and day am considering how to put matters straight. Please God, the mutineers will soon meet with the punishment they deserve, and my affairs will be arranged to the satisfaction of the British government. Certain persons of high position in these provinces have become rebellious; but I am watching carefully and closely every quarter. I trust to God for the opportunity of showing my sincere friendship for the British government, and for recovering my good name before the world.

George looked up from the letter. 'I don't see it as deceitful. What the amir is trying to say is that it's an extremely delicate situation in Kabul, and that he needs time to disarm the regular troops, raise new levies and punish all those involved in the massacre. To give him the opportunity to do this, he asks you to delay your advance on Kabul. This is because the mutinous soldiers come from all the tribes of Afghanistan, and if you were to invade now and crush them, there's a danger that the whole country will unite against us and the amir. Already there are many in Kabul who regard the amir as a traitor, because of the way he has thrown in his lot with us.'

'What do you make of this, FitzGeorge?' asked Roberts.

'I wouldn't trust Yakub an inch, Sir Frederick. We've already heard from several Afghan sirdars that he's hand-in-glove with the mutineers, and wants to delay our advance so that he can raise more troops to oppose us. Only yesterday we received corroboration from a local chief interviewed by young Sykes.'

George started at the mere mention of a name that, for him, was synonymous with cruelty and vindictiveness: the name of his fagmaster at school, Percy Sykes. But as he knew that Sykes had gone on to join the Grenadier Guards, a smart regiment that rarely fought in colonial wars, and that there were bound to be many officers of that name in the British Army, he saw no need to enquire further. Indeed, he was in no position to do so without jeopardizing his cover story. So, casting all thoughts of Percy Sykes from his mind, he responded to FitzGeorge's charge that the amir was playing a double game. 'I don't believe that for a minute, General. When I arrived at the royal palace on the day of the attack, Yakub seemed genuinely bewildered by events, and unsure how to react. He had already sent his commander-in-chief, Daoud Shah, and other emissaries to dissuade the mutineers from violence, but none had the desired effect, and Daoud Shah was badly beaten for his pains. I finally convinced him that he must send his loyal Kuzzelbashes to intervene. But it was too late – the Residency had fallen.'

'You say he did his best to save Cavagnari and the others, Harper,' said FitzGeorge, 'but it doesn't seem so to me. Instead of troops he sent a handful of emissaries who were never going to have the desired effect. He must have known that.'

'Possibly, but bear in mind that one of the emissaries he sent was his own son and heir, which was a courageous thing to do. He didn't go further, until it was too late, because he feared the mutineers would turn on him.'

'You seem determined to see the amir in a positive light,' said Roberts, 'and yet you hardly know him. Nor can someone of your tender years have much experience of this part of the world. How many times have you visited Afghanistan?'

'Only once.'

'*Once!* Yet you try to convince us that you know best. Do you know how long I've been dealing with these people?'

'No, General.'

'Almost thirty years. My first posting as a young subaltern was to Peshawar in fifty-two. It was there I met the late great John Nicholson, whose authority over the refractory tribes of the frontier was legendary. He taught me to judge the men of these parts by their deeds, not their words. It's a lesson you've yet to learn. But I'd be failing in my duty if I didn't pass on by telegraph the gist of the amir's letter, and your verbal clarification, to Lord Lytton at Simla. Then it will be up to him and his council to decide on our next move.'

'Quite right, Sir Frederick,' said FitzGeorge, 'and would it not make sense to ask Harper to deliver this response? He knows the amir, and has already crossed the ground between here and Kabul, so he is familiar with the route.'

Roberts smiled. 'Capital idea. And if he refuses we'll keep him here until we can verify his identity. So, what do you say, Harper? Will you carry our answer?'

'It seems I have no alternative.'

'Good. We'll leave you now, and later I'll send someone with a change of clothes. You're welcome to use the officers' mess, but go easy on the drink. As soon as I've heard back from Simla I want you in the saddle.'

A couple of hours later, wearing an assortment of ill-matched clothes that included a Gurkha officer's tunic and a pair of riding breeches, George entered the large tent that served as a staff officers' mess to howls of derision. 'I didn't know they'd mounted the Gurkhas,' called a young wag among a group sitting in easy chairs.

'Either that or it's fancy-dress night and the mess president forgot to tell us,' said another.

George ignored them and made for the trestle-table bar where he ordered a whisky. As he took his first gulp, a finger tapped him on the shoulder.

'George Hart. It *is* you, isn't it?' said a voice, a little the worse for drink.

This use of his real name caused George to freeze – until he remembered FitzGeorge's mention of a 'young Sykes', and silently cursed his ill luck. He turned to see a face that, in recent years, had appeared in only the occasional nightmare. It was a little fleshier and more weathered than he remembered, but the thin lips, piggy eyes and cruel sneer were unmistakably those of his schoolboy tormentor-in-chief, Percy Sykes, as was the broken nose, courtesy of George's right fist. That fight, which the lighter and younger George had won despite the handicap of a broken hand, had put a stop to the physical bullying if not the taunts, and Sykes's departure from Harrow School a year later had come as a huge relief. He had hoped never to set eyes on him again – yet here he was, on the Afghan border of all places, wearing the uniform of a staff officer and threatening to blow George's cover. 'I'm sorry,' replied George, feigning ignorance, 'you must have confused me with someone else.'

But Sykes was not fooled. 'Nonsense, I'd recognize you anywhere, even with a beard and in that damn stupid rig. The last I heard you'd been drummed out of the King's Dragoon Guards. So, what are you doing here?'

With heads turning, George made an instant decision to change tack and bring the hated Sykes into his confidence. 'You're right – I am Hart,' he whispered, a finger to his lips, 'but lower your voice, please. I'm travelling under an assumed name.'

'Are you indeed?' said Sykes, in a mock-conspiratorial voice. 'For what purpose, may I ask?'

George took him by the arm and led him to seats in a quiet corner of the mess. 'I'm on a secret assignment for the Foreign Office,' he said, once he was happy no one could overhear. 'I was briefed by Lord Beaconsfield himself.'

'To do what?'

'I can't say, but it's to do with our relations with Afghanistan.'

'What relations?' scoffed Sykes. 'Haven't you heard about the murder of our man at Kabul? We're at war again, or damn soon will be, only this time we won't make the mistake of withdrawing after victory.'

George could feel his temper rising. He could never look upon Sykes's face, its near permanent expression of disdain, without wanting to drive a fist into it. But to do so now would guarantee the failure of his mission and with difficulty he managed to control himself. 'Of course I know about Cavagnari's death. I was there. And it needn't result in a full-scale war if we're sensible, which means not invading until the amir has been given a chance to prove himself a reliable ally by re-establishing his authority and punishing those responsible for the attack on the Residency.'

'You were *there*, at the Residency? How did you get away when the others perished?'

'I went to the amir's palace to summon help, but by the time I'd persuaded him to intervene it was too late. A couple of weeks later, once I'd recovered from a sword cut to the hand, I agreed to the amir's request to carry a message to General Roberts. And here I am.'

'Just like that? Do you really expect me to believe all this cloak-and-dagger nonsense?'

'Whether you believe me or not, Sykes, is immaterial. General Roberts and Major FitzGeorge, on the other hand, are in no doubt as to the veracity of my tale and have asked me to deliver the Indian government's response to the amir's letter, which I've agreed to do.'

Sykes looked more incredulous than ever. 'You're working for the general? But you're not even a soldier.'

'I am, as it happens. I was granted a new commission, and promotion to captain, for services during the recent Zulu war.'

'What services?'

'It's a long story. Suffice to say, I'm not using my military rank in Afghanistan.'

'I *see*,' said Sykes, his eyes lighting up. 'So the general doesn't know you're a soldier?'

'No, and neither does Major FitzGeorge. I've told them I'm a British merchant, and was in Kabul on business when the mutiny occurred. And I'd appreciate it if you didn't disabuse them. Your career prospects might depend upon it.'

'My *prospects*? Are you threatening me?'

'Certainly not. I'm just letting you know how things stand. Few Guardsmen are seen in these parts and I'm assuming you came east to further your career and not to enjoy the weather. Am I right?'

'Perhaps.'

'And am I also correct in assuming your immediate loyalty is to your chief, General Roberts?'

'Of course. I'm on his staff.'

'Yes, but are you a member of his "ring", his inner circle of favoured staff officers?'

'Not yet, but I hope to be. Then I'll be guaranteed a plum appointment in any future campaigns. After all, he's the best fighting general in India. I'd be a fool not to tie myself to his star.'

'A fool indeed. But remember this: my assignment to Afghanistan was sanctioned by His Royal Highness the Duke of Cambridge. If you were to reveal my true identity to General Roberts and Major FitzGeorge, he would not thank you. So ask yourself this: who would you prefer to make an enemy of? General Roberts or the Duke of Cambridge? I know which one I'd choose.'

'You haven't changed, have you?' sneered Sykes. 'I knew you were a blackguard from the minute I clapped eyes on you at Harrow. How your Fenian *actress* mother got you into the school is anyone's guess. We all suspected she was pleasuring the head beak. But then someone suggested your mystery father must be a man of influence. Is that true? I can't think of any other reason why a dago bastard like you would be allowed into Harrow *and* Sandhurst.'

George let go of his whisky glass and curled his hand into a fist. He was on the point of leaping on Sykes and pummelling him to a pulp when another voice intervened: 'What did you just say, Lieutenant Sykes? Did you call this man a "dago bastard"?'

They both turned to see FitzGeorge standing beside them, his moustache bristling with indignation. 'Good evening, Major,' replied Sykes, hoping to placate his notoriously thin-skinned superior.

'Did you, or did you not, call this man a "dago bastard"?'

'I – I may have, but only to tease. We were both at Harrow. We're old school chums. Isn't that right?' said Sykes, turning to George but careful not to use his real name.

'Well, is it, Harper?' demanded FitzGeorge.

'Yes, Major, but I wouldn't go so far as to say we're chums. I was his fag.'

'Were you? Well, I was a fag too, at Eton, and I don't recall feeling anything other than contempt for my fagmaster, a sadistic bully called Fellowes who's now an under-secretary at the Home Office. But I'm also illegitimate, as the world knows, and thus a little sensitive to the use of the word "bastard" as an insult. Do you know, Sykes? When you spoke just then you reminded me of Fellowes, and he's not a person I care to be reminded of. I suggest you leave the mess, now, before I do something I'll regret.'

'Sir,' said Sykes, red-faced, 'I apologize if I said something to upset you. It was a light-hearted remark, not to be taken seriously.'

'Light-hearted?' said FitzGeorge. 'Are you certain? Because I could have sworn it was the opposite. It sounded to me as if you were voicing your incredulity that a "dago bastard" could have been admitted to Sandhurst. Well, I'm not a dago, but I *am* a bastard and I *did* go to Sandhurst. Do you think I should have been barred from entry as well?'

'No, sir, I don't think that at all.'

'But you do think that Harper should have been?'

'I . . . Well, no, sir, not really.'

'Then why say it? I'd like you to leave. Now!'

'But I haven't had dinner, sir.'

'You can go hungry. Now get out!'

'Sir,' said Sykes, saluting smartly before turning on his heel and leaving the tent.

FitzGeorge sat in the vacated armchair and beckoned the mess waiter with a raised arm. 'A chota peg and soda, please, Hanumant Singh,' he said to the bearded Sikh, immaculate in his starched white tunic. 'On second thoughts I'll have a double.'

Once his drink had arrived, FitzGeorge took a large gulp and stared at George for a moment. 'It seems,' he said, pursing his lips, 'that we have more in common than I thought. Why didn't you mention you'd served in the army?'

'I didn't think it was important.'

'I'm sure not. What happened?'

'I didn't see eye to eye with my commanding officer.'

'His name?'

'Sir Jocelyn Harris.'

'He drove you out, did he?'

'He didn't appreciate sharing a mess with . . . Now, how did he put it? Ah, yes, I remember, "a tawny Irishman of unknown paternity". It was after I left that I joined the Anglo-Indian.'

'I see. So you're Irish, are you?'

'On my mother's side, yes. Her father was a captain in the Twenty-Seventh Inniskillings.'

'And what of her? Did I hear Sykes say she's an actress?'

'Yes, though she rarely appears now.'

'What is her stage name?'

'Emma Hart,' said George, omitting to mention that that was also her real name.

'I think I've heard of her. She's quite exotic-looking, isn't she?'

'Her mother was Maltese,' said George. He didn't care to share his Zulu heritage with FitzGeorge. 'Hence my own dark colouring,' he added.

'I wondered about that. Thought you might have Indian blood. It used to be very common out here.'

'What was?'

'Consorting with the natives. Of course, all that changed with the arrival of British wives and daughters, the so-called "fishing fleet", in the thirties and the prissy moral standards imposed soon after by our sainted sovereign. Not that she's maintained those standards. According to Papa, she's long been under the spell of her ghastly Scotch gillie, John Brown, and many suspect their relationship of having crossed the bounds of propriety, hence the soubriquet "Mrs Brown". And she still refuses to receive my mother, or to acknowledge the existence of my brothers and me. The hypocrisy is not to be borne.'

'You sound bitter.'

'I am, and with good reason. I am of *royal* birth, for goodness' sake, yet I exist on the very fringes of society. All it would take to change that is a single invitation from Her Exalted Majesty to Windsor – or Balmoral, even. But it never comes,' he said, shaking his head, 'and I continue my ambivalent existence as an officer and a gentleman who is unwelcome in the best houses – all because my parents were not married at the time of my birth. You of all people must know how that feels.'

'I certainly do,' said George, with something close to empathy.

'And the worst of it is that my parents did marry eventually, before the birth of my brother Gussie, but it was never legal because my father failed to ask the Queen's permission and so contravened the Royal Marriages Act.'

'Would permission have been given, do you think?'

'Good God, no! Not in eighteen forty-six, when that arch-prig Albert was still alive, and probably not even now – notwithstanding John Brown. You see, my maternal grandfather was a common labourer, hardly a suitable father-in-law for a cousin of the Queen. Nor did it help that when my mother met Papa she already had two small children, Charles and Louisa.'

'My God! How *did* they meet?'

'Why, in the theatre, of course. Where else would a prince meet a commoner? Mother was playing Margaret in *Much Ado About Nothing* at Drury Lane. She was known as Sarah Fairbrother in those days, and considered a great beauty. Papa first set eyes on her at a royal performance – attended by the Queen and Prince Albert, no less – and at once pursued her. They've been together, on and off, ever since.'

'That's two advantages you have over me, Major. First, you know your father's identity. I don't. And, second, your parents still live together.'

'After a fashion,' said FitzGeorge, refilling their glasses from the whisky bottle. 'They share the same address, I'll grant you, but no longer the same bed – they haven't since my mother became an invalid ten years ago. Even before then Papa had many mistresses, and when my mother found out, as she invariably did, there were the most terrible rows. I remember one in particular, when I was about fourteen.

Mother was apoplectic with rage because the lady in question, if that's the right word, was also an actress, but much younger and still in her prime. Mother's a very jealous woman. Always has been.'

'Did I hear you correctly?' said George. 'Did you say your father had another mistress who was an actress?'

'He could never resist a pretty face.'

George was stunned. FitzGeorge's mention of his mother's jealousy had reminded him of something his mother had said a couple of years earlier when she had first confessed that his father hadn't died in shipwreck but was still very much alive. He had not been in a position to acknowledge George because, she had said, he was already 'married', as the duke had been, albeit illegally, when he had had an affair with a 'younger' actress. A tiny suspicion entered George's mind, and was just as quickly rejected, that his and FitzGeorge's father was one and the same man. Surely it couldn't be – or could it? There was one way to rule it out. 'Do you recall the year of the affair?'

'Yes. I was fourteen, so it must have been eighteen fifty-nine. Why do you ask?'

George's jaw fell. 'Oh, no reason,' he said, trying desperately to conceal from FitzGeorge the emotions that were swirling through his breast. The idea that his father was none other than His Royal Highness the Duke of Cambridge was almost beyond belief, yet it made sense. He knew from his mother that his father was a man of *considerable influence*, already married but with a predilection for actresses, who had given George financial incentives to do well as a soldier because his other sons in the military had *disappointed him*. The duke himself had said as much in May with the words: *If they'd been anyone else's sons they'd have been cashiered years ago*. At the time George had been surprised by the duke's willingness to talk about his family – but why wouldn't he to his own son? As for the mystery of how a half-breed like him was able to gain entry into Harrow, Sandhurst and a crack cavalry regiment, like the King's Dragoon Guards (not that that he had stayed long, thanks to Sir Jocelyn Harris), it was now explained. His father was not only a first cousin to the Queen but also Commander-in-Chief of the British Army, a man with the authority to send a member of Military Intelligence to keep an eye on him and make sure he reached Afghanistan safely. And Overton had done his job, even if it had cost him his own life.

As George pondered the revelation that his father might be one of the most powerful men in the British establishment, he felt nauseous and giddy, and put his hand on the table to steady himself.

'Are you all right, Harper?'

George looked closely at the man he now strongly suspected was his half-brother. His eyes were blue to George's hazel, but there were definite similarities. Both had symmetrical, classically handsome faces with square chins and prominent cheekbones. George's nose was a little broader, and slightly crooked, thanks to a schoolboy fistfight, and his upper lip was a little more generous, but their toothy smiles were the same, as were their tall, athletic frames. He was tempted – very tempted – to blurt out his suspicions. But then he came to his senses. He scarcely knew the man opposite him, even if they were related. And he had seen enough of FitzGeorge's haughty arrogance at their first meeting to be wary of too close an association. There was also the issue of FitzGeorge's cosy relationship with his chief, General Roberts, and that he had made no bones about his support for the Indian government's Forward policy in Afghanistan. As such he could not be trusted with the truth about George's previous dealings with the duke, still less the real reason he had been sent to Afghanistan. He could, of course, still voice his general inkling that they were related, but where was the proof? Only his mother could provide that – and she was in Ireland.

'I just feel a bit out of sorts,' George said. 'Too much sun, I expect.'

'Too much whisky, more like.'

'Perhaps. I'd better . . .' George paused. He had been about to say he would turn in but, having discovered common ground between himself and FitzGeorge, and possibly kinship, he was keen to take advantage of an opportunity that might not repeat itself. '. . . turn in,' he went on, 'but before I do, could I ask you about a rumour I heard in Kabul that the cloak said to belong to the Prophet Muhammad has been taken from its shrine in Kandahar and is bound for a rabble-rousing mullah in Ghazni?'

'The rumour is true.'

'How can you be certain?'

FitzGeorge tapped the side of his nose in a conspiratorial gesture. 'And I wouldn't be surprised,' he added, 'if it hadn't already reached its destination.'

George feigned puzzlement. 'But surely you wouldn't want that to happen when it would enable the mullah to declare a holy war against ourselves and Yakub.'

'And would that be disadvantageous to us? I think not. For one thing, it would flush our enemies out into the open and end the current unsatisfactory state of affairs whereby we have to rely on a pliable ruler for our influence in Afghanistan. That way we bite the bullet and absorb the whole country – lock, stock and barrel – into British India.'

'You think it will be so easy? If history teaches us anything in this region it's that Afghans do not submit lightly to outside political interference. Why should they? Do you think we would if the roles were reversed?'

FitzGeorge snorted. 'Well, they're not reversed, are they? We're the globe's dominant power with a long-established hegemony in this region and they're a backward agricultural society, dominated by feudal chiefs who think nothing of slitting each other's throats over a petty feud. They need to know we're not to be trifled with, that we're here to stay. A short, sharp war should do it. The only thing these people understand is force.'

George could have sworn he'd heard those exact sentiments expressed about the Zulus earlier in the year, and look how that conflict had unfolded. But he knew that to make the comparison would invite awkward questions about what an employee of the Anglo-Indian Trading Company knew about South Africa. 'That's true up to a point, Major, but they tend to meet force with force. And even if you do overcome the mutinous regiments, you've still to contend with tens of thousands of unruly tribesmen who, familiar with weapons from boyhood, know instinctively how to make the best use of cover, and can move from rock to rock with the nimbleness of a mountain goat. I know – I saw them in action a couple of days ago. Such proud, tough people, at one with their harsh terrain, are almost impossible to subdue by conventional military methods.'

'What do *you* know about conventional military methods? You were only in the army for five minutes, for God's sake, and you're wrong. We thrashed the Afghans last year, and we'll do it again. You talk about learning from history, and I assume you're referring to the disasters of the last war. Well, the lesson *I* take from that conflict was that we used *too little* force and trusted a ruler who did not have popular support. We made the same mistake in May. This time we won't. As for the martial capabilities of the Afghans, of which you've waxed so lyrical, I don't agree they're insurmountable. They can shoot straight, I'll give you that, but can they stand up to trained and disciplined troops, armed with the latest breech-loading weapons? I doubt it. In 1842 our smooth-bore muskets were outgunned by the Afghan *jezail*. Now our Martini-Henrys are far superior to anything they have. So don't quote history to me, Harper, unless you're sure of your facts.'

George could see no sense in continuing the discussion. As he'd suspected, FitzGeorge was a fully paid-up supporter of the Indian government's Forward policy and, as such, his solution to India's security problems was very different from the one George was pursuing for the home government. In truth their aims in Afghanistan were diametrically opposed and, brother or no, George would have to tread warily. He now knew there was very little chance the Indian government would give Yakub the time he had requested to re-establish his authority, which made it more imperative than ever for him to continue his mission. If he could get his hands on the cloak before the mullah used it to rouse the faithful, there was still time to prevent the national uprising that Roberts and the Indian government required to justify annexation. And if his conversation with FitzGeorge had revealed anything of importance, beyond their possible fraternal connection, it was that the cloak was indeed on the way to Ghazni, and he should be too.

'I bow to your superior historical knowledge, Major,' said George, hand raised in submission, 'and now I must get some rest.'

As he rose a final thought occurred to him. 'You spoke warmly of your mother, earlier. May I ask how often you write to her?'

'What business is it of yours?'

'None, of course, but if she's anything like my mother – and we know they have some similarities – she'd certainly appreciate a note from her son now and then. Just to know he's alive and well. You know how mothers are . . .'

'I'll thank you to keep your filial advice to yourself. What an odd cove you are, Harper,' said FitzGeorge, his brow furrowed. 'I can't make you out at all.'

'Not many can, Major. Not many at all.'

Early next morning, George was woken by a member of the headquarters staff and told that the general wanted to see him. Minutes later he was shown into a large whitewashed front room in the adjacent farmhouse, where he found Roberts sitting at the head of a long table.

'Ah, Harper, I trust you slept well,' said the general, his immaculately pressed uniform and jaunty tone a reproach to George's own thick head and rumpled appearance.

'Not really, sir. I couldn't get the stench of livestock from my nostrils, and my guide snored.'

'I noticed the odour myself when we first looked round these buildings. It's why we decided not to use the barn as our mess. Take a seat,' said Roberts, gesturing towards an empty chair on his left. To his right sat a thick-set colonel George did not recognise, with prematurely grey hair, a neat moustache and goatee covering the lower half of his tanned, leathery face. Next to the colonel sat FitzGeorge.

'You know my chief of intelligence,' said Roberts. 'This other officer is Colonel MacGregor, my chief of staff. He claims direct descent from Robert MacGregor, better known as the notorious Highland bandit Rob Roy, and I can easily believe him. Like me he was blooded in the Mutiny, and a more redoubtable soldier you would do well to find. He doesn't know the meaning of fear. His speciality is guns, capturing the enemy's or saving ours, and how he hasn't won a Victoria Cross is beyond me.'

'Me too,' said MacGregor, with a growl. 'I should have been given one for the action at Sinho in China in sixty, when I saved three guns and received five slugs for my pains, but that blighter Fane wouldn't recommend me.'

'Our good colonel has a temper, you see,' continued Roberts, 'that doesn't always endear him to his superiors. But he's a fine soldier and has travelled extensively in this region, reaching Herat in western Afghanistan in seventy-five and crossing Baluchistan a couple of years later. Like me, he believes that India will never be truly secure from a Russian invasion until we have Afghanistan in our possession.'

'Or at least part of it,' muttered MacGregor.

'Quite so. Which brings me to the point of this meeting. I've heard from Lord Lytton and his instructions are emphatic. British public opinion will not tolerate any delay in British troops entering Kabul and gaining retribution for the murder of the resident and his escort. We are, therefore, to continue our advance on Kabul as soon as possible, as are the other British columns at Kandahar and Peshawar. I have written all this in my reply to the amir, and the relevant passage is the one I have underlined,' he said, handing George a copy of the letter. It read:

I have carefully considered Your Highness's proposal that you yourself should be permitted to administer just punishment to the mutinous troops and others who shared in the treacherous and cruel attack on the British resident and his small escort, and thus save Her Majesty's troops the trouble, hardship, and privation that must necessarily be encountered by an advance on Kabul at this season of the year. I thank Your Highness most cordially on the part of the viceroy and government of India for this further proof of Your Highness's friendly feelings. Under ordinary circumstances such an offer would be gratefully and willingly accepted, but after what has recently occurred, I feel sure that the great British nation would not rest satisfied unless a British army marched to Kabul and there assisted Your Highness to inflict such punishments as so terrible and dastardly an act deserves.

George looked up with a frown. 'General, I must ask you to reconsider, or at least to ask Lord Lytton to do so. I'm convinced the amir had nothing to do with the attack on the Residency, and that if you invade now it will leave him in an impossible position. He is already a traitor in the eyes of some of his people for signing the treaty that allowed a British mission in Kabul in the first place. But if you cross the border again, only three unenviable options will be available to him: allying himself with the rebels in opposition to us, which will mean near certain military defeat; allying himself with us against the rebels, which will be like signing his own death warrant; or abdicating. Whichever he chooses, he will forfeit his throne.'

'And good riddance, as far as I'm concerned,' said Roberts,

and turned to FitzGeorge. 'Tell Harper the latest intelligence you've received about Yakub.'

'It's from a chief in the Logar valley,' replied FitzGeorge. 'He insists the amir is stirring up the frontier tribes to oppose our advance.'

'You see, Harper?' said Roberts, triumphantly. 'Yakub is not to be trusted, and the sooner he shows his true colours and sides with the rebels, the sooner we can break up this accursed country and annex the territory as far as the Hindu Kush. Then, and only then, will we be able to sleep safely in our beds, secure in the knowledge that the Russians are not about to pour down on us through the Afghan passes. So, no, I will not reconsider, and neither will the Indian government. MacGregor,' he said, turning to his chief of staff, 'what is the timetable of advance?'

'Yesterday General Baker's brigade advanced as far as Kushi, and set up camp there,' said MacGregor, gruffly, his voice betraying no hint of his Scottish ancestry. 'We follow with the rest of the column once we've gathered enough supplies and transport animals. That should take no more than a few days.'

In the meantime, Harper,' said Roberts, 'I expect you to carry out your side of the bargain and deliver my reply to the amir. Will you do that?'

George nodded. The Indian government's response had been disappointing, but no more so than he'd expected, and his priority now was to proceed to Ghazni and find the cloak. The slight detour to Kabul would provide the perfect cover.

'Splendid,' said Roberts. 'You'd better have some breakfast and be on your way. How long do you think it will take you?'

'Two days, I expect, with a stop at Kushi en route.'

'In that case it might be better not to wear your native togs until you leave the camp at Kushi. The men are a bit jumpy, and it wouldn't do to be shot by your own side.'

'No, it wouldn't,' said George, though the thought had occurred to him that he no longer knew which side he was on.

12

Advanced British Camp at Kushi, Afghanistan

The first streaks of daylight were visible to the east as George and Ilderim passed through the outer picket of Baker's camp, manned by wiry Gurkhas of the 5th Regiment, and joined the track to Kabul. They had reached the camp the evening before, after a difficult and slow two-day ride from Ali Khel, and George was anxious to press on with as little delay as possible. He had donned his Afghan garb once more and, with a rifle slung across his back, looked every inch the fierce tribesman he was trying to impersonate.

In a ravine to his left, he could just make out the village of Kushi, a veritable oasis of mud houses, abundant orchards and fertile land irrigated by the stream from the Dobundi defile. The camp, by contrast, was pitched on stony ground on the right bank of the ravine, which was three miles long and half a mile wide, each bank rising for more than a hundred feet.

They had been riding for some hours when, as they approached a low range of hills, Ilderim drew George's attention to a large dustcloud ahead. 'Many riders, *huzoor*, we must take care.'

'We'll hide in that building,' said George, pointing to a ruined fort on the side of the road, 'until we know who they are. If they *are* rebels, they're taking something of a chance in coming so close to Baker's camp.'

They rode through the fort's ramshackle main entrance and dismounted. 'Wait here with the horses,' said George. 'We might need to leave in a hurry. I'll take a look from the ramparts.'

He picked his way carefully up the crumbling steps to the parapet and, leaning his carbine against the wall, scanned the hills to the north. The dustcloud was still visible but nothing else. Then over the brow of the hill came a continuous stream of red-coated riders, their naked *tulwar*s glinting in the early-morning sun. 'I think they're rebel horsemen,' he shouted down to Ilderim. 'Get ready to move.'

Yet as George watched the cavalrymen were followed by other riders in a variety of rich clothes, a couple of horse-drawn carriages and, finally, a long baggage train of mules and more red-coated horsemen. It did not look to George like an army on the move; rather, an important retinue with its escort. But who would be foolish enough to venture so close to the British at a time like this? The answer came to him: Yakub Khan. Only the amir would risk such an association with an invading army. He was obviously about to place himself under the protection of the British. But why?

Ignoring the dangerous masonry, George ran down the steps, took his bridle from Ilderim and mounted. 'Let's go. The riders approaching are Yakub Khan and his escort.'

Ilderim's broad forehead creased in a frown. 'Has he come to negotiate with the British?'

'Judging by the number of baggage animals he has with him, he's here to stay. Something must have happened in Kabul to drive him out. Whatever it was, he's crossed the Rubicon now and there's no going back.'

'The Rubicon, *huzoor*?'

'It's a river in Italy . . . never mind. Unless . . .'

'What, *huzoor*?'

'Unless I can talk him into returning to Kabul. Quick, Ilderim, we have little time.'

Ilderim vaulted into his saddle and the pair cantered out of the fort and up the road towards the approaching calvacade. They were intercepted by the Kuzzelbash advance guard, which surrounded them with *tulwar*s outstretched. Once George had explained to their officer that he was carrying an important message for the amir from the British general, he and Ilderim were led along the column to where Yakub was waiting, mounted on a fine grey Arab, with Shah Mohammed and his leading sirdars behind him. The amir's eyes were bloodshot and he looked exhausted, as if the strain of ruling such a turbulent country had finally proved too much to bear.

'Your Highness,' said George, 'it is I, Captain Hart, the man who carried your last message to General Roberts. I was on my way back to you with his reply. Why have you left Kabul?'

'I had to,' said Yakub. 'When word reached the city that Angrez troops had entered Afghanistan and occupied Kushi, my uncle, Nek Mahomed, and the other rebel leaders came to my palace and offered me a choice: join them against the Feringhees or die. I chose life, but I had no intention of leading the fools in a war they cannot win. So yesterday morning I sent servants to erect tents in my pleasure garden at Beni Hissar, as I often do at this time of year, and followed later with my retinue, including my son and heir, Musa Khan. In the evening I sent the tents back to the Bala Hissar, as if to show my intention of returning. But instead I rode south through the night to Zergan Shah, and on to here.'

'You've ridden all night?'

'I have.'

'Then stop and rest while we talk.'

Yakub hesitated, as if worried that at any moment the rebels, having worked out his intention, would overtake him and return him to Kabul in chains. But exhaustion got the better of him and he agreed to halt for refreshments. Orders were shouted and servants came scurrying from the baggage train with carpets and cushions for the amir and his sirdars to sit on. Fires were lit and soon tea was being served in pretty china cups from a fine silver teapot. George took a sip. It was far too sweet for his taste, and he preferred it with milk, but he drank it anyway. With the niceties observed, he put down his cup and turned to Yakub, who was sitting cross-legged to his right.

'Your Highness, I must ask you to reconsider your decision to meet with General Roberts. It will be seen by your people as an act of betrayal.'

'What do you know of my people, Angrez? Nothing. Believe me when I tell you they will understand my reasons. It is the rebels I flee, not my people.'

'Quite right, Highness,' said his wazir, Shah Mohammed, seated to his right. 'Once those dogs have been defeated, we can return to Kabul with honour.'

George ignored the wazir. 'Do you really believe, Your Highness, that your people will forgive you for deserting to the British?'

'I am not deserting them,' said Yakub. 'I am removing myself from Kabul for my own safety.'

'But is that how they will see it?'

'They might, if I can persuade your General Roberts not to enter Kabul. All I need is time to restore order among my troops and to punish those who attacked the Residency. What does he say in his letter? Does he hold out any hope of a delay?'

'I'm afraid not,' said George, removing the message from inside his *kurta* and handing it over. 'He's determined to advance as quickly as possible to assist Your Highness in putting down the rebellion and carrying out the necessary punishments. He says that British public opinion won't accept any delay, and that other British columns are advancing on Kabul from the south and the east.'

Yakub read the letter, then passed it to his wazir. 'I must do something before it's too late,' he said to George, almost in tears. 'I must speak to General Roberts, face to face, and persuade him to change his mind.'

'He will not.'

'He may if I explain to him that an Angrez army at Kabul will provoke a national uprising.'

'I am not sure that will sway him.'

'Why?'

'Because,' said George, 'that's exactly what he and the hawks in the Indian government want. It will give them the excuse they need to depose you and annex the country. They're already blaming you for Cavagnari's death.'

'But I had nothing to do with it. You were there. You saw my efforts to stop the fighting.'

'Indeed I did,' said George, but did not add that the amir's efforts had been less than wholehearted. 'And I said as much to the general. But he seems only too happy to see the worst in you, and claims to have intelligence that you have been encouraging the hill tribes to oppose his advance.'

Yakub seemed caught off guard by the accusation, his eyes darting sideways to his wazir for reassurance. 'Lies, all lies,' he said, without conviction. 'Why would I do that?'

George raised his eyebrows, as if the answer was clear. 'To slow Roberts's advance, of course, and to give you a chance to shore up your authority and win kudos among your countrymen in the event of a British defeat. Who knows? But it's immaterial because Roberts has made up his mind that you're not to be trusted. Make no mistake, he'll welcome you with open arms and expressions of friendship but he'll watch you like a hawk and ignore any request you make to slow his advance. Kabul will be his in a matter of days.'

'In that case,' said Yakub, 'my family are doomed.'

'Is your family not with you?'

'Only my son, Musa Khan. He's seven and is travelling in one of the covered carriages. But the rest of my household – my sister Yasmin, my wives and servants – are still in the Bala Hissar. I wanted to bring them with me, but Shah Mohammed advised against it.'

'And with good reason, Highness,' interjected the stern-faced wazir. 'It would have been impossible to move them all in carriages to Beni Hissar without arousing the suspicion of the mutinous soldiery.'

'So instead you abandoned them to the depredations of those same soldiers.' George was appalled by Yakub's weak and unchivalrous behaviour, and no less furious with the wazir. 'How could you?'

'Shah Mohammed said it was for the best,' said Yakub, defensively. 'And I didn't abandon them. They still have Walidad Khan and the palace guard to protect them.'

'How strong is the guard?'

'Two hundred picked men.'

'And can they be trusted?'

'Of course. They have all sworn a personal oath of allegiance to me. But already they are outnumbered by mutineers, and if Roberts continues his advance, as you say he will, other regiments at Sherpur may break out and attack the citadel. If that happens, my family will be in grave peril.'

'All the more reason for you to return to Kabul, or at least send your escort back to collect them.'

'I . . . don't know,' said Yakub, hesitating. 'Shah Mohammed?'

'Ignore the Feringhee, Highness,' growled his wazir. 'The rebels will arrest you if you return, and if you don't they will never allow your family to join you. It's hard, I know, but the women must fend for themselves. You must put your throne before your family.'

Yakub nodded his assent. 'You see, Captain Hart? I have no choice. I must go on, and hope that General Roberts takes pity on my poor womenfolk.'

Fat chance of that, thought George. He looked from Yakub to his wazir – they were as bad as each other, with their weasel words and cowardly actions. Yakub in particular was beneath contempt and Afghanistan, he decided, would be better off without him. 'I can see that your mind is made up, and that any further discussion is pointless,' he said coldly. 'With your permission, therefore, I will take my leave.'

'What?' exclaimed Yakub. 'Will you not escort me as far as the British camp?'

'I promised General Roberts that I would see for myself the lie of the land as far as Kabul, and that is what I mean to do.'

'Goodbye, then, Captain Hart. And have a care. The country will be crawling with rebels anxious to oppose the Angrez invasion.'

'Or patriots, Your Highness,' was George's parting shot. 'They could be either.'

* * *

George cursed. He knew from the position of the sun, low to the west, that it would soon be dark and too dangerous to travel. Yet he also knew that the bridge over the river Logar at Zahidabad was barely a mile distant, and that it was the last major hazard he and Ilderim had to negotiate before the road divided: left, through the hills to Ghazni, a distance of fifty miles, and right along the familiar, shorter route to Kabul. Ilderim was expecting him to take the road to Ghazni, but George was seriously considering the alternative. It made little sense, he knew, but a voice inside his head kept telling him that Princess Yasmin was the last hope for Afghanistan.

Ilderim turned in his saddle. 'Is something wrong, *huzoor*?'

'It's nothing. I'm just anxious to get across the river this evening.'

'Never fear. There are two shallow fords nearby that we can use if we have to.'

It was dusk as they approached the stone bridge up a narrow road flanked with high banks and much cut up by dry canals and small water-channels. They could just distinguish the large village of Zahidabad to their left, between the road and a bend of the river, but there was little sign of life. The bridge, too, appeared to be deserted. But as they closed to within three hundred yards of the river Ilderim laid a hand on George's arm. 'I can see someone, *huzoor*.'

'Where?' whispered George, squinting into the darkness.

'Just beyond the bridge, to the left, a sentry with his rifle slung.'

George could see a shape that he would never have identified as a soldier, and marvelled again at Ilderim's eagle eyesight. 'Is he a rebel, do you think?'

'Almost certainly, *huzoor*. He's wearing uniform.'

'Are there others?'

'I can't see any, but their camp might be in the dead ground beyond.'

'In that case we'd better use the fords and hope they aren't guarded. Do you know exactly where they are?'

'No, *huzoor*, only that they lie to the right of the bridge.'

'We'll head in that direction, then,' said George, dismounting and leading his horse over the high bank and into the cultivated field beyond. Though harvested of standing crops, the land was still criss-crossed with irrigation channels, and it took them a good ten minutes to reach the willows at the edge of the river, and another five to locate the cut in the embankment that marked the ford, by which time they were thankful for the inky blackness. Before attempting to cross, they listened hard for any sounds that would indicate the ford was guarded. There were none, though they could hear voices and see the twinkle of fires closer to the bridge, confirming Ilderim's suspicion of a rebel camp.

'Let me go ahead, *huzoor*,' said Ilderim. 'If it's clear I'll hoot like an owl.'

George waited nervously as Ilderim led his horse into the river, the slap of hoofs against water sounding impossibly loud. At every moment he expected a challenge, or a gunshot, but the far bank was quiet and, after what seemed an age, Ilderim's comical hoot signalled the all-clear. With his carbine slung on his back, pistol in one hand and reins in the other, George edged forward into the river, the icy-cold river soaking his shoes and trousers, and causing goosebumps to rise on his thighs. By mid-stream, with the water waist-high, he was shivering. But the snap of a twig from the bank to his left banished all thoughts of discomfort and he paused, ears alert to further sounds. He heard a soft footfall.

Someone was approaching. He raised his pistol, ready to fire. The footsteps were closer. Then a loud groan, and they stopped.

'*Huzoor*, hurry!' hissed Ilderim, from the bank.

George splashed through the shallows, pulling hard on his uncooperative mount, as a voice called, from the direction of the camp, 'Have you been at the arrack, Hazrat Khan? I've heard less noise from a buffalo in a thicket.'

George was nearing the bank when the same voice cried, more urgent this time, 'Hazrat Khan? Have you fallen into the river?'

'Quick, *huzoor*,' whispered Ilderim, out of the darkness. 'It won't be long before they investigate.'

'What did you do with the body?'

'I left it in the shallows.'

A shout came from their left. George could see men running towards them with flaming torches. He swung into the saddle and dug in his heels, his horse following Ilderim's up the cut. As they reached level ground a soldier with a torch appeared to their left, dropped to his knee and fired, the bullet pinging uncomfortably close to George's ear. He fired back and instantly regretted it as the flash from his muzzle gave away his position. The response was a volley of shots, but all were fired in haste and passed harmlessly overhead.

'This way, *huzoor*,' shouted Ilderim. 'The road can't be far.'

George urged his horse on, praying it wouldn't stumble in a ditch, or a lucky bullet find its mark. Having reached the road unscathed, they turned away from the rebel camp and towards Kabul.

'Fear not, *huzoor*,' said Ilderim, once they had left the

shouts and gunshots far behind, 'we can work our way back to the Ghazni road later. There's a turning up ahead.'

'We won't need it. I've decided to make for Kabul first,' replied George, surprising even himself with the suddenness of his decision.

'I don't understand,' said Ilderim, drawing rein. 'When we left the amir you said our destination was Ghazni. That is where we will find the cloak, not in Kabul. Why not proceed by the quickest route?'

'Because there's something I must do in Kabul. I would have mentioned it before, but I've only just convinced myself it's the right thing.'

'What must you do, *huzoor*?' asked an exasperated Ilderim. 'What could be worth the risk of returning to that rebel-infested slum? Jewels? Bullion? And if it's not money there's only one thing I know that can cause a man to lose his senses, and that's a woman. But it can't be a woman because . . . because . . .'

Ilderim took George's silence as a bad sign. 'Please, *huzoor*, tell me it's not a woman.'

'I'm sorry but it is. That spineless amir has left the women of his household in the Bala Hissar with barely two hundred soldiers to protect them. They're at the mercy of the rebels and I must help them.'

'You return to save *all* of them, *huzoor*?'

'Just one. Princess Yasmin, the amir's sister.'

'What business is she of yours?'

'None, I suppose, but I'm making her my business. I met her once during my time at the palace and if you'd been there you'd understand. She's magnificent. I don't mean in her person, though she is very beautiful, but in the way she holds herself, the way she thinks. If her brother had half her spirit and determination your country would not be in the chaos it is.'

'I'm confused, *huzoor*. You've spoken to her just once and yet you'd risk all to save her from . . . from what, exactly?'

'From the rebels. Once they realize the amir has absconded to the British they're bound to sack the palace, and any women they find will be fair game.'

'So you'd risk our lives for her honour?'

'Yes, indeed, but it's more than that. It's hard to explain, but since leaving the amir's camp I haven't stopped thinking about her – and, no, not in *that* way.'

'In what way, then, *huzoor*?'

'In the way she encapsulates – by her nobility, courage and fortitude – all that's good about Afghanistan, because there's so much that's bad, as well you know. When you meet her you'll understand. Ilderim, there's something about her that offers this country hope. If she dies, I fear it will too. I know it's not rational – call it instinct, if you like – but I have to save her.'

'So your mind is made up.'

'It is.'

'And the cloak? Have you forgotten why you came to this country?'

'I intend to make for Ghazni as soon as I know the princess is safe. But I can't succeed in either endeavour without you, my friend. So will you help me?'

Ilderim sighed. 'I must be mad but, yes, I'll help you, *huzoor*. I think you're a fool to return to Kabul, but I told you many weeks ago that I would stay with you until you had completed your task or were killed in the attempt, and I never break a pledge.'

'Thank you, Ilderim. Now I'm in *your* debt.'

For a mile or so they rode in silence until, at last, Ilderim felt compelled to speak. 'Truly, *huzoor*, a woman's ability to scramble a man's brain is something to behold.'

'Isn't it just, my friend?' said George. 'And you should know.'

13

Near Kabul

George had never thought of himself as chivalrous. As a child who never quite fitted in – on account of his parentage and colour – he had concentrated on looking after number one, and the thought of others needing his assistance had never entered his head. Until, that was, he had met Jake Morgan at Sandhurst. Jake was also an outsider, the son of a Welsh colliery owner – and therefore 'trade' as far as his over-bred classmates were concerned – so the two of them had clung together like drowning swimmers in a sea of social prejudice. George would have done anything for Jake, but since his death at Isandlwana he had felt himself reverting back to his old selfish ways. Yet there were hopeful signs: he was proud of how he had treated Ishtar in letting her choose whether she wanted to spend the night with him, and now he was risking all for a woman he hardly knew. Was it chivalry? He couldn't decide. There was certainly an element of self-interest in that he knew himself to be highly attracted to both the princess's physical charms and her spirited nature. But he also sensed her importance to her dynasty and her country, and it was this motive for keeping her safe that George knew to be selfless.

Thoughts such as these had been swirling round his head

since the crossing of the Logar river. Now that he and Ilderim could see the Bala Hissar looming ahead, the jagged shadow of its lofty walls dominating the skyline, he registered the sheer insanity of what he was trying to achieve. Already they had passed a number of drunken mutineers, carousing by the roadside, and it was likely there would be many more inside the fortress.

'The gatehouse is ahead, *huzoor*,' whispered Ilderim, as they climbed the last rise and the track began to level off. 'I'll explain to the guards that we own shops in the bazaar.'

But the ruse was unnecessary because the gatehouse was unmanned, its huge wooden doors open to the world. 'We may be too late,' muttered George, as they rode through the empty vaulted entrance and into the fortress. 'There's not a soul about.'

The lane beyond was strewn with clothes, possessions and broken furniture, still just visible in the evening twilight. 'The place has been ransacked, *huzoor*,' said Ilderim, scanning the scene. 'There will be scavengers about. We should leave.'

'Not until I've seen the amir's palace.'

'Why? Do you think these dogs will have left it untouched?'

'No. But we've come this far,' said George, kicking his horse forward. 'I have to be certain.'

As they picked their way through the destruction, the sickly sweet smell of death was heavy in the air, though few corpses were visible. George covered his nose with a piece of his turban, and was glad when they reached the lane that ran alongside the amir's garden, and the smell of corruption was replaced by that of scented flowers.

George knew that at the end of the lane, barely three hundred yards further on, stood the empty ruins of the

Residency compound. He felt oddly drawn to the scene of the massacre. But a more pressing task was at hand, and this required him and Ilderim to take a right turn off the lane, away from the Residency, and on towards the huge palace gates. They, too, were unguarded, and George's heart quickened as he rode through the devastation of the once beautiful garden, its flowers and shrubs uprooted and scattered anyhow.

'Wait here with the horses,' he said, dismounting in front of steps that led up to the main entrance, its shattered door still attached by the lower hinge.

'Is that wise, *huzoor*? What if there are bandits inside?'

'Then I'll deal with them. This was my foolish idea and I'll see it through. Besides, someone has to keep an eye on our mounts – we won't get to Ghazni without them. If I'm not back in ten minutes, you're absolved of your promise.'

George entered the front door, cocked pistol at the ready. The only sound was the crunch of broken china and glass under his shoes. Otherwise the building was eerily silent and dark. George felt his way up the broad staircase to the first floor and listened. A clock was ticking in one of the durbar rooms, but there was still no sign of life. He had barely started up the next flight of stairs when his foot trod on a bulky obstacle. He knelt down to touch it and made contact with someone's face, the flesh cold and clammy. He quickly withdrew his hand and was about to step over the body when a blood-curdling scream pierced the night, then another. It was a woman's, and it was coming from the top floor of the palace where the princess had her apartments.

George hurdled the body and tore up the remaining two flights of stairs, his shoes ringing on the polished hardwood floor. He turned right at the top and, using the wall as a guide, raced down the corridor that led to the princess's apartments. The door was open and light from a lamp was spilling on to the landing. He paused in the doorway, shocked by the spectacle before him. At the far end of the room a member of the palace guard, still fully clothed but with his trousers pulled down, was ravishing a naked girl with brutal thrusts and animal grunts. She was sobbing.

As George ran towards them, the man swivelled his head in surprise and found himself staring down the barrel of an Adams .45. 'Please don't shoot!' begged the man in Pashto. 'You can have her after me.'

George pulled the trigger, the shot sounding impossibly loud in the enclosed space. The heavy lead bullet entered the man's eye and blew off the back of his head in a red and grey shower of blood and brains. He slumped lifeless to the ground, pinning his victim beneath him. She screamed again and tried to push him off, but he was too heavy. George rolled him to one side and at last recognised the girl as the princess's maid, Sufi. Her eyes were wide with terror, her face spattered with her attacker's gore.

'Where's your mistress?' asked George, covering her with her torn *shalwar kameez.*

She lay in shock, unable to speak.

'Where's your mistress?' demanded George, a second time.

'She's in her bedchamber,' said Sufi, her voice barely audible, 'with that brute Walidad Khan.'

George ran for the door to the next room and yanked it open. He had steeled himself for a sight similar to, or worse than, the one that had just greeted him. It was just as shocking, but for a different reason. The girl – Princess

Yasmin – was astride her attacker on the bed, and in her hand she clutched a long, curved dagger, stained red with blood. Walidad Khan was still, and appeared to be dead, but that did not deter the princess from again plunging the dagger into his chest with such force that the blade snapped. 'You think you can betray your master and dishonour me with impunity, you dog?' she said venomously, spitting in the dead man's face. 'You are mistaken.'

'Princess, are you hurt?' asked George, from the doorway.

She swung round to face him, her eyes still blazing with murderous anger. 'Who are you and what do you want? Because if you're another who would do me harm—'

'I'm not, Princess. My name is Captain George Hart. We spoke briefly after I escaped the attack on the Residency. Do you remember?'

'The Angrez soldier?' she asked, as she clambered off Khan's corpse and straightened her dishevelled clothes. 'Is it really you in that tribesman's garb?'

'It is, Princess.'

'What are you doing here? I thought you'd escaped to your people.'

'I had. But I was asked by my general to take a message to your brother, and when I met him near Kushi he told me that he had left you and the other women here with only the palace guard for protection.'

'He might as well have left us naked for all the protection the traitorous worms afforded us. Most abandoned their posts the day after my brother fled to the Angrez, and those who did not, Walidad Khan among them, were only too happy to join the mutinous soldiery and bazaar rabble in plundering the Bala Hissar. The other women and servants fled to the city, but I chose to stay,' she said, her chin tilted in defiance. 'It takes more than a disorganized rabble to hound me from my home.'

'I admire your spirit, Princess, but was it wise to remain here? If Walidad Khan and his accomplice hadn't come back, others would have.'

'And they'd have met the same fate. I may have the body of a woman, Angrez, but I have the heart of a tiger,' she said, tapping her chest.

'I know it, Princess, but your maid is not made of such stern stuff.'

'Poor Sufi! Is she alive?'

'Yes. I killed her attacker, but not before . . .'

The implication was obvious. 'I must go to her,' said the princess, rushing past George and into the main room. On seeing the distraught Sufi, she let out a wail of sympathy and scooped her into her arms.

George gave them a brief moment together, then said, 'We must go, Princess, before others come. They'll have heard my shot.'

The princess turned to him, her cheeks wet with tears. 'Yes, of course. Where are you making for?'

'I was rather hoping you'd suggest somewhere. We need a safe place to sleep that's away from Kabul.'

'We?'

'My Afghan guide and I. His name is Ilderim Khan. He's waiting with the horses outside.'

'How many horses?'

'Two, but you can ride behind us.'

'In that case we should go to my brother's pleasure garden at Beni Hissar. In it, well-hidden by a screen of trees, there is a small pavilion he had built for me. Only I have the key.'

'We'll stay there tonight and decide tomorrow what to do with you both.'

'First I must change into suitable clothes. Can you wait here? I'll be a couple of minutes.'

'Princess, we don't have time.'

'Please!'

'Two minutes, then, and not a moment longer,' said George.

'One more thing, Angrez.'

'Yes?' said George.

The princess came up to him, kissed both his cheeks and embraced him. He was anxious to be out of the palace, but the smell of her perfume and the feel of her supple body made him forget the danger. 'Thank you,' she whispered in his ear, 'with all my heart.'

Two hours later, George and Ilderim were enjoying a much-needed brandy in the sitting room of the princess's pavilion at Beni Hissar as the lady herself, in a curious case of role reversal, put her maid to bed. With most of the rebels already asleep, the ride to Beni Hissar had been straightforward enough, and required only one minor detour to avoid a noisy picket of soldiers. Of more concern was the princess's inability to find the key to the pavilion, but a lengthy search had finally located it under a small statue, enabling the exhausted quartet to enter the pretty wooden chalet without having to break a window.

George took a sip from his glass of brandy, the fiery liquid searing his throat and warming his chilled bones. 'Tomorrow,' he said to Ilderim, 'I want you to find a covered carriage and a driver to transport the princess and her maid to Baker's camp at Kushi. We'll escort them as far as Zahidabad and the road to Ghazni.'

'As you wish, *huzoor*,' said the big Afghan, with a knowing grin, 'though it seems a shame to part from two beautiful women after such a brief acquaintance.'

George snorted in disgust. 'Did I not tell you what both women have been through? The maid, in particular, could be forgiven for never wishing a man near her again. So keep your lascivious thoughts to yourself.'

'What lascivious thoughts?'

They turned to see the princess framed in the doorway, hands on hips. She looked particularly fetching in her riding habit of sleeveless sheepskin coat, or poshteen, jodhpurs and soft felt boots, her raven hair tied back from her face. But her stony expression was far from friendly, and George knew better than to elaborate. 'Just male banter, Princess. My guide can't take his drink.'

'Then he should forgo alcohol, like a good Muslim. I have no such problem,' she said as she poured herself a brandy, 'and like to drink to forget. What else were you discussing?'

'Our plan for tomorrow.'

'Which is?'

George explained.

'And after you leave us at Zahidabad, where will you go?'

George glanced at Ilderim for guidance. But the Afghan sat there expressionless, forcing George to make the decision. That he chose to tell her the truth was testament to the spell the princess, however inadvertently, had cast on him. 'To Ghazni. You remember our conversation about the Prophet's Cloak?'

'Yes.'

'We have good reason to believe it has been taken from its shrine in Kandahar and is either in Ghazni or on its way there, and will be used to rouse the faithful in a holy war.'

'By whom?'

'Mullah Mushk-i-Alam. Do you know him?'

'Of course. Who in Afghanistan does not? He's a firebrand, a religious fanatic, who opposed my brother's rule from the start. Now it begins to make sense,' said the princess, slowly. 'The cloak will confer legitimacy on the mullah. Once he has it he will declare himself Amir al-Mu'minin, or "Leader of the Faithful", and the Ghazis and tribesmen will flock to him. With such a force he will hope to defeat your troops and turn our kingdom into a theocracy. It will be the end of my dynasty. I cannot let that happen.'

'Neither can I,' said George. 'And not just because I was sent here to prevent such a war. I also want what is best for Afghanistan.'

'And that is?'

'A country ruled not by a religious fanatic but by a strong, forward-thinking ruler who is prepared to stand up to us and the Russians.'

Yasmin looked grave. 'You have a wise head on young shoulders, Angrez. Only such a ruler as you describe can hope to unite the different peoples of this country. And that ruler is not my brother. He calls himself a man but his actions are those of a coward, leaving women and children to fend for themselves while he flees to the British. He's a disgrace to his dynasty and to Afghanistan. But I will atone for his shame.'

'How?'

'By accompanying you to Ghazni.'

'*What?*' George was so shocked he had forgotten to whom he was speaking. He recovered himself. 'Forgive me, Princess,' he said, frowning, 'but that won't be possible.'

'Let me finish. My cousin Hamid Shah is governor of Ghazni. He will provide us with shelter and, with luck, information about the cloak. He has spies all over the city. If anyone can find the cloak, he can.'

'And his assistance will be very welcome, but there is no need for you to come with us if you would write us a letter of introduction.'

'That will not do. He will only help if I'm there to ask in person.'

George turned to Ilderim. 'What do you think? Should we take her?'

'No, *huzoor*. Ghazni is no place for a woman. If she comes we'll have to look after her as well as ourselves.'

'You insolent dog!' said the princess, narrowing her eyes. 'Did I need a man to save me from Walidad Khan? No, I took care of myself, and will do so again. As a child I was never content with a girl's lot and used to sneak off with my brothers to train as a warrior. I was the best rider, fencer and shot among them, and I'm a match for any man.'

George was loath to let a woman accompany them on such a dangerous mission – particularly a princess of royal blood – yet he accepted that her presence might be extremely useful and had seen at first hand her ability to look after herself. He knew he was falling for her, and tried not to let it influence him unduly. He pondered for a moment, then made his decision. 'You may come with us. Tomorrow Ilderim will find you a horse and arrange a carriage to take your maid to her family. But no more royal airs and graces. We're all equals now.'

Yasmin nodded, a smile playing on her rosebud lips as the old saying came back to her: *We are equals, but one must always come first.*

14

Near Ghazni, eastern Afghanistan, mid-autumn 1879

George buttoned his poshteen against the late-afternoon chill. Most of the two-day ride from Kabul had been in warm sunshine across a flat, dusty terrain, bounded by yet more barren mountains, with only the occasional patch of green produced by irrigation from a village stream. But as the track climbed towards the city of Ghazni, set on a high plateau at seven thousand feet, the temperature plummeted and the scenery brightened. The greys and browns gave way to lush pastures and the brilliant green foliage of fruit trees; and from the banks of streams wafted the beguiling perfume of the sunjyt tree, which grew among the willows.

With the stone marker by the side of the road showing just four miles to the city of Ghazni, Ilderim had volunteered to scout ahead for armed rebels, leaving George and Yasmin to enjoy the view. 'Not far now, Angrez,' said the princess, smiling, as she turned in her saddle, 'but first a reminder of the rapacity of your people. You see that village ahead, to the right of the track?'

George's eyes settled on a typical mud-built settlement, protected by a rude fort. 'What of it?'

'At its heart stands the tomb of Sultan Mahmud. Have you heard of him?'

The name sounded familiar to George from his background reading, but he couldn't place him. 'Remind me.'

Yasmin raised her eyebrows, seemingly in amusement, though it was hard for George to be sure because her mouth and nose were covered with a silk scarf. 'Mahmud,' she explained, 'was the founder of the Turkish Ghaznavid dynasty. He brought Islam to this country and, from the tenth to the twelfth centuries, ruled a huge empire from Ghazni that stretched from Persia to northern India. He was a fierce warrior who led many raids into India to destroy Hindu temples and bring back booty, and his most infamous items of loot were said to be the carved sandalwood doors from the temple of Somnath in Gujarat. For eight centuries these doors guarded the entrance to his tomb. Until your governor-general ordered them to be torn from their hinges and taken back to India.'

George smiled. 'Now I understand your reference to British rapacity, Princess. But were we any worse than this Mahmud fellow? After all, it sounds as though *we* were trying to return the gates to their rightful owners.'

Yasmin snorted. 'A noble sentiment, Angrez, but do you know what actually became of them? In India they were quickly identified as the wrong ones – not from Somnath at all – and they lie to this day in Agra Fort, while Mahmud's tomb remains open to the elements. Would you like to see your countrymen's handiwork?'

'Another time, princess. For now we have more important business to attend to, which I hope, if we're successful, will help to heal the rifts of the past.'

They could hear a rider approaching and, moments later, Ilderim appeared over the brow of the hill ahead and cantered down to them. 'It seems quiet enough, *huzoor*. I rode as far as the second minaret from where I could see the Kabul Gate into the city. Traders and villagers are coming and going, and nowhere could I see armed bands. The royal standard is flying from the citadel so it seems the princess's cousin still has authority.'

'That's a relief,' said George. 'We'd better make contact while the going's good. Does he live in the citadel, Princess?'

'As far as I know.'

They rode on, and from the second minaret that Ilderim had mentioned – a beautiful brick-built tower, 150 feet high, in the shape of an eight-pointed star – they could see the walled city laid out before them. It had been built on a plateau in the shadow of a ridge of hills, and consisted of a formidable outer fortification in the shape of an irregular pentagon, with sides varying from two hundred to four hundred yards in length, and an inner citadel sited on a rocky mound in the centre of the city. George noted approvingly that the outer walls were built on a scarped mound, at least thirty-five feet high, and were protected by a wide ditch and numerous towers giving an all-round field of fire. All in all it looked a hard nut to crack and he marvelled anew at General Keane's success in capturing the town in two hours during the first Afghan war.

At the Kabul Gate – its masonry still scarred by the British gunpowder that had blown the gates in 1839 – Ilderim explained to one of the guards, a slovenly fellow in a filthy uniform, that they had business with the governor at the citadel. 'You had better hurry then,' said the guard, ominously. 'Rumour has it that Hamid Shah will soon be leaving the city to seek refuge with his cousin the amir and the Feringhees.'

'Will it not be dangerous for you if he goes?' asked Ilderim.

'No, sir, safer. At present the people jeer at us in the streets. There are many Ghazis in the city, drawn from the country around to hear the mullah preach, and it won't be long before they turn on us. I hope Hamid Shah leaves soon, and I can replace my uniform with the clothes I wear in my home village.'

Ilderim gave George a pointed look – this was going to be harder than they had thought – and they rode on through the gate, heading south towards the citadel. The narrow streets were crowded with people out for an evening stroll, and at first they failed to notice that one of the three riders threading their way between them was a woman. But as they passed a fruit stall, the wizened trader called, 'Look, brothers, a woman sitting a horse like a man. It is not right.'

Others joined in the chorus and one burly ruffian, wearing a sword and a black turban, tried to grab Yasmin's bridle. George and Ilderim were about to draw their weapons, but Yasmin sent her assailant reeling with a smartly placed riding boot to his chest. 'This way!' she shouted, jabbing spurs into her horse's flanks and scattering pedestrians as she veered down a side-street, closely followed by her two companions.

Forced to avoid the main thoroughfares, it took them twenty minutes to find the paved road that led up to the citadel, a fort every bit as commanding as the Bala Hissar in Kabul. At the entrance gate the half-dressed guards hardly bothered to hear Ilderim's explanation before waving the trio through with bored complacency. After action in the Zulu war, George could recognise the signs of military indiscipline, and as they dismounted in the inner courtyard, he knew that time was of the essence.

They were met on the steps to the living quarters by a

slim, elegant man wearing red robes and a multi-coloured cummerbund. 'I'm Hamid Shah. Who are you?' he asked, his eyes flitting nervously from one new arrival to another. 'Do you have news from Kabul?'

'We do, cousin,' said the princess, unwrapping the scarf from her face.

His eyes widened in amazement. 'Yasmin! Can it really be you? What are you doing here? You must know it's not safe.'

'Safer than Kabul, cousin. For the moment, anyway. Let us go inside and I will explain.'

Hamid led them into the solid three-storey building and up two flights of stone steps to a large, airy room with beautiful views across the city to the mountains beyond. 'This is my private audience chamber. No one will disturb us. Rest yourselves,' said Hamid, indicating the bolsters and cushions on the floor. 'You must be tired after your long journey.'

Once everyone was sitting cross-legged, he turned to Yasmin. 'First tell me about your brother. Is it true he's joined the Angrez?'

'Yes,' she said bitterly. 'He skulked away from Kabul at dead of night with that snake Shah Mohammed and his other senior advisers, leaving me and the rest of his family to fend for ourselves.'

'Was his life in danger?'

'He thought so. A day earlier, on hearing that British troops were advancing from the Kurram valley, Nek Mahomed and the other rebel sirdars threatened him with death if he didn't join them. He said he would, but instead he fled.'

Hamid sighed. 'Has our dynasty fallen so far that a grandson of the great Dost Mahomed would behave in this way? Yakub should never have become amir. He was proud and wilful as a boy, but without the judgement and courage that a ruler requires. You have those qualities, Yasmin. It's a shame you were born a woman.'

'I don't think Walidad Khan would agree.'

'Walidad Khan? The commander of Yakub's Guard?'

'He was.' Yasmin related her killing of Walidad Khan and the timely arrival of her companions, who had finished off her maid's attacker.

'What an ordeal, cousin,' said Hamid, his eyes moist with tears. 'That faithless swine deserved to die.' He turned to George and Ilderim. 'And I thank you for helping my cousin. But who are you and why have you come to Ghazni? It's quiet now but it won't be for long.'

'That is why we're here,' said George, and explained his secret mission to stop the Mullah Mushk-i-Alam from using the Prophet's Cloak to launch a holy war against Yakub and the British.

'So you're an Angrez spy,' concluded Hamid.

'Yes, he is,' interrupted Yasmin. 'But his objective and ours are the same: to prevent Afghanistan from falling into the clutches of the extremist clerics and their Ghazi foot-soldiers who would impose a theocracy over us.'

'But won't that give the Angrez reason to invade and never leave?'

'Not all the Angrez,' said George. 'Only those members of the Indian government, including the viceroy, who would like to absorb Afghanistan as a bulwark against Russian encroachment. But their political masters in London – the people I work for – don't want that to happen because they fear a long, drawn-out war.'

'And they're right to fear it. Look what happened in Kabul when the Angrez tried to install a resident to control the amir. Ghazni will be next, mark my words, and the other provinces will follow.'

'Which is why we must find the cloak before the rebellion gets out of hand and the Indian government has its way.'

'So what have you heard, cousin?' asked Yasmin. 'Are we too late?'

'I fear so,' said Hamid. 'Earlier today one of my spies told me that the cloak is already in the mullah's possession. Now he waits only for a national rising to occur before he dons it in a formal ceremony outside the town.'

'Do you have any idea when that will be?' asked George.

'No. But I do know that the mullah is biding his time, sounding out the chiefs and sirdars, and identifying those who have the stomach for the fight. But soon he will act. Of that I'm certain.'

'And yet *you* are the ultimate authority in the city?'

'I am.'

'Then why do you not simply arrest him and search for the cloak?'

Hamid laughed. 'I am still governor, Angrez, but in name only. If I ordered my soldiers or police to arrest the mullah they would refuse, and some would turn on me. Even now I am planning to leave Ghazni. If I stay my enemies will kill me.'

'I understand your quandary, cousin,' said Yasmin. 'But before you go is there anything you can do to help us find the cloak?'

Hamid hesitated, as if weighing up the risk. 'There is one thing,' he said at last. 'I have an empty house in the old town that overlooks the mullah's compound. You can hide there and, if fortune smiles on you, you may discover where they keep the cloak. But you must be careful. That part of the city is swarming with the mullah's men.'

'Thank you, cousin. You're a brave man to have stayed in Ghazni until now. You'd have made a better ruler than my brother.'

'Perhaps – but I know who would have made the *best* ruler. Even as a child you had a commanding presence and the skill to make people do your bidding. You haven't lost it.'

'But I'm a woman still. Why do you not try to dissuade me from this dangerous enterprise, cousin?'

'Because, dear Yasmin, I know you too well. You wouldn't listen. You never did. Adieu, then, and may Allah be with all of you. You will need His blessing if you're to leave Ghazni alive.'

15

Old Town, Ghazni

'*Huzoor!* Wake up!'

George opened his eyes to see Ilderim crouching beside him. 'What is it?'

'I think I know where they're hiding the cloak.'

'Where?'

'Come up to the roof and I'll show you.'

George threw off the warm Kashmir shawl he had slept under, rose to his feet and followed Ilderim out of the first-floor room and up the handsome wooden staircase to the top of the house. They had arrived in darkness the night before and, having left the horses in a stable off the inner courtyard, had quickly settled for the night, George and Ilderim on cushions in the main room on the first floor, and Yasmin in the more salubrious quarters reserved for women on the third.

Now George climbed the last few steps to the zenana. Every piece of wood used as a support or in the partition walls had been carved and fretted with great skill, while the inner rooms were cut off from the glare outside by carved wooden screens in elaborate patterns. The walls were gay with frescos of every colour, the plaster covered with Afghan scrollwork, filled in with birds of startling plumage and flowers of many hues. The ceilings and cornices were similarly adorned, the latter set with mirrors in long, narrow strips that reflected the gorgeous artwork.

As George gazed around in awe, Ilderim was already halfway up the staircase that led to the roof. 'Wait,' said George, stopping him in his tracks. 'We must first wake the princess. Which room is she in?'

Ilderim groaned, muttered something about modern women not knowing their place, and pointed to the door at the far end of the hall. George walked over to it and knocked. There was silence. He slowly turned the handle and went in. The room was dark, but he could just make out the sleeping form of the princess on a pile of cushions. She looked so peaceful lying there – like a sleeping child – that he found it hard to wake her. A strand of hair had fallen over her face and, momentarily entranced by her beauty, he leant forward to move it away. But barely had his fingers touched it than his wrist was grabbed and Yasmin was sitting bolt upright. In her other hand she held a knife.

'It's Captain Hart,' said George. 'I'm sorry if I startled you.'

She let go of his wrist. 'Don't creep up on me like that, Angrez. What do you want?'

George repeated what Ilderim had told him.

'Give me a moment to dress and I will join you.'

'Of course,' said George, thankful that the darkened room was hiding his embarrassment. But as he reached the doorway he could not resist a quick glance behind him. Yasmin had her back to him and was balancing on one shapely leg as she pulled on her jodhpurs. It was a sight more erotic than if she'd been naked.

Minutes later, the three were lying flat on the roof and

peering down from the parapet to the mullah's compound, which lay to the south of Hamid's house, on the far side of a narrow lane. It looked to George like the typical dwelling of a wealthy Afghan, with suites of rooms at either end of an inner courtyard, and an outer compound housing servants' quarters, storerooms, and stables. The one difference was pointed out by Ilderim. 'You see that building to the left of the entrance gate, the one guarded by two armed men? It's a mosque. I'm convinced that's where they're keeping the cloak.'

George looked at the nondescript building, with its mud walls and simple roof, and found it hard to believe it was a place of worship. 'Are you certain it's a mosque?'

'Yes, *huzoor*.'

'What do you think, Princess? Could he be right?'

'Yes. But we must know for sure. Perhaps you should send Ilderim to the bazaar to buy supplies and listen to the gossip. It's the surest way to find out what is going on in any city.'

'Are you happy to do that, Ilderim?'

'Of course, *huzoor*.'

'Good. Meanwhile we'll keep a watch on who comes and goes.'

Once Ilderim had gone, the princess put her hand on George's and gave it a little squeeze. 'Thank you, Angrez, for everything you're doing for my country.'

George wanted to tell her the truth – that he was doing it as much for himself as for anyone else – but her touch had given him goose-pimples, and he was unwilling to destroy the intimacy of the moment. He felt a fleeting sense of guilt – as images of the two women he had left in South Africa, particularly Lucy, flashed before his eyes – but it did not last.

* * *

Two hours later, with Ilderim back from the bazaar, they retired to the main room on the first floor to eat and discuss their next move.

'Did you hear anything about the cloak?' asked George, between mouthfuls of pilau rice and boiled chicken, which Ilderim had bought from street vendors.

'The word is that the mullah is indeed keeping the cloak in his private mosque and will soon display it in public. This I was told by the shopkeepers, but also by many black-clad Ghazis who invoked Allah that it might be so. One told me that his only wish was to die a martyr and enter Paradise. Such fanatics feel they have nothing to lose and everything to gain by *jihad*.'

'Which is why,' said the princess, picking at her food with distaste, 'we must take possession of the cloak tonight. If we wait we may be too late.'

George shook his head. 'Tonight is far too soon. There are only three of us. We need to plan this properly. My suggestion is that we continue to observe the compound for another day or so, making a note of when the guards go off duty and when the cloak is easiest to steal.'

'I cannot agree, *huzoor*,' said Ilderim, licking his greasy fingers. 'The princess is right. Time slips away. We should act tonight.'

'But we don't even know how many men will be guarding the cloak. Surely it's better to wait a day if it increases our chances of success.'

'I know about the guards, *huzoor*. I climbed on to the roof last night and could see only one on the main gate and one at the mosque. The rest were sleeping in their barracks close to the inner courtyard. At first light the guards were doubled. So we must make our move while it's dark.'

George looked from Ilderim to Yasmin. Their expressions were fixed, their minds made up. 'All right,' he said, hands raised in surrender. 'I can see I'm outnumbered. But how do we deal with the guards? If we shoot them we'll wake the others, not to mention the hundreds of Ghazis camping on the wasteground beside the mullah's compound.'

'True, *huzoor*, which is why we use this,' said Ilderim, drawing his long Khyber knife from the scabbard on his belt.

George smiled. 'Is it my imagination, or do most Afghans actually enjoy killing?'

'It is not your imagination, *huzoor*.'

'So, we kill the guards with knives. But how do we get close enough without being seen?'

Ilderim shrugged his shoulders. 'I can kill a man at ten paces with a knife.'

'I'm sure you can. But what if you miss? We can't take that chance. We have to get close. The question is, how?' George mused. Suddenly the solution came to him. 'What if I stagger up the lane, pretending to be intoxicated, and distract the guard long enough for you to stab him in the back? Then you can dress in his clothes and call the second guard over. Once you've dealt with him you can get the cloak from the mosque while I cover the guardhouse with my carbine. How does that sound?'

'Risky, *huzoor* – but it might work.'

'Indeed,' said Yasmin, 'and what role, pray tell me, have you reserved for me?'

'I didn't . . . er . . . think you . . .' George coloured slightly.

'What? That I'd want to take part? Don't you know me by now, Angrez?'

'You're the sister of the amir, for Heaven's sake, and it wouldn't do to put you in harm's way.'

'Then don't,' said Yasmin. 'But I insist on taking part. I will hold the horses a short way up the lane while you two heroes recover the cloak. Then we'll leave by the Kabul Gate. Agreed?' she asked, one shapely eyebrow raised.

'Agreed.'

George peered round the edge of the wall and could just see by moonlight, barely fifty yards away, the lone guard on duty at the mullah's front gate. He had sent Ilderim to work his way round to the lane beyond the gate, and knew that by now he must be in position, lurking in the shadows. He turned to Yasmin, who was standing behind him, holding the reins of their three mounts. 'Don't forget,' he whispered, 'that if we are separated, we'll meet at Mahmud's tomb on the Kabul road. Wait there until daybreak, but no longer. If we haven't appeared by then, we'll either be dead or captured, so you must save yourself. Understand?'

She nodded, then leant forward to kiss him on the cheek. 'Be careful, Angrez. Your life is very precious. My country's future depends on your success.'

'What about you, Princess?' asked George, staring into Yasmin's large brown eyes. 'Is my life precious to you, too?'

'Of course. I am my country.'

'In that case,' he said, pulling her towards him, 'I'm sure you won't object to this, in case I don't come back.'

He kissed her full on the mouth, and she responded by moaning softly and pressing her body hard against him. After a few seconds they parted, and George turned away to collect his carbine from where he had left it leaning against the wall. He hid it under his long *kurta* and, without looking back, walked out into the lane and began stumbling up it, shouting a few incoherent oaths.

'Who's there?' roared the guard.

George ignored him, and continued to stagger along the lane, swearing as he went.

'A wastrel!' exclaimed the guard, his voice tinged with disgust. 'Hold your tongue, you dog! If you wake my master you'll pay with your life.'

'Go to the devil!' replied George.

'Why, you . . .' The guard drew his pistol and advanced from his post in front of the wicket-gate, his teeth bared in a snarl.

Suddenly George feared that Ilderim wouldn't react in time. He was about to pull out his carbine to defend himself but he needn't have worried. At that moment a dark figure ran up behind the man, clamped a huge hand on his mouth and stabbed him in the neck. The guard twitched for a second or two, and was still. Ilderim lowered him gently to the ground and began to remove his turban and clothes. Once he had put them on he beckoned George to follow him.

The wicket-gate was open and they peered through it. Fifty yards to the right lay the guardhouse and beyond that the door to the inner courtyard; about the same distance to the left, on the far side of the compound, was the small mosque. Outside it stood the second guard, his face turned towards them. 'Abdul! Who was shouting?'

'Just a wastrel, brother,' replied Ilderim, his hand muffling his voice, 'who'll wake up with a headache.'

The guard grunted. 'I hope you didn't hit him too hard, or we'll have to get rid of the body.'

'Now you have me worried, brother. I'll check his pulse.' Ilderim waited for a few seconds, then shouted, 'He's not breathing!'

The guard uttered an oath and strode across the compound

towards the wicket-gate. But something aroused his suspicion, possibly the sight of Ilderim's huge frame, and he retraced his steps. 'Abdul! Come out where I can see you properly.'

'What's wrong, brother?' asked Ilderim.

'Nothing. I just want to see that you're all right. For all I know you might have a knife to your throat.'

'What? Let a wastrel overpower me? Never. Now come and help me revive this fool.'

'First you must show yourself. You have five seconds, and then I'll raise the alarm. One.'

Ilderim drew his knife and looked at George.

'Two.'

George nodded.

'Three.'

Ilderim moved a step closer to the second guard, as far as he could risk without being identified.

'Four.'

Ilderim hurled his knife as hard as he could. It seemed to take an age to reach its target, turning end over end, and finally embedding itself in the soft wood of the door frame, two inches from the guard's neck, with a loud thwack. Shocked by this closest of shaves, the guard looked at the quivering knife, then back at Ilderim before raising his rifle. But George was quicker. A gunshot rang out and the guard toppled backwards.

'I thought you never missed!' scolded George.

'He must have moved, *huzoor*.'

'Never mind that now. Get the cloak. I'll try to hold off the other guards.'

As Ilderim ran towards the mosque, George made for the cover of a small godown between the gate and the guardhouse. From there he could hear shouts and see armed men emerging into the night with lighted torches. He shot one, causing the others to fling themselves to the ground and return fire. Bullets were slamming into the front wall of the godown, sending splinters of wood slicing through the air. George flinched as one shot whistled narrowly past his face. More men, waving rifles and swords, were emerging from the door behind the guardhouse that led to the mullah's private dwelling. George fired at one, and saw him crumple, but others kept coming, and soon the storm of fire against the godown had forced him to duck out of sight. 'Ilderim!' he shouted, towards the mosque. 'For God's sake, hurry!'

Seconds later, Ilderim emerged from the doorway of the mosque, wearing a bag across his chest that had to contain the cloak. In spite of the danger all around, George's heart skipped a beat as he took in the significance of the moment: at last, after all they'd been through, they had in their possession a piece of clothing that had belonged to the Prophet Muhammad. But for how long?

The guards had spotted Ilderim and a great roar of fury went up as they realized what he was carrying. Bullets were kicking up the ground as he ran, but he made it unscathed to the main gate where he stopped and raised his carbine to give George covering fire. 'Run, *huzoor*!' he bellowed, firing and loading as fast as he could.

George set off for the gate with shoulders hunched, doing his best to keep the godown between him and the mullah's guards. He could see bullets striking the gate post above Ilderim's head, and inwardly rejoiced that the Ghazis were such bad shots. But with barely five yards to go he felt a searing pain in his right calf and pitched heavily to the ground, his carbine clattering along the cobblestones. Barely able to look, he put his hand to his leg and felt a penny-sized hole close to the fibula. It was seeping blood. He felt sick, and the pain was so acute he was close to blacking out.

Strong hands were lifting him. It was Ilderim who, seemingly without effort, hauled him up onto his shoulder and quickly covered the remaining distance to the gate. Once through it, he turned left and ran as fast as his burden would allow him towards the junction where Yasmin was waiting with the horses. He could hear shouts and running feet from inside the compound, and knew that the mullah's men were in pursuit, and would soon have a clear shot at his back. Just as he neared the junction, a bullet zipped past his ear. More shots rang out, but none found its mark, and he and George reached the cover of the building at the junction. Twenty yards further down the side lane Yasmin sat on her mount, holding the reins of the other horses in one hand and a pistol in the other. 'Princess!' shouted Ilderim, as he ran towards her. 'Help me get the sahib on to his horse. His leg is wounded.'

'No,' she said, pointing the pistol at Ilderim's chest. 'Put the Feringhee and your weapon on the ground and give me the cloak. If you don't I'll kill you.'

'What? This is no time for jokes, Princess. Those fiends from hell will be here at any moment. Get off your horse and help me.'

Yasmin aimed and fired, the bullet striking sparks from the ground at Ilderim's feet before ricocheting harmlessly away. 'Hand me the cloak,' she said coldly.

Cursing her faithlessness, Ilderim dropped his carbine before gently lowering George to the ground. He then unhooked the large bag from across his chest and handed it to Yasmin. She opened it to inspect the contents. Satisfied, she refastened the tie at the neck and placed it in her saddlebag. 'I'm taking the horses so you can't follow me,' she said, 'but I'll tether them in the compound of Mahmud's tomb.'

George looked up at her from the ground and, through a fog of pain and disbelief, uttered a single anguished word: 'Why?'

She gazed down at him, a tear in her eye. 'Forgive me, Angrez, but I have my reasons.'

Before George could respond, she had turned her horse and was cantering down the lane and away from the mullah's compound, trailing the two mounts behind her.

Ilderim picked up his carbine and was about to fire a shot after her when George intervened: 'Forget her and save yourself. Quickly, before the mullah's men arrive.'

'And leave you?'

'You must. Now go.'

As Ilderim continued to hesitate, a Ghazi poked his weapon round the wall and fired, the bullet narrowly missing the prone George. This made up Ilderim's mind for him. He fired a single shot in reply, gave George a nod of encouragement, then ran down the lane and into the night.

Suddenly George was alone and immobile. He drew his revolver, fully determined to keep the last bullet for himself. But he was still in a state of shock – the effects of his injury compounded by Yasmin's desertion – and did not register the approaching footsteps until it was too late. As he swung round to fire, a foot kicked the pistol from his grasp, while another man leapt on him and held a knife to his throat. More shadowy figures ran up. 'Does he have the cloak?' asked one in a gruff baritone.

'No, master. The other robber must have it. He ran up the lane.'

'Then after him, you fools, and don't come back without it.'

Another voice barked orders and part of the crowd – some on horseback, others on foot – set off after Ilderim. The rest were baying for George's blood. 'Only say the word, master,' said the man sitting on George's chest, 'and I will send this dog to hell.'

'No. To kill him now would be a kindness. First I must know he who is and why he seeks the cloak. Only then will I put an end to his suffering.'

16

A hilltop fort, near Ghazni, late autumn 1879

George lay naked and shivering on the straw-covered floor of a freezing cell. The pain from his wounded calf had receded to a dull throb but it was ever present, as was his hunger and thirst. Far harder to endure was his sense of betrayal. Why had she done it? he kept asking himself. Why had she cheated him after all he and Ilderim had done, were doing, for her and her country? Why had she drawn him into her web, like a spider, by pretending to like him – love him, even – before leaving him to his enemies with no hope of escape? The only answer that made sense to George was that she wanted the cloak for her own ends. But what ends? That was the question, and the more George asked it the further he seemed from a satisfactory answer. He had, in any case, more immediate concerns.

He had been brought to the fort blindfolded five days earlier, and had no idea of its location, though he suspected from the length of the journey and the incline of the route that it lay in the hills close to Ghazni and was the property of an acolyte of the mullah. The routine was always the same. Sustenance arrived once a day in the form of half a pint of water and scraps from the kitchen. Barely had he fallen into a fitful sleep than two guards would enter the cell and douse him with a pail of cold water. All this George could just about bear, but not the regular sessions of torture in the room up the corridor.

It had started mildly enough, with punches and slaps interspersing the questions of who he was and what he was doing in Afghanistan. But as his answers had failed to convince, the methods of his interrogators had become more brutal. He had been beaten with a weighted club, his head held under water until he almost drowned, and his hands tied with leather bonds that were kept wet so that they dug into his wrists and cut off all circulation. And all the while he was hooded and unable to see his tormentors, and barely conscious from lack of sleep. Thus far he had only confessed his name and military rank. But he was at the end of his tether and feared that during the next session he would tell all to end his pain. He would have done so earlier had it not been so obvious that they were only keeping him alive to extract information that might help them recover the cloak.

He started at the sound of footsteps in the corridor, aware of what they heralded. A key sounded in the lock and the heavy wooden door swung open.

'Greetings, Feringhee. It's time for your morning interview,' cackled one of the guards, as he pulled a black hood roughly over George's face.

Two men grabbed his arms, then dragged him out of the cell and along a stone-flagged corridor to the interrogation room, ignoring his cries of pain as his wounded leg bumped against the floor. He was thrown face down into the room and the door clanged shut behind the departing guards. Normally the interrogation began immediately. But this time there was silence and George assumed he was alone. 'I can't take much more of this,' he whispered to himself. 'I'd rather die.'

'Patience, Feringhee, all in good time,' said a nasal voice that George recognised as his usual interrogator's. 'Just tell us what we need to know: why did you steal the cloak and how can we get it back?'

George said nothing, his teeth chattering from the cold. Footsteps got closer until George sensed the man was standing above him. He tensed his body against the inevitable blow but when it came it was far more excruciating than any before. The man had placed his foot against George's wounded calf and was slowly exerting pressure. The pain was so bad George was convinced the leg was fractured and let out a guttural roar. Tears of anguish began to flow down his face.

'Tell me, Feringhee,' said the interrogator, lifting his foot slightly, 'and the pain will stop.'

'All right,' said George, gasping with relief. 'I'll tell you. I was sent by my government in London to prevent the cloak being used to promote *jihad*.'

'Being used by whom?'

'The Ghazni mullah, your master.'

'And why did your government think that might happen?'

'They received intelligence from a spy.'

'And your plan once you had the cloak?'

'To keep it safe until the country had settled down and a pro-British ruler was secure on the throne.'

'That will never happen, Feringhee, be assured of it. But your spy spoke the truth. My master needs the cloak to establish his legitimacy in the eyes of the faithful. So where has your accomplice taken it?'

'I don't know,' said George, half relieved that the princess's role in the theft had not been discovered. 'We didn't discuss what we'd do once we had the cloak.'

'You lie!' said the interrogator, treading hard on George's right calf.

George screamed. 'I'm telling the truth. I don't know where he's taken it.'

'Who is your accomplice?'

Even through the fog of pain, George knew he could never admit Ilderim's true identity. 'He's a Ghilzai,' he gasped, 'a former Guide called Firoz Khan. He lives in the Khyber country.'

'Where exactly?'

'He never told me.'

'Liar!' shouted the interrogator, exerting more pressure on George's injury.

George screamed again.

'Tell me the truth.'

'I am telling the truth,' sobbed George. 'I *don't know*!'

'Enough!' said a second voice, the same gruff baritone he had heard the night he was captured 'The dog doesn't know. No man would endure such pain for another when he knows the truth will put an end to his misery. Tomorrow morning we will give him what he wants. You will execute him in the courtyard. But he will die by inches: genitals first, then hands, limbs and finally his head, which will adorn the gate of the fort. In the meantime I want you to send out riders to search for this elusive Firoz Khan. And when you've found him and recovered the cloak, I want you to destroy all trace of his line. Do you understand?'

'Yes, master.'

That night, George was woken from his feverish sleep by the sound of his cell door swinging open. Ilderim was standing there, lighted torch in hand. 'You!' George was astounded. 'How did you get past the guards?'

'I'll explain later, *huzoor*,' replied Ilderim. 'We must leave before they come back.'

George stood up on his good leg, hiding his nakedness with a hand. 'They took my clothes.'

'I can see that,' said Ilderim, with a grin. 'Wrap this turban around your waist.'

George caught the cloth and, despite his predicament, couldn't help laughing. With his modesty covered, he hopped over to the doorway, which Ilderim was guarding with a pistol.

'Which way?' he asked.

'Up, of course. Follow me.'

Ilderim led the way up a flight of stone steps with George hopping behind. Halfway up, George stopped. 'Ilderim –' he was gasping for breath '– you'll have to carry me.'

Ilderim muttered an oath and was on the point of descending the steps towards him when a shout came from below. 'Oh, God!' exclaimed George. 'They must have seen the empty cell.'

'Yes, which means, *huzoor*, that I must leave you now.'

'You can't! I'm to be killed in a few hours.'

'Better one than two. I'll never escape if I have to carry you. Goodbye, *huzoor*,' said Ilderim, and and fled up the steps.

George looked below. Black-turbaned guards were racing upwards. One held a *tulwar* above his head, ready to strike. George screamed Ilderim's name, but no sound came out. He screamed again – and woke. He was in his cell, lying on straw. He felt sick. It had all been a dream, and he would still die an agonizing death.

As he lay there, waiting for the mullah's men to take him to his execution, he thought of the people who would regret his passing: his mother, certainly; his father too, if indeed he was the Duke of Cambridge; Fanny Colenso and Lucy Hawkins, the latter without question; Ilderim, because he hadn't been paid; and possibly Lords Beaconsfield and Salisbury, but only because his death would signify the failure of his mission. And that was it. His only real friend, Jake, had died earlier that year. Would they meet in Heaven?

Once again the cell door opened, but this time George knew he wasn't dreaming. Two guards entered and one, a tall man with a jagged scar down his cheek, threw George the clothes that had been taken from him when he arrived. 'Put these on, Feringhee.'

George raised one eyebrow. 'Am I to be dressed for death?'

'Do as I say, or you'll feel the edge of my whip.'

George dressed, taking care not to bump his wounded calf, which, without proper care, had swollen to twice its normal size. Not that it mattered any more. Once he had finished, the guards placed him on a makeshift stretcher and carried him up endless flights of steps, grumbling all the while, until they reached level ground and the door that led to the main courtyard. The morning sun dazzled George as they passed through the doorway and his eyes took a moment to adjust to natural light. He had been expecting to confront some form of scaffold, and despite his earlier calm his heart was beating fast. But instead all he could see was a large group of men on horseback, eyeing him as he was brought out into the courtyard.

'Bring the Feringhee to me,' said one of the mounted men, in the same baritone that George remembered from the night before. It could only be the Mullah Mushk-i-Alam, George reasoned, the man who was plotting a holy war against the British and their Afghan allies, the man from whom they had stolen the cloak to prevent such a war. It was the first time George had seen him in the flesh. He was dressed in black, tall and broad-shouldered, with a thin, wrinkled face and a bushy white beard that indicated a man in his sixties, if not older. Yet he seemed to have lost none of his physical vigour, and he sat his grey Arab with the ease of a seasoned horseman.

As George was brought before him, he spat on the ground. 'Allah has granted you a temporary stay of execution, Feringhee,' said the mullah, his lip curled in derision. 'You should be grateful.'

George could scarcely believe what he was hearing. 'What? I don't understand.'

'Then listen well. Last night a messenger from Ghazni brought a note from your accomplice. In it he offers the cloak for your life, and suggests the exchange takes place today at noon in a defile five miles north of Ghazni. He wants you and two of my men to ride to a point just beyond the narrowest part of the defile where you will find, hanging from the branch of a willow tree, a bag containing the cloak. As soon as my men are happy that the bag is genuine, they are to release you and leave with the bag. Your accomplice says he will be watching nearby in case of treachery.'

'And you agreed?'

'Of course. I must have that cloak. The future of my country depends upon it. But mark my words, Feringhee. If that bag does not contain the cloak, you will not leave the defile alive. My men,' he said, indicating the riders behind him, 'will see to that.'

By the time the mullah and his calvacade of mounted men reached the entrance to the defile, after an hour's hard ride, it was almost midday and the sun was high in the sky. George was sore and thirsty, having been forced to ride with his hands bound and his mouth gagged, yet he felt more hope than he had at any time since his capture. Ilderim was hiding in the defile and would, he felt sure, have devised a plan to rescue him without handing over the cloak. How he would do so was another matter: George was fairly certain that Ilderim didn't have the cloak. Or did he? Had he somehow caught up with Princess Yasmin and recovered it? It seemed hard to believe.

George was still mulling over his chances of surviving the encounter when the mullah called forward his two best men to give them last-minute instructions. 'As soon as you have the cloak you're to release the infidel. If it isn't there, kill him. Do you understand, Ahmed?'

'Yes, master,' lisped the older of the two, a hawk-nosed villain with a broken front tooth. 'But what if his friend is hidden with a rifle nearby?'

'What if he is? There are two of you and one of him. And the rest of my men will join you as soon as they hear shots. You have nothing to fear. Now go. It's time.'

Ahmed nodded, grabbed George's bridle and led his pony into the defile with the other rider following. Both had left their rifles behind, as Ilderim had requested, but beneath their coats they had hidden pistols and knives, which they fingered nervously as they followed a path along the bank of a small stream. At first the width of the defile was a good fifty yards, with the side walls rising at a shallow angle. But the further they rode the steeper and closer the walls of rock and scree became, until they were barely six yards apart and the path was so narrow that the riders could only proceed in single file. A perfect place for an ambush, thought George, as he craned his neck in an effort to see the ridge above the defile, but no one was visible. Once through this narrow stretch, which only lasted for a hundred yards or so, the floor of the defile widened dramatically, though it was covered with brushwood and small boulders, and still not easy to negotiate.

'There it is!' shouted Ahmed, pointing to a willow tree on the bank of the stream ahead, just below the path. Hanging from one of its lower branches was a multi-coloured shoulder bag that George had never seen before, and which convinced him more than ever that Ilderim did not have the cloak.

'Fazel,' said the leader to the second man, 'go and see if it contains the cloak. If it does, raise your right hand and I will release the Feringhee. If it doesn't, show your left and I'll kill him.'

Fazel nodded and rode on. Once level with the tree, he dismounted and scrambled down the bank. George's heart was in his mouth as the man unhooked the bag and looked inside. His left hand was on the point of being raised when a shot rang out. The man staggered and fell down the rest of the bank into the stream.

'Treachery!' shouted Ahmed, as he scrabbled for his pistol. With his hands bound and helpless, George could only pray that Ilderim wouldn't miss with his second shot. But he did, the bullet pinging harmlessly off the rock behind Ahmed who, by now, had drawn his pistol and was swinging it round to fire. In desperation, George dug his heels into his pony and sent it barrelling into Ahmed's mount, the shock enough to spoil the Afghan's aim. The bullet passed a couple of inches above George's head, the explosion ringing in his ears. Ahmed aimed again and, knowing that he wouldn't miss a second time, George threw himself from his pony as the Afghan fired, hitting the ground hard with his right shoulder and jarring his wounded leg. Ignoring the pain, he looked up, expecting a third shot. But Ahmed's saddle was empty, his crumpled body lying beside his mount. Ilderim, George realised, must have fired simultaneously, and this time he hadn't missed.

George waited anxiously for Ilderim to appear, fearful that the mullah and his men would have heard the shots and be rapidly approaching. The sound of hoofbeats provided confirmation and George began to panic. Did Ilderim think he was dead? He tried to cry out that he was alive, but his gag muffled the sound. The hoofbeats were getting louder and George knew that the game was almost up. He tried to drag his battered body into the cover of some nearby bushes, but had covered barely half the distance when a noise like an oncoming train sounded on the hillside above him. He looked up to see a huge rock bounding down the hillside, loosening scores of smaller ones as it went. The landslide gathered pace and crashed into the floor of the defile at the moment that the first of the mullah's riders emerged from the narrow path, consuming both horses and men in its lethal torrent of earth and rock.

As the dust settled, and the cries of wounded men and horses echoed along the defile, George understood why Ilderim had chosen this location for the 'exchange'. The rockfall had sealed the entrance of the narrow section to a height of more than fifteen feet. It would take the mullah's men hours to remove the obstacle, giving George and Ilderim plenty of time to escape. George shook his head in admiration. The resourcefulness of his Afghan companion knew no bounds.

Minutes later Ilderim appeared, leading the two horses that Yasmin had taken. He ran over to George, who was still prone on the ground, and released his gag. 'It's good to see you with your skin in one piece, *huzoor*,' he said, with a grin.

'You too,' replied George, his swollen tongue making his voice barely recognizable. 'Now cut my ties and help me on to a horse.'

Ilderim did as he was asked, and after twenty minutes of hard riding they were clear of the defile and into open country, heading north towards Kabul. But the action of riding over broken ground soon proved too painful for George and he signalled to Ilderim to slow to a walk. 'Would you like to stop and rest, *huzoor*?'

'No,' said George, though he would have liked nothing better. 'We must put as much distance between ourselves and the defile as possible. I'll feel better in a while, and we can press on. But thank you for saving my life again. You didn't have to come back for me. Why did you?'

Ilderim smiled. 'Because I like you, *huzoor*, and because my father would never have forgiven me if I'd returned without you.'

George nodded. 'And the cloak?'

'That faithless bitch has it still. When I recovered the horses at Mahmud's tomb, she was long gone and the cloak with her.'

'Have you any idea where she may be and why she took it?'

'No, *huzoor*. Though it's possible she went north to Kohistan.'

'Why there?'

'Her mother was a Kohistani. She's dead, but the princess has other family in the north.'

'Does she now? Well, if that is so, we must follow.'

'*Huzoor*, you're in no condition to ride that far. You must rest until your leg is better.'

'There isn't time. But you're right: I can't ride all that way. You'll just have to find me some alternative transport. For now I'll have to grit my teeth and bear the pain. Let's go,' he said, jabbing the pony with his one good leg.

That night they camped in hills seven miles north of the defile. Again George slept fitfully, and dreamt of dungeons and falling rocks. When he woke the air was chilly and the fire Ilderim had built to keep them warm had dwindled to a few smoking embers, yet his skin was burning. He threw off his blanket and tried to sit up, but he lacked the strength and slumped back to the ground.

Ilderim stirred. '*Huzoor*?'

'My skin's hot and I feel as weak as a newborn.'

Ilderim came over and placed a palm on his forehead. 'You have a fever, *huzoor*. Let me look at your leg.' He carefully unravelled the soiled bandages that covered George's right calf and gasped. The puckered entry hole at the right rear of the swollen muscle was neat enough, but on the far side the jagged exit wound was the size of a crown and crawling with tiny white maggots. 'It's infected, *huzoor*, and if it's not treated soon you will die.'

'Are you certain?' asked George.

'I've seen enough bullet wounds to know when one is infected. And likely the bone is broken too, or chipped at best. Either way you need rest.'

'Very well,' said George, his palms raised in submission. 'I'll rest for a while. But where?'

'My uncle Sher Afzul, my mother's brother, has a house in the hills south-west of Kabul. I haven't seen him for many years, but he always liked me and will surely help us. Anyway, he has to – he's family.'

'How far?'

'Twenty miles. Can you make it that far on horseback, or shall I steal a cart?'

'I can make it.'

17

Sher Afzul's fort, south-west of Kabul

George sat up in bed, and looked round the bare, unfamiliar room. Its few sticks of furniture were rough-hewn and of poor quality, but the view through the open window of snow-capped mountains, their peaks bathed in morning sunshine, was one of the most beautiful he had seen.

Where on earth am I? he wondered. And then he remembered the conversation with Ilderim about his uncle, and the long, difficult ride through the hills to Sher Afzul's fort, by the end of which he had been barely conscious and had had to be tied to his saddle.

'Greetings, Angrez,' said a voice from the door. 'You're awake at last. I'm Sher Afzul, Ilderim's uncle.'

The speaker was of middle height and thick-set, with a white beard and an easy smile. His *kurta* and sash were clean and well made, rather than extravagant, and denoted a man of means, but not great wealth or power. He pulled up a chair and sat down.

George nodded. 'I remember arriving, but nothing after that. How long have I been here?'

'Three weeks.'

'Three *weeks*? Have I been unconscious all that time?'

'For most of it, yes,' said Sher Afzul. 'You were very

feverish when you arrived and rambling. My wife made up a poultice for your leg and at last it seems to have worked. She tells me the wound is healing well and that the bone is unbroken.'

George touched his lower leg. 'It's still a little sore, but much better. Will you thank her for her kindness?'

'You may thank her yourself.'

'I will. But what of Ilderim? Is he still in the fort?'

Sher Afzul shook his head. 'He waited two weeks for you to recover. When you did not, he went to visit his father. He should be back soon.'

'I'm glad. I have much to thank him for. He saved my life three times. Did he tell you that?'

'No, Angrez, but he did say you had both been in great danger, and were fortunate to be alive.'

'Very fortunate,' said George. 'But, tell me, what news of the British? Have they taken Kabul?'

'They took it in early October, after dislodging the rebels from a strong position in the hills above Charasiab. But much has happened since then, and none of it to the credit of the Angrez chief.'

'I take it you mean General Roberts?'

'I do. Since reaching Kabul he has levied a huge fine, placed the entire city to a distance of ten miles under martial law, and set up military courts to try those responsible for the death of the resident. He has also made the carrying of any weapon – firearms, swords *and* knives – an offence punishable by death, and ordered the arrest of the amir's chief advisers for complicity in the massacre at the Residency and the resistance at Charasiab.'

'Is the wazir among them?

'He is. Do you know him?'

'Not well, and what I saw I didn't like. But accusing Shah Mohammed Khan of conspiracy is tantamount to accusing the amir himself. Do they have any credible evidence that he was involved?'

'I couldn't say, Angrez. What I *have* heard is that scores of Afghans have been executed without any proof of their guilt.'

'But not Yakub's advisers?'

'Not yet. But the other killings have created much bad feeling, as has the Angrez practice of collecting grain and forage supplies by force, leaving the people with nothing for themselves. This leaves them easy prey to the hotheads and religious extremists who talk of *jihad*, and who, only two days ago, killed Mohammed Hussein Khan, the man appointed by the Angrez general to rule the region to the east of here.'

'Was Mullah Mushk-i-Alam of Ghazni involved?'

'I'm certain of it. Most believe the assassination was the work of Bahadur Khan, a Ghilzai chief in the Dara Nirikh valley, whose villages were destroyed because they refused to hand over supplies. But if he did it, he was acting on the orders of the mullah and his military commander, Mohammed Jan. For weeks the mullah has been gathering large bodies of armed men with his fiery speeches at Ghazni. He even sent emissaries here to ask if I would join the fight.'

'Were they looking for me?'

'I think not.'

'So how did you get rid of them?'

'It wasn't easy,' said Sher Afzul, stroking his beard. 'I told them I'd consider their proposal. But they'll be back, and when they come I'll find it even harder to refuse them. Since Yakub's abdication, I can no longer plead loyalty to the amir.'

'Yakub has *abdicated*? When?'

'A few days ago. The Angrez general issued this proclamation,' said Sher Afzul, producing a yellow slip of paper from his pocket and handing it to George. It read:

I, General Roberts, on behalf of the British government, hereby proclaim that the amir, having by his own free will abdicated, has left Afghanistan without a government. In consequence of the shameful outrage upon its resident and suite, the British government has been compelled to occupy by force of arms Kabul, the capital, and to take military possession of other parts of Afghanistan.

The British government now commands that all Afghan authorities, chiefs, and sirdars do continue their functions in maintaining order, referring to me whenever necessary.

The British government, after consultation with the principal sirdars, tribal chiefs, and others representing the interests and wishes of the various provinces and cities, will declare its will as to the future permanent arrangements to be made for the good government of the people.

George handed back the proclamation. 'I can understand why Yakub did it: ever since joining Roberts at Kushi he's been a virtual prisoner of the British. And by abdicating he's revealed Roberts and the Indian government for what they are – not allies here to help, but foreign invaders, plain and simple. Well, now that they have Kabul *and* the government of the country, they won't relinquish it without a fight.'

'Then that's what they shall have, Angrez, mark my words. Already the countryside is ungovernable for your people, and each day the armed opposition will grow. Unless, that is, you and Ilderim can recover the cloak.'

George's jaw fell. 'You *know* about the cloak?'

'Of course. Ilderim explained. Afghan families have no secrets.'

'Did he tell you that the princess took the cloak from us at the point of a gun?'

'I told you, I know everything.'

'So you agree with Ilderim that the princess has probably gone north?'

'I suspect she planned this all along. She has many relatives and supporters among the Kohistan tribes, and is probably making her own play for leadership of the uprising.'

'You think she intends to fight the British?'

'I'm sure of it. How else can she hope to gain popular support for her rule?'

Suddenly all became clear to George. He remembered the words of Pir Ali: *You must never forget, Hart Sahib, that the cloak means power.* Sher Afzul was right, he decided. The princess had taken the cloak because she wanted to rule in her own right. And while the revelation made her betrayal a little easier to take, George was not optimistic about her chances of success. 'From what I've seen of your people, Sher Afzul, I find it hard to believe they'll accept a female ruler. Would you?'

'It depends, Angrez. All most of us want is a ruler who is strong, just and only a little rapacious. That seems as much as we Afghans can hope for, and if Princess Yasmin is all of those things then I, for one, would back her at the *loya jirga* we tribal chiefs attend to approve a new amir. Whether the mullahs and the more traditional chiefs would ever consent to be ruled by a woman is another matter. I doubt it.'

'So do I. But are you saying, Sher Afzul, that you'd support a war against the British?'

'Of course, if your people intend to stay in Afghanistan. I have nothing against you, Angrez, but it's the patriotic duty of every Afghan to repel the foreign invader. I would not fight for the mullahs and the extremists, but I would take sides with a strong moderate like Sher Ali, our former amir, or even Princess Yasmin if she proves her worth.'

'I understand. And may I point out that Roberts and his kind are not my people, as you put it. I was sent here to prevent the Indian government from provoking an all-out war that would give it the excuse to annex Afghanistan, and that is still my aim.'

'Then we see eye to eye, Angrez.'

'So it seems. But do you really believe there's still a chance we can stop the war by recovering the cloak?'

'Yes, Angrez, I do. The mullahs and the extremists will fight with or without the cloak. But many moderate Afghans will only join a *jihad* if they believe it's legitimate. The cloak gives it that legitimacy.'

'But did you not say a moment ago you would join a *jihad*?'

'Not a *jihad*. I would fight to free my country. There's a difference. Put it like this, Angrez. If the Ghazni mullah succeeds in raising a national *jihad*, the Angrez troops at Kabul will be slaughtered and your government will have no choice but to return to avenge them, never to leave. Then even I would be forced to fight, and I'd most likely die. But if the rising is local, it will be defeated. Then there is still some hope that your government will see sense and, with its honour intact, withdraw its troops and leave us to our own devices.'

'Good Lord,' said George, impressed, 'you'd put a philosopher to shame with your sophistry. But even if you're right, and we can still make a difference by recovering the cloak, we've first got to find it. And then there's the issue of time. We're more than three weeks behind the princess, who must have reached her destination long ago. She may, at this very moment, be marching south at the head of a huge army.'

'True, Angrez, she may indeed. But never forget it takes many weeks for a man to gather an army, and for a woman even longer, so you and Ilderim may yet be in time.'

'I hope you're right,' said George, thinking it over. The odds, he knew, were stacked against them. It would be hard enough finding the cloak, let alone stealing it from the princess and her armed adherents. But he had to try or his mission would fail and Afghanistan would suffer. There was also the small matter of forfeiting the two-thousand-pound bonus he desperately needed to save the family home.

'I've made up my mind,' said George, after a long pause. 'We'll leave as soon as Ilderim returns.'

'Leave for where, *huzoor*?'

George turned to see Ilderim's smiling face and huge frame, covered with dust from his ride, taking up most of the doorway. 'You're back,' he said lamely, incapable of doing justice to the pleasure he felt at the sight of his comrade in arms.

'Yes, *huzoor*.'

'And your father is well?'

'He is, *huzoor*, as are you, I see.'

'Much better.'

'I'm glad. But you haven't answered my question. Where are we going?'

George rolled his eyes. 'Why, to Kohistan, of course. Where else?'

18

Near Gulbahar, Kohistan, winter 1879

'Wait here, *huzoor*,' instructed Ilderim, 'while I ride into the town and make enquiries. It will be better for both of us if I go alone.'

'Very well,' replied George, blowing into his hands to warm them. 'But don't be too long. It looks like snow again and we need to find shelter before dark.'

They had left Sher Afzul's fort two days earlier and, resolved to give the British at Kabul a wide berth, had passed to the west of the city through the fertile pastures and shady orchards of the Chardeh valley, rejoining the main route north at Karez Mir. Another day's hard ride had brought them close to Gulbahar where the Shamali plains rose to meet the foothills of the Hindu Kush, the towering range of mountains that divides northern from southern Afghanistan, which the proponents of the Forward policy in Simla had long hoped to acquire as the 'scientific' northern frontier of British India. And George could see why. The most prominent of the snow-capped peaks in the distance rose to a height of twenty thousand feet, and even the smaller ones seemed to form an unbroken wall of jagged ridges and deep ravines. There were, moreover, only a limited number of passes over the natural barrier, easy to control and blocked in winter.

As Ilderim continued down the snow-covered hill to Gulbahar, a small town of flat-roofed houses at the head of the Panjshir valley, George dismounted and led his horse off the road into a forest of conifers and weeping spruce. About fifty yards in he came upon a small clearing where he knee-haltered his horse and sat down on a rock with his carbine to wait. But after half an hour, with the chill seeping into his bones, he rose to stretch his legs and ease the ache in his recently healed calf. The clearing was too small for any proper exercise, so he shouldered his carbine and struck off into the trees in an easterly direction, away from the main road, and soon came upon a forest track that led gently downhill. He followed it for about four hundred yards and was about to turn back when he heard the faint sound of raised voices. They seemed to be coming from further down the path. George walked towards them, hugging the treeline, until he came to the edge of the forest where he stopped, open-mouthed.

Directly below him, strung out along a fast-flowing river at the foot of the valley, was a huge tented encampment with a brushwood enclosure for hundreds of horses. Near the centre of the camp was a large bonfire and round it sat a vast crowd of Afghan tribesmen, listening to and occasionally heckling a man who was addressing them. They were too far away for George to hear what was being said, or to recognize faces, and he was again on the point of retracing his steps when he saw a second figure rise from the edge of the crowd and join the original speaker by the fire. Two things caught George's attention: from her gait and outline, the new speaker was almost certainly a woman; and she was wearing a heavy red cloak with tan sleeves, the jewels of its clasp sparkling at her throat.

'It can't be,' muttered George. But he knew it was. He had found Yasmin and the cloak.

For a moment he stared transfixed, his heart pounding at his first sight of the woman who had drawn him into her web only to betray him. He didn't feel anger, just sadness, and a determination to hear from her lips the answer to the question: why? Yet he forced himself to put all personal feelings aside and to concentrate on the matter in hand, which was how to steal the cloak from under the noses of a band of armed and dangerous Afghans. He knew he couldn't do it alone, and was about to return to the clearing to wait for Ilderim when a strong hand gripped his right arm, causing him to start. His spirits sank as he imagined an Afghan sentry had sneaked up on him. But when he swung round he found Ilderim, finger to his lips.

'How did you find me?' whispered George.

Ilderim snorted. 'It wasn't difficult, *huzoor*. You left tracks in the snow a child could have followed. What's down there?'

'It looks to be some sort of tribal gathering. A man was speaking, now a woman. I think she's Princess Yasmin, and she's wearing a red cloak with tan sleeves. It must be the Prophet's Cloak.'

'It is, *huzoor*. I heard talk in the bazaar at Gulbahar of a big meeting of Kohistani chiefs and their men by the Panjshir river. This is surely it. So if that Hell-cursed bitch is here, wearing the cloak, she must be trying to win them over. But why?'

'To march on Kabul. She's making her play for the throne, and her means to that end is to defeat Roberts in battle. I'm sure of it.'

Ilderim frowned. 'No Afghan will follow a woman into battle.'

'Are you certain about that?'

'I am.'

'We'll soon find out. But first we need to get closer to the camp so we can hear what they're saying. Luckily the light's fading,' said George, as he eyed the sun setting to the west, 'and we should be able to cross the fields below without being seen. We'll make for that orchard just above the camp.'

'We can do that, *huzoor*, but what hope have we of stealing the cloak with so many men against us?'

'Not much, it's true. But we did it once and we can do it again. I say we wait until they've all gone to sleep, then sneak in and take it. The princess will have it with her. We need to find out which is her tent. Keep close,' said George, unslinging his carbine before setting off from the wood in a stooped trot.

The camp lay six hundred yards below them, across two maize fields separated by an irrigation ditch. On the far side of the second field was the orchard of walnut trees that George had identified as the ideal place to lie up. After a nervous minute or two spent crossing open ground in the half-light, with Ilderim cursing silently as he slipped a foot into the icy water of the irrigation ditch, they reached it unobserved. Now just eighty yards from the camp, and even less from the crowd round the fire on a plateau just above the tents, they crawled on their bellies to the bottom of the orchard where a small mound provided a convenient rest for their carbines. All eyes in the crowd, meanwhile, were on the woman speaking.

Beneath the cloak she was dressed in the same green tightly fitting jacket and white jodhpurs that she had worn on the night they had taken the cloak from the mullah. She was also veiled, presumably as a sop to the conservative Kohistani tribesmen, but her clothes, flashing eyes and extravagant hand gestures left George in no doubt that she was Princess Yasmin. Her words provided the confirmation. 'I won't deny,' she cried, straining to make herself heard at the back of the gathering stretched out before her, 'that the shame my brother has brought on his family, and on Afghanistan, by throwing off his dynastic responsibilities is a stain that cannot easily be wiped clean. But with Allah's help, and your assistance, I will try. I know there are many here who would question my right to rule . . .'

Whistles sounded from one or two in the crowd.

'. . . but I say to you, cast aside your prejudices and let me prove myself. Did not Lakshmibai, Rani of Jhansi, show herself to be a worthy ruler, as valiant in battle as she was wise in counsel, during the sepoy rebellion against the Angrez?'

Someone in the crowd shouted that the rani was a Hindu not a Muhammadan, and that no Afghan would shame himself by hiding behind a woman's skirts.

'Did her religion make her any less inspiring to her people?' responded Yasmin. 'No. And if you need an example of a Muhammadan woman ruler, begums have been ruling the princely state of Bhopal in central India for more than fifty years.'

This last remark prompted a grey-bearded chief to rise from the front row and take the floor. 'What you say is true, Princess, but the begums of Bhopal are pawns of the Angrez. Is that how you would rule, a petticoat imitation of your lapdog brother?'

'How dare you suggest such a thing, Sher Khan?' snapped Yasmin, her eyes narrowed in fury. 'Would I have urged you to march on Kabul, with myself at your head, if I was planning to throw myself at the feet of the Angrez? No! I swear to you all that in return for your allegiance I won't rest until the Angrez have been driven from our land.'

A handful of tribesmen cheered their assent, but they were quickly silenced by glares from their maliks and headmen, at which point a second younger chief, gorgeously attired in an emerald green *kurta* with a yellow sash and matching yellow turban, rose to say his piece. He was lighter-skinned than most Pathans, with blue eyes and a reddish tint to his immaculately trimmed and carefully oiled beard. 'We all admire your spirit, Princess,' declared the young dandy, 'but to defeat the Angrez we will require more than that: a general needs cunning, determination and military experience. I possess all of those qualities, and you do not.'

Yasmin paused before answering, as if aware of the serious threat this chief posed to her ambitions. 'I won't deny you've seen more fighting than I have, Mir Bacha. What man has not? But it's rumoured that years of peace under my father Sher Ali have made you soft, more interested in women and fine clothes than in the rigours of a campaign.'

A few in the crowd sniggered, while Mir Bacha glared and Yasmin nodded knowingly. 'And there's one more thing you lack, cousin,' she continued, 'and that's the royal blood of the Barakzais that flows through *my* veins. Without it, how can you imagine the people of this country will accept you as their ruler?'

'Why do you think I want to rule, Princess? We are not here to decide the next amir. That is for the *loya jirga* to decide, though I won't deny my preference is for your uncle Wali Mahomed. We are here today to choose a military commander for the thousands of Kohistani tribesmen who, in a few days, will march on Kabul and destroy the Angrez. I want to be that commander. It is my destiny.'

Listening intently from his hiding place, George could sense that the charismatic young chief was getting the upper hand and that the princess had one last chance to win over the crowd.

'No, Mir Bacha. It is *my* destiny. Am I not wearing the sacred cloak of our Prophet?' she asked, arms spread wide to illustrate the fact. 'Did I not pluck it from the undeserving hands of the Ghazni mullah, a man who would hope to impose a medieval theocracy over our country that would set it back hundreds of years?'

Boos rippled through the crowd as the princess realized she had underestimated the mullah's popularity with the conservative Kohistani chiefs. 'How dare you malign one of Afghanistan's holiest men?' said Mir Bacha, accusingly. 'The mullah has no ambition to rule. His call for a *jihad* to rid this country of its foreign invaders is a patriotic act, not a selfish one, and all true believers have a duty to respond. We have done that, and I for one will co-operate with the mullah's troops, under Mohammed Jan, when we reach the capital.'

'Then you're a fool, cousin. He will use you to defeat the Angrez, then take control.'

'I don't agree. But let us give my fellow chiefs and maliks their say, shall we?'

'As you wish,' answered Yasmin, convinced that the cloak would win her a majority.

Mir Bacha turned to the crowd. 'Which of you would choose Princess Yasmin to lead you into battle?'

Not a single voice or hand was raised in her support.

'And which of you would choose me?'

A forest of arms went up.

'The council has spoken,' declared Mir Bacha. 'I will lead the advance on Kabul. It only remains, Princess, for you to hand over the cloak. I will see that it is returned to its keepers in Kandahar.'

'Give you the cloak so you can use it for your own ends? Never!' vowed Yasmin, her hands placed defiantly on her hips.

'If you will not give it to me, I shall have to take it,' said Mir Bacha.

But as he reached Yasmin and tried to spin her round so that he could remove the cloak, she whipped out a tiny pistol from her cummerbund and pointed it at her cousin's head. 'Take your hands off me,' she warned. 'You shall have this cloak over my dead body.'

Seeing the princess produce a weapon, a number of Mir Bacha's adherents drew theirs, but their chief merely laughed. 'Does the cloak mean so much to you that you'd kill one of your kinsmen to keep it? What then, Princess? You wouldn't get five yards.'

'With you dead, no. But that is your choice. Now, tell your men to place their weapons on the ground or I'll put a bullet in your brain.'

Mir Bacha hesitated, not certain that she had the nerve to carry out her threat. But a look into her unblinking brown eyes, fixed like a cobra on its prey, assured him that she did. 'Put down your weapons,' he ordered.

One by one his men complied. Yasmin then directed Mir Bacha, her gun still to his head, towards the brushwood enclosure where she instructed him to saddle a horse. 'You will regret this,' he snarled, as he put a bridle on the nearest mount. 'Princess or no, I will hunt you down, and when I do you will wish you had killed me first.'

'Save your idle threats, cousin. If we do meet again, it is you who will be begging for mercy. Now, hand me the reins and hurry with the saddle.'

From his vantage point above the camp, George had held his breath as the princess drew her weapon and pointed it at the young chief, convinced she was just seconds from death. But her luck had held and now, incredibly, it looked as if she might get away. He admired her steely nerve and silently chided the Kohistanis for refusing to recognize her outstanding qualities.

'*Huzoor!*' whispered Ilderim, pointing to the left of the enclosure. 'A gunman is aiming at her.'

George followed the line of Ilderim's gesture, but could see nothing. 'Where?'

'There! He's behind a rock with a rifle.'

A slight movement caught George's eye. He squinted harder and could just make out the top of someone's head, poised above a rifle barrel. He lifted his carbine and lined up the sights on the Afghan's head. He knew that if he fired the tribesmen would swarm up the hill like a hive of disturbed bees, but if he did not the princess would be killed. He fired, the noise reverberating across the valley as the bullet thudded into the gunman's temple, jerking his head sideways.

The crowd scattered, some taking cover while others ran for their tents to retrieve their rifles. Yasmin mounted in the confusion and urged her horse up the track that led to Gulbahar as Mir Bacha shouted at his men to follow her. Two heeded his call, not even bothering to saddle their horses, but neither got further than the perimeter of the camp. One had his horse shot by Ilderim and was pitched headlong into the road; the other became George's second victim. By now the tribesmen were returning fire and George knew it was time to go. He signalled to Ilderim and they scrambled back up the hill, stopping every hundred yards or so to fire at their pursuers who, thanks to the gloom, had little to aim at.

Once under the cover of the trees, they hurried along the track to where they had left their horses, pausing only to tighten their girths before rejoining the road to Charikar where they hoped to intercept Yasmin as she fled south. A mile short of the town, they pulled off the track, and hid behind some rocks. It was now dark, though the half-moon and clear sky provided enough light to see the track, and the temperature had plummeted to well below zero. The only sound was the distant howl of a wolf. Then, faintly at first, and slowly getting louder, they picked up the regular beat of a horse approaching at the trot, its rider preferring not to canter by moonlight. George peered round the rocks and confirmed that it was the princess.

They waited until Yasmin was almost level with them before spurring on to the road. Uncertain who they were, she tried to get away by swerving her horse round George, but Ilderim managed to grab her reins and bring the animal to a halt. He looked up and found himself staring at the barrel of a pistol.

'Don't shoot, Princess!' shouted George, as he rode up. 'It's Captain Hart and Ilderim. We saved your life back at the camp.'

She kept her weapon levelled at Ilderim. 'It was *you* who shot the man sneaking up on me?'

'Yes, and the two horsemen who tried to follow you.'

'Why would you help me after I left you at Ghazni?'

'Because I now know what you were trying to do, and I sympathize, and because you still have the cloak. Now hand it over.'

'Why should I? I could kill you both.'

'No, Princess,' said George, pointing his carbine with one hand. 'You might kill one of us, but not both.'

She thought about the odds for a moment and saw sense, lowering her pistol and jamming it into her cummerbund. Then she began to take off the cloak, which, close up, was even more striking than George had imagined. The sleeves were plain enough, but the body was a mixture of many different strands of fine thread – reds, blues, greens, yellows and blacks – that had been beautifully worked into a single garment.

'Look after it,' said Yasmin, as she handed it over. 'It's very delicate.'

George took it and was stunned by the brilliance of the jewelled clasp, the centrepiece of which was a diamond the size of a thumbnail, surrounded by scores of smaller gems. The solitaire alone must have weighed ten carats. As for the cloak's material, it felt as soft as silk, but not so fine. 'What is it made from?' asked George.

'Camel hair,' replied Yasmin. 'But not the hair of any camel, only those that reside in Paradise. Legend has it that the cloak was woven by the Prophet Enoch, and presented by Allah to Muhammad after the great Prophet's Night Journey and Ascension to Heaven. It is said to have the power to cure disease, convert the faithless, and end national disasters. You should handle it with respect.'

A shiver went down George's spine as he grasped the historical significance of the 1300-year-old garment in his hands. To a Muhammadan it would be like holding a piece of the True Cross. He could sense the weight of history between his fingers, and was fiercely determined that the cloak would come to no harm. 'I will,' he replied, carefully folding the garment and stowing it in his saddle-bag. 'And now we must leave before your Kohistani friends find us.'

'And go where?'

'I haven't yet decided but away from here.'

Three hours later, having left the hills for the wide expanse of the Shamali plains, they were sitting round a camp-fire, wrapped in blankets to keep out the bitter cold. Ilderim was snoring softly, but George and Yasmin were awake, both aware that the other needed to talk. Yasmin spoke first.

'I'm sorry for what I did at Ghazni,' she said, staring intently into the flames, 'but I had my reasons.'

'I understand.'

'You should hate me, and yet you tell me you understand.' She turned to look at George who met her gaze. 'Would you have done the same in my position?'

'I don't know.'

'No – how could you? You're an Angrez, after all. Your empire reaches every corner of the globe. How can you imagine what it feels like to see your country invaded by a foreign power, its soldiers given licence to plunder and rape? You can't. But I'm going to tell you. It shames you. It boils your blood and turns your heart to stone. It leaves you determined to do everything in your power to see that foreign presence removed. That is why I betrayed you. I needed the cloak. I thought it would cause others to follow me, and together we would free Afghanistan. But I was wrong. Did you see those fools back there? They can't or won't admit that a woman might make a better ruler than a man. I might as well have been wearing sackcloth for all the good the cloak did me. So much for its fabled power,' she said bitterly, tears streaking her beautiful face.

George reached across and took one of her hands in his. 'I heard what you said to them and they *are* fools. I would have followed you. I *do* understand your strength of feeling. You may think I'm a typical Angrez officer but I'm not. I was born in Ireland, a country that has long felt itself occupied by the Angrez, and I have Zulu blood.'

'Zulu? What is that?'

'An African tribe. My mother is half Zulu, yet earlier this year I fought for the British against the Zulus in a war I knew to be wrong.'

'Why?'

George sighed. 'It's hard to explain. I didn't agree with the war, but I felt it might have a positive outcome for the Zulus if it resulted in the destruction of their king's brutal system of rule.'

'And did it?'

'Time will tell. But I wanted you to know that I'm not what I seem to be. This,' he said, indicating his tanned skin, 'should give you a clue.'

Yasmin smiled. 'You're not very different in colour from me. I thought you'd been too long in the sun. But I'm glad you understand why I acted as I did.'

George nodded. 'There's just one thing that still bothers me. Did you feign your affection for me to get close to the cloak?'

'At first, yes. I *do* like you, more than any man I've met – not that my family has exposed me to many – but my personal feelings will always come second to my duty.'

'So you don't regret betraying me?'

'I did it for the noblest of reasons. But I am sorry that my actions might have caused you pain, Angrez. Tell me what happened at Ghazni. How did you escape the mullah's men?'

'I didn't.'

'But . . . here you are.'

'I got away eventually, thanks to him,' said George, nodding towards Ilderim's sleeping form.

'And before that? Were you badly treated?'

'I'd prefer not to talk about it,' said George, staring intently into the flames.

Yasmin leant closer to him and gently stroked his face. 'I'm sorry, Angrez, I truly am.'

George turned to face her. 'It's forgotten, in the past. What matters now is that we work together to end the war and the British occupation.'

'I'm with you, Angrez. But how do we do that?'

'By keeping the cloak out of the hands of the Ghazis and tribesmen converging on Kabul, and by warning General Roberts that he's about to be attacked. Because if Roberts *is* taken by surprise, and his force at Kabul is destroyed, the Indian government will send more troops and use the defeat as an excuse to annex the whole country.'

'You're asking me to betray my own people? I won't do it!' she said, with a shake of the black mane hanging loose down her back.

'You wouldn't be betraying your people, just those who would seek to profit from war,' said George, patiently. 'Surely most Afghans would choose peace over war.'

'Yes, but not at the cost of their independence.'

'It need not come to that if we give Roberts sufficient warning of an attack.'

Yasmin seemed unconvinced. 'But even if we *do* save your General Roberts, what makes you think he and all the other Angrez soldiers will then want to leave?'

'They won't. Not immediately. They'll go when they're

ordered to by London, of course, but that will not happen if our troops have been defeated in the field. So it's vitally important to prevent that.'

'So what you're saying, Angrez, is that your people are *less* likely to leave if they've been defeated in battle?'

'A defeat will give the Indian government the excuse it needs to send more troops to occupy Afghanistan permanently. The government in London, on the other hand, does not want this to happen because it fears the financial and human cost of occupation. It was to prevent this that I was sent to Afghanistan in the first place. But a lot has happened since then, including Cavagnari's murder, and for reasons of prestige the British government would be bound to support its subordinates in Simla if one of its armies was defeated. Do you understand?'

'I think so. But the choice is not a happy one for me, Angrez. To serve my country I must betray some of my people, my family even. It does not seem right.'

'I was faced with a similar dilemma in Africa, but I made the right choice in the end. You will too.'

'It is strange you have such faith in me, Angrez, after the way I treated you. But I'm about to repay that faith.'

'What do you mean?'

'What would you say if I told you I knew when Mir Bacha was planning to attack the Angrez at Kabul?'

'When?'

'First tell me what you'd say.'

'I'd say you hold in your hand the key to the battle, and that if you tell me you will be doing me and your country a service.'

'Then it is right for me to tell you, and you can make what use of it you will. Mir Bacha's plan is to join with the Ghazni mullah and attack the Angrez camp at Sherpur north of Kabul at first light on the last day of the Shia festival of Mohurram. The festival commemorates the martyrdom of the Prophet's grandson, Imam Hussain, and runs for ten days at the start of the Muhammadan New Year. It's regarded as an auspicious date.'

'Are you saying Roberts and his men are at Sherpur? I thought they'd be holed up in the Bala Hissar.'

'Some of them were, but they evacuated the fortress after the magazine exploded in October. The whole Angrez force is now concentrated at the Sherpur cantonment, a much weaker defensive position.'

'I see. When is the last day of Mohurram?'

'A week from now.'

'At least that gives us time to warn Roberts. What will you do? Will you come with us?'

She nodded. 'On one condition.'

'Name it.'

'That you make no mention of the cloak to General Roberts. If he discovers we have it, he will either destroy it or remove it from Afghanistan. I can't allow that. Will you promise?'

George hesitated. He had been ordered by Lord Salisbury to do exactly what she was asking him to promise he would try to prevent: namely, the removal of the cloak to Britain. But as the payment of his bonus depended upon it, he decided to reassure her, and defer a final decision on the fate of the cloak until after the battle. He consoled himself with the thought that he would not, strictly speaking, be lying if he simply assured her he would keep all mention of the cloak from Roberts and his staff.

'I promise,' he said at last, a lump in his throat. 'But are you certain you want to do this? Once you're in Roberts's clutches, he won't easily let you go.'

'I'm certain,' she said, her gaze steady. 'There's nothing left for me here. My people have made their choice, and my duty now is with my brother in exile. Will you take me to him, if we survive the fighting?'

George blinked in surprise, taken aback that this once spirited woman was willing to go so meekly into exile. Could she be luring him into a false sense of security, he wondered, so that she could make off again with the cloak? Or had she genuinely given up all hope of personal rule? He couldn't decide, which was why he resolved to watch her and the cloak like a hawk until they were safely within the walls of the Sherpur cantonment. But, of course, he said nothing of this to her. 'It would be an honour,' he replied.

'Thank you, Angrez,' she said, closing her eyes and raising her lips to his. He hesitated for the briefest moment as images of Fanny and Lucy, particularly the latter, swam before him. But ignoring them he leant forward to kiss her, gently at first, and then more urgently as she pressed her upper body against his. He raised his hand to cup the gentle swelling of her right breast and she pulled away abruptly.

'I'm sorry,' said George, flushed with embarrassment. 'Please forgive me.'

'There is no need to apologize. I was enjoying it – too much. But now is not the time. Not here, in front of him,' she said, nodding towards Ilderim's sleeping form.

'Of course not.'

'Goodnight, then, Angrez,' said Yasmin, with a final kiss, before pulling her blanket over her and settling down for the night.

'Goodnight, Princess.'

19

Near Sherpur cantonment, Kabul, winter 1879

Ilderim turned and put his finger to his lips as they approached the Afghan pickets a mile to the east of the British fortified post at Sherpur. Well wrapped in poshteens and thin scarves called *pugri*s to keep out the cold, they were leading their horses through a snow-covered field to the right of the main road, hoping that the Afghan guards ahead would not see them in the failing light.

A day earlier, at Koh-i-Daman, they had picked up the alarming news that the mullah's army had already attacked Roberts at Kabul, badly mauling a column of cavalry. Roberts himself had been present at the action and, according to the bazaar gossip, had only narrowly escaped with his life, as had the bulk of his troops. More skirmishes had taken place in the days following this initial contact, but so numerous were the insurgents that Roberts had eventually chosen to withdraw all his troops inside the relative safety of the Sherpur cantonment. Since then they had been besieged by the mullah's army, fifteen thousand strong and led in the field by Mohammed Jan, though the mixed quality of the Afghan fighters – some of whom were trained soldiers, some fanatical Ghazis and some tribesmen out for plunder – had convinced George that it would not be too difficult to pass through their screen of pickets. Ilderim and Yasmin had agreed, so here they were, risking their lives to take news of the impending attack to a general whom none of them had any time for and whose reputation and promising career, tarnished by the setbacks of the last few days, hung in the balance.

George peered nervously to his left front and could just make out the twinkle of a fire and two sentries standing near it, stamping their feet to keep warm. 'Let's hope they're too distracted by the cold to notice us,' he whispered to Yasmin, who was walking beside him.

She nodded, a weak smile betraying the anxiety she was bound to feel as she sought to enter the camp of her country's occupiers.

All three tensed as they drew level with the picket, barely three hundred yards to their left. There was no shouted challenge, no shot, and they pressed on, convinced the worst was over. But as they remounted on the road beyond the picket, barely half a mile from the cantonment, they could hear riders behind them. Ilderim swung round in his saddle to see dark shapes coming up the road at speed. 'They've seen us, *huzoor*, we must hurry!' he shouted, urging his horse into a canter.

The others fell in behind him, their horses' hoofs thudding into the thin layer of snow on the paved surface. They had discussed the danger of approaching the cantonment at speed, and decided that it was worth the risk if they were being pursued. Now, as they clattered onwards in the dark, George was not so certain. 'Ilderim!' he called. 'Let me go first. They'll see I'm a European.'

Barely had the words left his mouth than a shot lit the darkened battlements ahead, followed by more, the flashes of flame spreading along the rampart. Bullets were striking the road all around them and George knew it was only a matter of time before one of them was hit. 'Stop firing!' he shouted, waving his free hand. 'I'm British!'

But they couldn't have heard him because, if anything, the rate of fire increased. George crouched lower on his horse's neck and continued to shout his name as the road swung sharply to the left to reveal the dark shadow of the main gate, no more than three hundred yards away. Now bullets were coming from two directions as their pursuers, fearful of losing their prey, had opened fire from horseback. Through this crossfire they rode, miraculously untouched, until even George dared to imagine that they might get through unscathed. He looked back to see the princess close behind him, her beautiful face grimly determined; Ilderim, now bringing up the rear, had his pistol out and was firing the occasional shot over his shoulder. It seemed to George that some invisible shield was deflecting the storm of lead and protecting them from harm.

Then something thudded into his horse's chest, causing the large gelding to stumble and fall. Time seemed to slow as the ground rose to meet George's right shoulder. The impact was softened a little by the light covering of snow, yet it still drove the air from his lungs and left him sprawled on his back. Beside him lay the still form of his dead horse.

Too stunned to move, George gazed up at the night sky, its blackness relieved by scores of brilliant stars. Then his view was obscured by a bearded face. '*Huzoor!* Can you hear me?'

'Yes,' replied George, half forgetting his predicament. 'No need to shout. Where's the princess?'

'I'm here, Angrez,' she answered, from behind Ilderim.

'What about the horsemen?'

'They turned tail when the defenders spotted them and switched targets. They've ceased firing now. They must think we're all dead.'

Ilderim helped George up into a sitting position, but as he did so the main gates of the cantonment were thrown open and out rode a troop of lancers with lighted torches who made directly for them.

'I'm British!' George shouted, as the horsemen surrounded them with lowered lances. 'My name is James Harper.'

'You don't look British to me,' said the troop officer, a tall man with a pencil-thin moustache.

'That's because I'm in disguise,' said George, with more than a hint of sarcasm, his mood not improved by the pain in his shoulder. 'But I can assure you I am. Major FitzGeorge will vouch for me.'

'We'll see about that. What about your accomplices? Who are they?'

'The man's my guide. The lady's a member of the Afghan royal family.'

'Is she now?' said the officer, peering at Yasmin with new respect. 'You can explain everything to the Major. But quite what you think you were doing, charging through the enemy lines and appearing unannounced below our walls, is anyone's guess. It's a miracle you weren't all killed. Fortunately for you, an eagle-eyed sentry spotted the Afghans in pursuit and eventually put two and two together. But not before your horse was hit, I see. Can you ride or do you need a litter?'

'I can ride,' said George, rising to his feet with Ilderim's help. 'My shoulder's a little sore, but otherwise I'm all right.'

'Good. Jump up behind me. We'll have you in the fort in a jiffy. I'm Captain Fanshawe, Ninth Lancers, by the way,' he said, extending his hand.

George took it. 'A Delhi spearman, eh?' he responded, using the nickname for the 9th that had been earned during the Indian Mutiny.

'Yes,' said Fanshawe, helping George up behind him. 'Though I suspect we might be given a less respectful soubriquet after the regiment's poor show in the Chardeh valley the other day. Let's go, before the Afghans see what we're up to.'

Barely a minute later they were clattering through the gateway and into the fortified cantonment, which had, only three months earlier, housed the Herat regiments responsible for the attack on the Residency. Now it had become a place of refuge for General Roberts's army of invasion and would soon, George knew, be the focus of a huge attack by those Afghans – notably the Ghazni mullah and Mir Bacha – who were determined to remove the British by force.

Once through the gate, guarded by the familiar big-boned soldiers of the 5th Punjabis, they drew rein and dismounted. Though it was dark and hard to pick out detail, George could tell by the spread of camp-fires that the cantonment covered a huge area and would, as a result, be extremely difficult to defend.

'This way, if you please,' said Fanshawe, leading them towards a cluster of buildings close to the gate they had just passed through. He knocked on the door of a single-storey house.

'Who is it?' asked a familiar voice.

'It's Captain Fanshawe of the Ninth Lancers. I've just brought in a man called James Harper. He's here with his guide and, um, an Afghan princess. Harper says he knows you.'

Hurried footsteps, and the door swung open to reveal the handsome features of Major FitzGeorge. 'Harper! Is that you?' he said, catching sight of the heavily bearded George in his Afghan garb. 'My God, it is. It must be almost three months since I last saw you at Ali Khel. Yet here you are again, safe and sound, with your faithful guide. And this is?' he asked, inclining his head towards Yasmin.

'Yakub's sister, Her Highness Princess Yasmin.'

FitzGeorge gave her an admiring glance. She was still clad in her masculine riding garb, her face streaked with dust and grime, but there was no disguising her beauty.

'I'll be damned,' he said, shaking his head. 'So you're the cause of all that firing. I thought it was the sentries getting the jitters. But do come in, all of you. And thank you, Fanshawe, I'll take charge from here.'

They filed past FitzGeorge into a large, whitewashed room, part of which was wreathed in shadows. The rest was lit by a single oil lamp, and contained a table covered with papers, a few scattered chairs and, most welcome of all, a small wood-burning stove. 'Do sit down,' said FitzGeorge. 'Would any of you like a drink or something to eat?'

George repeated the question to Yasmin in Pashto.

'Yes, but no pork,' she said, placing a chair close to the stove and rubbing her arms for warmth.

'She'd like . . .'

'I know,' interrupted FitzGeorge. 'I speak Pashto. What about your guide?'

'He'll have what she has.'

'Fine. I'll get my servant to rustle something up. I won't be a moment,' said FitzGeorge, opening the door and disappearing into the night.

Minutes later he was back. 'Brrr. It's cold out there. The refreshments are on their way. In the meantime, Harper,' said FitzGeorge, lighting a second oil lamp, 'can I have a word with you in private?'

'Of course,' said George, turning to Yasmin. 'He wants to speak to me alone. I won't be long.'

Yasmin nodded her assent, though George could tell she was unhappy at being excluded. He followed FitzGeorge through to his bedroom, a Spartan affair with a camp-bed, a trunk and a mahogany chest of drawers.

'Where did you get that?' asked George, pointing at the chest.

'I liberated it from one of the palaces in the Bala Hissar before we abandoned the place. Handsome, isn't it?'

'Yes, it is, but I wouldn't let the princess see it if I were you. It's technically her property – or, at least, her brother's.'

'Don't be such a prig, Harper. It's a legitimate spoil of war. Do sit down while I get you a whisky.'

George sat on the camp-bed while FitzGeorge poured the drinks.

'I'm relieved to see you again, Harper,' said FitzGeorge, handing him a glass containing a more than generous dram. 'But I won't deny I'm surprised. When Yakub came into our camp shortly after you'd delivered the general's message, and there was no word from you, we all assumed you'd been killed. What happened to you? And how did you find the princess?'

George took a large gulp from his glass, letting the fiery liquid warm his throat. He knew he couldn't tell FitzGeorge everything so decided to stick as close to the truth as possible. 'My intention was to deliver the message to Yakub and then leave the country. But when Yakub told me he had left his family defenceless in the Bala Hissar at Kabul, I was so angered by his cowardly behaviour that I decided to return with Ilderim to see if we could help. I had met the princess while I was recovering from the wound I received during the attack on the Residency, and I was worried for her safety.'

'Having seen the princess, I can well understand your eagerness,' said FitzGeorge, with a lascivious wink. 'She's a fine piece. But I still can't believe you'd risk returning to a city teeming with armed rebels, any one of whom would have happily slit your throat, for the sake of a woman, however beautiful. There must be more to it than that.'

'I don't know what you're talking about,' said George, flustered. 'I went back to save the princess, that was all.'

'So you say – but let's not fall out over this. I didn't really care why you returned to Kabul. The fact is you did, and by doing so you may have come across vital intelligence. So, please, tell me everything.'

George sat there for a moment, mulling things over. He knew there was a strong chance that the prickly, self-serving individual before him was his half-brother. There were just too many coincidences for that not to be true. But that didn't mean he had to like him. Neither did he have to help him. But this wasn't about helping Harry FitzGeorge. It was about saving an army and, with a bit of luck, preventing the Indian government from absorbing yet another unwilling country into the British Raj. To do that he would have to tell FitzGeorge the truth, or most of it anyway.

So George related exactly what had happened in the Bala Hissar, only diverging from the truth when they had taken refuge in the pleasure garden at Beni Hissar. At that point, George claimed, the princess had persuaded him to escort her north to Kohistan where she had family and knew she would be safe.

'*Safe?* She'd have been a darned sight safer with us. Why didn't you bring her to join her brother?'

George had expected this question and had his answer ready. 'Because, Major, she didn't want to. She didn't agree with Yakub's decision to leave Kabul for our camp, and was furious that he did so without telling anyone, leaving her and his wives to the tender mercies of the mutineers and, as it turned out, his own guard. With her father dead, it was only natural that she would seek refuge with her mother's family in Kohistan.'

FitzGeorge nodded. 'Yes, I can see that. So what happened next?'

'On the way north we were waylaid by bandits and, in the scrimmage, I was shot in the calf.' George lifted his trouser leg to show the purple scar tissue. 'We got away, just, thanks to Ilderim, but it was many weeks before I could walk again. During that time the princess caught wind of the plan by the principal Kohistani chiefs, led by her cousin Mir Bacha, to join forces with the Ghazni rebels to attack you here at Sherpur.'

'Well, if that was the plan, the mullah's men have jumped the gun because they and other tribesmen from the Kabul area attacked us in force a week ago in the Chardeh valley.'

'Yes,' said George, 'we heard of the fighting on the way down here, and Lieutenant Fanshawe mentioned something about it. What went wrong?'

'Everything. We knew that trouble was afoot in late November when we started to receive reports that large bands of men were collecting in the Ghazni area at the instigation of the local mullah.'

'Do you mean Mullah Mushk-i-Alam?'

'That's the fellow. Anyway, apparently at his instigation, villagers in the area to the south-west of Kabul began to refuse to hand over supplies and forage. We sent Baker's brigade to knock a few heads together, take some headmen as hostages, that sort of thing, but it only made matters worse, and as the armed opposition grew we were forced to withdraw. A couple of days later our local appointee as governor was murdered.'

'I heard about that,' said George.

'Did you? Then you must also have known about the growing unrest in Kohistan. Naturally we feared a coalition between the two groups and tried to forestall it by sending columns out to intercept them. But we were the ones taken by surprise when the mullah's men appeared in force in the Chardeh valley, twelve thousand strong, and almost wiped out a brigade of cavalry under Massy.'

George was appalled that a general as experienced as Roberts had made the same elementary mistakes – dividing his forces, inadequate intelligence – that had cost Lord Chelmsford a camp full of supplies and more than thirteen hundred lives in Zululand at the start of the year. But he made no mention of this, for fear of revealing his recent military past, and instead asked FitzGeorge how Roberts had managed to pull the chestnuts from the fire.

'With a lot of good fortune. We arrived on the scene as Massy began his retreat, and as soon as the chief saw the seriousness of the situation he ordered infantry from Sherpur to hold the two passes into the Chardeh valley. He also ordered a charge by some of Massy's cavalry so that four guns of horse artillery could be extricated. But the charge made little impact and we had difficulty rallying the Ninth Lancers who began to panic. In the confusion the guns were abandoned in a ditch near the Ghazni road and many of our men were killed. The chief was almost one of them. He was helping a dismounted trooper out of the ditch when he was attacked by a knife-wielding villager. Fortunately a sowar of the First Bengal Cavalry intervened and we got him safely away. What saved us from total disaster was the arrival in the enemy's rear of one of our columns under Brigadier Macpherson. It deflected the enemy from the Nanachi Pass, which leads directly here and was then unguarded, and gave our troops time to secure the southern pass, the Deh Mazang, through which we retired. But it was a close-run thing.'

'It sounds it. What of the guns? Were they lost to the enemy? asked George, well aware that the loss of a single artillery piece was a professional disgrace from which few generals recovered.

'Only for a time, thanks to Colonel MacGregor. During the retreat, he managed to rally about fifty cavalrymen and with them joined Macpherson's column. Later that day, with the help of some of Macpherson's infantry, he recovered all four guns.'

'How fortunate for General Roberts,' said George, sarcastically. 'But it doesn't alter the fact that we came off worst.'

'No, it doesn't, but we got our own back a couple of days later when the Seventy-Eighth Highlanders drove the rebels from the Asmai Heights above the city.'

'Indeed?' said George, raising his eyebrows. 'And yet here you are, cooped up in a fort while the rebels rule the roost. Why *is* that?'

'Their numbers just kept growing. We'd drive them from one position only to find that more had appeared somewhere else. It became impossible to protect our outposts so the chief decided, after much soul-searching, to withdraw everyone into the cantonment.'

'But I thought you told me when we last met that our troops wouldn't have any problem defeating the Afghans.'

'Nor did they at Charasiab, on the march to Kabul, but these blighters don't know when they're beaten and the scale of the recent uprising has, er, rather taken us by surprise.'

'Has it now?' said George, enjoying the major's obvious discomfort. 'That's quite a confession for a chief of intelligence to make.'

'Yes, but there it is. Anyway, we're safe enough in here while we wait for reinforcements.'

'Are any on their way?'

'Yes. We can still get messages out by heliograph, and the last we had back was that Brigadier General Gough's brigade had got as far as Jagdalak, which is about twenty-five miles from here.'

'And you expect him when?'

'We don't know. The Ghilzais have risen in the eastern passes and Gough will have to fight every step of the way.'

'How many men have you here already?' asked George.

'About seven thousand.'

'And the rebel strength?'

'It's hard to say with any certainty, but at least thirty thousand.'

'You can double that number when the Kohistanis arrive.'

'How long have we got before they do?'

'Not long. According to the princess, a joint attack by the mullah and Mir Bacha's men is planned for the last day of Mohurram in three days' time.'

'That soon? Good God!' said FitzGeorge, shaking his head. 'I doubt Gough will be able to get here by then. Is she certain?'

'She's a cousin of Mir Bacha and heard about the attack from the horse's mouth. Ask her, if you don't believe me.'

'I will. I'm just curious as to why she would want to give us this information. I doubt she approves of our presence here.'

'No, she doesn't,' said George. 'But neither does she wish

her country to be ruled by the mullahs or even by her cousin. What she hopes for, above all else, is the fighting to stop and us to leave. Her fear is that if we're defeated we will return in force and never leave.'

FitzGeorge cleared his throat. 'She's no fool, is she? And now, I think, it's time for her side of the story. But before we do I'll rouse the chief. He'll want to hear this in person.'

Ten minutes later, by which time George had rejoined Yasmin and Ilderim and was helping them to demolish the last of a heaped plate of mutton and rice, the door opened and in strode the diminutive General Roberts, with FitzGeorge close behind. The general was as dapper as ever, in a freshly pressed uniform with a silver-topped cane beneath his arm. But his eyes seemed to have lost some of their sparkle, and his bushy beard was greyer than George remembered. The strain of the previous two weeks had clearly taken its toll.

'Harper! This is a turn-up for the books,' said the general, without enthusiasm. 'And I see you still have your Pathan guide with you.'

'Yes, sir,' replied George, putting down his fork and gesturing towards Yasmin. 'And this is Her Highness Princess Yasmin, the sister of the former amir.'

'I'm delighted to make your acquaintance, Your Highness,' said Roberts, doffing his blue and gold cap.

Yasmin barely nodded in response.

Roberts turned back to George. 'Major FitzGeorge tells me the princess has news of an impending attack. Can you ask her to elaborate?'

George repeated the question to Yasmin in Pashto, and she responded in more detail than he had expected. When she had finished, he turned back to Roberts. 'It seems, General, that a day or two before the attack the rebels will occupy several forts to the east of the cantonment from which they will launch their assault. It will take place during the early hours of the twenty-third, the signal being the lighting of a bonfire on the Asmai Heights by the Mullah Mushk-i-Alam himself. The first effort will be directed against the western end of the southern wall with scaling ladders, but this is only a feint. Once you've shifted the bulk of your forces there the rebels will make their main attack against Bimaru village and the east wall, which they've identified as your weak spot. If that attack is successful they will resume the pressure on the south wall in the hope of crushing us by sheer weight of numbers.'

Roberts's eyes widened. 'She's certain of this.'

'Yes, General,' replied George. 'She heard it from her cousin Mir Bacha, leader of the Kohistani rebels, who has long been in communication with the mullah and his military commander, Mohammed Jan.'

Roberts snorted. 'Well, they may have agreed on a military course of action, but politically they're poles apart. Yesterday we received two separate offers of peace: one from Mohammed Jan, offering us safe passage to Peshawar if we agreed to support the amirship of Yakub's son, Musa Khan, the other from Mir Bacha who says he will accept Yakub's uncle, Wali Mahomed, as amir if we march away without concerning ourselves further with Afghan matters.'

'Is Yakub Khan's son still at large?' asked George.

'Unfortunately he is. When his father went into exile earlier this month, the son was spirited to Ghazni and is now a puppet in the hands of the mullah and Mohammed Jan. They need him, no doubt, to give the new regime a whiff of legitimacy. But their day will never come, and neither will the Kohistanis'. Of course I sent both messengers back with a flea in their ear. Do they take me for a fool? The last British general at Kabul to do a deal with besieging Afghans was Elphinstone in forty-two, and look what happened to him.'

George was only too aware that Elphinstone's army of sixteen thousand soldiers and civilians had been cut to pieces in the eastern passes as it tried to withdraw to India, while the general himself had died in captivity. 'What of the rebels' battle plan, General?' he asked. 'Does it make sense?'

'Yes,' replied Roberts. 'It's a good plan, and it might succeed because our position here is not uniformly strong. Major FitzGeorge will explain.'

'What the general means is this,' said FitzGeorge. 'The cantonment was designed as a huge defensive square that should have taken in the Bimaru Heights to our north. But when we arrived in early November, only the south wall and part of the west wall had reached the required height of sixteen feet with bastions to provide flanking fire. The east wall was just seven feet high and finished well short of the heights, while the northern wall hadn't even been started. Since then we've tried to plug the gaps by constructing earthworks along the crest line of the Bimaru Heights and connecting them to the ends of the eastern and western walls with ditches, wagon laagers and wire entanglements. We've also loopholed Bimaru village and built a wooden stockade in front of the lower east wall. But it's far from impregnable, and the rebels are right to identify the east wall as our weak point.'

'Is there anything we can do to make it stronger?' asked George.

'Not in the time available,' said Roberts. 'I've already assigned the bulk of my best troops to the east wall, including the Guides and the Twenty-Eighth Punjab Infantry. I can move a couple more regiments there tomorrow, and strengthen the reserve, which I've placed in the depression at the centre of the Bimaru Heights so that it can move rapidly to either one of the most vulnerable sectors. But I have to be careful. I've only got seven thousand men to guard a perimeter of eight thousand yards, and that's not enough. What I wouldn't give for the arrival of Gough's brigade *before* the battle. But that doesn't seem likely, though we're daily urging him on.'

'What about artillery pieces, General?' asked George.

'Twenty-six field guns, most of them nine-pounders, and two Gatlings. They're spread around the perimeter with four in reserve.'

'And ammunition?'

'We've got three hundred rounds per man. Why do you ask?'

'Because at Rorke's Drift we had almost that amount yet by morning were down to our last box and a half.'

Roberts gaped. '*You* were at Rorke's Drift?'

George cursed himself for this first slip of the tongue since his arrival in Afghanistan. His first instinct was to say he had been joking, but then it occurred to him that, with his mission almost over, there was no longer any need for secrecy. And he suspected that Roberts would be more willing to let him take part in the battle if he was aware of his true military rank. 'Indeed I was,' he admitted.

'But you said you worked for a British trading company.'

'I know. That was the cover story I was given. In fact I am Captain George Hart of the Third Sixtieth Rifles. I'm currently on attachment to the Foreign Office, and was sent here on a secret assignment by Lord Beaconsfield himself.'

'I'll be damned,' interjected FitzGeorge. 'I knew all along you weren't a businessman.'

'Quiet!' barked Roberts, his hand raised. 'You say you're an army officer on a mission for the British government. Why wasn't I informed?'

'Because no one in India was told about my mission, not even the viceroy. The only people who know are the Prime Minister, the Foreign Secretary, the Commander-in-Chief and one or two senior officials at the Foreign Office.'

'I'm sorry Harper – or Hart, or whatever you're calling yourself now – I don't believe you. The home government knows very well that Afghanistan is within our sphere of influence, and that all intelligence gathering is co-ordinated by Simla. It would never send agents without letting us know. We're on the same side, after all.'

'I know that, General, but this is an exceptional case and the Prime Minister has his reasons.'

'Which are?'

'I'm not at liberty to say.'

'Not at *liberty*!' exploded Roberts, his face red with fury. 'Who do you think you are? You arrive at my headquarters with some cock-and-bull story about a secret mission and you expect me to believe you? I'm beginning to wonder if the princess's warning of an attack on our east wall isn't a ruse to get us to weaken our defences elsewhere. I'm tempted to shoot you all as spies.'

'It's not a ruse, General, and I'm not a spy – at least, not for the rebels.'

'How can I be sure? You're swarthy enough to be an Afghan.'

'I was brought up in Ireland and my mother is half Maltese. But everything I've told you about my military rank and mission is true.'

'Do you have any proof? You must have something in writing.'

'No, General, I do not. But there is one man on your staff who can vouch for me.'

'Name him.'

'Lieutenant Sykes.'

'*Sykes?* How does *he* know you?'

'He was with me at Harrow We met by chance in the mess at Ali Khel, and I decided to tell him the truth of my mission for fear he'd reveal my identity.'

Roberts turned to FitzGeorge. 'Did Sykes say anything to you?'

FitzGeorge gulped. 'Only that he and Harper had known each other at school. When I asked Harper about this he said they hadn't got on. He also said he'd since left the army.'

'Why didn't you tell me about this?'

'I don't know, sir. I suppose I didn't think it was important.'

'Well, it is. Fetch Sykes. We'll soon get to the bottom of this.'

'Yes, sir,' said FitzGeorge, less than happy to be forced out into the cold for the second time that night.

Minutes later he returned with Sykes. 'You asked to see me, General?'

'Do you know this man?' said Roberts sharply, gesturing at George.

At first Sykes failed to recognise his former fag beneath the beard and Afghan clothes. 'He looks familiar, but I can't . . .'

George interrupted, 'It's me, you fool. George Hart.'

Sykes's eyes widened in shock. 'Good Heavens, it *is*.'

'So you *do* know him?' said Roberts.

'Um . . . yes, sir. We were at Harrow together.'

'And do you know why he's in Afghanistan?'

Sykes paused, causing George to hold his breath. He knew that if Sykes lied, there was every chance he would be locked up until the battle was over.

At last Sykes spoke: 'I only know what he told me, sir.'

George exhaled slowly in relief

'And what was that?' asked Roberts.

'That he was sent here by the Prime Minister on a secret mission.'

'Did he tell you the nature of that mission?'

'Only that it was to do with our relations with Afghanistan.'

'He didn't elaborate?'

'No, sir.'

'And you didn't think to mention this either to myself or Major FitzGeorge?'

'No, sir . . . That is, I did think about it, but Hart warned me that if I said anything my career would suffer.'

'And you believed him?'

'Yes, sir. He said that his mission had been authorized by the Commander-in-Chief himself, and that I would be jeopardizing my prospects of promotion if I revealed what he was up to.'

Roberts exploded: 'You self-serving fool! As a member of my staff, your first loyalty should always be to *me* – yet you think of your own advancement and keep vital information from your chief! If I didn't need every man I could muster for the battle ahead, I'd lock you up and throw away the key. As it is, you're finished on the staff. From tomorrow you'll serve with the Ninth Lancers as a supernumerary. Maybe together you can regain your honour. Now get out of my sight.'

'But, sir, I was only doing what—'

'Get out!' shouted Roberts. 'Or, so help me, God . . .'

'Sir,' said Sykes, pausing only to glare at George before he saluted, turned on his heel and left.

'It seems,' said Roberts to George, 'that you are who you *now* say you are. Whether the rest of your story is true is another matter. But as there's no way to verify it, I'll have to let the matter rest until after the battle. In the meantime, I'm sending you and your Afghan companion to assist Colonel Jenkins of the Guides Infantry. He's a good man, one of the best I've got, and is in charge of the vulnerable eastern sector, which, if the princess is right, will face the brunt of the assault. He'll need every man he can get.'

'I'm glad to help where I can,' said George, 'as is Ilderim Khan. He served for many years in the Guide cavalry, retiring as a subadar, and may still know some of the officers. Will we retain our ranks?'

'No, your ranks are unverified and mean nothing to me. You'll both serve as privates. But remember this: if you're playing me false, you'll suffer the consequences. I promise you that. As for the princess, she'll be kept within these walls until it's possible for her to join her brother in exile.'

'You mean to keep her under lock and key?' George was aghast.

'No, no, nothing like that,' said Roberts, waving dismissively. 'She'll be given a guard of honour, as befitting her royal status.'

'And if she tries to leave the cantonment before the battle?'

'Then she'll be, um – how can I put it? – dissuaded. She'll be much safer here. I'd be grateful if you could explain that to her.'

'I'll try, but she won't like it.'

'Maybe not, but there it is. Goodnight, then,' said Roberts, bowing slightly to Yasmin as he rose from his chair.

'FitzGeorge will arrange your quarters and the princess's guard.'

Once Roberts had departed, George turned to Yasmin and translated what the general had said.

'Great God!' responded Yasmin, eyes blazing. 'Am I to be kept here against my will?'

'I'm afraid so. At least until the battle is over.'

'That's not *quite* how the general put it,' interrupted FitzGeorge, also speaking Pashto.

'Isn't it, Major?' said George. 'Then perhaps you'd care to explain what he *did* mean.'

'Simply that it wouldn't be safe for the princess to leave while the rebellion is in full spate.'

'So you won't allow me to, is that it?' asked Yasmin.

'Um, yes,' said FitzGeorge, 'but for your own good.'

'What nonsense! Why can't you admit I'm your prisoner?'

'Because it's not true, Your Highness,' said FitzGeorge, lamely. 'You should think of yourself, instead, as a guest with restricted movement. Now, if you'll allow me, I'll show you to your quarters.'

George was lying fully clothed on a camp-bed in his room over the main gate, mulling over the events of the evening, when a knock sounded at his door. 'Who is it?'

'FitzGeorge. I've a message from the princess.'

George rose wearily from the camp-bed, padded to the door and opened it. FitzGeorge was standing there, his head cocked to one side, a half-smile on his lips.

'What message?'

'She wanted you to know that she doesn't blame you for what's happened, and that she trusts you'll stick to your side of the bargain. I'm intrigued as to what she means by that.'

'Oh, it's nothing,' said George, more than a little irked that Yasmin felt she needed to remind him to keep the cloak secret. 'Was there anything else?'

'I meant to ask you earlier if you ever found out what became of the cloak.'

So surprised was George by the question that he just stared, open-mouthed. 'The cloak? What cloak?' he said at last, playing for time.

'You know perfectly well what cloak. The Prophet's Cloak, of course. You asked me about it at Ali Khel, and I confirmed it was on its way to the mullah at Ghazni. The question is, did it get there?'

'I've no idea,' said George, trying to keep his gaze away from the saddle-bag beside the bed. 'But, given the success of the mullah's call to arms, I'd say it's a safe bet he has it.'

'You'd think so, wouldn't you? But none of my spies has mentioned it, which they would have done if he'd worn it in public.'

'Maybe he's waiting for the right moment.'

'That moment's been and gone. The only logical explanation is that he doesn't have it yet. But if that's so, who does?'

'Does it matter?'

'I don't suppose so. Either way the tribes have risen and if Lytton holds his nerve we'll soon have them licked. Then we can choose at our leisure which bits of the country we'd like to keep hold of.'

'This is what you've been planning for all along, isn't it?' asked George. 'To break up the country, divide and rule.'

'Of course. It will secure India's frontiers and give us the opportunity to extend British trade.'

'What do you care about trade?'

'Nothing, ordinarily,' said FitzGeorge. He paused. 'But

I'm a little short of cash at the moment and an Armenian merchant, prominent in the Calcutta business community, has offered me a very generous sum if I secure for him a monopoly over certain Afghan exports.'

'Which ones?'

'Fruit and nuts, to begin with. Have you tried them? They're excellent.'

'What else?'

'Opium. My merchant friend is keen to find out if Afghanistan, particularly the Helmand province in the south-west, is suitable for the production and export of high-grade opium. The Chinese can't get enough of it.'

'And why is that?' asked George, indignantly. 'It's because twice in the last forty years we've fought wars to force the Chinese to open their ports to our trade, particularly opium grown in India. Why do you think we acquired Hong Kong in forty-two if not as a base for opium smuggling? And why do you think in sixty we destroyed the Imperial Summer Palace at Peking, one of the wonders of the world, if not to promote free trade? It certainly seems to have worked because this year, according to *The Times*, we exported twice as many chests of opium to China as we did in eighteen sixty. The result is that three of every four Chinese males are addicts – and you're happy to extend this wicked trade here, as if the Afghans haven't got enough to worry about. What kind of a monster are you?'

FitzGeorge snorted with derision. 'Don't get pious with me, Hart. We're all in it for something, even you. And why shouldn't my Armenian friend take over? He'll make more money out of the opium and fruit trades than the Afghans ever could. I wouldn't be surprised if, in a few years' time, they name a Kabul street after him.'

'How much?'

'How much what?'

'How much is your cut?'

'He's offered me a lakh of rupees, which is ten thousand pounds to you, but I'm sure I can squeeze a little more out of him.'

George looked at FitzGeorge scornfully, almost ashamed now that they might be brothers. 'Aren't you forgetting one thing?'

'What's that?'

'There's a battle looming that we might not win. Much good ten thousand pounds will do you when you're cold and in your grave – if the Afghans can be bothered to bury you, that is, which I very much doubt they will. Goodnight,' said George, and shut the door before FitzGeorge could respond.

20

North-east corner of the Sherpur cantonment, Kabul, 23 December 1879

George blew on his hands for warmth as he peered across the cantonment to the Asmai Heights where, if Yasmin's intelligence was correct, the Mullah Mushk-i-Alam would light a fire to signal the start of the battle. He and Ilderim were keeping watch behind a raised parapet on the roof of the native field hospital, a walled enclosure that was the keystone to the otherwise makeshift defences in the cantonment's north-east corner. It was pitch black and bitterly cold, and most of their new comrades in the 28th Punjab Infantry were still asleep in their tents.

The day before, in line with General Roberts's instructions, George and Ilderim had reported to Colonel Jenkins, a tall, snowy-haired officer in charge of the cantonment's eastern defences that stretched from the trenches on the lower slopes of the Bimaru Heights to the corner bastion facing the Siah Sang hills. After a breezy welcome, Jenkins had posted them to the 28th, which was holding the unfinished east wall as far as the native hospital. Ilderim had wanted to join his old comrades in the Guides, manning the trench system that linked the hospital to the loopholed village of Bimaru, but Jenkins would not relent, even when George told him they had fought alongside the doomed Guides at the Residency. 'We're all desperate to avenge our fallen comrades,' he had said, 'but you can do that just as well in the Twenty-Eighth as with us. They've lost quite a few men in recent days, and will welcome the reinforcement.'

So George and Ilderim had been directed to the headquarters of the 28th, a low building set back from the unfinished wall, where a red-faced quartermaster had issued them with Sniders and the battalion uniform of light blue turbans, short black boots, khaki tunics and trousers, and white cross-belts holding a bayonet and ammunition pouches for forty rounds. Then they were assigned to a company of a hundred men defending the hospital. The company commander, in turn, had put them on night sentry duty, which was why they were standing alone on the hospital roof with orders to rouse Havildar Singh as soon as they saw the first sparks of a fire on the distant Asmai Heights.

'Can you see anything?' asked George, as he stared into the inky blackness.

'No, *huzoor*, but I can hear something being dragged across the snow.'

George listened hard and could just make out a swishing sound, like a sledge. 'What do you think it is?'

'They might be bringing ladders closer to the wall.'

George shivered again and this time it wasn't the cold. He knew, as did every defender in the improvised fort, that if the Afghans broke in they would give no quarter. It was Isandlwana all over again, only this time they knew an assault was imminent, and from which direction. 'If the princess is correct,' said George, 'they'll attack the south wall first, but their main effort will be against us. Why is it that we always find ourselves in the thick of the action?'

Barely had George spoken than the garrison clock struck the hour, its six chimes heralding the near approach of dawn. George looked again to the Asmai Heights away to the south-east. On the topmost crag he could just see the spark of a tiny fire. Fed by oil, or ghee, and brushwood, it quickly grew until it was a blazing beacon, its flames and sparks shooting skywards and casting a reflection upon the fort below.

'That's the signal, Ilderim,' said George. 'Tell Havildar Singh.'

Ilderim sprinted across the rooftop and down the steps. Within minutes the battalion had been roused and a hundred tall Sikhs and Punjabi Muhammadans were pouring into the loopholed lower rooms of the native hospital and onto its roof. The hurried spectacle was being repeated across the cantonment as the bulk of four British and twelve Indian regiments hurried to their allotted places on the perimeter. All of the 'martial races' so beloved of the British were represented – Sikhs, Pathans, Gurkhas and kilted Highlanders – and the majority of the best regiments, the 28th included, had been placed on the southern and eastern walls.

As the Punjabis fell in on either side of George, each man cocking and loading his Snider with practised ease, a single rifle shot rang out from the direction of the amir's garden, a walled enclosure just a few hundred yards from the south wall that had been occupied by the rebels a few days earlier. More shots came from the villages on the south-east and eastern flanks, and one or two whistled over the top of the hospital, causing George and others to duck their heads.

'Hold your fire until I give the order,' bellowed Havildar Singh, an imposing figure of a man with a long black beard and a ready smile. But he needn't have worried, because it was still too dark to see individual objects and the first attack, as everyone knew, would come from the south. It was heralded by a rolling thunder of musketry against the south wall as thousands of Afghans, hidden behind every conceivable scrap of cover, opened a covering fire designed to keep the defenders' heads down.

Then, from the amir's garden and a fort to its right, came the sound of sandals slapping against snow as small groups of men with huge ladders broke from cover and made for the centre of the southern wall, a sector held by the dismounted troopers of the disgraced 9th Lancers and the 14th Bengal Lancers. The cavalrymen held their fire until star shells had lit up the battlefield, revealing numerous clusters of Afghans as they closed in on the walls. At last the order was given and the south wall exploded in a storm of carbine and howitzer fire, the bullets sweeping the open ground and the shells targeting the strongholds beyond. Scores of Afghans were hit, while their comrades ditched their ladders and sought cover behind broken walls and in ditches.

So much for the diversionary attack, thought George, as he watched from the hospital roof. The star shells were still arcing up into the night sky and throwing an eerie light onto the now empty battlefield in front of the south wall. There was a brief lull and then the storm broke with increased ferocity on George's sector.

It began with a mighty roar as ten thousand Afghan throats shouted their battle cry '*Allahu Akbar!*' ('God is Great!') and a storm of fire was opened onto the unfinished wall, the field hospital and the entrenchment that linked it to Bimaru village. Then, as the two sounds mingled in a deafening clamour, the Afghans attacked in human waves. At first George found it hard to distinguish the attacking masses in the grey dawn, but as they got closer he could see they were led by fanatical Ghazi warriors dressed in white and waving green standards, and backed up by tribesmen in black and former soldiers in red. The majority seemed to be heading for the shallow trench system and wooden stockade on George's left that covered the four-hundred-yard gap between the hospital and Bimaru village.

'Wait for it! Wait for it!' shouted Havildar Singh.

George squinted down the sights of his Snider, the trigger cold against his finger. The nearest Afghans were four hundred yards away, and well within range, but still the havildar waited because Roberts had ordered the troops to hold fire until the very last moment. George glanced to his left, past Ilderim to the trenches beyond, and wondered what the Guides were thinking as thousands of Afghans bore down on their exposed position. George himself was in a relatively secure spot, behind a parapet twenty feet above the ground, yet his mouth still felt dry and his palms sweaty. He wiped his trigger hand on his trousers and took a last swig from his water bottle. The liquid tasted brackish and he spat it over the parapet.

On raced the Ghazis, and the range was down to a hundred and fifty yards or so, and virtually point blank, when the havildar bellowed, 'Fire!'

George gently squeezed the trigger and felt a buzzing in his ears and a sharp pain in his shoulder as the rifle recoiled, throwing the foresight off the big Ghazi he had been aiming at. For a few seconds his view, and that of his neighbours, was obscured by a thick wreath of smoke from the black cartridges they had fired. As it cleared he could see no sign of the Ghazi and assumed he was one of many lying prone in the snow, their gaping wounds staining the white landscape with vivid patches of red. But for every casualty another twenty warriors were racing towards the east wall, determined to get to grips with the hated infidel.

At Singh's command, the men on the hospital fired successive volleys into the onrushing mass, as did the troops on either side. Shell fire and case shot from the artillery on the heights added to the maelstrom of flying lead and steel. Yet still the attackers kept coming, though they had resorted, like the Zulus at Isandlwana, to short rushes from one piece of cover to the next, while others used their marksmanship to pick off the defenders.

George was leaning forward to load his Snider when a bullet ricocheted off the parapet in front of him and into the neck of the soldier on his right. The man tried to staunch the flow of bright red arterial blood with his hand, but it kept spurting between his fingers, spraying George and even Ilderim beyond. George tore open a dressing and clamped it on the wound, only to find a much bigger gash on the back of the man's neck where the bullet had exited. A second dressing was applied, but by now the soldier was choking on his blood, his frightened eyes pleading for help. George wanted to lay him down, to comfort him in his last few minutes of life, but he was reminded of the harsh realities of war by Havildar Singh.

'Leave him and pick up your rifle, you bloody fool! If those buggers down there get a foothold in the fort, we're done for,' he shouted, drawing his hand across his throat.

Horrified by the havildar's callousness, George was about to tell him to go to hell. But then he remembered that the havildar was, for the moment, his military superior and, more importantly, he was right. This was no time for sentiment. So he held his tongue, wiped the dying man's sticky blood from his face and resumed his place on the parapet.

The noise of battle was, if anything, even louder, yet the smoke from the defensive fire had drifted across the battlefield, making it hard for the defenders to target their foe. Many Ghazis had taken advantage of this and George could see groups of the white-clad warriors emerging from the obstacles of telegraph wire that had been placed just thirty yards ahead of the trench to their left. He snapped off a shot and missed as more Afghans broke through the obstacle and raced for the barrier of trees that protected the trench. 'Havildar, look!' shouted George, pointing towards the danger. 'The Guides are about to be swamped. Let me take thirty men to reinforce them.'

The havildar swivelled his head and, for just a moment, considered the seriousness of the situation. George fully expected him to refuse permission and a row to ensue. But the havildar surprised him. 'Go, and take every other man from the parapet. We're safe enough here.'

George called out the order and the men fell in. 'Shall I come too, *huzoor*?' asked Ilderim who, by the havildar's calculations, was supposed to stay.

'Of course you must come,' said George, with a grin. 'I doubt I'd survive without you.'

George led the twenty or so men down the steps to the rear of the hospital where they joined one of the covered walkways that criss-crossed the cantonment and gave protection to the soldiers as they moved from one point to another. They soon came to a door that was roughly opposite the centre of the trench and George flung it open. Bullets were tearing up the ground all around, and smacking into the plastered wall on either side of the door, and it seemed the height of madness to leave the cover of the walkway. But one glance at the trench ahead was enough. The Ghazis had broken through the wooden barricades and were fighting hand-to-hand with the hard-pressed Guides in the trench, their curved *tulwar*s slicing easily through bone and flesh.

'Fix bayonets!' howled George, as he drew from the scabbard his own triangular bayonet, just under two feet long, and fixed it to the muzzle of his Snider with a snap of his wrist. Satisfied that Ilderim and the men had done likewise, George led them out of the doorway with a yell. The centre of the trench, the scene of the heaviest fighting, was barely a hundred yards distant. Yet ten Punjabis fell crossing the exposed ground, and George felt his lungs might burst as he sprinted the last twenty yards, almost grateful to join the struggling mass and escape the hail of fire above ground.

He slithered into the shallow trench, little more than four feet deep with an earth parapet facing the enemy, and saw to his right two Ghazis about to despatch a fallen Guide with their Khyber knives. He quickly raised his Snider and shot one, causing the other to turn on him. With no time to reload, he lowered the weapon and skewered the charging Ghazi on his bayonet. But as he did so he saw from the corner of his eye another Afghan with upraised sword. Hauling his bayonet free, he swung round and parried the blow, the sound of steel on steel ringing out above the din and the impact jarring his arm. His wiry opponent glared at him and uttered an oath. George saw hatred in the Ghazi's eyes, and the complete absence of fear he would witness only in a religious warrior who believed he would go to Paradise if he fell in battle. George was far less sanguine about the afterlife and had no desire to find out the truth sooner rather than later. But as he made his move, thrusting his bayonet with as much force as he could muster, the Ghazi stepped deftly to the side and raised his *tulwar* for the killing blow. With no time to parry, George tensed his muscles in anticipation of the razor-sharp blade cutting into the unprotected flesh of his shoulder. But before the Ghazi could strike, his body stiffened and the sword fell from his lifeless fingers. Ilderim had shot him from the rear lip of the trench.

George waved his gratitude as the rest of their party leapt into the trench, tipping the balance the defenders' way. As the last Ghazi was cornered and killed, his body thrown from the trench, George felt his hand grasped by that of a young subaltern with a blond moustache and ice-blue eyes. 'I'm Lieutenant Duggan. You saved my life.'

'You were the soldier on the ground?'

'I was, and about to meet my Maker when you intervened. I'm very grateful.'

'Glad I could help.'

Dawn had broken at last and, with the repulse of the Ghazis' determined attack, a temporary lull seemed to have settled on George's sector of the battlefield. It was as if the Afghans were gathering their strength for a final effort and many of the defenders, George included, were fingering their trigger guards nervously as they peered over the earth parapet to the corpse-strewn ground beyond.

When the attack was resumed ten minutes later, it was directed not against the trench but against the fortified village of Bimaru to its left, and another small village called Khatir, only lightly held, that occupied the tactically vital gap between Bimaru and the heights above it. Looking north, George could see thousands of tiny figures advancing on both objectives, and he and the rest of the trench's defenders fired into the enemy host as fast as they could load. But so numerous were the attackers that this counter-fire had a negligible effect and it seemed to George that the assault must carry all before it. He held his breath as wave after wave of Afghans neared and then recoiled from the loop-holed houses on the edge of Bimaru village, shot down in their hundreds by the rifles of the Guides.

Further north at Khatir, though, the attackers appeared to have gained a foothold. This was confirmed a short while later by Colonel Jenkins, the Guides' commander, who had come down to the trench from his command post in Bimaru village to thank the Punjabis for their timely intervention. 'Who's commanding the Twenty-Eighth here?' asked Jenkins.

'I suppose I am, sir,' said George, stepping forward.

'You? But you're a private.'

'Actually, I'm a captain, but General Roberts chooses not to recognise my rank.'

'Why ever not?'

'It's a long story, sir. I'd be happy to tell you when the battle's over.'

'I might hold you to that. In the meantime, please give my compliments to your company commander and tell him that his prompt action in sending you and your men to help us may have saved the garrison.'

'It wasn't his idea, sir. It was mine.'

'Yours?'

'Yes, sir.'

'Well, I'm very grateful to you, then, Captain . . .?'

'Hart, sir.'

'Well, Captain Hart, you'd better get back to your post. The Afghans have captured the village of Khatir, to the north of Bimaru, and from there can launch fresh assaults on both Bimaru and the heights. This fight is far from over.'

'Does General Roberts know, sir?'

'Of course. General Gough, who's in command of the heights and Khatir, sent him a message by internal telegraph, requesting reinforcements. Roberts's reply was that no men could be spared, as we were hard pressed elsewhere, and that Gough was to "hold on" at all costs.'

'But what if he can't?'

'Then we're all in trouble.'

George shook his head in disbelief. 'This is madness. If Roberts was on the spot, instead of safe in his headquarters, he'd surely release part of Baker's reserve. It's only a mile away, in the lee of the heights, and could be here in no time.'

'I agree with you, Hart. But as I'm a mere colonel, and he's a major general with a Victoria Cross, I'm hardly in a position to tell him that. Then again,' said Jenkins, scratching his beard, 'it wouldn't do any harm to repeat the original message. If I write it out, will you agree to carry it? Your personal observations just might make a difference.'

'Of course I will, sir, if you'll inform the Twenty-Eighth of my whereabouts.'

'Consider it done.' Jenkins pulled a pencil and notebook from his pocket, scribbled a quick message and handed it to George. 'Tell the general that I support Gough's request for reinforcements. The dyke's sprung a leak and we need to plug it.'

George smiled at the colonel's choice of metaphor. 'I will, sir. But may I take this man with me?' he asked, nodding towards Ilderim. 'He's my lucky charm.'

'By all means. If something happens to you, he can carry the message.'

* * *

Proceeding at a jog-trot, with Ilderim complaining most of the way, it took them a good fifteen minutes to negotiate the two miles that separated the north-east corner of the cantonment from Roberts's headquarters in the centre of the west wall. With the battle still raging, particularly against the south wall where the firing was incessant, George was grateful for the protection given by the covered walkways from stray bullets that rattled the tiles above them like rain.

At last they emerged into the low winter sunlight, close to the headquarters gate, and were shown the way to Roberts's office on the ground floor of the bastion by a private of the 5th Punjab Infantry, one of the regiments defending the west wall. Two more tall Punjabis guarded the entrance to the office, but George walked straight past them, leaving Ilderim to explain their business.

Having opened the door, George paused on the threshold. He was struck by the tense atmosphere in the room as Roberts and his staff – FitzGeorge among them – stood grouped round a central table spread with a huge map of the cantonment and the surrounding area, listening intently to a telegraph clerk delivering the latest situation report. It was from Brigadier General Macpherson, and seemed to confirm that the attack on the south wall was still at its height, though as yet no breach had been made.

'Very good,' said Roberts, still unaware of George's presence. 'Tell Macpherson to hold on. They can't keep this up for too much longer.'

The clerk saluted and returned to the telegraph room, at which point George announced his presence with a cough. All eyes turned to the doorway, though it was FitzGeorge who spoke first. 'Hart! What are you doing here? Who gave you permission to leave your post?'

'Colonel Jenkins. I have a message from him for the general,' said George, nodding towards Roberts.

'And why didn't he send it by telegraph?' asked Roberts.

'Because, sir, he wasn't convinced that a telegraph message would have the desired effect.'

'Ye gods!' snapped Roberts, his quick temper and bloodshot eyes showing the strain he was under. 'I'm plagued by little Napoleons. Well, bring it to me, then.'

George handed Roberts the slip of paper. Having read it, he frowned. 'This repeats General Gough's message.'

'I know, sir. Like General Gough, Colonel Jenkins is of the opinion that if you do not release reinforcements *now* we might not be able to hold on. By capturing Khatir, the Afghans are perfectly placed for further assaults, either against the heights or Bimaru village itself. They could break through at any time.'

'Yes, and they could break through elsewhere too. Do Gough and Jenkins think they're the only ones under attack?'

'Of course not.'

'Well, they're damn well behaving as if they do. That firing you can hear is coming from the south wall. It's been under attack for the best part of three hours and, according to the report we've just heard, the Afghan dead are piled before it in heaps. So if I do release the reserves, and there's a breakthrough at the south wall, what then?'

George could hardly believe that a general famed for his tactical brilliance was being so cautious. But now, he realized, was not the time for sarcasm. 'I can't speak for General Gough or Colonel Jenkins, sir, but I doubt either of them is expecting you to send the whole reserve force to assist them, just some of it. The north-east section of the wall is, after all, the one the princess identified as the Afghans' chief target.'

'Certainly she did – but can we rely on her word?'

'I think we can, sir. The pattern of attacks so far seems to back up her assertion.'

Roberts turned to his chief of staff. 'What do think, MacGregor?'

The hard-bitten old soldier fingered his salt-and-pepper goatee. 'I don't suppose it would hurt, General,' he said, 'to send Gough a wing of Third Sikhs from Colonel Hills's sector above us. His men have hardly fired a shot. And that way we'll still have the reserve if we need it.'

'An admirable solution,' said Roberts, nodding. 'Give the order at once.'

'Of course, sir,' said MacGregor, scribbling a note and then handing it to an assistant.

Roberts turned to George. 'Satisfied?'

'It was not I, sir, who requested reinforcements.'

'No, but you've made it quite clear you agree with the request.'

'I do, sir, and so would you if you had seen at first hand the hair's breadth by which we held on to the trench between the hospital and Bimaru village.'

'Are you daring to criticize my generalship?' asked Roberts, his voice rising.

'No, sir, I'm simply saying the situation in the north-east sector is a little more precarious than you've been led to believe.'

'Is it? Then you won't mind telling us your solution to the problem, will you?'

George was a little taken aback by the question and took a moment to weigh his response. 'Well, as you ask, General, I'd recommend an immediate sortie by cavalry and horse artillery through the gap in the Bimaru Heights to take the Afghans in Khatir village in the flank. They might be expecting an assault from the front, but not the side.'

Roberts's eyes widened – he appeared to be looking at George with new respect. 'That's not a bad idea, young Hart. Not a bad idea at all. MacGregor, what do you think?'

'I think his plan has merit, General,' said the chief of staff, 'but now is not the time. The Afghans are still attacking in huge numbers and we need to weaken them further before we can risk a sortie.'

'But that's my point,' said George, his hands clasped. 'If we wait too long they may force a breach. At least this way we'd keep the initiative.'

Roberts seemed in two minds. 'Anyone else like to voice an opinion?'

'Yes, sir, I would,' said FitzGeorge. 'We know from spies' reports that our attackers number at least sixty thousand men. I doubt half that number has yet entered the fray, which means it might be extremely dangerous to take the initiative. Remember what happened the last time our cavalry got caught in the open by Afghan foot soldiers?'

'Only too well,' said Roberts, shaking his head at the memory. 'So you'd advise caution?'

'Yes, General. My feeling is that we should only unleash the cavalry when we know the Afghans are beaten. But if Hart here is looking to be a hero, why don't you assign him to the flying column that will pursue Mir Bacha and the Kohistanis? He's been among them, after all, and will know what Mir Bacha looks like.'

'You've already planned the pursuit?' said George, horrified. 'Isn't that a little over-confident?'

'Of course not,' said Roberts. 'A sensible general always plans ahead. As soon as I knew the rebels' battle plan, I was confident we could hold out here. My next priority is to crush the rebellion, and the quickest way to do that is to arrest the leading players. Hence the flying columns: one to go after Mir Bacha, another to chase the Ghazni mullah and Mohammed Jan. And Major FitzGeorge is quite right: you'd do us a great service if you'd agree to accompany the column bound for Kohistan. So, will you volunteer? It's dangerous work, but nothing a resourceful fellow like you can't handle.'

Even George had to admit that Roberts was right: the sooner they caught the leading rebels, the sooner they could re-establish some kind of rule of law; and the sooner they could do that, the sooner the chance of a political settlement that would allow the British to withdraw from some or all of the country with their honour and, more importantly, their prestige intact. First, however, George needed reassurance. 'If I agree to go, and we catch Mir Bacha, what guarantees can you give me that you'll try to bring this bloodshed to an end by withdrawing from Kabul?'

The general's eyebrows shot up. 'What an extraordinary request. Why do you care if we stay or go?'

'I have no personal interest one way or another,' said George, less than truthfully, 'but I was sent here by the British government to try to prevent another Afghan imbroglio and, thus far, I've failed. But if we can cut our losses now my mission won't have been entirely in vain.'

Roberts shook his head in astonishment. 'You're either a fantasist or you really were sent by London, Hart, and I'm inclined to believe the latter. But I can't give you any guarantees about our future policy here. I'm a soldier, not a politician. All I can say is that, from my own perspective, a long-term British presence in Kabul is not feasible. We're clearly not wanted, and may be doing more harm than good.'

'So when things settle down you'll advise the viceroy to withdraw?'

'From Kabul, certainly. The scale and violence of the uprising here has made it plain to me that Kabul can only be ruled by Afghans.'

'Sir,' interrupted FitzGeorge, 'I must protest. I thought the policy was to keep control of the country as far as the Hindu Kush.'

'That was the theory, Major. But my experience on the ground tells me that it's no longer possible. The best we can hope for now, I suspect, is a ruler on the throne whom we can do business with, rather than one we control.'

'Is there a chance that Yakub will be restored?' asked George.

'I doubt it. He's too closely connected to the attack on the Residency and poor Sir Louis's murder. But I'm sure any future amir will be a member of the Barakzai dynasty, though preferably one not tainted by the current uprising.'

George's thoughts turned to Yasmin. Was this an opportunity for her to prove her worth to the British, and to push herself up the pecking order of viable alternatives to Yakub? It seemed so. 'I will volunteer, General,' he said, after a pause, 'but on one condition.'

'Which is?'

'That you also let Princess Yasmin join the Kohistan flying column.'

'The princess? A woman? It's out of the question.'

'Hear me out, General. She's a cousin of Mir Bacha and if anyone can persuade him to surrender she can. She's also a skilled horsewoman, no slouch with a sword or carbine, and can take care of herself, if that concerns you.'

'It does, partly. But I'm just as fearful that she'll play us false.'

'If she meant you harm, she would never have told you the rebels' battle plan, which, you have to admit, they're following to the letter.'

Roberts stroked one side of his moustache. 'You're right about that. And you'll vouch for her safety? It wouldn't do to lose a royal princess in battle.'

'I will, sir. She'll be safe as houses with my guide Ilderim Khan to look after her.'

'Is he the big Pathan?'

'Yes, sir.'

'Very well, you may take her with you. And you can tell her from me that I'll look favourably on her cause, and that of her family, if she can deliver up Mir Bacha. She sounds quite the Amazon, this Princess Yasmin. But does she play straight?'

'If you're straight with her.'

'That makes a change in this Godforsaken country. I tell you, Hart, the Afghans could do a lot worse than have a woman like her as their ruler. It hasn't done us any harm.'

'My thoughts exactly, General.'

'Well, off you go to fetch the princess. But don't dawdle. I need you ready to move at a moment's notice. Major FitzGeorge will arrange your mounts. On second thoughts, he can go with you. He's studied the photographs of the rebel leaders and knows who we're looking for. He can also keep an eye on the princess and, if he's lucky, pick up some worthwhile intelligence. That is, after all, what he's trained to do – though you wouldn't always know it,' said Roberts, with a chuckle. 'Eh, FitzGeorge?'

'Quite, sir,' said the major, flustered. 'But wouldn't I be of more use to you here?'

'No, frankly, you wouldn't. Not when the battle's as good

as won, which it will be by the time I send out the flying columns. You'll be my eyes and ears.'

'Yes, General,' said FitzGeorge, without enthusiasm.

Roberts scribbled a note on a scrap of paper and handed it to George. 'The princess's quarters are in the double-storey house to the east of here that the Royal Engineers officers are using as their mess. Give that to the officer in charge of the princess's guard. If she agrees to accompany you, escort her to the cavalry lines below the Bimaru Heights where Major FitzGeorge will be waiting with your mounts. Quick as you can.'

George saluted and left the room, gathering up Ilderim outside. As they made their way up the covered walkway to the Engineers' mess, he had one or two misgivings that he was putting Yasmin in the way of danger. But her reaction to the plan was enough to dispel them instantly. 'Of course I'll come with you!' she said, her face as radiant as a child's. 'Anything to escape this prison.'

'Are you certain, Princess? We'll be hunting your own kin.'

'I know that, Angrez. But they rejected me. And if I have to turn in that slippery toad Mir Bacha to safeguard my family's rule, I'll do it.'

George was tempted to mention the general's complimentary remarks, and the possibility that the British might even recognize her as ruler of Kabul, but he didn't want to risk her becoming even more reckless than usual so he held his tongue. Instead he told her that General Roberts had come to his senses and, once the battle was over and the rebellion put down, would recommend to his political masters in Simla that Kabul be restored to an Afghan ruler.

'I wish I could believe that, Angrez. But even if he is true to his word, who will rule the rest of the country?' she asked.

'He didn't say, and it may well be that they'll try to hold on to Kandahar and the south. But at least the rest of Afghanistan will be rid of foreign control.'

'If I were amir,' said Yasmin, her pretty chin raised defiantly, 'I wouldn't rest until the *whole* country was free.'

'I can believe it, Princess,' said George, marvelling again at her fierce patriotism. 'But let's take one step at a time. Mir Bacha is our priority today.'

'You're right, Angrez,' she said, buttoning up her poshteen, 'one step at a time.'

21

They found Major FitzGeorge waiting impatiently with a groom and their horses at the entrance to the cavalry lines, a large tented encampment in the lee of the Bimaru Heights. 'Where have you been?' he demanded. 'The general has already sent out the Fifth Punjab Cavalry and four horse artillery guns to drive the rebels from Khatir, as you suggested. We could be ordered after them at any moment.'

'I'm glad to hear it, Major,' said George. 'As for our tardiness, we came as quickly as we could. The princess had to change her clothes.'

FitzGeorge turned to Yasmin who, as before, looked remarkably fetching in her riding garb of jodhpurs, boots, poshteen and turban. In her cummerbund was stuffed a short dagger with a jewelled hilt and pistol. 'Of course. Please accept my apologies, Your Highness. It's just that the general has impressed upon me the importance of overtaking the Kohistan rebels before they reach the Khair Khana Pass to the north-west.'

'And so we will, Major,' replied Yasmin, stern-faced. 'Many of the Kohistanis are on foot and the Khair Khana is a good five miles from here.'

'That's true, Your Highness, but Mir Bacha and his lieutenants are the prize and they're horsed. So if you would care to select a mount, we can join the rest of the flying column at the gap in hills.'

The horses were typical cavalry mounts, big-boned and none under fifteen hands. George picked out a fine bay for Yasmin.

'How many sabres are we?' he asked FitzGeorge, as he helped Yasmin into the saddle.

'Two hundred. A squadron each of the Ninth and Fourteenth Bengal Lancers. Will that be enough?'

'I hope so,' said George, tightening Yasmin's girth. He then mounted his own horse, a sturdy black Waler leaving Ilderim with the grey. All three animals, he noted with satisfaction, were equipped with leather buckets containing carbines. But he also knew that a sword was a more effective weapon at close quarters. 'I don't suppose you have a spare sabre?' he asked FitzGeorge.

'I'm afraid not. I suggest you try to cadge one from the lancers. Now can we go?'

'By all means. Lead on.'

The sound of firing was fairly constant from most parts of the perimeter, but it rose in intensity as they neared the narrow gap in the centre of the Bimaru Heights – more a shallow depression than an interval between two separate features – through which the 5th Punjab Cavalry and four guns had already passed. George could hear artillery fire from beyond the hills, and assumed that the horse artillery was already in action.

The two squadrons of blue-coated Lancers – one composed of whey-faced Britons of medium height, the other of tall Jats from northern India – were waiting for them on the road ahead, just beyond a barrier of trees and wire that had been hastily pulled aside. Each trooper was holding a nine-foot bamboo lance with a red and white pennon and tipped with a steel three-sided point, its metal shoe resting in a special holder attached to the right stirrup. Across their backs were slung carbines, while the officers were armed with pistols and swords.

Major FitzGeorge rode up to one of these officers, a young cornet of the 9th Lancers, and asked him who was in charge. 'Captain Fanshawe was, sir, but he was wounded a short time ago by a stray bullet.'

'I'm sorry to hear that,' said George, concern in his voice – Fanshawe was the officer who had escorted them in.

'So who's replaced him?' asked FitzGeorge.

'I have, Major,' said a voice behind them. They all turned to see Percy Sykes approaching on horseback with a bugler in tow. 'How can I help?'

'By saluting a superior officer, for a start,' said FitzGeorge, testily.

Sykes quickly did so, the bugler too.

'That's better. The flying column's task is to capture Mir Bacha, the Kohistani leader. Is that right?'

'Yes, sir. We're to make for the Khair Khana Pass as soon as the rebels break off the attack.'

'We're coming with you.'

Sykes looked from one to another, his face darkening as he recognised George. 'All of you? Captain Hart and the princess included?'

'That's right. Any objections?'

'Only that this is a military operation, and no place for part-time soldiers and women.'

George bristled at the insult and was about to respond in kind, but FitzGeorge got in first. 'So you know what Mir Bacha looks like, do you, Lieutenant Sykes?'

'No, sir.'

'Does anyone under your command?'

'I don't think so, sir.'

'Well, both Princess Yasmin and Captain Hart do, as does Captain Hart's companion, Ilderim Khan. Their task is to identify and capture Mir Bacha with your assistance. Do you understand?'

'Yes, sir,' said Sykes, through gritted teeth. 'May I ask who's responsible for the princess's safety?'

'You are, so make sure she returns in one piece. Now, before we set off, Captain Hart would like to borrow a sabre.'

Sykes looked at George. 'You were in the cavalry so briefly I'm surprised you know how to use one.'

'Just get him the sword, Lieutenant,' said FitzGeorge.

'Yes, sir,' said Sykes, and instructed the bugler to fetch his spare.

He did so, and George was buckling it to his waist when a galloper arrived with a message from the heights. FitzGeorge read it. 'The good news,' he announced, 'is that our sortie has worked: the rebels have been outflanked by our horse artillery guns and are streaming back from Khatir. The issue of the battle, it seems, is no longer in doubt. The bad news for us is that the Kohistanis are well on their way to the Khair Khana Pass, and had probably begun their withdrawal before the cavalry and guns left the cantonment. We must move now, Lieutenant, to have any chance of success.'

'Sir,' responded Sykes. 'Bugler, sound the advance!'

With Sykes and FitzGeorge leading, followed closely by George, Yasmin, Ilderim and successive troops of Lancers riding four abreast, the column trotted through the gap in the hills and out into the plain beyond. A few bullets whistled close, but the vast majority of rebels were more concerned with escape than continuing the fight. As far as the eye could see figures were fleeing, some taking refuge in the villages and dry watercourses called nullahs that dotted the plain, others heading for the more certain refuge of the high ground to the north and west.

'Keep to the roads,' shouted FitzGeorge over his shoulder, 'and ignore any stragglers. We must get to the pass before the Kohistanis do.'

For ten minutes they rode through the slush of a narrow dirt track, mud and ice spattering the clothes of the riders behind. Once of twice they were fired at from villages they passed, prompting a fusillade in response, but otherwise their passage was unimpeded as rebels melted from their path. Having skirted the southern edge of a lake, they turned north and finally sighted their prey. Spread out ahead was a huge array of horse and foot, many thousands strong, swarming across the plain towards the safety of the pass. They seemed to be wearing all the colours of the rainbow, and were armed with a wide variety of weapons, ancient and modern, from swords and spears to muskets and breech-loading rifles. The rear of this retreating mass was barely a mile ahead; the front was nearing the spur that hid the entrance to the pass.

FitzGeorge at once called a halt. 'God almighty!' he exclaimed. 'We can't take them all on with our tiny force. What do we do?'

'You're the senior officer, Major,' said Sykes, sourly. 'You tell me.'

George nudged his horse forward. 'Gentlemen, we're wasting time. If we don't take the initiative we'll lose track of Mir Bacha and the other chiefs, and neither of you will want to explain why to General Roberts. In any case, retreating troops are terrified of cavalry and will fly at our approach.'

'How can you be certain?' demanded FitzGeorge. 'Have you charged an enemy on the move?'

'No, but I've read enough military history to know that pursuits are rarely opposed. Moreover they have no artillery to use against us. We must advance and take our chances.'

'I hate to admit it, Major,' said Sykes, 'but I agree with Hart. In any event, if we don't attack we might as well write off our military careers.'

This last point seemed to make up FitzGeorge's mind. 'Very well, then. We'll advance. But I won't take the blame if this ends in disaster.'

George looked scornfully at FitzGeorge, and wondered how it was possible that two brothers – if indeed they were – could have such different characters. But then he remembered the crucial distinction between them: FitzGeorge was white and had always known of his royal status, albeit one tainted by illegitimacy, whereas he was a quarter black African and, until recently, had assumed his father was a gentleman but no more. Was it any wonder that FitzGeorge saw the world from the embittered perspective of a man born into, yet never truly accepted by, the British ruling class while he, thanks to his Irish-African heritage, had a broader outlook and tended to sympathize with the underdog? The answer was no.

'What are your orders, Major?' asked Sykes.

'To advance, to charge – as you've both suggested.'

'I didn't suggest that, sir, and neither did Hart. If we charge now,' advised Sykes who, like George, had served in a cavalry regiment, 'the horses will arrive blown. Better to close the distance at a trot.'

'And when we do, how do we find Mir Bacha? They all look the same to me.'

'To you maybe,' said George, 'but not to the princess.' He

turned to Yasmin. 'Can you see anything, Princess,' he asked in Pashto, 'that would enable us to pinpoint your cousin?'

She scanned the many standards being carried by the retreating Kohistanis and soon found what she was looking for. 'Look to the centre of the throng, Angrez,' she said, pointing, 'and you will find a large body of cavalry and a huge green and gold flag. Do you see it?'

'Yes.'

'That's Mir Bacha's personal standard. He will not allow it to be captured.'

'So if we aim for the standard, we'll find Mir Bacha?'

'Yes.'

George repeated what she had said to the two officers.

'Very good,' said FitzGeorge. 'The standard will be our target. Tell your men, Sykes, that whoever captures it will earn himself ten guineas.'

'And the man who captures Mir Bacha himself?' asked Sykes.

'A hundred.'

Sykes whistled softly. 'That's quite an incentive, Major, but can you be sure the general will pay out?'

'I'm certain of it. His priority now is to secure the rebel leaders. If he could do that for a hundred guineas a man, he'd pay up willingly.'

Sykes grinned. 'I'll inform the men,' he said, turning his horse to find the nearest NCO.

As George waited for the order to move, his horse impatiently pulling on its bridle, he felt a hand on his forearm. 'If anything happens to me, Angrez,' said Yasmin, her eyes brimming with tears, 'I want you to know that I am grateful for all you've done.'

'Thank you,' said George, putting his hand over hers. 'But

you mustn't talk like this. You'll come safely through. We both will.'

She gave a thin smile and nodded, but George could tell she was unconvinced. He was about to speak more words of encouragement when Sykes returned to the head of the column and spoke to the bugler. He at once played the seven notes that all cavalrymen dream of hearing on active service: 'Form line!'

The two squadrons formed up side by side, in two lines, their combined front extending for more than three hundred yards. FitzGeorge and Sykes took their place at the head of the right squadron, the 9th Lancers, with George, Yasmin and Ilderim close behind. George surveyed the ground between them and the retreating Kohistanis and noted with relief that it was flat and uncultivated, with only the occasional ditch and clump of trees providing an obstacle. It was almost ideal for cavalry.

By now the closest Kohistanis had seen what was happening and many were fleeing for the nearest high ground, while a few of the bolder types had turned to stand their ground. Mir Bacha and his horsemen, on the other hand, were continuing their orderly withdrawal down the centre of the plain as if they had all the time in the world.

Taking his lead from FitzGeorge and Sykes, George drew his sword and carefully wrapped the loop of cord dangling from its three-bar hilt around his wrist in case he lost his grip. Then he tested the edge of the three-foot straight blade with his thumb and felt a prick of pain as it drew blood. It was razor sharp.

He looked beyond Yasmin to Ilderim and felt a surge of brotherly affection for the big Afghan who, thus far, had seen him through so much danger. As ever, Ilderim seemed to be enjoying the prospect of combat, and was sitting on his grey with a half-smile on his handsome bearded face, the stock of his carbine resting lazily on his left thigh.

'Ilderim,' called George.

'Yes, *huzoor*?'

'Don't worry about me today. Stay close to the princess.'

Ilderim nodded, and as he did so Sykes gave the order to advance. The bugle sounded the familiar three notes, repeated once, and the two lines began to move forward: first at a walk, then a trot and finally, as the distance to the nearest Kohistanis closed to under two hundred yards, a gallop.

Once again George felt that strange mix of fear and exhilaration as his horse tore across the plain, kicking clods of snow onto the grim-faced troopers behind them, their fearsome lances extended like the quills of a porcupine. Bullets were zipping through the air and the odd one found its mark, knocking a trooper from his horse, or bringing his mount down. But no sooner had one rider dropped out than the nearest officer cried, 'Close up! Close up!' and the line formed a new unbroken front.

Most of the Afghans on foot were running from the wall of horsemen, which must have seemed as unstoppable as the incoming tide. But a few brave souls had stopped to face the foe, and they were the first to be consumed by sword and lance as the line swept over them. George saw a lone rifleman to his right front, and changed direction so that he could cut at him right-handed. But at the last moment the Afghan went to ground and George's swing passed harmlessly over his head. It was left to a trooper behind to skewer the Afghan with his lance, a weapon from which no man on foot without cover could hide.

Up ahead, Mir Bacha and a few of his horsemen had at last recognized the danger and were galloping for the safety of the pass, the huge green and gold standard marking their progress through the scattered remnants of the Kohistani army. Yet the bulk of Mir Bacha's escort, presumably under orders from their chief, had turned to meet the Lancers and was firing a last ragged fusillade before the two forces collided. More saddles emptied behind George, yet he and the others rode on unscathed.

The bugler sounded the charge and a great cheer rose from the throats of the Lancers as they swept towards their prey. But George had eyes only for the green and gold standard, which, billowing out behind its bearer, was nearing the spur at the entrance to the pass. 'Leave the fighting to the Lancers and follow me,' he shouted across to Yasmin and Ilderim. 'We must catch up with the standard before it's too late.'

Yasmin nodded and, with barely fifty yards between them and the much bigger block of Afghan horsemen, George veered off to the right in an effort to outflank the obstacle. Yasmin and Ilderim followed, and it seemed for a moment as if they would make it unimpeded, giving them a clear run at Mir Bacha. But just as Sykes, FitzGeorge and the front rank of Lancers smashed into the waiting body of Afghan horse amid screams, cries and shots, half a dozen Afghans wheeled to the right in an attempt to block George's manoeuvre. Yasmin killed one with her pistol, and Ilderim another with his carbine, which he was firing one-handed. But the rest closed with *tulwar*s and George found himself attacked from two directions. He parried one cut with a loud ringing of steel, and ducked the second, before countering with a thrust that pierced his first assailant's lower abdomen. The man screamed with pain and clutched his stomach as George turned back to the second Afghan, who had closed to take advantage. It was too late to block the Afghan's slashing cut, which was arcing towards his head. But it never made contact because, halfway through his stroke, the Afghan reared up in his saddle as a bullet passed through his midriff, his *tulwar* dropping from his grip. His expression was a mixture of agony and amazement as he toppled from his saddle.

'Come, Angrez!' shouted Yasmin, smoking pistol in hand. 'There's still time to catch my cousin.'

George put spurs to his mount and was relieved to see that all three of them had come through the scrimmage, though Ilderim was tightening a bloody strip of material round his left forearm with his teeth. 'How is it?' yelled George, as they rode for the spur.

'A scratch,' replied Ilderim. 'Unlike the wound I inflicted in return.'

George looked back to see a boiling mass of men and horses, hacking, stabbing and shooting at each other. Though his view was partly obscured by smoke, he could see that the discipline and skill at arms of the Lancers was giving them the upper hand against a numerically superior opponent. Yet it seemed unlikely that any would break free in time to join their pursuit of Mir Bacha and his diminished escort who, by now, had disappeared round the corner of the spur. They were on their own.

George began to have his doubts as to the sense of their headlong dash into the pass and voiced them to Yasmin, whose horse was surging ahead. 'Princess!' he shouted. 'We should stop. There's no knowing how many snipers are guarding the sides of the pass. It's madness to rush in without support.'

She pulled hard on her reins, slowing her horse and almost

causing George and Ilderim to collide with her. 'Are you afraid, Angrez?' she asked.

George felt a surge of anger that she should suggest such a thing. 'Not afraid,' he snapped, 'just realistic about our chances. It was worth making the attempt, but we're too late. If we enter that pass alone we won't come out alive.'

'Then return to your people. I must go on.'

'Why?'

'Because I would rather not be remembered as the Afghan princess who betrayed her people and was forced into exile.'

'That won't happen. General Roberts knows the contribution you've already made to our cause, and will certainly look favourably upon your claim to the throne when we leave.'

Yasmin shook her head sadly. 'You're so young and still have much to learn, Angrez. General Roberts will support the strongest claimant, whatever I do today. I know now I will never be ruler, and that whoever takes over will not forgive my actions of these last few days. I also know I can never leave Afghanistan.'

'But you said before that—'

'I was angry with Mir Bacha and the Kohistanis for rejecting me, and didn't see the sense of remaining in a country that offers no outlet for a woman's talent or ambition. But I know that I could never be happy in exile. So here, today, is where it must end. And if, before I die, I can kill my cousin and help bring peace to my country, my life won't have been in vain.'

George tried to think of something – anything – that would change her mind. In desperation, he blurted out, 'I love you.'

She raised her eyebrows. 'You *love* me? How can you after I left you at Ghazni?'

'I don't know, but I do.'

Yasmin blinked as if holding back the tears. 'Maybe you do love me, Angrez – and maybe I have feelings for you too. But it doesn't change anything.'

'Why not? My mission is almost over and tomorrow, if I survive this jaunt, I'll leave this country for ever. Why don't you come with me?'

'To where?'

'To England. To South Africa. Does it matter?'

'Indeed it matters. These places are as alien to me as Afghanistan is to you. I know what you're doing. You're hoping to delay me long enough for your cavalry to arrive and force the pass. But that will be too late. Mir Bacha will be long gone. I must go now.'

'Princess, please, I beg you not to go. It will mean certain death.'

'I know that.'

'Then why do it?'

'Because it's my destiny. Goodbye, Angrez.' She gave George a last look of regret before she turned her horse towards the pass and dug in her heels.

George was about to follow when Ilderim grabbed his reins. 'What are you doing?' demanded George. 'We have to help her.'

'No, *huzoor*. She has chosen to die. I prefer life.'

'Let go of my reins, Ilderim,' said George, raising his sword. 'Or, by Christ, I'll sever your arm.'

'As you wish, *huzoor*,' he said, releasing the reins with a flourish. 'But I will not come with you.'

'It's your choice,' said George, as he put spurs to his horse and thundered after Yasmin who, already, was two hundred yards ahead and nearing the entrance to the pass.

'Princess!' yelled George, as he rode. 'Wait!'

She either didn't hear or didn't want to, and was soon into the pass and out of view. George used the flat of his sword's blade to urge his mount to go faster, but it made little difference, and every yard he expected to hear the gunshot that would signal Yasmin's demise. It never came and, as he neared the rocky spur that marked the southern entrance to the pass, he began to hope that Mir Bacha and his Kohistanis had kept running. But once past the spur, and into the pass, his optimism was dashed. Lining the heights on either side of the narrowest part of the pass ahead, perched behind every bush and rock, were hundreds of armed Afghans, while the stony track through the defile was barred by a thorn barricade protected by yet more riflemen and, beyond, a small cluster of horsemen with Mir Bacha's green and gold standard in their midst. All eyes seemed focused on a single stationary rider – Yasmin – who had reined in halfway between George and the barricade.

George pulled up before he, too, was caught in the trap, his horse's hoofs slipping on loose stones as he guided it off the track and up a short incline to the minimal cover of a juniper tree. At that moment his thoughts were centred on Yasmin's predicament, and how to get her out of it. He was about to shout a warning, though he knew it to be pointless, when he noticed activity at the barricade. A section was removed and a lone rider came through. George at once recognised the rider's green *kurta* and yellow turban. It was Mir Bacha himself.

George watched transfixed as the Kohistani chief approached Yasmin at the trot, stopping just yards from her. He seemed to be saying something, his right hand chopping through the air like an axe. George could imagine Yasmin's spirited response, and silently urged her not to do anything stupid. Inevitably she did, drawing her pistol in a blur and pointing it directly at Mir Bacha's chest. But before she had the chance to pull the trigger, a single shot rang out, quickly followed by two more. Yasmin's body twitched, and George knew she had been shot by a hidden marksman.

He looked on in horror as her hand dropped the pistol and she toppled from the saddle. *No!*

He wanted to ride over to her, to cradle her in his arms, though he knew such an act to be every bit as suicidal as hers. While he hesitated – choked with emotion – Mir Bacha leant from his saddle and applied the *coup de grâce* to Yasmin's inert form, the gunshot echoing down the canyon. This final callous act was too much for George to take and, his face pale with shock and his chest heaving with anger, he kicked his horse back down the incline, determined to kill Mir Bacha or die in the attempt.

He had barely reached the track when a horse galloped up from behind and a huge fist grabbed his reins. 'No, *huzoor*,' said Ilderim, shaking his handsome, weatherbeaten face. 'It is too late. She is dead and we must go.'

This time George didn't try to free himself. He knew that Ilderim was right, and that it would serve no purpose to sacrifice his own life. It wouldn't bring her back. And so, as quickly as it had flared, his anger ebbed away, to be replaced by an almost crushing sadness for what might have been: for Yasmin and for Afghanistan.

'*Huzoor!*' repeated Ilderim, more urgently this time. 'We *must* leave or we'll join her in the dust.'

A bullet whizzed by and pinged off a rock behind them. Then more shots, until the ground around them was erupting in little puffs of dust that caused the horses to shy and back away. This proximity to death brought George to his senses and, with a last look back at Yasmin's crumpled body, he turned his horse and galloped after Ilderim, the occasional bullet following them until they had rounded the spur. Directly ahead, riding fast towards them, was the remnant of the two Lancer squadrons, led by Sykes and FitzGeorge. George raised his hand and the ragged column, containing many wounded Lancers and others with their red and white lance pennons encrusted with blood, clattered to a halt in front of them.

'Why have you stopped us?' demanded FitzGeorge, his bridle hand shaking from the nervous shock of combat. 'And where's the princess?'

'She's dead. And so will you be if you enter the pass. Mir Bacha has barricaded the track and lined the heights with riflemen. Fortunately for you, the princess sprang the trap and paid with her life.'

FitzGeorge's face drained of blood. 'We've failed twice over: Mir Bacha has got away and we've lost a royal princess. What am I going to tell the general?'

'Tell him the truth – that we did our best.'

'Doing your best cuts no ice with Roberts,' observed FitzGeorge, bitterly. 'He's only interested in success. He'll never forgive me for this, or any of us.'

'I said it was a mistake to bring her,' said Sykes. 'What I want to know, though, is how Hart survived and she didn't.' He turned to George. 'Can you explain that?'

'What are you suggesting, Sykes?' said George, his face screwed up with contempt. 'That I stood by and let her die?'

'I'm not suggesting anything. I'm asking you a simple question.'

'You're forgetting that I outrank you so I don't answer to you.'

'But you don't outrank *me*,' said FitzGeorge. 'So what happened? The general will want to know.'

George looked away as the memory of Yasmin's death came back to him in all its tragic detail, sending a shiver down his spine. 'I tried to stop her but . . .'

'But what?' asked FitzGeorge.

'. . . she *wanted* to die.'

22

General Roberts's headquarters, Sherpur cantonment, winter 1879

'Ah, Hart, do come in,' said the general, rising from his desk and gesturing towards a chair opposite. 'FitzGeorge here has already told me his side of the story. Now I'd like to hear yours.'

George looked across at the major, who was writing at a separate table, in the hope of gleaning a hint as to whether his report had been favourable or not. But FitzGeorge kept his head down and George was forced to conclude the worst. 'There's not much to tell,' he said woodenly. 'By the time we cut our way through the Kohistani cavalry, Mir Bacha had reached the safety of the pass where he'd set up an ambush for any pursuers. If the princess hadn't gone in first and sprung the trap, we'd all have been killed.'

'Yes, so I gathered from Major FitzGeorge. But the princess wasn't alone, was she? You and your Afghan bodyguard were with her. Why did you let her go on? Why didn't you wait for the rest of the cavalry?'

'I wanted to, and said as much to her. But she wouldn't listen.'

'Why?'

George thought back to their final conversation and shook his head. 'It's as I told Major FitzGeorge, General. She wouldn't listen because she welcomed death.'

'She *wanted* to die?'

'Yes.'

'Why?'

'Because, having sided with us, she couldn't see a future for herself in Afghanistan, and neither could she contemplate a life in exile.'

'She told you that?' asked Roberts.

'Yes.'

Roberts slowly shook his head. 'I'll never understand these people, and I've served in India for twenty-five years.'

'Perhaps that's the point, General.'

'What point?'

'We'll never understand each other, which is why we – the British – should stop trying to impose our culture and system of rule on unwilling and ungrateful foreigners.'

Roberts rubbed his beard in contemplation. 'You may be right. But the problem we face in Afghanistan, when we do withdraw, is who to leave in control.'

'So your mind is fixed then, General? You *will* advise Simla to pull our troops out of the whole country?'

'Yes, I will.'

'Sir,' interrupted FitzGeorge, who had ceased writing, 'I thought we'd agreed that our advice would be to pull out of the north only and retain Kandahar and Helmand provinces as an extra buffer between us and the Russians.'

'I've changed my mind.'

'Sir,' persisted FitzGeorge, clearly worried that he would lose the commission on the trading concessions he had promised to secure, 'are you sure you've thought this through? If we relinquish the whole country are we not back to where we started from?'

'No, Major, we are not. Because I also intend to

recommend a break-up of the country. If these last few weeks of fighting have taught me anything, it's that the Afghans will never accept foreign rule. So our best course of action is to restore a strong Afghan ruler favourable to our policies. The question is, do we restore one ruler, or many? I favour the latter. A strong, united Afghanistan is only desirable if we can be certain that its interests and ours will always remain identical. But history has taught us that we can't be certain, and that even if the man we were to choose as amir were to remain perfectly loyal, there is no guarantee that his successor would. Which is why I'm going to advise the Indian government to divide the country into two or three smaller states, each run by a different ruler, and never again attempt to place the whole country under a single sovereign.'

'Sir,' said FitzGeorge, 'I think you're making a mistake. The security of our Indian empire depends upon our retaining at least a foothold in Afghanistan.'

'Not in my opinion. Now, I won't hear any more on the subject, Major. Have you finished the text of the proclamation I asked you to write?'

'Yes, sir.'

'Well, let me see it.'

Glum-faced, FitzGeorge walked over to Roberts's desk and handed over the paper he had been working on. Roberts read it and nodded with satisfaction. 'Very good, Major.'

'Thank you, sir,' said FitzGeorge, without enthusiasm. 'Is there anything else? Because if not I have reports to write.'

'No, there's nothing else. Off you go.'

As the door closed, Roberts pushed the paper across the desk to George. 'What do you think, Hart? Will it do?'

George was not hopeful. He had already seen and heard enough of Roberts's smug self-importance and casual brutality to doubt that this proclamation would be any different from the previous ones. But he was about to be pleasantly surprised. It read:

At the instigation of some seditious men, the ignorant people, generally not considering the result, raised a rebellion. Now many of the insurgents have received their reward, and as subjects are a trust from God, the British government, which is just and merciful, as well as strong, has forgiven their guilt. It is now proclaimed that all who come in without delay will be pardoned, excepting only Mohammed Jan of Wardak, Mir Bacha of Kohistan, and Mullah Mushk-i-Alam of Ghazni. Come and make your submission without fear. The British government has no enmity towards the people. All who come in without delay need have no fear or suspicion. The British government speaks only that which is in its heart.

George looked up from the paper. 'You mean to offer an amnesty to all but the leading rebels?'

'I do. It's a pity we failed to capture any yesterday, but the victory we gained yesterday was so complete – with more than three thousand Afghans killed, while we lost just five killed and thirty or so wounded – that I have no doubt the great tribal confederation is broken for good. Why, only this morning we reoccupied Kabul and the Bala Hissar, and tomorrow I will send cavalry further afield to harry the retreating rebels. But this proclamation will do more to bring the rebellion to a speedy conclusion than any military action could. Lord Canning tried something similar during the Mutiny of fifty-seven and it was a great success. I hope it will be again, because I can't set up a new Afghan ruler here until order has been restored.'

'Do you have anyone in mind, General?'

'Well, I *had* Princess Yasmin in mind, as I told you, but she's no longer with us, and I wonder if the Afghans could have accepted a female ruler – I doubt it. Which leaves only two credible candidates, in my view: Ayub Khan, Yakub and Yasmin's younger brother, and the current governor of Herat; and Abdur Rahman, their first cousin, whose father fought and lost the throne to his younger brother, Sher Ali, in the sixties. My personal preference is for Abdur Rahman because he was in exile in Russian Turkestan when the attack on the Residency took place, and therefore cannot be implicated. I can't say the same for Ayub Khan, not least because the troops that mutinied were from his province.'

'Do you know where this Abdur Rahman is now?'

'No, but Major FitzGeorge is doing all he can to find out. We'll track him down sooner or later, never you fear. So, what's next for you, Hart? I imagine you're keen to return home and make your report.'

'I am, General,' said George, taken aback, 'but I half suspected you'd want to keep me here for a while.'

'Not at all,' said Roberts, waving his hand dismissively. 'You've done your bit, and more, both before and during the battle. If you hadn't brought the princess in we'd never have learnt the rebels' battle plan, and during the fighting you provided valuable tactical advice, and courage in action. The only black mark against you is the loss of the princess, a death I'll be hard put to explain to the authorities, let alone her family, but hardly your fault. So, no, I'm happy for you to leave Afghanistan as soon as you consider the route to be secure. Before you go, however, I'd like to know what you intend to write about me in your report to His Royal Highness the Duke of Cambridge.'

'I'm sorry, General, but that's confidential.'

'Yes, yes. I'm aware of that. But I'd consider it a special favour – and one that I'd be happy to reciprocate – if you could tell me the gist of what you'll write.'

George remembered a similar offer – you scratch my back, I'll scratch yours – being made to him in Zululand by Lord Chelmsford's chief of staff. But the crucial difference now was that he wasn't being asked to lie, just to provide information. Moreover, the man asking was a general who, despite his flaws, was clearly heading for the very top of the army, a man he should try not to cross.

After a pause, George said, 'I'll give you a brief pointer. On the one hand I fully understand you've had a difficult job to do and feel, on the whole, that you've carried out your military responsibilities with professionalism and no little skill. On the other I think you were far too quick to invade, and that you let your own strategic priorities – notably your wish to see part of Afghanistan fall under British rule – cloud your judgement of the political situation, notably Yakub's responsibility for the massacre. And even after the invasion you made mistakes, alienating the locals with your harsh proclamations and, even worse, underestimating their military capabilities, hence the recent siege and the close-run battle yesterday.'

Roberts raised his palm in acknowledgement. 'I accept I've made mistakes, Hart. All generals do. All I ask is that you present the duke and the Cabinet with the full picture. Yes, there was a minor setback in the Chardeh valley a couple of weeks ago, I'm not denying that. But we put that right yesterday and I'd hope to have British troops out of the country before next summer at the latest.'

'Can you guarantee that we'll have left by then?'

'Too many variables are involved for that, not least the agreement of Lord Lytton and his council. But I'll do my best. You have my word.'

'Good. And in turn I promise to include in my report the fairest possible account of your actions during these last few months.'

Roberts extended his hand with a smile. 'Then let's shake on it, like gentlemen.'

'Gladly,' said George, satisfied that he had promised nothing more than to tell the truth. But as he took the small bony hand offered, Roberts widened his bright blue eyes and tilted his head slightly as if an unspoken pact had passed between them.

The spell was broken by a knock at the door. 'Yes?' responded Roberts.

A young staff officer entered and saluted. 'Sorry to interrupt you, General, but the Lancers have just brought in the princess's body.'

'Thank you, Jarvis, I'll be out directly.' Roberts turned back to George, whose face had paled. 'You all right, Hart?'

'Yes . . . I . . . I think so. It's the shock of her death. I still can't believe she's gone.'

'No, I can see that. Well, I must arrange the funeral. Ordinarily we'd return the body to the family, but there's no time. Muhammadans are never embalmed, as I'm sure you know, and must be buried as soon after death as possible.'

'So you'll bury her today?'

'Yes.'

'May I see her first?'

'Of course. Follow me.'

They left the headquarters office and found the horse-drawn ambulance and a Lancer guard of honour just beyond the main gate. As they reached the rear of the ambulance, the princess's body was being removed on a makeshift stretcher of lances and blankets.

'Present arms!' shouted an officer. The guard responded by lowering their lances to the horizontal position, with the butt resting in the armpit, a sign of respect. Roberts and the assembled officers saluted, as did George, feeling sick at what he was about to witness.

Roberts strode forward and lifted the blanket covering Yasmin's face. He shook his head slowly, as if deploring the waste of a young life, let the blanket fall and moved a few paces away. George was next. As he lifted the blanket, and saw that it was indeed her, he felt a wave of grief wash over him and shuddered. But it was some comfort to see that her face was unmarked by injury, though it was flecked with blood and grime, and that in the stillness of death she was, if anything, even more beautiful. Her lips were parted slightly and George could have sworn, or at least consoled himself with the thought, that at the moment of death she had been smiling. He leant down and kissed her cold forehead.

'Goodbye, Princess,' he whispered, a single tear falling from his face onto hers.

George's body felt heavy with exhaustion as he trudged up the stone steps to his room above the gatehouse. With Roberts's permission, he had decided to leave with Ilderim for the Khyber Pass that very afternoon, and it only remained to don his old Afghan disguise and gather up his kit. It was some small consolation to him that, though he had failed to stop the war or save Yasmin's life, he at least had possession of the cloak. Now all he needed to do, to claim the reward that would enable him to pay off his mother's creditors, was get it back to England in one piece.

But as George reached the door to his room he found it slightly ajar. He crept forward and looked through the narrow gap. The room was dark, with its curtains still drawn, but he could just make out a shadowy form by the bed, rifling through his saddle-bags. He flung open the door and tore across, driving his shoulder into the small of the intruder's back and knocking him to the floor.

'Aaargh!' roared the man in pain and surprise, before springing nimbly to his feet. He was an inch or so taller than George, and though he could have run off he didn't. Instead he came at George and the two of them wrestled, crashing into a wall, then the bed and finally the floor. The man had one hand on George's throat and was slowly throttling him. In desperation George slammed a fist into the intruder's kidney and the pressure on his thoat eased, enabling him to roll away, gasping for breath. But when he looked back the man had drawn a tiny pistol and was pointing it at his chest.

'Don't shoot!' said George, instinctively. 'Just take what you want and go.'

'Gladly,' came the reply, 'if you'll pass me the saddle-bags.'

The voice was unmistakable. 'FitzGeorge?'

'Who else?'

'What are you doing here, skulking about like a thief?'

'I would have thought that was obvious. First you lie to me about the cloak, which you had in your possession all along. Then you persuade the general to withdraw from Afghanistan. Don't you understand what that means? Without the commission from the trading concessions, I won't be able to pay my debts and will have to resign from the Army. I'll be ruined and my father will disown me. Which is why I need money from somewhere, and that somewhere is the cloak. So pass me the saddle-bags, there's a good chap, and we'll say no more about it.'

'You can't mean to sell it to the highest bidder,' said George, appalled.

'Why not? If it's as precious to the Afghans as they claim, they'll pay handsomely for it.'

'I'm sure they will,' said George, massaging his bruised throat. 'But what if it finds its way into the hands of someone who'll use it for their own ends, as the mullah tried to do?'

'What if it does? We're pulling out, thanks to you, so what do I care? Anyway, don't take the moral high ground with me. For all I know you were planning to sell it too. You certainly weren't going to hand it back to its rightful owners, I'm quite sure of that.'

'No, Major, you're right. I wasn't planning to hand it back because I've been ordered by my superiors, your father among them, to see it safe to London.'

'To *London*? I don't believe you.'

'It's true. They want to keep it out of the clutches of the religious fanatics.'

'But we're leaving. It's no longer our business.'

'Isn't it? What if our preferred candidates as rulers of the separate provinces are toppled by opponents using the cloak? It'd be our business then.'

FitzGeorge mulled over George's words. 'Yes,' he said, after a considerable pause. 'I suppose you're right. I tell you what. I'll do you a deal. I need money, you need the cloak to complete your mission. So why don't I take the jewelled clasp and you can keep the rest? After all, the clasp is not even part of the original garment. I read somewhere that it was added by Ahmad Shah Durrani, one of Yakub's ancestors, in the eighteenth century.'

'That's possible, I suppose,' said George, not entirely convinced. 'I certainly didn't hear any mention of it until I saw the cloak for the first time in Kohistan. But, even so, I can't let you take it.'

FitzGeorge laughed, waving the end of the pistol. 'You're hardly in a position to stop me, now, are you?'

'Are you serious?'

'Deadly.'

'You'd shoot me for the clasp?'

'Yes,' said FitzGeorge, jutting his jaw defiantly.

'You must be desperate.'

'I am.'

George considered playing the trump card of their probable kinship. But would FitzGeorge believe him? And even if he did, would it be enough to curb his avarice? After all, they hardly knew each other and had little in common beyond a slight physical resemblance. And something else prevented George showing his hand: an instinct that, once his royal connections were known, everything would change. He certainly wasn't ashamed of them, far from it, but neither did he wish to be known thereafter as a royal bastard whose career was dependent on his father's patronage. He preferred to make his own way in life, and he knew he could only do that if he kept his suspicions about his father's identity to himself. So he stayed silent.

FitzGeorge raised his eyebrows. 'What's this? The garrulous Hart for once struck dumb? I'll take that as acceptance of my offer, then, shall I?'

George nodded.

'Good. Well, if you'll do the honours,' said FitzGeorge, pointing towards the saddle-bags.

George did as he was asked, unclasping one of the bags and pulling out the cloak. Then, having taken a deep breath, he wrenched off the clasp and handed it to FitzGeorge. 'I hope you can live with yourself, Major.'

'Oh, I think I can,' said FitzGeorge, with a wink. 'The question is, can you?'

'What do you mean by that?'

'I think you know. Goodbye, Hart. I doubt our paths will cross again.'

'Don't be too sure, Major.'

23

Near Torkham, the Afghan gateway to the Khyber Pass, late December 1879

It was a beautiful day to bid farewell to Afghanistan. The sun was glinting off the snow-covered ground, the air crisp and clear, as they crested the final ridge to reveal the border crossing at Torkham in the valley below. George turned in his saddle to the man who had seen him through so many dangers, and from whom he would now have to part. 'So, my old friend, it's time to say goodbye.'

'Yes, *huzoor*,' said Ilderim, stony-faced, trying hard not to show his true feelings.

'This is for you,' said George, pulling the money-belt and its remaining sovereigns from his saddle-bag, and handing it to Ilderim. 'I've kept back a few coins to get me as far as Karachi. The rest are for you.'

Ilderim opened the belt and counted the sovereigns. 'Twenty-nine, *huzoor*? This is more than you owe me.'

'Maybe so,' said George, with a grin, 'but no more than you deserve. No amount of money can repay the service you have done me. I'm for ever in your debt.'

'No, *huzoor*. You have repaid me handsomely by reconciling me with my father.'

'That was for my benefit too, if you remember. But I'm

glad it's worked out. I could tell how much he loves you, and must have missed you. I'd give my eye teeth to be as close to my own father.'

'Why are you not, *huzoor*?' asked Ilderim.

'It's a long story, for another time. Before I go, I have one more thing for you.'

'A gift, *huzoor*?'

'No, not a gift, more a responsibility.' George felt behind him in his saddle-bag and brought out the cloak, neatly folded into a square. 'I didn't tell you this before because I knew you wouldn't approve, but my superiors wanted me to take this to my country so that it could never be used again to rouse the Afghan people against us. They even promised me a reward of money, a lot of money, which I desperately need. But I can't bring myself to do it. The cloak belongs here in Afghanistan so I'm entrusting it to you. Will you swear to return it, when the time is right, to its shrine in Kandahar?'

'Of course, *huzoor*, on my father's life.'

'Then take it,' said George, handing it over, 'and let us say our goodbyes like the brothers we've become.'

George leant from his saddle and clasped Ilderim in an awkward bear hug. At last releasing his grip, he nodded to the Afghan before urging his horse forward down the track.

'If you ever need me, *huzoor*,' shouted Ilderim after him, 'you only have to ask and I will come.'

George raised his arm in acknowledgement, but didn't look back.

He was still mulling over the consequences of his decision to leave the cloak as he approached the same Torkham border crossing he and Ilderim had used to enter Afghanistan four months earlier. Then it had consisted of a couple of sentries and a single whitewashed building; now it was guarded by a fortified camp containing tents for at least two hundred men. 'That's far enough, Mahomed,' called a soldier, covering him with a rifle from the parapet of the fort. 'State your business.'

'I am Captain George Hart. I'm on my way to Karachi, via Peshawar, and have a passport signed by General Roberts.'

'Wait there. I'll get my officer,' said the soldier, disappearing from the parapet, though George could see that other soldiers had him in their sights.

Minutes later the gate to the fort swung open and a young subaltern of the 67th Foot emerged on foot. 'May I see your papers, Captain?'

George dug out Roberts's letter and handed it over. The subaltern took one look at general's signature and snapped off a salute. 'Welcome to Torkham, Captain Hart. I apologize for the sentry's abrupt manner but even you will admit you don't look much like a British officer in that get-up.'

'No,' said George, 'I'll grant you that. Well, if there's nothing else I'll be on my way.'

'Actually there is something,' said the subaltern, pulling a piece of folded paper from his tunic pocket. 'I have a message for you from General Roberts. It arrived last night by heliograph.'

Oh, no, thought George. Don't tell me he's changed his mind and wants me to stay after all. With heart racing, he opened the sheet of paper:

Dear Captain Hart

It gives me great pleasure to inform you that today, after the receipt of reports from Colonel Jenkins, Major FitzGeorge and Lieutenant Duggan, I sent a recommendation to HRH the Duke of Cambridge, Commander-in-Chief, that you be awarded the Victoria Cross for gallantry during the fighting of 23 December.

Both Jenkins and Duggan state in their reports that but for your bold initiative the Afghans would have captured the trench beside the native hospital, a loss that might have proved fatal for the whole garrison. Duggan, moreover, states that you personally saved his life. FitzGeorge says that you initiated and led the charge that routed the Kohistani cavalry, and then followed Princess Yasmin into the enemy-held Khirskhana Pass in a vain attempt to save her life.

Of course my recommendation has to be confirmed by both HRH the Duke and HM the Queen before an award can be made. But I cannot foresee any circumstances in which that would not happen.

May I, therefore, offer you my congratulations, and my thanks for all you've done during the recent campaign.

I am, etc.,

Sir Frederick Roberts, VC

George stared at the page, dumbfounded that his self-centred 'brother' had helped to secure this very welcome – but wholly unexpected – recommendation. Was it guilt? A *quid pro quo* for George having let him take the jewelled clasp? He couldn't be sure, but what did it matter? At the age of twenty he had as good as won the Victoria Cross and would get the money he needed after all: not from the government but from his father the Duke of Cambridge; and not two thousand pounds but ten thousand. It would be enough to keep his mother in comfort and let him get on with the rest of a career that now seemed destined, after this, to go from strength to strength. Tears of joy – and relief – welled in his eyes, and he could contain himself no longer. 'Hurrah!' he shouted, punching the air with his free hand.

'Good news, sir?' asked the subaltern.

'Yes, very good. I've been recommended for the VC.'

'How marvellous!' said the subaltern, gazing at George with heightened respect. 'Please accept my congratulations.'

'Thank you,' said George, but already the euphoria was being replaced by nagging doubt. Was Roberts, like Chelmsford before him, offering George the sweetener of a Victoria Cross in return for his silence about the errors made before and during the rebellion? He wouldn't put it beyond him. But then it occurred to George that this time *he* held all the cards: unlike Chelmsford, who had made his recommendation dependent on George's co-operation, Roberts had *already* recommended him for a VC, and any benefit that accrued to the general was entirely at George's discretion; a discretion that, when he wrote his report, he was determined to exercise with extreme caution.

Two weeks later – still dusty from the journey, though by now recognizably European having shaved off his beard, cut his hair and changed into his own clothes – George entered the Metropole Hotel in Karachi and was greeted at the front desk by the manager, Mr Beresford.

'Welcome back, Mr Harper. I trust your business transactions up-country were successful?'

'Yes, thank you. Very successful.'

'I'm glad to hear it. I have a letter for you from South Africa.'

George took the proffered envelope and scanned the handwriting. It was Lucy's. Three months earlier that might have disappointed him, but not now. With his heart racing, he tore the letter open and read the single sheet:

The Lucky Strike
Long Street
Kimberley
Cape Colony

Dearest George

When I received your reply to my previous letter, I fully intended to follow your advice to sit tight and do nothing until you arrived in South Africa. But last week I received another letter from Colonel Harris. In it he claimed to have heard from Mr Thompson's brother that when you met in London you confessed both to the murder and the fact that I was your accomplice. He also warned me that he'll be paying a visit to Kimberley in the New Year, and that if I refuse to return to England he'll expose me as an accessory to murder.

With you in Asia, thousands of miles away, the only person I could turn to was my employer, Mr Barnato. He's offered to protect me from Harris, and to spend whatever it takes on legal fees to prevent my forcible repatriation, but on one condition: that I marry him. I have agreed and the marriage will take place on 20 January 1880.

I don't love him, George. I love you. But I had no choice.

Your loving friend

Lucy

As he read the last few lines, George felt sick – and it suddenly occurred to him that his feelings for Lucy were much stronger than he had ever allowed himself to admit. What if he'd loved her all along, and was only able to acknowledge it now that he was on the verge of losing her for ever? It was certainly possible, he conceded, not least because he knew that if he wedded a girl of working-class origins like Lucy he would forfeit fifteen thousand pounds of his father's legacy: five thousand for marrying 'respectably' and the ten-thousand-pound bonus for complying with all three conditions in the time allotted.

But where did that leave his professions of love for Fanny Colenso and, more recently, Princess Yasmin? He could only assume that, since her last seemingly final rejection of him, he'd fallen out of love with Fanny and had never been truly smitten by the princess. Yes, he'd told her he loved her, but that had been in a vain attempt to save her life; even at the time his half-truth hadn't sat comfortably with him. He'd been infatuated with her, certainly, and may even have been falling in love. But he wasn't 'in' love, and that may have been Lucy's doing.

With his true feelings now clearer in his mind, he still couldn't decide on the best course of action. Would it not, he asked himself, be doing Lucy a service to let the marriage go ahead as planned? After all, Barney Barnato was only a few years her senior, and a man with enough money to keep her safe from her enemies for the rest of her life. Yet seven words kept coming back to him: *I don't love him, George. I love you.* He knew what he had to do.

Looking up, he caught the hotel manager's eye. 'When does the next packet leave for Durban?'

'At eight this evening.'

'Reserve me a cabin.'

Author's Note

Historical fiction always takes liberties with the 'truth': it compresses time, invents conversations and motives that real people never had, and generally tampers with the historical record for the purposes of plot. The trick is to minimize those liberties, and to make sure that when you're writing about historical figures you stay true to the spirit of that person. A made-up character, of course, gives the author the greatest license, but even he or she must conform to the standards/mores/thought patterns of the time.

It helps, too, if the plot is credible. I first came across the Prophet's Cloak – my chief plot device – when I read David Loyn's excellent history of foreign engagement in Afghanistan, *Butcher & Bolt* (see below). From that book and other sources, I discovered that the cloak was said to have been brought to Afghanistan from Central Asia in the 1760s by the first Amir of Kabul, Ahmad Shah Durrani, and today is kept in a locked silver box in the Kharka Sharif shrine in Kandahar. Its last public appearance was in the spring of 1996 when the leader of the Taliban, Mullah Omar, wore it to rally support for his movement's stalled attempt to capture Kabul, proclaiming himself *Amir al-Mu'minin* ("Leader of the Faithful"). Weeks later Kabul fell to the Taliban. A hundred and fifty years earlier, and for much the same reason, it was donned by Amir Dost Mahomed when he launched a *jihad* against the first British invasion of Afghanistan. Dost was restored to power when the British withdrew in 1842.

There is, however, no evidence that the cloak was used by Mullah Mushk-i-Alam, or any other leader, during the Afghan rebellion of 1879 (part of a conflict known to historians as the second Anglo-Afghan War). But it easily might have been: it seems inconceivable, given the precedent set by Dost Mohamed a generation earlier, that the advantage to be gained by displaying it in public did not occur to them. The mullah certainly proclaimed a *jihad* that was hugely popular until it suffered the crushing military defeat at Sherpur, on 23 December 1879, which is the climax to this book.

Nor is it beyond the bounds of possibility that the British government in London would have sent an agent to acquire the cloak in 1879. Disraeli was furious that Lord Lytton, the Viceroy of India, had exceeded his brief by invading Afghanistan in the first place in 1878, and by the following year he and his Cabinet colleagues were doubly determined to avoid a fresh outbreak of hostilities. Lytton and many senior political and military figures in India, on the other hand, were convinced that the sub-continent's security depended upon the annexation of all or part of Afghanistan (the so-called 'Forward' policy), and the attack on the Residency was just the excuse they needed for a fresh invasion. After the victory at Sherpur, the preferred plan was to break up the country and only annex Kandahar. But even that province was relinquished when the British, following defeat at Maiwand, finally withdrew in early 1881. Soon afterwards the country was reunited by Britain's preferred choice of amir, Abdur Rahman, who ruled for the next 20 years without foreign interference (though Britain exercised a nominal control over the amir's foreign policy).

My three main characters – George Hart, Princess Yasmin and Ilderim Khan – are all fictional, but most of the people they come into contact with really existed: Sir Louis Cavagnari, Lieutenant Walter Hamilton V.C., William Jenkyns and Doctor Kelly (all of whom perished during the attack on the Residency); Yakub Khan and his wazir, Shah Mohammed Khan; Lieutenant-General Sir Frederick 'Bobs' Roberts (who went on to command the British Army), Brigadier-General Thomas Baker and Colonel Charles MacGregor; and the rebel leaders Mullah Mushk-i-Alam and Mir Bacha. As far as possible I have tried to stay true to the historical record of where these figures were and what they were up to (even, in places, using recorded speech and letters), and the main events in Afghanistan from September to December 1879 – including the sack of the Residency, the re-invasion by Sir Frederick Roberts, Yakub Khan's abdication, Roberts's reverse in the Chardeh valley, and the final British victory at Sherpur cantonment – were as I describe. Yakub Khan, moreover, did abandon his wives and close relatives in the Bala Hissar when he left to join the British in late September.

During my research I used a number of excellent histories and first-hand accounts. For those readers who would like to delve further, I recommend the following:

Giles St Aubyn, *The Royal George, 1819-1904: The Life of H.R.H. Prince George Duke of Cambridge* (1965)

J. Duke, *Recollections of the Kabul Campaign 1879 & 1880* (1883)

T.A. Heathcote, *The Afghan Wars: 1839-1919* (2007)
David Loyn, *Butcher & Bolt: Two Hundred Years of Foreign Engagement in Afghanistan* (2008)
Field Marshal Lord Roberts of Kandahar, *Forty-One Years in India: From Subaltern to Commander-in-Chief* (1898)
Brian Robson, *The Road to Kabul: The 2nd Afghan War 1878-1881* (2008)
William Trousdale (ed.), *War in Afghanistan, 1879-80: The Personal Diary of Major General Sir Charles Metcalfe MacGregor* (1985)

Switching from history to fiction is never easy. Fortunately I've been guided by an excellent editorial team at Hodder – notably my publisher Nick Sayers and his (former) assistant and now editor Anne Clarke – and once again they've come up trumps. I have Nick to thank for suggesting I consult the screenwriter Guy Meredith while I was plotting this book (in an attempt, no doubt, to iron out the wrinkles of its predecessor) and Guy's input has been invaluable. And to everyone else at Hodder who has worked so hard on the book – Laura, Kerry, Claudette, Helen, Mark, as well as Auriol, Lucy, Jason and their teams, in particular Aslan – not to mention my excellent freelance copy-editor Hazel Orme, proof-reader Barbara Westmore, and Martin Collins who drew the maps, I'm extremely grateful.

Thanks, also, to Richard Foreman and Peter Robinson, my publicist and agent respectively, who between them made this transition to fiction possible; and, last but not least, to my wife Louise for reading the manuscript (and enjoying it for a change), and making the extremely sensible suggestion that I should leave the writing of sex scenes to those 'who know what they're doing'.